# THE

# SHEIKH'S

*Desert Conquest*

# THE SHEIKH'S

## COLLECTION

January 2016

February 2016

March 2016

April 2016

# THE
# SHEIKH'S
## *Desert Conquest*

**SUSAN STEPHENS**
**GAIL DAYTON**
**CAROL GRACE**

MILLS
BOON

First Published in Great Britain 2016
by Mills & Boon, an imprint of HarperCollins*Publishers*
1 London Bridge Street, London, SE1 9GF

THE SHEIKH'S DESERT CONQUEST © 2016 Harlequin Books S.A.

*Diamond in the Desert* © 2013 Susan Stephens
*Hide-and-Sheikh* © 2001 Gail Dayton
*Her Sheikh Boss* © 2008 Carol Culver

ISBN: 978-0-263-91842-7

23-0416

Our policy is to use papers that are natural, renewable and recyclable products and made from wood grown in sustainable forests.
The logging and manufacturing processes conform to the legal environmental regulations of the country of origin.

Printed and bound in Spain
by CPI, Barcelona

# DIAMOND IN THE DESERT

## SUSAN STEPHENS

*For all my wonderful readers who love the mystery of the desert and the romance of a sheikh.*

**Susan Stephens** was a professional singer before meeting her husband on the tiny Mediterranean island of Malta. In true Modern Romance style they met on Monday, became engaged on Friday, and were married three months after that. Almost thirty years and three children later, they are still in love. (Susan does not advise her children to return home one day with a similar story, as she may not take the news with the same fortitude as her own mother!)

Susan had written several non-fiction books when fate took a hand. At a charity costume ball there was an after-dinner auction. One of the lots, 'Spend a Day with an Author', had been donated by Mills & Boon author Penny Jordan. Susan's husband bought this lot, and Penny was to become not just a great friend but a wonderful mentor, who encouraged Susan to write romance.

Susan loves her family, her pets, her friends and her writing. She enjoys entertaining, travel and going to the theatre. She reads, cooks, and plays the piano to relax and can occasionally be found throwing herself off mountains on a pair of skis or galloping through the countryside.

Visit Susan's website at www.susanstephens.net—she loves to hear from her readers all around the world!

If you love reading about the Skavanga family dynasty, take a look at their website: http://www.susanstephens.com/skavanga/index.html

looked forward to meeting her. A deal with the added spice of down time in the bedroom held obvious appeal. There was no sentiment in business and he certainly wasted none on women.

'Why do you get all the fun?' Roman complained, frowning when Sharif told the other men about his plan.

'There are plenty to go round,' he reassured them dryly as the other two men studied the photographs of the sisters. Glancing at Raffa, he felt a momentary twinge of something close to apprehension. The youngest sister, whom Raffa was studying, was clearly an innocent, while Raffa was most certainly not.

'Three good-looking women,' Roman commented, glancing between his friends.

'For three ruthless asset strippers,' Raffa added, devouring the last piece of orange with relish. 'I look forward to stripping the assets off this one—'

Raffa's dark eyes blackened dangerously as Sharif gathered the photographs in. Sharif hardly realised that he was caressing the photograph of Britt Skavanga with his forefinger while denying Raffa further study of Leila, the youngest sister.

'This could be our most promising project to date,' the man known to the world as the Black Sheikh commented.

'And if anyone can land this deal, Sharif can,' Roman remarked, hoping to heal the momentary rift between his friends. He could only be thankful their interest wasn't in the same girl.

Raffa's laugh relaxed them all. 'Didn't I hear you have some interesting sexual techniques in Kareshi, Sharif? Silken ties? Chiffon blindfolds?'

Roman huffed a laugh at this. 'I've heard the same

thing. In the harem tents it's said they use creams and potions to send sensation through the roof—'

'Enough,' Sharif rapped, raising his hands to silence his friends. 'Can we please return to business?'

Within seconds the Skavanga girls were forgotten and the talk was all of balance sheets and financial predictions, but in one part of his mind Sharif was still thinking about a pair of cool grey eyes and a full, expressive mouth, and what could be accomplished with a little expert tutelage.

An absolute monarch, bred to a hard life in the desert, Sharif had been trained to rule and fight and argue at council with the wisest of men—women being notable by their absence, which was something he had changed as soon as he took over the country. Women in Kareshi had used to be regarded as ornaments to be pampered and spoiled and hidden away; under his rule they were expected to pull their weight. Education for all was now the law.

And who would dare to argue with the Black Sheikh? Not Britt Skavanga, that was for sure. Staring at Britt's photograph and seeing the steely determination so similar to his own in her eyes only reinforced his intention to check out all the assets in Skavanga personally. Britt possessed the generous, giving mouth of a concubine, with the unrelenting gaze of a Viking warrior. The combination aroused him. Even the severity of the suit she was wearing intrigued him. Her breasts thrusting against the soft wool stirred his senses in a most agreeable way. He adored severe tailoring on a woman. It was a type of shorthand he had learned to read many years ago. Severe equalled repressed, or possibly a player who liked to tease. Either way, he was a huge fan.

'Are you still with us, Sharif?' Raffa enquired with

amusement as his friend finally pushed Britt's photograph away.

'Yes, but not for long as I will be leaving for Skavanga in the morning, travelling in my capacity of geologist and advisor to the consortium. This will allow me to make an impartial assessment of the situation without ruffling any feathers.'

'That's sensible,' Raffa agreed. 'Talk of the Black Sheikh descending on a business would be enough to send anyone into a panic.'

'Have you ever *descended* on a tasty business prospect without devouring it?' Roman enquired, hiding his smile.

'The fact that this mysterious figure, conjured by the press and known to the world as the Black Sheikh, has never had a photograph published will surely be an advantage to you,' Raffa suggested.

'I reserve judgement until we meet again when I will be in a position to tell you if the claims that have been made about the Skavanga Diamonds are true,' Sharif said with a closing gesture.

'We can ask for no more than that,' his two friends agreed.

'Well, clearly, I must be the one to meet him,' Britt insisted as the three sisters sat round the interestingly shaped—if not very practical, thanks to the holes the designer had punched in it—blonde wood kitchen table in Britt's sleek, minimalist, barely lived-in penthouse.

'Clearly—why?' Britt's feisty middle sister, Eva, demanded. 'Who says you have the right to take the lead in this new venture? Shouldn't we all have a part in it? What about the equality you're always banging on about, Britt?'

'Britt has far more business experience than we have,' the youngest and most mild-mannered sister, Leila, pointed out. 'And that's a perfectly sensible reason for Britt to be the one to meet with him,' Leila added, sweeping anxious fingers through her tumbling blonde curls.

'Perfectly sensible?' Eva scoffed. 'Britt has experience in mining iron ore and copper. But diamonds?' Eva rolled her emerald eyes. 'You must agree the three of us are virgins where diamonds are concerned?'

And Eva was likely to remain a virgin in every sense if she kept on like this, Britt thought, fretting like a mother over her middle sister. Eva had been a glass-half-empty type of person for as long as Britt could remember and sadly there were no dashing Petruchios in Skavanga to prevent Eva from turning into a fully-fledged shrew. 'I'm going to deal with this—and with him,' she said firmly.

'You and the Black Sheikh?' Eva said scornfully. 'You might be a hotshot businesswoman here in Skavanga, but the sheikh's business interests are global—and he runs a country. What on earth makes you think you can take a man like that on?'

'I know my business,' Britt said calmly. 'I know our mine and I'll be factual. I'll be cool and I'll be reasoned.'

'Britt's very good at doing stuff like this without engaging her emotions,' Leila added.

'Really?' Eva mocked. 'Whether she can or not remains to be seen.'

'I won't let you down,' Britt promised, knowing her sisters' concerns both for her and for the business had prompted this row. 'I've handled difficult people in the past and I'm well prepared to meet the Black Sheikh. I realise I must handle him with kid gloves—'

'Nice.' Eva laughed.

Britt ignored this. 'We would be unwise to underestimate him,' she said. 'The ruler of Kareshi is known as the Black Sheikh for a very good reason—'

'Rape and pillage?' Eva suggested scathingly.

Britt held her tongue. 'Sheikh Sharif is one of the foremost geologists in the world.'

'It's a shame we couldn't find any photographs of him,' Leila mused.

'He's a geologist, not a film star,' Britt pointed out. 'And how many Arab rulers have you seen photographs of?'

'He's probably so ugly he'd break the camera,' Eva muttered. 'I bet he's a nerd with pebble glasses and a bristly chin.'

'If he is he would be easier for Britt to deal with,' Leila said hopefully.

'A ruler who has moved his country forward and brought peace sounds like a decent man to me, so, whatever he looks like, it doesn't matter. I just need your support. Fact: the minerals at the mine are running out and we need investment. The consortium this man heads up has the money to allow us to mine the diamonds.'

There was a silence as Britt's sisters accepted the truth of this and she breathed a sigh of relief when they nodded their heads. Now she had a chance to rescue the mine and the town of Skavanga that was built around it. That, together with all the fresh challenges ahead of her, made her meeting with the so-called Black Sheikh seem less of a problem.

She was feeling slightly less sanguine the following day.

'Serves you right for building up your hopes,' Eva said as the girls gathered in Britt's study after hearing her groan. 'Your famous Black Sheikh can't even be bothered to meet with you,' Eva remarked, peering over Britt's shoulder at the email message on the computer screen. 'So he's sending a representative instead,' she scoffed, turning to throw an I-told-you-so look at Leila.

'I'll get some fresh coffee,' Leila offered.

Eva's carping was really getting on Britt's nerves. She'd been up since dawn exchanging emails with Kareshi. It was practically noon for her, Britt reflected angrily as Leila brought the coffee in. Her sisters loved staying in the city with her, but sometimes they forgot that, while they could lounge around, she had a job to do. 'I'm still going to meet with him. What else am I going to do?' she demanded, swinging round to confront her sisters. 'Do you two have any better ideas?'

Eva fell silent, while Leila gave Britt a sympathetic look as she handed her a mug of coffee. 'I'm just sorry we're going back home and leaving you with all this to deal with.'

'That's my job,' Britt said, controlling her anger. She could never be angry with Leila. 'Of course I'm disappointed I won't be meeting the Black Sheikh, but all I've ever asked for is your support, Eva.'

'Sorry,' Eva muttered awkwardly. 'I know you got landed with the company when Mum and Dad died. I'm just worried about what's going to happen now all the commodities are running out. I do realise the mine's sunk without the diamonds. And I know you'll do your very best to land this deal, but I'm worried about you, Britt. This is too much on your shoulders.'

'Stop it,' Britt warned, giving her sister a hug. 'Whoever the Black Sheikh sends, I can deal with him.'

'It says that the man you're to expect is a qualified geologist,' Leila pointed out. 'So at least you'll have something in common.' Britt's degree was also in Geology, with a Master's in Business Management.

'Yes,' Eva agreed, trying to sound as optimistic as her sister. 'I'm sure it will be fine.'

Britt knew that both her sisters were genuinely concerned about her. They just had different ways of showing it. 'Well, I'm excited,' she said firmly to lift the mood. 'When this man gets here we're another step closer to saving the company.'

'I wish Tyr were here to help you.'

Leila's words made them all silent. Tyr was their long-lost brother and they rarely talked about him because it hurt too much. They couldn't understand why he had left in the first place, much less why Tyr had never contacted them.

Britt broke the silence first. 'Tyr would do exactly what we're doing. He thinks the same as us. He cares about the company and the people here.'

'Which explains why he stays away,' Eva murmured.

'He's still one of us,' Britt insisted. 'We stick together. Remember that. The discovery of diamonds might even encourage him to return home.'

'But Tyr isn't motivated by money,' Leila piped up.

Even Eva couldn't disagree with that. Tyr was an idealist, an adventurer. Their brother was many things, but money was not his god, though Britt wished he would come home again. She missed him. Tyr had been away too long.

'Here's something that will make you laugh,' Leila said in an attempt to lift the mood. Pulling the newspaper towards her, she pointed to an article in the newspaper that referred to the three sisters as the Skavanga Diamonds. 'They haven't tired of giving us that ridiculous nickname.'

'It's just so patronising,' Eva huffed, brushing a cascade of fiery red curls away from her face.

'I've been called worse things,' Britt argued calmly.

'Don't be so naïve,' Eva snapped. 'All that article does is wave a flag in front of the nose of every fortune-hunter out there—'

'And what's wrong with that?' Leila interrupted. 'I'd just like to see a man who isn't drunk by nine o'clock—'

This brought a shocked intake of breath from Britt and Eva, as Leila had mentioned something else they never spoke about. There had long been a rumour that their father had been drunk when he piloted the small company plane to disaster with their mother on board.

Leila flushed red as she realised her mistake. 'I'm sorry—I'm just tired of your sniping, Eva. We really should get behind Britt.'

'Leila's right,' Britt insisted. 'It's crucial we keep our focus and make this deal work. We certainly can't afford to fall out between us. That article is fluff and we shouldn't even be wasting time discussing it. If Skavanga Mining is going to have a future we have to consider every offer on the table—and so far the consortium's is the only offer.'

'I suppose you could always give the sheikh's representative a proper welcome, Skavanga style,' Eva suggested, brightening.

Leila relaxed into a smile. 'I'm sure Britt has got a few ideas up her sleeve.'

'It's not my sleeve you need to worry about,' Britt commented dryly, relieved that they were all the best of friends again.

'Just promise me you won't do anything you'll regret,' Leila said, remembering to worry.

'I won't regret it at the time,' Britt promised dryly.

'Unless he truly is a boffin with pebble glasses—in which case I'll just have to put a paper bag over his head.'

'Don't become overconfident,' Eva warned.

'I'm not worried. If he proves difficult I'll cut a hole in the ice and send him swimming. That will soon cool his ardour—'

'Why stop there?' Eva added. 'Don't forget the birch twig switches. You can always give him a good thrashing. That'll sort him out.'

'I'll certainly consider it—'

'Tell me you're joking?' Leila begged.

Thankfully, Britt's younger sister missed the look Britt and Eva exchanged.

# CHAPTER TWO

BRITT WAS UNUSUALLY nervous. The breakfast meeting with the Black Sheikh's representative had been arranged for nine and it was already twenty past when she rushed through the doors of Skavanga Mining and tore up the stairs. It wasn't as if she was unused to business meetings, but this one was different for a number of reasons, not least of which was the fact that her car had blown a tyre on the way to the office. Changing a tyre was an energetic exercise at the best of times, enough to get her heart racing, but the circumstances of this meeting had made her anxious without that, because so much depended on it—

'I'll show myself in,' she said as a secretary glanced up in surprise.

Pausing outside the door to the boardroom, she took a moment to compose herself. Eva was right in that when their parents were killed Britt had been the only person qualified to take over the company and care for her two younger sisters. Their brother was... Well, Tyr was a maverick—a mercenary, for all they knew. He had been a regular soldier at time, and no one knew where he was now. It was up to her to cut this deal; there was no one else. The man inside the boardroom could save the company if he gave a green light to the consortium.

And she was late, an embarrassment that put her firmly on the back foot.

*Back foot?*

Forget that, Britt concluded as the imposing figure standing silhouetted against the light by the window turned to face her. The man was dressed conventionally in a dark, beautifully tailored business suit, when somehow she had imagined her visitor would be wearing flowing robes. This man needed no props to appear exotic. His proud, dark face, the thick black hair, which he wore carelessly swept back, and his watchful eyes were all the exotic ingredients required to complete a stunning picture. Far from the bristly nerd, he was heart-stoppingly good-looking, and it took all she'd got to keep her feet marching steadily across the room towards him.

'Ms Skavanga?'

The deep, faintly accented voice ran shivers through every part of her. It was the voice of a master, a lover, a man who expected nothing less than to be obeyed.

Oh, get over it, Britt told herself impatiently. It was the voice of a man and he was tall, dark and handsome. So what? She had a company to run.

'Britt Skavanga,' she said firmly, advancing to meet him with her hand outstretched. 'I'm sorry, you have me at a disadvantage,' she added, explaining that all she had been told was that His Majesty Sheikh Sharif al Kareshi would be sending his most trusted aide.

'For these preliminary discussions that is correct,' he said, taking hold of her hand in a grip that was controlled yet deadly.

His touch stunned her. It might have been disappointingly brief, but it was as if it held some electrical charge that shot fire through her veins.

She wanted him.

*Just like that she wanted him?*

She was a highly sexed woman, but she had never experienced such an instant, strong attraction to any man before.

'So,' she said, lifting her chin as she made a determined effort to pitch her voice at a level suitable for the importance of the business to be carried out between them, 'what may I call you?'

'Emir,' he replied, more aloof than ever.

'Just Emir?' she said.

'It's enough.' He shrugged, discarding her wild fantasy about him at a stroke.

'Shall we make a start?' He looked her up and down with all the cool detachment of a buyer weighing up a mare brought to market. 'Have you had some sort of accident, Ms Skavanga?'

'Please, call me Britt.' She had completely forgotten about the tyre until he brought it up, and now all she could think was what a wreck she must look. She clearly wasn't making an impression as an on-top-of-things businesswoman, that was for sure.

'Would you like to take a moment?' Emir enquired as she smoothed her hair self-consciously.

'No, thank you,' she said, matching his cool. She wasn't about to hand over the initiative this early in the game. 'I've kept you waiting long enough. A tyre blew on my way to the office,' she explained.

'And *you* changed it?'

She frowned. 'Why wouldn't I? I didn't want to waste time changing my clothes.'

'Thank you for the consideration.' Emir dipped his head in a small bow, allowing her to admire his thick, wavy hair, though his ironic expression suggested that

Emir believed a woman's place was somewhere fragrant and sheltered where she could bake and quake until her hunter returned.

*Was he married?*

She glanced at his ring-free hands, and remembered to thank him when he pulled out a chair. She couldn't remember the last time that had happened. She was used to fending for herself, though it was nice to meet a gentleman, even if she suspected that beneath his velvet charm Emir was ruthless and would use every setback she experienced to his advantage.

No problem. She wasn't about to give him an inch.

'Please,' she said, indicating a place that put the wide expanse of the boardroom table between them.

He had the grace of a big cat, she registered as he sat down. Emir was dark and mysterious compared to the blond giants in Skavanga she was used to. He was big and exuded power like some soft-pawed predator.

She had to be on guard at all times or he would win this game before she even knew it had been lost. Business was all that mattered now—though it was hard to concentrate when the flow of energy between them had grown.

Chemistry, she mused. And no wonder when Emir radiated danger. The dark business suit moulded his athletic frame to perfection, while the crisp white shirt set off his bronzed skin, and a grey silk tie provided a reassuring sober touch—to those who might be fooled. She wasn't one of them. Emir might as well have been dressed in flowing robes with an unsheathed scimitar at his side, for seductive exoticism flowed from him.

She looked away quickly when his black gaze found hers and held it. *Damn!* She could feel her cheeks blazing. She quickly buried her attention in the documents in front of her.

Britt's apparent devotion to her work amused him. He'd felt the same spark between them that she had, and there was always the same outcome to that. He generally relied on the first few minutes of any meeting to assess people. Body language told him so much. Up to now Skavanga had not impressed him. It was a grey place with an air of dejection that permeated both the company and the town. He didn't need the report in front of him to tell him that the mineral deposits were running out, he could smell failure in the air. And however good this woman was at running the business—and she must be good to keep a failing company alive for so long—she couldn't sell thin air. Britt needed to mine those diamonds in order to keep her company alive, and to do that she needed the consortium he headed up to back her.

The town might be grey, but Britt Skavanga was anything but. She exceeded his expectations. There was a vivid private world behind those serious dove grey eyes, and it was a world he intended to enter as soon as he could.

'You will relate our dealings verbatim to His Majesty?' she said as they began the meeting.

'Of course. His Majesty greets you as a friend and hopes that all future dealings between us will bring mutual respect as well as great benefit to both our countries.'

He had not anticipated her sharp intake of breath, or the darkening of her eyes as he made the traditional Kareshi greeting, touching his chest, his mouth and finally his brow. He amended his original assessment of Britt to that of a simmering volcano waiting to explode.

She recovered quickly. 'Please tell His Majesty that I welcome his interest in Skavanga Mining, and may I also welcome you as his envoy.'

Nicely done. She was cool. He'd give her that. His senses roared as she held his gaze. The only woman he knew who would do that was his sister, Jasmina, and she was a troublesome minx.

As Britt continued to lay out her vision of the future for Skavanga Mining he thought there was a touching innocence about her, even in the way she thought she would have any say once the consortium took over. Her capable hands were neatly manicured, the nails short and unpainted, and she wore very little make-up. There was no artifice about her. What you saw was what you got with Britt Skavanga—except for the fire in her eyes, and he guessed very few had seen that blaze into an inferno.

'You must find the prospect of mining the icy wastes quite daunting after what you're used to in the desert,' she was saying.

He returned reluctantly to business. 'On the contrary. There is a lot in Skavanga that reminds me of the vast-ness and variety of my desert home. It is a variety only obvious to those who see it, of course.' As much as he wanted this new venture to go ahead, he wanted Britt Skavanga even more.

As hard as she tried to concentrate, her body was mak-ing it impossible to think, but then her body seemed tuned to Emir's. She even found herself leaning to-wards him, and had to make herself sit back. Even then his heat curled around her. His face was stern, *which she loved,* and his scent, spicy and warm, sandalwood, maybe, it was a reminder of the exotic world he came from. Her sisters had already teased her mercilessly about Kareshi supposedly being at the forefront of the erotic arts. She had pretended not to listen to such nonsense, especially when they insisted that the people of Kareshi had a potion they used to heighten sensation. But she'd heard them. And now she was wondering if anything they'd said could be true—

'Ms Skavanga?'

She jerked alert as Emir spoke her name. 'I beg your pardon. My mind was just—'

'Wandering? Or examining the facts?' he said with amusement.

'Yes—'

'Yes? Which is it?'

She couldn't even remember the question. The blood rush to her cheeks was furious and hot, while Emir just raised a brow and his mouth curved slightly.

'Are you ready to continue?' he said.

'Absolutely,' she confirmed, sitting up straight. She was mad for this man—crazy for him. No way could she think straight until the tension had been released.

'There are some amendments I want to discuss,' he said, frowning slightly as he glanced up at her.

She turned with relief to the documents in front of her.

'I need more time,' she said.

'Really?' Emir queried softly.

She swallowed deep when she saw the look in his eyes. 'I don't think we should rush anything—'

'I don't think we should close any doors, either.'

Were they still talking about business? Shaking herself round, she explained that she wouldn't be making any decisions on behalf of the other shareholders yet.

'And I need to take samples from the mine before I

can involve the consortium in such a large investment,' Emir pointed out.

He only had to speak for alarm bells to go off in every part of her body, making it impossible to think about anything other than long, moonlit nights in the desert. Not once since taking over at Skavanga Mining had she ever been so distracted during a meeting. It didn't help that she had thought the Black Sheikh's trusted envoy would be some greybeard with a courtly air.

'Here is your copy of my projections,' she said, forcing her mind back to business before closing her file to signify the end of the meeting.

'I have my own projections, thank you.'

She bridled at that before reminding herself that just a murmur from the Black Sheikh could rock a government, and that his envoy was hardly going to be a push-over when it came to negotiations.

'Before we finish, there's just one here on the second page,' he said, leaning towards her.

'I see it,' she said, stiffening as she tried to close her mind to Emir's intoxicating scent. And those power-ful hands…the suppleness in his fingers…the strength in his wrists…

He caught her staring and she started blushing again. This was ridiculous. She was acting like a teenager on her first date.

Exhaling shakily, she sat back in the chair deter-mined to recover the situation, but Emir was on a roll.

'You seem to have missed something here,' he said, pointing to another paragraph.

She never missed anything. She was meticulous in all her business dealings. But sure enough, Emir had found one tiny thing she had overlooked.

'And this clause can go,' he said, removing it with a strike of his pen.

'Now, just a minute—' She stared aghast as Emir deconstructed her carefully drawn-up plan. 'No,' she said firmly. 'That clause does not go, and neither does anything else without further discussion, and this part of the meeting is over.'

He sat back in his chair as she stood up, which explained why she wasn't ready for him moving in front of her to stand in her way.

'You seem upset,' he said. 'And I don't want the first part of our meeting to end badly.'

'Bringing in investors is a big step for me to take—'

'Britt—'

Emir's touch on her skin was like an incendiary device, but the fact that his hand was on her arm at all was an outrage. 'Let me go,' she warned softly, but they both heard the shake in her voice. And surely Emir could feel her trembling beneath his touch. He must feel the heated awareness in her skin.

He murmured something in his own language. It might as well have been a spell. She turned to look at him, not keen to go anywhere suddenly.

'It seems to me we have a timing problem, Britt. But there is a solution, if you will allow me to take it?'

Emir's eyes were dark and amused. At first she thought she must have misunderstood him, but there was no mistake, and the solution he was proposing had been in her mind for some time. But surely no civilised businessman would be willing to enter into such a risky entanglement within an hour of meeting her?

As Emir's hand grazed her chin she moved into his embrace, allowing him to turn her face up to his. This was no meeting between business colleagues. This was a meeting between a man and woman who were hot for each other, and the man was a warrior of the desert.

Emir promised pleasure. He also promised a chance to forget, and, for however short a time, the prospect of that seemed preferable at this moment to doing battle endlessly on every front. How would it feel to have this big man hold her and bring her pleasure? She must have swayed towards him, for the next thing she knew he was holding her in front of him.

'Why, Britt,' he said with amusement. 'If I'd known how badly you wanted this I'm sure we could have arranged something before the meeting.'

Emir's blunt approach should have shocked her— annoyed her—but instead it made her want him all the more, and as he brushed her lips with his she found herself instantly hungry, instantly frantic, for more pressure, more intimacy, and for everything to happen fast.

But Emir was even more experienced than she had realised, and now he took pleasure in subjecting her to an agonising delay. As the clock ticked, the tension built and he held her stare with his knowing and faintly amused look. She guessed Emir knew everything about arousal, and could only hope it wouldn't be long before he decided she had suffered enough. She voiced a cry of relief when he cupped her face in his warm, slightly roughened hands, and another when her patience was rewarded by a kiss that began lightly and then brutally mimicked the act her body so desperately craved.

It was in no way subjugation by a powerful man, but the meeting of eager mates, a fierce coupling between two people who knew exactly what they wanted from each other, and as Emir pressed her back against the boardroom table and set about removing her clothes she gasped in triumph and began ripping at his.

He tossed her jacket aside. She loosened his tie and dragged it off, letting it drop onto the floor. As he ripped her blouse open she battled with the buttons on his shirt. She exclaimed with pleased surprise when he lifted her and she clung to him as he stripped off her tights and her briefs. Suddenly it was all about seeing who could rid themselves of any barriers first. She was mindless sensation—hot flesh brushing, touching, cleaving, in a tangle of limbs and hectic breathing, while Emir remained calm and strong, and certain. He felt so good beneath her hands...so very good—

*Too good! You have never felt like this about a man before—*

*Danger! This man can change your life—*

*You won't walk away from this with a smile on your face—*

Using sheer force of will, she closed off her annoying inner voice. She wanted this. She needed it. This was her every fantasy come true. Even now as Emir took time to protect them both she saw no reason not to follow her most basic instinct. Why shouldn't she? Emir was—

Emir was enormous. He was entirely built to scale. Was she ready for this?

He made her forget everything the moment he caressed her breasts. Moaning, she rested back and let him do what he wanted with her. Just this once she wanted to feel that she didn't have to lead or fight. Just this once she could be the woman she had always dreamed of being—the woman who was with a man who knew how to please her.

*And I wonder what he thinks about you—*

To hell with what he thinks about me, she raged silently.

*To hell with you, don't you mean?*

# CHAPTER THREE

BRITT WAS BEAUTIFUL and willing and he had needs. Willing? She was a wild cat with a body that was strong and firm, yet voluptuous. Her breasts were incredible, uptilted and full, and he took his time to weigh them appreciatively, smiling when she groaned with pleasure as he circled her nipples very lightly with his thumbnails. She was so responsive, so eager that her nipples had tightened and were thrusting towards him, pink and impertinent, and clearly in need of more attention. He aimed to please. Kissing her neck, he travelled down, part of him already regretting that they had wasted so much time. She shuddered with desire as he blazed a trail through the dust she had collected when she changed her tyre. 'You're clean now,' he said, smiling into her lust-dazed eyes.

She laughed down low in her throat in a way he found really sexy, and then weakened against him as she waited for him to continue his sensory assault.

'Shall I take the edge off your hunger?' he offered.

'Yours too,' she insisted huskily.

'If that's what you want, you tell me what you'd like.'

Her gaze flicked up and her cheeks flushed pink. She wasn't sure whether to believe him or not.

'I'm serious,' he said quietly.

'Please—'

As she appealed to him he decided that the time he had allowed for this visit to Skavanga wouldn't be enough. He ran his fingers lightly over her beautiful breasts before moving on to trace the swell of her belly. Lifting her skirt, he nudged her thighs apart. She made it easy for him, so he repaid her gesture by delicately exploring the heated flesh at the apex of her thighs. When she whimpered with pleasure it was all he could do to hold back. So much for his much-vaunted self-control, he mused, as Britt thrust her hips towards him, trying for more contact. He wanted nothing more than to take her now. Clutching his arms, she tilted herself back against the table, moaning with need. Opening her legs a little more for him, she showed him a very different woman from the one in the starchy photograph he had examined in London, but this was the woman he had suspected Britt was hiding all along.

'You're quite clinical about this, aren't you?' Britt panted in a rare moment of lucidity as he watched her pleasure.

Duty could do that to a man. He never let himself go. Growing up the second son of the third wife had hardly been to his advantage as a youth. He had been forced to watch the cruelty inflicted on his people by those closer to the throne than he was on a daily basis. So, yes, he was cold. He'd had to be to overthrow tyrants that were also his relatives. There was no room now in his life for anything other than the most basic human appetite.

'Don't make me wait,' Britt was begging him.

She needn't worry. His preference at this moment was to please her.

This was insane. Emir was cold, detached—and the

sexiest thing on two legs. He was frighteningly distant, but she was lost in an erotic haze of his making. She needed more—more pressure, more contact—more of him. The more aloof he was, the more her body cried out to him. The ache he'd set up inside her was unbearable. She had to have more of his skilful touches—

An excited cry escaped her throat when she felt the insistent thrust of his erection against her belly. She rubbed herself shamelessly against it, sobbing with pleasure as each delicious contraction of her nerve endings gave some small indication of what was to come. Emir's hard, warrior frame was even more powerful than she had imagined, and yet he used his hands so delicately in a way that drove her crazy for him. Lacing her fingers through his thick black hair, she dragged him close. He responded by cupping the back of her head to keep her in place as he dipped down and plundered her mouth. Sweeping the table clear, he lifted her and balanced her on the edge. Moving between her legs, he forced them apart with the width of his body. 'Wrap your legs around me,' he commanded, pushing them wider still.

She had never obeyed a man's instructions in her life, but she rushed to obey these. Resting her hands flat on the table behind her, she arched her spine, thrusting her breasts forward, while Emir reared over her, magnificent and erect.

*Like a stallion on the point of servicing a mare?*

With far more consideration than that—

*Are you sure?*

She was sure that any more delay would send her crazy. She was also sure that Emir knew exactly what he was doing.

'Tell me what you want, Britt,' he demanded fiercely.

'You know what I want,' she said.

'But you must tell me,' he said in low, cruel voice.

Her throat dried. The harsher he got, the more arousing she found it. No one had ever pushed her boundaries like this before. And she had thought herself liberal where sex was concerned? She was a novice compared to Emir.

She had also thought herself emotion-free, Britt realised, but knew deep in her heart that something had changed inside her. Even when she plumbed the depths of Emir's cold black eyes she wanted to be the one to draw a response from him—she wanted to learn more about him, and in every way.

'Say it,' he instructed.

Her face blazed red. No one spoke to her like that—no one told her what to do. But her body liked what was happening, and was responding with enthusiasm. 'Yes,' she said. 'Yes, please.' And then she told him exactly what she wanted him to do to her without sparing a single lurid detail.

Now he was pleased. Now she got through to him. Now he almost smiled.

'I think I can manage that,' he said dryly. 'My only concern is that we may not have sufficient time to work our way through your rather extensive wish list.'

On this occasion, she thought. 'Perhaps another time,' she said, matching him for dispassion. But then she glanced at the door. How could she have forgotten that it was still unlocked? Just as she was thinking she must do something about it, Emir touched her in a way that made it impossible for her to move.

'Don't you like the risk?' he said, reading her easily.

She looked at him, and suddenly she loved the risk.

'Hold me,' he said softly. 'Use me—take what you need.'

She hesitated, another first for her. No one had ever given her this freedom. She moved to do as he said and found it took two hands to enclose him.

'I'm waiting,' he said.

With those dangerous eyes watching her, she made a pass. Loving it, she made a second, firmer stroke—

Taking control, Emir caught the tip inside her. She gasped and would have pulled away, but he cupped her buttocks firmly in his strong hands and drew her slowly on to him. 'What are you afraid of?' he said, staring deep into her eyes. 'You know I won't hurt you.'

She didn't know him at all, but for some reason she trusted him. 'I'm just—'

'Hungry,' he said. 'I know.'

A sound of sheer pleasure trembled from her throat. She had played games with boys before, she realised, but Emir was a man, and a man like no other man.

'Am I enough for you?' he mocked.

She lifted her chin. 'What do you think?'

He told her exactly what he thought, and while she was still gasping with shock and lust he kissed her, and before she could recover he thrust inside her deeply to the hilt. For a moment she was incapable of thinking or doing, and even breathing was suspended. This wasn't pleasure, this was an addiction. She could never get enough of this—or of him. The sensation of being completely inhabited while being played by a master was a very short road to release.

'No,' he said sharply, stopping her. 'I'll tell you when. Look at me, Britt,' he said fiercely.

On the promise of pleasure she stared into Emir's molten gaze. She would obey him. She would pay whatever price it took for this to continue.

He was pleased with her. Britt was more responsive

than even he had guessed. She was a strong woman who made him want to pleasure her. He loved the challenge that was Britt Skavanga. He loved her fire. He loved her cries of pleasure and the soft little whimpers she made when he thrust repeatedly into her. What had started as a basic function to clear his head had become an exercise in pleasuring Britt.

'Now,' he whispered fiercely.

He held her firmly as she rocked into orgasm with a release so violent he trusted his strength more than the boardroom table and held her close, though he could do nothing about the noise she was making, which would probably travel to the next town, and so he smothered it with a kiss. When he let her go, she gasped and called his name. He held her safe, cushioning her against the hard edge of the table with his hands as he soothed her down. Withdrawing carefully, he steadied Britt on her feet before releasing her. Smoothing the hair back from her flushed, damp brow, he stared into her dazed eyes, waiting until he was sure she had recovered. The one thing he had not expected was to feel an ache of longing in his chest. He had not expected to feel anything.

'Wow,' she whispered, her voice muffled against his naked chest.

He liked the feeling of Britt resting on him and was in no hurry to move away. If she had been anyone else the next move would have been simple. He would have taken her back to Kareshi with him. But she was too much like him. There would be no diamond mine, no town, no Skavanga Mining, without Britt. Just as he belonged in Kareshi, she was tied here. But still he felt a stab of regret that he couldn't have this exciting woman. 'Are you okay?' he murmured as she stirred.

She lifted her chin to look at him, and as she did this

she drew herself up and drew her emotions in. As she pulled herself together he could almost see her forcing herself to get over whatever it was she had briefly felt for him.

'There are two bathrooms,' she informed him briskly. 'You can use the one directly off the boardroom. I have my own en suite attached to my office. We will reconvene this meeting in fifteen minutes.'

A smile of incredulity and, yes, admiration curved his lips as he watched her go. She walked across the room with her head held high like a queen. It might have seemed ridiculous had anyone else tried it, but Britt Skavanga could pull it off.

He showered down quickly in the bathroom she had told him about, and was both surprised and pleased by the quality of the amenities until he remembered that Britt had a hand in everything here. There were high-quality towels on heated rails, as well as shampoo, along with all the bits and pieces that contributed to making a freshen-up session pleasurable. Britt hadn't forgotten anything—at which point a bolt of very masculine suspicion punched him in the guts. Had she done this before? And if so, how many times?

And why should he care?

He returned to the boardroom to find Britt had arrived before him. She looked composed. She looked as if nothing had happened between them. She looked as she might have looked at the start of the meeting if she hadn't been forced to change a tyre first. She also looked very alone to him, seated beneath the portraits of her forebears, and once again he got the strongest sense that duty ruled Britt every bit as much as it ruled him.

They both imagined they were privileged and, yes, each was powerful in their own way, but neither of them could choose what they wanted out of life, because the choices had already been made for them.

She hated herself, *hated herself* for what she had done. Losing control like that. She hadn't even been able to meet her sex-sated reflection in the bathroom mirror. She had weakened with Emir in a way she must never weaken again. She put it down to a moment of madness before she closed her heart. But as her mind flashed back to what they'd done, and the remembered feeling of being close to him, for however short a time, she desperately wanted more—

She would just have to exercise more control—

'Is something distracting you, Britt?' Emir demanded, jolting her back to the present.

'Should there be something?' she said in a voice that held no hint that Emir was the only distraction.

'No,' he said without expression.

They deserved each other, she thought. But she was curious all the same. Did he really feel nothing? Didn't his body throb with pleasurable awareness as hers did? Didn't he want more? Didn't he yearn to know more about her as she longed to know more about him? Or was she nothing more than an entertainment between coffee breaks for Emir?

And rumour had it she was the hardest of the Skavanga Diamonds?

What a laugh!

Tears of shame were pricking her eyes. She could never make a mistake like this again—

'Hay fever,' she explained briskly when Emir glanced suspiciously at her.

'In Skavanga?' he said, glancing outside at the icy scene.

'We have pollen,' she said coldly, moving on.

She wasn't sure how she got to the end of the second half of their meeting, but she did. There was too much hanging on the outcome for her to spoil the deal with a clouded mind. So far so good, Britt concluded, wrapping everything up with a carefully rehearsed closing statement. At least she could tell her sisters that she hadn't been forced to concede anything vital, and that Emir was prepared to move on to the next stage, which would involve a visit to the mine.

'I'm looking forward to that,' he said.

There was nothing in his eyes for her. The rest of Emir's visit would be purely about business—

And why should it be anything else?

She hated herself for the weakness, but she had expected something—some outward sign that their passionate encounter had made an impression on him… but apparently not.

'Is that everything?' Emir said as he gathered up his papers. 'I imagine you want to make an early start in the morning if we're going to the mine.'

The mine was miles away from anywhere. The only logical place for them to stay was the old cabin Britt's great-grandfather had built. It was isolated—there were no other people around. Doing a quick risk-assessment of the likely outcome, knowing the passion they shared, she knew she would be far better off arranging for one of her lieutenants to take him…

But Emir would see that as cowardice. And was she frightened of him? Could she even entrust the task of taking him to the mine to anyone else? She should be there. And maybe getting him out of her system once and for all would allow her to sharpen up and concentrate on what really mattered again.

'I would like to make an early start,' she said, 'though I must warn you there are no luxury facilities at the cabin. It's pretty basic.' Somehow, what Emir thought about the cabin that meant so much to her mattered to her, Britt realised. It mattered a lot.

Emir seemed unconcerned. 'Apart from the difference in temperature, the Arctic is another wilderness like the desert.'

'My great-grandfather built the cabin. It's very old—'

'You're fortunate to have something so special and permanent to remember him by.'

Yes, she was, and the fact that Emir knew this meant a lot to her.

They stared at each other until she forced herself to look away. This was not the time to be inventing imaginary bonds between them. Better she remembered Eva's words about a true Nordic welcome to contain this warrior of the desert. It would be interesting to discover if Emir was still so confident after a brush with ice and fire.

# CHAPTER FOUR

HE LEARNED MORE about Britt during the first few hours of their expedition than he had learned in any of the reports. She was intelligent and organised, energetic and could be mischievous, which reminded him to remain on guard.

She had called him at five-thirty a.m.—just to check he was awake, she had assured him. He suspected she hadn't slept after their encounter, and guessed she was hoping he'd had a sleepless night too. He gave nothing away.

It couldn't strictly be called dawn when her Jeep rolled up outside his hotel, since at this time of year in Skavanga a weak grey light washed the land for a full twenty-four hours. Only Britt coloured the darkness when she sprang down and came to greet him. He was waiting for her just outside the doors. Her hair gleamed like freshly harvested wheat and she had pulled an ice-blue beanie over her ears to protect them from the bitter cold. Her cheeks and lips were whipped red by the harshest of winds, and she was wearing black polar trousers tucked into boots, with a red waterproof jacket zippered up to her neck. She looked fresh and clean and bright, and determined.

'Britt—'

'Emir.'

Her greeting was cool. His was no more than polite, though he noticed that the tip of her nose was as red as her full bottom lip and her blue-grey eyes were the colour of polar ice. She gave him the once-over, and seemed satisfied by what she saw. He knew the drill. He might live in the desert, but he was no stranger to Arctic conditions.

'Was the hotel okay?' she asked him politely when they were both buckled in.

'Yes. Thank you,' he said, allowing his gaze to linger on her face

She shot him a glance and her cheeks flushed red. She was remembering their time in the boardroom. He was too.

She drove smoothly and fast along treacherous roads and only slowed for moose and for a streak of red fox until they entered what appeared to be an uninhabited zone. Here the featureless ice road was shielded on either side between towering walls of packed snow. She still drove at a steady seventy and refused his offer to take over. She knew the way, she said. She liked to be in control, he thought. Except when she was having sex when she liked him to take the lead.

'We'll soon be there,' she said, distracting him from these thoughts.

They had been climbing up the side of a mountain for some time, leaving the ice walls far behind. Below them was a vast expanse of frozen lake—grey, naturally.

'The mine is just down there,' she said when he craned his neck to look.

He wondered what other delights awaited him. All he could be sure of was that Britt hadn't finished with him yet. She liked to prove herself, so he was confident the test would include some physical activity. He looked forward to it, just as he looked forward to a return bout with her in the desert.

Emir seemed utterly relaxed and completely at home in a landscape that had terrified many people she had brought here. She knew this place like the back of her hand, and yet, truthfully, had never felt completely safe. Knowing Emir, he had probably trialled every extreme sport known to man, so what was a little snow and ice to him?

'Penny for them,' he said.

She made herself relax so she could clear her mind and equivocate. 'I'm thinking about food. Aren't you?'

She was curious to know what he was thinking, but as usual Emir gave nothing away.

'Some,' he murmured.

She glanced his way and felt her heart bounce. She would never get used to the way he looked, and for one spark of interest from those deceptively sleepy eyes she would happily walk barefoot in the snow, which was something Emir definitely didn't need to know.

'The food's really good at the mine,' she said, clinging to safe ground. 'And the catering staff will have stocked the cabin for us. The food has to be excellent when people are so isolated. It's one of the few pleasures they have.'

'I wouldn't be too sure about that,' he said dryly.

'There are separate quarters for men and women,' she countered promptly—and primly.

'Right.' His tone was sceptical.

'You seem to know a lot about it,' she said, feeling a bit peeved—jealous, maybe, especially when he said,

'It's much the same for people who work in the desert.'

'Oh, I see.'

'Good,' he said, ignoring her sharp tone and settling back. 'I'm going to doze now, if you don't mind?'

'Not at all.'

Sleep? Yeah, right—like a black panther sleeps with one eye open. There was no such thing as stand down for Emir.

Emir could play her at her own game, and play it well, Britt realised as she turned off the main road. She could be cool, but he would be cooler, and now there was no real contact between them as he dozed—apparently—which she regretted. He wanted her to feel this way—to feel this lack of him, she suspected.

'Sorry,' she exclaimed with shock as the Jeep lurched on the rutted forest track. The moment's inattention had jolted Emir awake and had almost thrown them into the ditch.

'No problem,' he said. 'If you want me to drive...?'

'I'm fine. Thank you.' She'd heard that the ruler of Kareshi was introducing change, but not fast enough, clearly. Emir probably resented her running the company too. He came from a land where men ruled and women obeyed—

She gasped as his hand covered hers. 'Take it easy,' he said, steadying the steering wheel as it bounced in her hands.

'I've been travelling these roads since I was a child.'

'Then I'm surprised you don't know about the hazards of melting snow.'

He definitely deserved a session in the sauna and a dip in the freezing lake afterwards, she concluded.

'We're nearly there,' she said.

'Good.'

Why the smile in his voice? Was he looking forward to their stay at the isolated cabin? She squirmed in her seat at the thought that he might be and then wondered angrily why she was acting this way. It was one thing bringing her city friends into the wilderness for a rustic weekend, but quite another bringing Emir down here when there could only be one outcome—

Unless he had had enough of her, of course, but something told her that wasn't the case. She'd stick with her decision to enjoy him and get him out of her system, Britt concluded, explaining that the nearest hotel was too far away from the mine to stay there.

'You don't have to explain to me, Britt. I like it here. You forget,' Emir murmured as she drew to a halt outside the ancient log cabin, 'the wilderness is my home.'

And now she was angry with him for being so pleased with everything. And even angrier with herself because Emir was right, the wilderness was beautiful in its own unique way, she thought, staring out across the glassy lake. It was as if she were seeing it for the first time. Because she was seeing it through Emir's eyes, Britt realised, and he sharpened her focus on everything.

'This is magnificent,' he exclaimed as they climbed down from the Jeep.

She tensed as he came to stand beside her. Her heart pumped and her blood raced as she tried not to notice how hot he looked in the dark, heavy jacket and snow boots. Emir radiated something more than the confidence of a man who was sensibly dressed and comfortable in this extreme temperature. He exuded the type of strength that anyone would like to cling to in a storm—

He looked downright dangerous, she told herself sensibly, putting a few healthy feet of fresh air between them. But the lake was beautiful, and neither of them was in any hurry to move away. It stretched for miles and was framed by towering mountains whose jagged peaks were lost in cloud. A thick pine forest crept up these craggy slopes until there was nothing for the roots to cling to. But it was the silence that was most impressive, and that was heavy and complete. It felt almost as if the world were holding its breath, though she had to smile when Emir turned to look at the cabin and an eagle called.

'I'll grab our bags,' he said.

As he brushed past her on his way to the Jeep she shivered with awareness, and then smiled as she walked towards the cabin. She was always happy here—always in control. There would be no problems here. She'd keep things light and professional. Here, she could put what had happened between them in the boardroom behind her.

Emir caught up with her at the door, and his first question was how far was it to the mine? With her back to him, she pulled a wry face. Putting what had happened behind her was going to be easier than she had thought. They hadn't even crossed the threshold yet and Emir's mind was already set on business.

Which was exactly what she had hoped for—

*Was it?*

Of course it was, but she wasn't going to pretend it didn't sting. Everyone had their pride, and everyone wanted to feel special—

Hard luck for her, she thought ruefully.

'So, how far exactly is it to the mine?' he said. 'How long will it take by road?'

'Depending on the weather?' She turned the key in the lock. 'I'd say around ten minutes.'

'Is there any chance we can take a look around today, in that case?' Emir asked as he held the door for her.

He was in more of a hurry than she'd thought. Well, that was fine with her. She could accommodate a fast turnaround. 'The mine is a twenty-four-hour concern. We can visit as soon as you're ready.'

'Then I'd like to freshen up and go see it right away—if that's okay with you?'

'That's fine with me.' She had to stop herself laughing at the thought that she had never met anyone quite so much like her before.

As she used to be, Britt amended, before Emir came into her life. Taking charge of her bag, she hoisted it onto her shoulders. 'Welcome,' she said, walking into the cabin.

'This is nice,' Emir commented as he gazed around.

He made everything seem small, she thought, but in a good way. The cabin had been built by a big man for big men, yet could be described as cosy. On a modest scale, it still reflected the personality of the man who had built it and who had founded the Skavanga dynasty. With nothing but his determination, Britt's great-grandfather had practically clawed the first minerals out of the ground with his bare hands, and with makeshift tools that other prospectors had thrown away. There was nothing to be ashamed of here in the cabin. It was only possible to feel proud.

'What?' Emir said when he caught her staring at him.

'You're the only man apart from my brother who makes me feel small,' she said, managing not to make it sound like a compliment.

'I take it you're talking about your brother, Tyr?'

'My long-lost brother, Tyr,' she admitted with a shrug.

'I can assure you the very last thing on my mind is to make you feel small.'

'You don't—well, not in the way you mean. How tall are you, anyway?'

'Tall enough.'

She could vouch for that. And was that a glint of humour in Emir's eyes? Maybe this wouldn't be so bad, after all. Maybe bringing him to the cabin wasn't the worst idea she'd ever had. Maybe they could actually do business with each other *and* have fun.

*And then say goodbye?*

Why not?

'Are you going to show me to my room?' Emir prompted, glancing towards the wooden staircase.

'Yes, of course. '

Ditching her bag, she mounted the wooden stairs ahead of him, showing Emir into a comfortable double bedroom with a bathroom attached. 'You'll sleep in here,' she said. 'There are plenty of towels in the bathroom, and endless hot water, so don't stint yourself— and just give me a shout if you need anything more.'

'This is excellent,' he called downstairs to her. 'Thank you for putting me up.'

'As an alternative to having you camp down the mine?' She laughed. 'Of course, there are bunkhouses you could use—'

'I'm fine here.'

And looking forward to tasting some genuine Nordic hospitality, she hoped, tongue in cheek, as she glanced out of the window at the snow-clad scene.

'Britt—'

'What?' Heart pounding, she turned. Even now with all the telling off she'd given herself at the tempting thought of testing out the bed springs, she hoped and smiled and waited.

'Window keys?' Emir was standing on the landing, staring down at her. 'It's steaming hot in here.'

Ah… 'Sorry.'

She stood for a moment to compose herself and then ran upstairs to sort him out. The central heating she'd had installed was always turned up full blast before a visit. She could operate it from her phone, and thoughts of turning it down a little had flown out of the window along with her sensible head thanks to Emir. 'I suggest you leave the window open until the room cools down.' Fighting off all feelings about the big, hard, desirable body so very close to her, she unlocked the window and showed him where to hang the key.

'This is a beautiful room, Britt.'

The room was well furnished with a thick feather duvet on the bed, sturdy furniture, and plenty of throws for extra warmth. She'd hung curtains in rich autumnal shades to complement the wooden walls. 'Glad you think so.'

Now she had to look at him, but she lost no time making for the door.

'Are these your grandparents?'

She did not want to turn around, but how could she ignore the question when Emir was examining some sepia photographs hanging on the wall?

'This one is my great-grandfather,' she said, coming to stand beside him. The photographs had been hung on the wall to remind each successive generation of the legacy they had inherited. Her great-grandfather was a handsome, middle-aged man with a moustache and a big, worn hat. He was dressed in leather boots with his heavy trousers tucked into them, his hands were gnarled and he wore a rugged jacket, which was patched at the elbows. Even the pose, the way he was leaning on a spade, spoke volumes about those early days. Family and Skavanga Mining meant everything to her, Britt realised as she turned to leave the room.

She had to ask Emir to move. Why was he leaning against the door? "Excuse me…'

Straightening up, he moved aside. Now she was disappointed because he hadn't tried to stop her. What was wrong with her? She had brought a man she was fiercely attracted to to an isolated cabin. What did she think was going to happen? But now she wondered if sex with Emir would get him out of her system. Would anything?

At the top of the stairs she couldn't resist turning to see if he was still watching her.

Something else for her to regret. And what did that amused look signify—the bed was just a few tempting steps away?

And now the familiar ache had started up again. They were consenting adults who made their own agenda, and, with the mine open twenty-four seven, it wasn't as if they didn't have time—

*And if she gave in to her appetite, Emir would expect everything to be on his terms from hereon in—*

'I'll take quick a shower and see you outside in ten,' she called, running up the next flight of stairs to her own room in the attic. Slamming the door, she rested back against it. Saying yes to Emir would be the easiest thing in the world. Saying no to him required cast-iron discipline, and she wasn't quite sure she'd got that.

She had to have it, Britt told herself sternly as she showered down. Anything else was weakness.

Britt's bedroom was one of three at the cabin. She

had chosen it as a child, because she could be alone up here. She had always loved the pitched roof with its wealth of beams, thinking it was like something out of a fairy tale. When she was little she could see the sky and the mountains if she stood on the bed, and when she was on her own she could be anyone she wanted to be. Over the years she had collected items that made her feel good. Her grandmother had worked the patchwork quilt. Her grandfather had carved the headboard. These family treasures meant the world to her. They were far more precious than any diamonds, but then she had to remember the good the diamonds could do—for Skavanga, the town her ancestors had built, and for her sisters, and for the company.

She had to secure Emir's recommendation to his master, the Black Sheikh, Britt reflected as she toyed with some trinkets on the dressing table. They were the same cheap hair ornaments she had worn as a girl, she realised, picking them up and holding them against her long blonde hair so she could study the effect in the mirror. She hadn't even changed the threadbare stool in front of the dressing table, because her grandmother had worked the stitches, and because it was a reminder of the girl Britt had been, like the books by her bedside. This was a very different place from her penthouse in the centre of Skavanga, but the penthouse was her public face while this was where she kept her heart.

*And to keep it she must cut that deal to her advantage—*

With a man as shrewd as Emir in the frame?

She had never doubted her own abilities before, Britt realised as she wandered over to a window she could see out of now without standing on the bed. Skavanga

Mining had meant everything to her parents, but they hadn't been able to keep it—

*Because her father was a drunk—*

She shook her head, shaking out the memory. Her parents had tried their best—

*Leaving little time for Britt and her siblings.*

So she had picked up a mess. Lots of people had to do that. And somehow she would find a way to cut a favourable deal with the consortium.

Staring out of the window drew her gaze to the traditional sauna hut, sitting squat on the shore of the lake. With its deep hat of snow and rows of birch twigs switches hanging in a rack outside the door, it brought a smile to her face as she remembered Eva's teasing recommendation—that she bring Emir into line here. There were certainly several ways she could think of to do that. If only there weren't a risk he might enjoy them too much…

Seeing Emir's shadow darkening the snow outside, she quickly stepped back from the window. Tossing the towel aside, she pulled out the drawers of the old wooden chest and picked out warm, lightweight Arctic clothing—thermals, sweater, waterproof trousers and thick, sealskin socks. She resented the way her heart was drumming, as if she were going out on a date, rather than showing a man around a mine so he could make vast sums of money for his master out of generations of her family's hard work. She also hated the fact that Emir had beaten her to it downstairs. She was endlessly competitive. Having two sisters, she supposed. Determined to seize back the initiative, she knocked on the window to capture his attention, and when she'd got his attention she held up five fingers to let him know she'd be down right away. Almost. She'd brush her hair and put some lip gloss on first.

*Traitor.*

Everyone likes to feel good, Britt argued firmly with her inner voice. This has nothing to do with Sharif.

He had the cabin keys as well as the keys to the Jeep, and was settled behind the wheel by the time Britt appeared at the door. Climbing out, he strolled over to lock the cabin. She held out her hand to take charge of the keys.

'I'll keep them,' he said, stowing them in the pocket of his lightweight polar fleece.

Britt's crystal gaze turned stony.

'I'm driving too,' he said, enjoying the light floral scent she was wearing, which seemed at complete odds with the warrior woman expression on her face.

She was still seething when she swung into the passenger seat at his side. 'I know where we're going,' she pointed out.

'Then you can guide me there,' he said, gunning the engine. 'I'll turn the Sat Nav off.'

She all but growled at this.

'Why don't you let me drive?' she said.

'Why don't you direct me?' he said mildly, releasing the brake. 'It doesn't hurt to share the load from time to time,' he added, which earned him an angry glance.

They drove on in silence down the tree-shrouded lane. He noticed she glanced at the sauna on the lakeside as they drove past. He guessed his trials might begin there. The sauna was all ready and fired up. She wasn't joking when she'd said the people at the mine looked after her. The consortium would have to work hard to win hearts and minds as well as everything else if they were going to make this project a success. Perhaps they needed Britt's participation in the scheme more than he'd thought at first.

The snow was banked high either side of the road. The tall pines were bowed under its weight. The air was frigid with an icy mist overhanging everything. Snow was falling more heavily by the time they reached the main road. It had blurred the tyre tracks behind them and kept the windscreen wipers working frantically. 'Left or right?' he said, slowing the vehicle.

'If you'd let me drive—'

He put the handbrake on.

'Left,' she said impatiently.

As he swung the wheel Britt tugged off her soft blue beanie and her golden hair cascaded down. If she had been trying to win his attention she couldn't have thought up a better ruse, he realised as the scent of clean hair and lightly fragranced shampoo hit him square in the groin. He smiled to himself when she tied it back severely as if she knew that he liked it falling free around her shoulders. The fact that Britt didn't want to flaunt her femininity in front of him told him something. She liked him and she didn't want him to know.

'You must be tired,' he said, turning his thoughts to the stress she was under. It wasn't easy trying to salvage the family business, as he knew only too well. Whether it was a town or a country made no difference when people you cared about were involved. Her thoughts were with all the people who depended on her, as his were with Kareshi.

'I'm not as fragile as you seem to think,' she said, turning a hostile back on him as she stared out of the window.

She wasn't fragile at all. And if Britt tired at any

point, he'd be there. Crazy, but somehow this woman had got under his skin—and he had more than enough energy for both of them.

# CHAPTER FIVE

EMIR HAD WHAT was needed to take the mine to the next level summed up within the first half hour of him visiting the immense open-cast site. Digging down into the Arctic core would require mega-machines, as well as an extension to the ice road in order to accommodate them, and that would take colossal funding.

With such vast sums involved he would oversee everything. Second in command—second in anything—wasn't his way. Britt was beginning to wonder how Emir managed to work for the sheikh—until he handed over the car keys.

As she thanked him she couldn't have been more surprised and wondered if she had earned some respect down the mine? She had known the majority of the miners most of her life, and got on with everyone, and, though her brother Tyr would have been their first choice, she knew that in Tyr's absence the miners respected her for taking on the job. Some of them had worked side by side with her grandfather, and she was proud to call them friends. She would do anything to keep them in employment.

Emir broke the silence as she started the engine. 'Once I've had the samples tested, we can start planning the work schedule in earnest.'

'I'm sure you won't be disappointed with the result of the test. I've had reports from some of the best brains in Europe, who all came to the same conclusion. The Skavanga mine is set to become the richest diamond discovery ever made.' If they could afford to mine the gems, she added silently. But surely now Emir had seen the mine for himself he wouldn't pull back. *He mustn't pull back.*

She tensed as he stretched out his long legs and settled back. 'So what do you think of the mine now you've seen it? Will you put in a good report? I have had other offers,' she bluffed in an effort to prompt him.

'If you've had other offers you must consider them all.'

Emir had called her bluff and left her hanging. Who else did he think could afford to do the work? It was the consortium or nothing. 'I would have liked Tyr to be involved, but we haven't seen him for years.'

'That doesn't mean he isn't around.'

'I'll have a word with our lawyers when we get back—to see if they can find him. I imagine you'll need to consult with your principal before making the next move?' She glanced across, but the only fallout from this was a heart-crunching smile from Emir. She turned up the heating, but there was ice in her blood. The fact remained that only three men had the resources to bring the diamonds to the surface.

'Why don't you stop by the sauna?' Emir suggested as she shivered involuntarily.

She was shivering, but at the thought of all the battles ahead of her.

*Battles she hadn't looked for in a job she didn't want—*

No one must know that. No one would *ever* know

that. She had accepted responsibility for the mine because there was no one else to do so, and had no intention of welching on that responsibility now. 'The sauna sounds like a good idea. I'm sure you'll enjoy it—'

'I'm sure I will too.'

It would be interesting to see if Emir felt quite so confident by the time they left the sauna.

Shock at the sudden dramatic change in temperature as they climbed out of the Jeep rendered them both silent for a few moments. The sky was uniform grey, though the Northern Lights had just begun to sweep across the bowl of the heavens as if a band of giants were waving luminescent flags. It was startling and awe-inspiring and they both lifted their heads to stare. The air was frigid, and mist formed in front of their mouths as they stood motionless as the display undulated above them.

The ice hole was probably frozen solid, Britt realised as the cold finally prompted them to move. They kept a power saw at the hut and that would soon sort it out. The sauna hut looked like a gingerbread house with a thick white coat of snow. It was another of her special places. Taking a sauna was a tradition she loved. It was the only way to thaw out the bones in Skavanga. And it was a great leveller as everyone stripped to the buff.

'No changing rooms?' Emir queried.

'Not even a shower,' she said, wondering if he was having second thoughts. 'We'll bathe in the lake afterwards.'

'Fine by me,' he said, gazing out across the glassy skating rink the lake had become.

As his lips pressed down with approval her attention was drawn to his sexy mouth. There wasn't much about Emir that wasn't sexy, and she couldn't pretend that she wasn't looking forward to seeing him naked. So far their encounters had been rushed, but there was no rushing involved in a traditional sauna. There would be all the time in the world to admire him.

She left him to open the locked compartment where the power saw was kept, but Emir wasn't too happy when she started it up. She turned, ready to give him a lecture on the fact that she had been cutting holes in the ice since she was thirteen, and stalled. That man could take his clothes off faster than anyone she knew. And could cause a ton of trouble just by standing there. How was she supposed to keep her gaze glued to his face?

'I'll cut the ice. You go inside. The sauna's been lit for some time. It should be perfect. Just ladle some more water on the hot stones—'

She hardly needed steam at this point, Britt reflected as Emir pushed through the door and disappeared. He was a towering monument to masculinity.

*And she was going to share some down time with him?*

She'd always managed to do so before with people without leaping on top of them—

*And they all looked like Emir?*

None of them looked like Emir.

Having cut the hole in the ice, she stripped down ready for the sauna. She kept her underwear on. She'd never done that before. Not that it offered much protection, but she felt better. And maybe it sent a message. If not, too bad; for the first time she could remember ever, she felt self-conscious, so the scraps of lace helped her, if no one else.

She found Emir leaning back on the wooden bench, perfectly relaxed, and perfectly naked as he allowed the steam rising from the hot stones on the brazier to roll over him.

She sat down in the shadows away from him, but couldn't settle.

'Too hot?' he asked as she constantly changed position.

*Try, overheating…*

And that was something else he didn't need to know. Emir's eyes might be closed, but she suspected he knew everything going on around him. If she needed proof of that, his faint smile told her everything. And as if she needed any more provocation with those hard-muscled legs stretched out in front of him, and his best bits prominently displayed—should she be foolish enough to take a look. She transferred her gaze to his face. His eyelashes were so thick and black they threw crescent shadows across his cheekbones, while his ebony brows swept up like some wild Tartar from the plains of Russia…

*Or a sheikh…*

Waves of shock and faintness washed over her, until she told herself firmly to give that overactive imagination of hers a rest. 'I'm going outside to cool off.'

Emir went as far as opening one eye.

'I'm going for a swim in the swimming hole—'

'Then I'm coming with you—'

'No need,' she said quickly, needing space.

Too late. Emir was already standing and taking up every spare inch in the hut. Regret at her foolishness replaced the shock and faintness. They should have said goodbye in Skavanga. She could have sent a trusted employee to the mine.

*Could you trust anyone else to do this deal but you?*

Whatever. There had to be an easier way than this.

'You can't go swimming in an ice lake on your own,' Emir said firmly, as if reading her.

'I've been swimming in the lake since I was a child.'

'When you were supervised, I imagine.'

'I'm old enough to take care of myself now.'

'Really?'

Emir's mockery was getting to her. And what did he think he was looking at now?

*Oh...* She quickly crossed her arms over her chest.

'I'm coming anyway,' he said, still with a flare of amusement in his eyes.

So be it, she thought, firming her jaw. In fairness, the golden rule at the cabin was that no one *ever* went swimming in the frozen lake alone. But did Emir have to tower over her to make his point?

He grabbed a towel on his way out, which he flung around her shoulders. 'You'll need it afterwards,' he said.

She gave him a look that said she didn't need his help, especially not here, and then gritted her teeth as she thought about the icy shock to come.

Running to the lake, she tossed her towel away at the last minute and jumped in before she had chance to change her mind.

She might have screamed. Who knew what she did or said? Once the icy water claimed her, rational thought was impossible. She was in shock and knew better than to linger. She was soon clambering out again—only to find Emir standing waiting for her with a towel.

'You didn't need to do that.'

He tossed the towel her way without another word, and then dived into the lake before she could stop him. She ran to the edge, but there was no sign of him— just loose ice floating. Panic consumed her, but just as she was preparing to jump in after him he emerged. Laughing.

*Laughing!*

Emir had barely cracked a smile the whole time he'd been in Skavanga, and *now* he was laughing?

She repaid the favour by tossing him a clean towel, which he wrapped around his waist. She didn't wait to see how securely he fixed it. She just pelted for the sauna and dived in. Emir was close behind and shut the door.

'Amazing,' he said, like a tiger that, finding itself in the Arctic, had played with polar bears and found it fun.

He shook his head, sending tiny rainbow droplets of glacier flying around the cabin like the diamonds they were both seeking.

'You enjoyed it, I see?' she said as the spray from him hissed on the hot stones.

'Of course I enjoyed it,' he exclaimed. 'I can think of only one thing better—'

She could be excused for holding her breath.

'Next you rub me down with ice—'

Before it melted? She doubted that was possible.

'I definitely want more,' he said, glancing through the window.

Oh, to be a frozen lake, she thought.

As Emir settled back on the wooden bench and closed his eyes she realised she was glad he had embraced her traditions, which led on naturally to wondering about his. She had to stop that before her thoughts took a turn for the seriously erotic.

'You love this place, don't you?' he said.

'It means a lot to me,' she admitted, 'as does the cabin.'

'It's what it represents,' Emir observed.

Correct, she thought.

'If I lived in Skavanga, I'd come here to recharge my batteries.'

Which was exactly what she did. She sometimes came to the cabin just for a change of pace. It helped her to relax and get back in the race.

And it was high time she stopped finding points of contact between them, Britt warned herself, or she'd be convincing herself that fate was giving her a sign. There was no sign. There was no Emir and Britt. It seemed they got on outside sex and business, but that was it.

'What are you thinking?' he said.

She was resting her chin on her knees when she realised Emir was staring at her.

'Why don't you take your underwear off?' he suggested. 'You can't be comfortable in those soggy scraps.'

'They'll soon dry out,' she said, keeping her head down.

Out of the corner of her eye she saw him shrug, but his expression called her a coward. And he was right. She was usually naked before she reached the door of the sauna—and she'd had sex with this man. Plus, she was hardly a vestal virgin in the first place. But somehow with Emir she felt exposed in all sorts of ways, and her underwear was one small, tiny, infinitesimal piece of armour—and she was hanging onto it. 'I'm going outside,' she announced.

'Excellent. I'm ready for my ice rub, Ms Skavanga.'

'Okay, tough guy, bring a towel. And don't blame me if this is too hard core for you.' Her grand flounce off was ruined by the sight of Emir's grin.

She had used to swim through the snow when she was a little girl—or pretend to—and so she plunged straight in. It wasn't something you stopped to think about. The shock was indescribable. But there was pleasure too as all her nerve endings shrieked at once. The soft bed of snow was cold but not life threatening. It was invigorating, and wiped her mind clean of any concerns she had—

*But where was Emir?*

She suddenly realised he wasn't with her. Springing up, she looked around. Nothing—just silence and snow. She called his name. Still nothing.

Had he gone back to the hut?

She ran to the window and peered in. It was empty.

*The lake—*

Dread made her unsteady on her feet as she stumbled towards the water, but then she gusted with relief…and fury as his head appeared above the surface. 'You're mad,' she yelled. 'You never go swimming in the lake on your own. What if something had happened to you?'

'You stole my line,' he said, springing out. 'I'm flattered you'd care.'

'Of course I'd care,' she yelled, leaning forward hands on hips. 'What the hell would I tell your people if I lost you in a frozen lake? Don't you dare laugh at me,' she warned when Emir pressed his lips together. 'Don't you—'

'What?' he said sharply. Catching hold of her arms, he dragged her close, but she saw from his eyes that he was only teasing her. 'Didn't I tell you I wanted more?' he growled.

His brows rose, his mouth curved. She could have stamped on his foot—much good it would do her in bare feet. They stared at each other for a long moment, until finally she wrestled herself free. 'You're impossible! You're irresponsible and you're a pig-headed pain in the neck.'

'Anything else?'

'You deserve to freeze to death!'

'Harsh,' he commented.

Wrapping both towels around her, she stormed off.

'You're a liability!' she flashed over her shoulder, unable to stare at the gleaming lake water streaming off his naked body a moment longer.

'Come back here. You haven't fulfilled your part of the bargain.'

She stopped at the door to the sauna. Emir's voice was pitched low and sent shivers down her spine. This was another of those 'what am I doing here?' moments…

And as soon as she turned she knew. There was nowhere else on earth she'd rather be. 'My part of the bargain?' she queried.

'Ice,' he said, holding her gaze in a way that shot arousal through her.

'I can't believe you haven't had enough yet.'

'I haven't had nearly enough.'

*Those black eyes—that stare—that wicked, sexy mouth—*

'You asked for this,' she said, scooping up a couple of handfuls.

She was right about ice melting on Emir. Even now, fresh from the lake, he was red hot, and as the ice scraped across his smooth, bronzed skin it disappeared beneath the warmth of her hands, leaving her with no alternative but to explore the heat of his body.

'That's enough,' she said, stepping back the instant her breathing became ragged. She had been wrong to think she could do this—that she could play with this man—toy with him—amuse herself at his expense. Emir was more than a match for her, and the strength she'd felt beneath her hands had only confirmed her thoughts that his body was hard, while hers was all too soft and yielding.

She didn't need to see his face to know he was smiling again as she went back to the sauna hut. Her hands were trembling as she let herself in, and hot guilt rushed through her as she curled up on the bench with her knees tucked under her chin and her arms wrapped tightly round them. By the time Emir walked in, she had put safety back at the top of her agenda. 'Let me know if you plan any more solo trips in the lake. Forget the sheikh—I don't even have a contact number for your next of kin.'

'Your concern overwhelms me,' Emir said dryly as he poured another ladle of water onto the hot stones.

'Where are you going now?' she said as he turned for the door.

'To choose which birch switch I would like to use,' he said as if she should have known. 'Would you care to join me?'

Talk about a conversation stopper.

# CHAPTER SIX

SHE WAS TWISTED into a ferment of lust. Her heart was beating like a drum as she watched Emir selecting a birch twig switch. She loved that his process of elimination was so exacting. She loved that he examined each bunch before trying them out on his muscular calves. Each arc through the air…each short, sharp slap against his skin…made her breath catch. Her head was reeling with all sorts of erotic impressions, though she couldn't help wondering if he ever felt the cold. She had grabbed a robe and fur boots before exiting the hut and was well wrapped up.

He started thrashing his shoulders. This was like an advanced lesson in how to watch, feel and suffer—from the most intense frustration she had ever known.

'What do you think?' His dark eyes were full of humour.

'I think I'll leave you to it,' she said, shaking her head as if to indulge the tourist in him.

'Why so prudish, suddenly?' Emir challenged as she turned to go.

Yes. Why was she so strait-laced with Emir when thrashing the body with birch twigs was a normal part of the traditional sauna routine in Skavanga?

'Don't you want to try it?' Emir called after her with amusement in his voice.

She stopped, realising that however high she raised the bar he jumped over it and raised it yet more for her.

Where would this end?

'I can do it any time,' she said casually. He didn't need to know she was shivering with arousal rather than cold as she headed for the door. She swung it open and the enticing warmth with the mellow scent of hot wood washed over her.

'It's not like you to run away from a challenge, Britt.'

She hadn't closed the door yet. 'You don't know anything about me.'

'Are we going to debate this while our body temperatures drop like a stone?'

His maybe. 'You could always join me in the sauna…' she suggested.

'Or you could join me with the birch twigs.' As Emir laughed she made her decision.

'In your dreams. And you might want to put some clothes on,' she added, heading for the sauna hut.

Slamming the door behind her, she leaned back against it, exhaling shakily. Damn the man! Did nothing faze him? She had dreamed of meeting her match, but now she'd met him she wasn't so sure it was such a good idea. They were too similar—too stubborn—too set on duty—too competitive—too everything.

It was too exhausting!

Flopping down on the bench, she closed her eyes, but that didn't help to blank out the fact that a connection of some sort, that wasn't sex, was growing between them. Crashing into the hut in a blast of energy and frigid air, Emir exclaimed, 'Make room for me,' before she could progress this thought.

'Close the door!'

'Wuss,' he murmured in a way that made her picture his sexy mouth curved in that half-smile.

'I don't like the cold,' she muttered, hugging her knees and burying her face so she didn't have to look at him.

'You could have fooled me! But I guess you'd love the desert,' he said.

She went very still and then forced herself to reach for the ladle so she didn't seem too impressed by this last comment.

'You can't still be cold?' Emir commented as she ladled water onto the hot stones. 'That's enough!'

The small hut was full of steam. She had been ladling the water on autopilot, trying not to think about the possibility of travelling to the desert with Emir, and in doing so was threatening to steam them alive. 'Sorry.' She lifted her shoulders in a careless shrug. 'I got carried away.'

'You certainly did,' Emir agreed as he towelled down.

'It's a long time since I've done the whole sauna ritual thing. I'd forgotten—'

'What fun it was?' Emir interrupted.

'How cold you get,' she argued, picking up the ladle again.

He laughed and took it from her. 'That's enough,' he said as their hands brushed. 'Sit down.' He towered over her, blocking out the light. 'If you want to raise the temperature, just ask me.'

'Very funny.' She glanced up.

Emir shrugged and smiled faintly, making her glad she was wearing a towel. He had no inhibitions, and, in fairness, most people went naked in the sauna, but that only worked if they had no sexual interest in each other.

'How about I build a fire in the fire pit outside?' Emir suggested. 'You don't want to be cooped up in here much longer.'

She had always enjoyed sitting round a blazing fire surrounded by snow and ice, and it would be one heck of a lot safer than this intimate space. 'That's a great idea.'

'I'll call you when I'm ready.'

You do that, she thought, banking Emir's sexy smile.

Her heart thumped on cue when he rapped on the door. Sliding off the bench, she went outside to join him. Emir had built an amazing fire…roaring hot and set to last.

'Nights in the desert can be freezing,' he explained. 'And in some parts a fire is essential to keep mountain lions away. We have amazing wildlife,' he added as she sat down and stretched her feet out. 'Kareshi is a country of great contrasts. We have big modern cities as well as a wilderness where tribal traditions haven't changed in centuries.'

Why was he telling her this? Was he serious about her visiting Kareshi? They were staring at each other again, Britt realised, turning away to pretend interest in the fire. There was no point in getting any closer to Emir when their relationship, such as it was, wasn't going anywhere. Lifting his chin, he stared at her as if he were expecting her to say something. Who knew that Britt Skavanga, lately hotshot businesswoman, as her sisters liked to teasingly call her, could feel so awkward, even shy?

*Maybe you should get out of the office more often.*

Maybe she should, Britt thought wryly, lacking the

energy for once to argue with her contrary inner voice. Emir had gone quite still, she noticed.

'Do you see them?' he said, looking past her into the trees.

'The deer? Yes,' she murmured. A doe and a fawn were watching them from the safety of the undergrowth. 'They're so beautiful,' she whispered, hardly daring to breathe. 'I always feel close to nature here,' she confided in another whisper.

'As I do in the desert,' Emir murmured back.

There was that connection thing again. It was there whether she liked it or not. And now she stiffened, remembering the warning her mother had given her when Britt was a child. Now she understood why her mother had said the things she had, but as a little girl she had thought her father loud rather than violent, and playful, rather than bullying. Now she knew he'd been a drunk who had prompted her mother to warn all her daughters that men kept you down. Her girls were going to be warriors who went out into the world and made their own way. Britt had grown up with the determination that no man would ever rule her engraved on her heart. And Emir was a forceful man...

His touch on her arm made her flinch, but then she realised he was pointing to the deer watching them. The animals were considering flight, and she wondered if it was Emir's inner stillness holding them. Their brown eyes were wide in gentle faces, and though Emir had moved closer to her he kept space between them, which made her feel relaxed. He had that sort of calming aura—which didn't mean she wasn't intensely aware of him. It was a special moment as they watched the deer watching them. It was as if humans and animals had come together briefly.

'What an amazing encounter,' she breathed as the deer turned and picked their way unhurriedly back through the maze of trees into the depth of the forest.

'Now I'm certain you'd love the desert,' Emir said, turning to smile at her. 'Many think it's just a barren space—'

'But we know better?'

He huffed a laugh, holding her gaze in a way that said he was glad she had understood.

'Maybe one day I'll make it to the desert,' she said, trying not to care too much.

'I'll make sure of it,' Emir said quietly. 'If this deal goes through I'll make sure you visit Kareshi.'

'I'd love to,' she exclaimed impulsively.

How much longer are you going to wear your heart on your sleeve? Britt wondered as Emir flashed her an amused glance and raised a brow. But she could see that a whole world of possibility was opening up, both for her and for Skavanga, and she couldn't pretend that the thought of visiting an emerging country where the vigorous young ruler had already done so much for his people didn't excited her.

'I want you to see what the money from the diamonds can accomplish,' Emir remarked.

Yes, there were benefits for both their countries. 'I will,' she said, more in hope than expectation. 'I think you miss Kareshi,' she added in an attempt to shift the spotlight onto him.

'I love my country. I love my people. I love my life in Kareshi. I love my horses—they're a real passion for me. I breed pure Arabs, though sometimes I strengthen the line of my breeding stock with Criolla ponies from the Argentine pampas.'

'You play polo?'

'Of course, and many polo players are my friends. You will have heard of the Acosta brothers, I'm sure.'

She had heard of the Acosta brothers. Who hadn't? 'I learned to ride at the local stable,' she admitted. 'Just old nags compared to the type of horses you're talking about, but I loved it all the same. I love the sense of freedom, and still ride whenever I get the chance.'

'Something we have in common,' he said.

Something else, she thought, inhaling steadily. Friendships were founded on sharing a passion for life, and there was no doubt that they were opening up to each other. So much for her mother's warning. And, yes, it was dangerous to reveal too much of yourself, but if you didn't, how could you ever get close to anyone?

She had to face facts. Once he had collected the information he needed, Emir would go home—and inviting her to Kareshi was probably just talk. Making her excuses, she stood up to go. Emir stood too.

'No birching?' he asked wryly.

She gave him a crooked smile. 'I'm warm enough, thanks to you.'

'That's right,' he called after her as she walked away. 'You probably deserve a good birching—probably even want it. But you're not getting it from me—'

Britt shook her head in wry acceptance, but Emir didn't turn around as she huffed a laugh. He didn't need to. There was a new sort of ease between them—an understanding, almost.

He caught her at the door of the hut, and, lifting a switch from the rack, he shot her a teasing look. 'Are you quite sure?'

'Certain,' she said, but there was laughter in both their eyes.

Laughter that died very quickly when Emir ran the

switch of twigs very lightly down between her breasts
and over her belly to the apex of her thighs. She was instantly aroused and couldn't move, even had she wanted
to. She remained motionless as he increased the pressure just enough, moving the bunched twigs with exactly the right degree of delicacy. Her breath came out
in a noisy shudder, and all this time Emir was holding
her gaze. His eyes told her that he knew exactly what
she wanted him to do. Her breathing stalled when he
used the switch to ease her legs apart.

'Why deny yourself, Britt?'

'Because I need to get inside where it's warm,' she
said lightly, pulling herself together.

Physically, she yearned for everything Emir could
give her, Britt realised as she quickly shed her underwear, while emotionally she was a wreck. She felt such
a strong connection to him, and knew she would never
be able to ignore those feelings—

Better she end this now.

He joined her in the hut. That was a foregone conclusion. The stag didn't abandon the doe when it was cor-
nered. The stag knew what the doe wanted and tracking
it was part of the game. They sat opposite each other
with the hot stones sizzling between them, and, leaning back, Emir gave her a look—just a slight curve at
the corner of his sexy mouth.

'What?' she said, knowing he could hardly have
avoided noticing that she was naked.

'Now we get really hot,' he said.

# CHAPTER SEVEN

As Emir's familiar warmth and scent flared in her senses and his arms gathered her in, Britt felt a new energy flooding through her. She even spared a foolish moment to wish it could always be like this—that he was really hers, and that these strong arms and this strong body would sometimes take over so she could take time out occasionally. But that was so ridiculous she had no difficulty blanking it out. She took one last look at a world where desire for a man could grow into friendship, and where that friendship could grow into love. That was just childhood fantasy. She'd settle for lust.

Holding her face between his hands, Emir made her look at him. Gazing into the burning stare of a man who knew so much about her body made it easy to forget her doubts. Her face must have shown this transition, because he brushed her lips with his. And from there it was an easy slide into a passionate embrace that ended with Emir manoeuvring her into a comfortable position on the bench—which just happened to be under him.

'Is there any part of this you don't like?' he said, smiling down at her.

She liked everything—too much—and at what risk to her heart? Right now she didn't care as another part of Britt Skavanga, warrior woman, chipped off and floated away. At one time sex was little more than a normal function for her, like eating or sleeping, but now...

Now that wasn't nearly enough.

But Emir's hands were distracting her, and as he traced the line of her spine she embraced the feelings inside her. They were so strong she could hardly ignore them. She wanted this man. She wanted him so badly. She wanted to be one with him in every way. Unfortunately, Emir's approach to sex was much like hers had used to be, and being on the receiving end of that was very different from doling it out. But then her mind filled with pleasure as his lips caressed her neck. He knew just how to work her hot spots until she softened against him and relaxed. She had always taken the lead in the past—she had been the one who knew what she was doing and where she was going, the one who was completely in control—but with Emir there was no control. She was his.

'I love your body,' he said as she writhed beneath him.

'I love yours too.' How could she not?

Emir was built on a heroic scale. She doubted she had ever met a bigger man. There wasn't a spare inch of unnecessary flesh on his hard, toned body, and each muscle was clearly delineated after his strenuous physical exercise in the lake. He was every bit the soldier, the fighter, the leader, yet he had the most sensitive hands. She groaned as he massaged her scalp with his fingertips.

'What do you want, Britt?' he murmured.

'Do you really need me to answer that?'

'I like you to tell me,' he said.

Emir's voice had the power to arouse her almost as

much as the man himself. Raising her chin, she took a deep breath and then told him what she wanted.

'So open your legs wider,' he said.

Her first thought was, No. I can't do that—not while you're looking down at me.

'Wider,' he said.

She wanted this. He excited her—

'Wider still…'

'I can't—you're merciless—'

'Yes, I am,' he agreed in the same soft tone.

'Enough,' she begged him, reaching out. She needed human contact. She needed closeness more than anything. She needed a kiss—a tender kiss. She still longed for the illusion that they were close in every way, Britt realised, feeling a pang of regret for what could never be.

He had never seen anything more beautiful than Britt at this moment, when every part of her was glowing and aroused. His desire to be joined to her was overwhelming, but something as special as this could not be rushed. It must be appreciated and savoured. One of the so-called erotic secrets of Kareshi was nothing more than this lingering over pleasure. Making time for pleasure was a so much a national pursuit he had been forced to persuade the Kareshi people to balance their country's business needs against it, but he would never wish these old traditions to die out. In fact, he had every intention of fostering them, and as Britt reached for him he took her wrists in a firm grip. 'Not yet,' he whispered.

'Don't you want me?' she said, arching her back as she displayed her breasts to best advantage.

She had no idea how much.

He held her locked in his stare as she sat up. He even

allowed her to lace her fingers through his hair, binding him to her. Britt was easy to read. She was already on the edge. Intuition had always helped him in the past— in all sorts of situations, and now this. With Britt he mastered his own desires by channelling his thoughts into all the things that intrigued him about her.

'How can you bear to wait?' she complained.

'I bear it because I know what's best for you,' he said. 'I know what you need and I know the best way to give it to you.'

'How do you know?' she said, writhing with impatience.

On the sexual front that was all too obvious, but knowing Britt wasn't so hard. She was the oldest child, always trying to do her best, the lab-rat for her sisters, the one who would have been given the strictest upbringing by her parents. Britt was used to bearing the weight of responsibility on her shoulders, and with duties at home and then duties in the business she hadn't had much time to explore life, let alone discover the nuances of sex and how very good it could be.

'So, how did you like our Nordic traditions?' she murmured against his mouth.

Distracted, he brushed a kiss against her lips. 'I like them a lot. I'd like to know more. I'd like to know more about you—'

The look of surprise on her face almost broke the erotic spell for him, and then she said with touching honesty, 'I'd like to know more about you and your country.'

'Maybe you will.'

Closing his eyes, he inhaled her wildflower scent, and realised then that the thought of never smelling it again was unthinkable. He was still on guard, of course.

There was still a business deal to do and it would be unwise to underestimate Britt Skavanga. She was everything he had been warned to expect…and so much more.

When Emir kissed her she was glad of his arms supporting her, because he didn't just kiss her breath away, he kissed her thoughts away too. It felt so good to drop her guard and lose herself in sensation, shut out the business robot she had become. It was good to feel sensation spreading in tiny rivers of fire through her veins, and even better to feel Emir's erection resting heavily against her thigh, because that said he wanted her as much as she wanted him. She groaned with anticipation when he nudged her thighs apart. Moving between them, he started teasing her with delicate touches until she thought she would go mad for him.

'Wrap your legs around me,' he instructed, staring deep into her eyes.

'Don't make me wait,' she warned, but in a way she was glad when he soothed her with kisses and caresses first. She cried out and urged him on. There were no certainties other than the fact that she was being drawn deeper into a dangerous liaison with him.

As if sensing her unease, he took her face in his big, warm hands and drugged her with kisses. Gentle to begin with, they grew deeper and firmer as the embers inside her sparked and flared. She loved it when he took possession of her mouth, and loved it even more when he took possession of her body. She loved being held so firmly. She loved the powerful emotions inside her.

'Have you changed your mind?' he said as she tried to rein them in.

She denied this, and then he did something so amazing she couldn't have stopped him if she had tried. A shaking cry escaped her throat as he sank slowly deep inside her. She could never be fully prepared for Emir. The sheer size of him stole the breath from her lungs. He was such an intuitive lover. He understood every part of her and how she responded. He knew her limits and never stepped over them, while his hands and mouth worked magic. Today he was using the seductive language of Kareshi—soft and guttural, husky and persuasive—to both encourage and excite her. It must have succeeded because she found herself pressing her legs wide for him with the heel of her palms against her thighs.

'Good,' he approved, thrusting even deeper.

She cried out his name repeatedly as he moved rhythmically and reliably towards the inevitable conclusion. But suddenly some madness overcame them, and control was no longer possible as they fought their way to release.

She was still shuddering with aftershocks minutes later. Her internal muscles closed around him gratefully, to an indescribably delicious beat.

Neither of them spoke for quite a while. They had both experienced the same thing—something out of the ordinary, she thought as Emir stared down at her. At last his eyes were full of everything she had longed to see.

'I take it you enjoyed that?' he murmured, and, withdrawing gently, he helped her to sit up.

'And you?' she said, resting her cheek against his chest.

'I have one suggestion—'

She glanced up.

'Next time we try a bed.'

His grin infected her. 'Now there's a novel thought,'

she agreed, but after she had rested on him for a moment or two harsh reality intruded and she remembered who she was, who he was, and the parts they played in this drama.

Lifting her chin, she put on the old confident face. 'Don't get ahead of yourself, mister. I sleep alone.'

'Who mentioned sleeping?' Emir argued.

'Do you always have to show such perfect good sense?'

'With you, I think I do,' he said, smiling, unrepentant.

Emir was probably the one man she was prepared to take instruction from, Britt concluded as she showered down later in her en-suite bathroom at the cabin, if only because the pay-off was so great. And she wasn't just thinking about the sexual pay-off, but the pay-off that was making her sing and waltz around the bathroom like a fruit-loop—the pay-off that made her feel all warm and fuzzy inside—and optimistic about the future—about everything. She felt suddenly as if anything could happen—as if the boundaries of Skavanga and her job had fallen away, leaving a world full of possibility. And the desert kingdom of Kareshi was definitely the stand out country in that world waiting to be discovered.

Of course, she must visit Emir's homeland as he had suggested. If the deal went through it would be wrong to accept the consortium's investment without wanting to know as much as she possibly could about the benefits the diamonds would bring to both countries. Perhaps there could be reciprocal cultural and educational opportunities—anything was possible. She longed to get stuck into it—to get out of the office and

meet people at last. Her mind was blazing with ideas.
No dream seemed too far-fetched.

Showering down after his unique encounter with Britt,
Sharif's thoughts were arranged in several compart-
ments. The first was all to do with Britt the businesswoman. She was meticulous and had held the company
together when many would have failed. Her attention
to detail was second to none—as he had learned when
it had taken him several hours, rather than the usual
five minutes, to pore over her first agenda and find a
hole. She was clear-headed and quick-thinking in her
business life—

*And an emotional mess when it came to anything
else.*

Her life was tied up in duty, but she wanted it all.
He guessed she heard the clock ticking, but she didn't
know how to escape from her work long enough to find
the fulfilment she craved—the satisfaction of raising
her own family and extending her sphere of influence
in the workplace too. She did everything she could to
support her sisters while they studied and campaigned
for this and that, but they didn't seem to stop and think
that Britt deserved some fulfilment too.

And neither should he, he reminded himself. He had
one duty, one goal, and one responsibility, which was to
the men who had come in with him on this deal. Business always came first, because business fed improve-
ments in Kareshi, and only then could he afford to pause
to wonder if there was anything missing from his life—

*Britt?*

Any man would be missing a woman like Britt in his
life. She was exceptional. She was an intriguing mix
of control and abandonment, and it seemed to him that

the only time Britt let go was during sex, which made cutting the best deal possible a challenging prospect, but not impossible.

Business, always business, he thought, towelling down. He liked that Britt was part of that business. He had always loved a challenge and Britt was a challenge. Securing the towel around his waist, he picked up his razor to engage in the one battle he usually lost. His beard grew faster than he could shave it off, but at least the ritual soothed him and gave him time to think.

Shaking his head as if that could shake thoughts of Britt out of it, he rinsed his face and raked his thick, unruly hair into some semblance of order. The deal was a tantalising prospect and he would bring it in. Between them he and his friends had the means and the skill and the outlets necessary to transform dull, uncut diamonds into sparkling gems that would shimmer with fire as they shivered against a woman's skin. Britt believed she held all the cards, and could cut the better deal, but he held the joker.

Stepping into jeans, he tugged on a plain back top, and fastened his belt before reaching for the phone. Some decisions were harder to take than others, and this was harder than most. Britt had all the instincts of a man inside the body of a woman, but she had a woman's emotions, which held her back when it came to clear thinking in a deal like this where family was involved. He wished he could protect her from the fallout from this call, but his duty was clear. This wasn't for him alone, but for the consortium, and for Kareshi. In the absence of her brother, Britt led her tribe as he did, making her a worthy adversary. He just had to hope she could handle this new twist in the plot as competently as she had coped with other obstacles life had thrown at her.

He drummed his fingers impatiently as he waited for the call to connect. Three rings later the call was answered. He hesitated, which was definitely a first for him, but the die had been cast on the day he had sat down to research the share structure of Skavanga Mining and had discovered that the major shareholder was not in fact the three sisters, but their missing brother, Tyr Skavanga. More complicated still was that, for reasons of his own, Tyr didn't want his sisters to know where he was. Having given his word, Emir would have to keep that from Britt even though Tyr's long-distance involvement in the deal would swing the balance firmly in the consortium's favour.

'Hello, Tyr,' he said, settling down into what he knew would be a long call.

# CHAPTER EIGHT

HE WAS PACKING? *Emir was packing?* She had come downstairs after her shower expecting to find him basking in front of a roaring fire—which he would have banked up, perhaps with a drink in hand and one waiting for her on the table. She had anticipated more getting-to-know-you time. That was what couples did when they'd grown closer after sex...

And they had grown closer, Britt reassured herself, feeling painfully obvious in banged-up jeans, simple top and bare feet. She felt as if, in this relaxed state, all her feelings were on display. And all those feelings spoke of closeness and intimacy with Emir. She had dressed in anticipation of continuing ease between them. She had dressed as she would dress when her sisters were around. And now she felt vulnerable and exposed. And utterly ridiculous for having let her guard down so badly.

*How could she have got this so wrong?*

She watched him from the doorway of his bedroom as Emir folded his clothes, arranging them in a bag that he could sling casually over his shoulder. He must have known she was standing there, but he didn't say a word. The chill seemed to creep up from the floor and consume her. Even her face felt cold.

*What had gone wrong?*

What was wrong was that Emir didn't care and she had refused to see that. He had come here to do a job and his job was done. He had taken samples for analysis and had seen the mine for himself. He had weighed her up and interviewed her colleagues. His only job now was to pack up and leave. What had she been? An unexpected bonus on the side? She had no part to play in Emir's plans, he'd made that clear. Why had she ever allowed herself to believe that she had? All that talk of Kareshi and the desert was just that—talk.

Her throat felt tight. Her mouth was dry. She felt numb. Anything she said in this situation would sound ridiculous. And what was the point of having a row when she had no call on this man? She had enjoyed him as much as he had enjoyed her. Was it his fault if she couldn't move on?

All this was sound reasoning, but reason didn't allow for passion, for emotion—for any of the things she felt for Emir. And out of bitter disappointment at his manner towards her—or rather his lack of…anything, really—came anger. What had he meant by staring into her eyes and suggesting they should take sex to the bedroom next time? Was that concern for her? Or was Emir more concerned about getting grazes on his knees? She had laughed with and trusted this man. Everything had changed for her, because she'd thought… Because she'd thought…

She didn't have a clue what she'd thought, Britt realised. She only knew she had given herself completely to a man, something she'd never done before, and now, just as her mother had predicted, she was paying the price. But she would not play the role of misused mistress and give him the chance to mock.

'You're leaving?' she said coolly. 'Already?'

'My job here's done,' Emir confirmed, straightening up. He turned to face her. 'My flight plan is filed. I leave right away.'

When did he file his flight plan? Immediately after making love to her?

'Do you have transport to the airport?' She wasn't so petty she would let him call a cab. She would take him to the airport if she had to.

'My people are coming for me,' he said, turning back to zip up his bag.

Of course. 'Oh, good,' she said, going hot and cold in turn as she chalked up the completeness of his plan as just one more insult to add to the rest. He'd had sex with her first and then had called his people to come and get him. He'd used her—

*As she had used men in the past.*

Her heart lurched as their eyes met. Mistake. Now he could see how badly she didn't want him to go.

'I have to report back to the consortium, Britt,' he said, confirming this assumption.

'Of course.' She cleared her throat and arranged her features in a composed mask. She had never been at such a disadvantage where a man was concerned. But that was because she had never known anyone like Emir before and had always prided herself on being able to read people. She had not read him. They were like two strangers, out of sync, out of context, out of time.

She stood in embarrassed silence. With no small talk to delay him, let alone some siren song with which to change his mind, she could only wait for him to leave.

'Thank you for your hospitality, Britt,' he said, shouldering the bag.

*Her hospitality?* Did that include the sex? Her face

was composed, but as Emir moved to shake her hand she stood back.

Emir didn't react one way or the other to this snub. 'I'll wait for test results on the samples, and if all goes well you will hear from my lawyers in the next few weeks.'

'Your lawyers?' Her head was reeling by now, with business and personal thoughts hopelessly mixed.

'Forgive me, Britt.' Emir paused with his hand on the door. 'I meant, of course, the lawyers acting for the consortium will be in touch with you.'

Suddenly all the anger and hurt inside her exploded into fury, which manifested itself in an icy question. 'And what if I get a better offer in the meantime?'

'Then you must consider it and we will meet again. I should tell you that the consortium has been in touch with your sisters, and they have already agreed—'

'You've spoken to Eva and Leila?' she cut in. He'd done that without speaking to her? She couldn't take any more in than she already had—and she certainly couldn't believe that her sisters would do a deal without speaking to her first.

'My people have spoken to your sisters,' Emir explained.

'And you didn't think to tell me?' *They didn't think to tell me?* She was flooded with hurt and pain.

'I just have.' A muscle flicked in his jaw.

'So all the time we've been here—' Outrage boiled in her eyes. 'I think you'd better go,' she managed tensely. Suddenly, all that mattered was speaking to her sisters so she could find out what the hell was going on.

Meanwhile, Emir was checking round the room, just to be sure he hadn't forgotten anything, presumably. He didn't care a jot about her, she realised with a cold rush of certainty. This had only ever been about the deal. How convenient to keep her distracted here while the consortium's lackeys acted behind her back. How very clever of Emir. And how irredeemably stupid of her.

'If you've left anything I'll send it on,' she said coldly, just wanting him to go.

How could her heart still betray her when Emir's brooding stare switched to her face?

'I knew I could count on you,' he said as her stupid heart performed the customary leap.

Emir's impassive stare turned her own eyes glacial. 'Well, you've got what you wanted from me, so you might as well go. You'll get nothing else here.'

The inky brows rose, but Emir remained silent. She just hoped her barb had stabbed home. But no.

'This is business, Britt, and there is no emotion in business. I wish I could tell you more, but—'

'Please—spare me.' She drew herself up. 'Goodbye, Emir.'

She didn't follow him out. She wouldn't give him the satisfaction. She listened to him jog down the stairs, while registering the tenderness of a body that had been very well used, and heard him stride across the main room downstairs where they had been so briefly close. It was as if Emir were stripping the joy out of the cabin she loved with every step he took, and each of those departing steps served as a reminder that she had wasted her feelings on someone who cared for nothing in this world apart from business.

Apart from her sisters and Tyr, that had been how she was not so very long ago, Britt conceded as the front door closed behind Emir.

She hadn't even realised she had stopped breathing

until she heard a car door slam and she drew in a desperate, shuddering breath.

There were times when he would gladly exchange places with the grooms who worked in his stables and this was one of them, but harsh decisions had to be made. He thought he could feel Britt's anguished stare on his back as he held up his hand to hail the black Jeep that had come to collect him. His men would take him back to the airport and his private jet. His mind was still full of her when he climbed into the passenger seat and they drove him away. It was better to leave now before things became really complicated.

Her sense of betrayal by Emir—and, yes, even more so by her sisters—was indescribable. And for once both Eva and Leila were out of touch by phone. She had tried them constantly since Emir had left, prowling around the cabin like a wounded animal, unable to settle or do anything until she had spoken to them. Even her beloved cabin had let her down. It failed to soothe her this time. She should never have brought Emir here. He had tainted her precious memories.

Not wanting to face the fact that she had been less than focused, she turned on every light in the cabin, but it still felt empty. There was no reply from her sisters, so all she could do was dwell on what she'd seen through the window when he'd left—Emir climbing into a Jeep and being driven away. She'd got the sense of other big men in the vehicle, shadowy, and no doubt armed. Where there were such vast resources up for grabs, no one took any chances. She had been kidding herself if she had thought that bringing investors in would be easy to handle. She was up against a power-

ful and well-oiled machine. She should have known
when each man in the consortium was a power in his
own right, and she was on her own—

So? Get used to it! There was no time for self-pity.
This was all about protecting her sisters, whatever
they'd done. They weren't to blame. They had no idea
what it took to survive in the cut-throat world of business—she didn't want them to know. She would protect
them as she always had.

She nearly jumped out of her skin when the phone
rang, and she rushed to pick it up. Mixed feelings when
she did so, because it was Eva, her middle and least
flexible sister, calling. 'Eva—'

'You rang?' Eva intoned. 'Seven missed calls, Britt?
What's going on?'

Where to begin? Suddenly, Britt was at a loss, but
then her mind cleared and became as unemotional as
it usually was where business was concerned. 'The
man from the consortium just left the cabin. He said
you and Leila signed something?' Britt waited tensely
for her sister to respond, guessing Eva would be doing
ten things at once. 'So, what have you signed?' Britt
pressed, controlling her impatience.

'All we did was give permission for the consortium's
people to enter the offices to start their preliminary investigations.'

'Why didn't you speak to me first?'

'Because we couldn't get hold of you.'

And now she could only rue the day she had left Skavanga to show Emir the mine.

'We thought we were helping you move things on.'

Britt could accept that. The sooner the consortium's
accountants had completed their investigations, the
sooner she could bring some investment into Skavanga

Mining and save the company. 'So you haven't agreed to sell your shares?'

'Of course not. What do you take me for?'

'I don't want to argue with you, Eva. I'm just worried—'

'You know I don't know the first thing about the business,' Eva countered. 'And I'm sorry you got landed with it when our parents died. I do know there are a thousand things you'd rather do.'

'Never mind that now—I need to help people at home. I'm coming back—'

'Before you go, how did you get on with him?"

'Who?' Britt said defensively.

'You know—the man who was at the mine with you—the sheikh's man.'

'Oh, you mean Emir.'

'What?'

'Emir,' Britt repeated.

'Well, that's original,' Eva murmured with a smile in her voice. 'Did the Black Sheikh come up with any more titles to fool you, or just the one?'

Britt started to say something and then stopped. 'Sorry?'

'Oh, come on,' Eva exclaimed impatiently. 'I guess he was quite a man, but I can't believe your brain has taken up permanent residence below your belt. You know your thesaurus as well as anyone: emir, potentate, person of rank. Have I rung any bells yet?'

'But he said his name was—' Hot waves of shame washed over her. She was every bit as stupid as she had thought herself when Emir left, only more so.

'Since when have you believed everything you're told, Britt?' Eva demanded.

Since she met a man who told her that his name was Emir.

She had to speak to him. She would speak to him, Britt determined icily, just as soon as she had finished this call to her sister.

'You haven't fallen for him, have you?' Eva said shrewdly.

'No, of course not,' Britt fired back.

There was a silence that suggested Eva wasn't entirely convinced. Too bad. Whatever Britt might have felt for Emir was gone now. Gone completely. Finished. Over. Dead. Gone.

'You should have taken him for a roll in the snow so you could both cool down.'

'I did,' she admitted flatly. 'He loved it.'

'Sounds like my kind of guy—'

'This isn't funny, Eva.'

'No,' Eva agreed, turning serious. 'You've made a fool of yourself and you don't like it. Turns out you're not the hotshot man-eater you thought you were.'

'But I'm still a businesswoman,' Britt murmured thoughtfully, 'and you know what they say.'

'I'm sure you're going to tell me,' Eva observed dryly.

'Don't get mad, get even.'

'That's what I was afraid of,' Eva commented under her breath. 'Just don't cut off your nose to spite your face. Don't screw this deal after putting so much effort into it.'

'Don't worry, I won't.'

'So what are you going to do?' Eva pressed, concern ringing in her voice.

For betraying her—for allowing his people to approach her sisters while Britt and he were otherwise engaged?

'I'm going to follow him to Kareshi. I'm going to track him down. I'm going to ring his office to try and find out where he is. I'll go into the desert if I have to. I'm going to find the bastard and make him pay.'

# CHAPTER NINE

*KARESHI*...

She was actually here. It hardly seemed possible. For all her bitter, mixed-up thoughts when it came to the man she had called Emir and must now learn to call His Majesty Sheikh Sharif al Kareshi, Britt couldn't help but be dazzled by her first sight of the ocean of sand stretching away to a purple haze following the curve of the earth. She craned her neck, having just caught sight of the glittering capital city. It couldn't stand in greater contrast to the desert.

Just as her thoughts of the man the world called the Black Sheikh couldn't have stood in starker contrast to the universal approval the man enjoyed. How could he fool so many people? How could he fool her?

That last question was easily answered. Her body had done that for her, yearning for a man when it should freeze at the very thought of him—if she had any sense.

As the city came into clearer view and she saw all the amazing buildings she got a better picture of the Black Sheikh's power and his immense wealth. It seemed incredible that she was here, and that His Majesty Sheikh Sharif had been her lover—

That she had been so easily fooled.

'The captain has switched the seat-belt sign on.'

'Oh, yes, thank you,' she said glancing up, glad of the distraction. Any distraction to take her mind off that man was welcome.

Having secured her belt, she continued to stare avidly out of the window. Her life to date hadn't allowed for much time outside Skavanga, and from what she could see from the plane Kareshi couldn't have been more different. The thought of exploring the city and meeting new people was exciting in spite of all the other things she had to face. An ivory beach bordered the city, and beyond that lay a tranquil sea of clear bright blue, but it was the wilderness that drew her attention. The Black Sheikh was down there somewhere. His people had told her this in an attempt to put her off. They didn't know her if they thought she would be dismayed to learn His Majesty was deep in the desert with his people. She would find him and she would confront him. She had every reason to do so, if only to learn the result of the trials on the mineral samples he had taken from the mine. She suspected he would agree to see her. His people were sure to have told him that she had been asking for him and, like Britt, the Black Sheikh flinched from nothing.

Another glance out of the window revealed a seemingly limitless carpet of umber and sienna, gold and tangerine, and over this colourful, if alien landscape the black shadow of the aircraft appeared to be creeping with deceptive stealth. The desert was a magical place and she was impatient to be travelling through it. Would she find Sheikh Sharif? The ice fields of Skavanga were apparently featureless, but that was never completely true, and where landmarks failed there was always GPS. Tracking down the ruler of Kareshi would be a challenge, but not one she couldn't handle.

* * *

Shortly after she reached the hotel Britt received a call
from Eva to say that one of their main customers for
the minerals they mined had gone down, defaulting on
a payment to Skavanga Mining, and leaving the company dangerously exposed. It was the last thing she
needed, and her mind was already racing on what to
do for the best when Eva explained that the consortium
had stepped in.

'I think you need to speak to the sheikh to find out
the details.'

'That's my intention,' Britt assured her sister, feeling that the consortium's net was slowly closing over
her family business.

As soon as she ended the call she tried once again to
speak to a member of the sheikh's staff to arrange an
appointment as a matter of urgency. Audience with His
Majesty was booked up for months in advance, some
snooty official informed her. And, no, His Majesty had
*certainly not* left any message for a visitor from a *mining* company. This was said as if mining were some
sleazy, disreputable occupation.

So speaks a man who has probably never got his
hands dirty in his life, Britt thought, pulling the phone
away from her ear. She had been placing calls non-stop
from her bedroom for the past two hours—to Sharif's
offices, to his palace, to the country's administrative
offices, and even to her country's diplomatic representative in the city.

Okay. Calm down, she told herself, taking a deep
breath as she paced the room. Let's think this through.
There was a number she could call, and this really was
a wild card. Remembering Emir telling her about his

love of horses, she stabbed in the number for His Majesty's stables.

The voice that answered was young and female and it took Britt a couple of breaths to compute this, as her calls so far had led Britt to believe that only men worked for the sheikh and they all had tent poles up their backsides.

'Hello,' the pleasant female voice said again. 'Jasmina Kareshi speaking…'

The Black Sheikh's sister! Though Princess Jasmina sounded far too relaxed to be a princess. 'Hello. This is Britt Skavanga speaking. I wonder if you could help me?'

'Call me Jazz,' the friendly voice on the other end of the line insisted as Jazz went on to explain that her brother had in fact been in touch some time ago to warn her that Britt was due to arrive in the country.

'How did he find out?' Britt exclaimed with surprise.

'Are you serious?' Jazz demanded.

Jazz's upbeat nature was engaging, and as the ruler of Kareshi's sister proceeded to tell Britt that her brother knew everything that was going on in Kareshi at least ten minutes before it happened Britt got the feeling that in different circumstances Jazz and she might have been friends.

'As he's not here, I'm supposed to be helping you any way I can,' Jazz explained. 'I can only apologise that it's taken so long for the two of us to get in touch, but I've been tied up with my favourite mare at the stables while she was giving birth.'

'Please don't apologise,' Britt said quickly. She was just glad to have someone sensible to talk to. 'I hope everything went well for your horse.'

'Perfectly,' Jazz confirmed, adding in an amused

tone, 'I imagine it went a lot better for me and my mare
than it did for you without a formal introduction to my
brother's stuffy staff.'

Diplomacy was called for, Britt concluded. 'They
did what they could,' she said cagily.

'I bet they did,' Jazz agreed wryly.

This was really dangerous. Not only had she fallen
for the Black Sheikh masquerading as Emir, but now
she was starting to get on with his sister.

'My brother's in the desert,' Jazz confirmed. 'Let
me give you the GPS—'

'Thanks.'

Jazz proceeded to dispense GPS coordinates for a
Bedouin camp in the desert as casually as if she were
directing Britt to the local mall. Britt was able to draw
a couple of possible conclusions from this. Sharif had
not wanted his staff to know about the connection between them—possibly because as she was a woman in
a recently reformed and previously male-dominated
country they wouldn't treat her too well. But at least
he had entrusted the news of her arrival to Jazz. She'd
give him the benefit of the doubt this one time. Just before signing off, she checked with Jazz that the car hire
company she had decided on had the best vehicles for
trekking in the desert.

'It should be the best,' Jazz exclaimed. 'Like practically everything else in Kareshi, my brother owns it.'

Of course he did. And he thought Skavanga Mining
was in the bag too. Not just an investment, but a takeover. There was no time to lose. Having promised to
keep in touch with Jazz, she cut the line.

She had a moment—a fluttering heart, sweaty palms
moment—when she knew it would have been far safer
to deal with the Black Sheikh from a distance, prefer-

ably half a world away in Skavanga. Sharif was too confident for her liking, telling his sister about Britt's arrival in Kareshi as if he knew all her arrangements. According to Jazz it was very likely that he did, Britt reasoned, more eager than ever to get into the desert to confront him. And this time she would definitely confine their talks to business. She might be a slow learner, but she never made the same mistake twice.

He wasn't surprised that Britt had decided to track him down in the desert. He would have been more surprised if she had remained in Skavanga doing nothing. He admired her for not taking anything lying down. Well, almost anything, he mused, a smile hovering around his mouth. He did look forward to taking her on a bed one day.

Stretching out his naked body on the bank of silken cushions in the sleeping area of his tent, he turned his thoughts to business. Business had always been a game to him—a game he never lost, though with Britt it was different. He wanted to include her. He knew about the customer going bankrupt leaving Skavanga Mining in the lurch. He also knew there was nothing Britt could have done about it even had she been in Skavanga, though he doubted she would see it that way. He had been forced to get in touch with Tyr again to fast-track the deal, and with Britt on her way to the desert maybe he would get the chance to put her straight. He didn't like this subterfuge Tyr had forced upon him, though he could understand the reasons for it.

He rose and bathed in the pool formed by an underground stream that bubbled up beside his sleeping quarters. Donning his traditional black robes, he ran impatient hands through his damp black hair. Jasmina had contacted him to say that Britt had landed safely and would soon be joining him. Not soon enough, he thought as one of the elders of the tribe gave a discreet cough from the entrance to the tent to attract his attention.

A tent was a wholly inadequate description for the luxurious pavilion in which this noble tribe had insisted on housing him, Sharif reflected as he strode in lightweight sandals across priceless rugs to greet the old man. A simple bivouac would have been enough for him, but this was a palatial marquee fitted out as if for some mythical potentate. It was in fact a priceless ancient artefact, full of antique treasures, which had been carefully collected and preserved over centuries by the wandering tribesmen who kept these sorts of tents permanently at the ready to welcome their leader.

The elder informed him that the preparations for Britt's arrival were now in place. Sharif thanked him with no hint of his personal thoughts on his face, but it amused him to think that an experienced businesswoman like Britt had shown no compunction in attempting to throw him off stride by introducing him to a variety of Nordic delights. It remained to be seen how she would react when he turned the tables on her. How would she like being housed in the harem, for instance?

The elderly tribesman insisted on showing him round the harem tent set aside for Britt. It was a great deal more luxurious than even Sharif's regal pavilion, though admittedly it was a little short on seating areas. The large, luxuriously appointed space was dominated by an enormous bank of silken cushions carefully arranged into the shape of a bed enclosed by billowing white silk curtains. The harem tent had one purpose and one purpose only—a thought that curved his lips in a smile, if only because Britt would soon realise where she was staying, and would be incensed. Teasing her was one of his favourite pastimes. How long was it going to take her to realise that?

Thanking his elderly guide, he ducked his head and left the tent. Pausing a moment, he soaked in the purposeful bustle of a community whose endless travels along unseen paths through a wilderness that stretched seemingly to infinity never failed to amaze him. He didn't bring many visitors to the desert, believing the change from their soft lives in the city to the rigours of life in an encampment would be too much for them, but Britt was different. She was adventurous and curious, and would relish every moment of a challenge like this.

Spending time with his people was always a pleasure for him. It gave him a welcome break from the constant baying of the media—to see his face, to know his life, to know him. And, more importantly, it gave him the chance to live alongside his people and understand their needs. On this visit the elders had asked for more travelling schools, as well as more mobile clinics and hospitals. They would have them. He would make sure of it.

No wonder he was passionate about the diamond deal, Sharif reflected as some of the children ran up to him, clustering around a man who, in their eyes, was merely a newcomer in the camp. He hunkered down so they were all on eye level, while the children examined his prayer beads and the heavily decorated scabbard of his *khanjar*, the traditional Kareshi dagger that he wore at his side.

This was his joy, he realised as he watched the children's dark, inquisitive eyes, and their busy little hands as they examined these treasures. They were the future of his country, and he would allow nothing to put a dent in the prospects of these children. He had banished his unscrupulous relatives with the express purpose of allowing Kareshi to grow and flourish, and he would support his people with whatever it took.

He was still the warrior Sheikh, Sharif reflected as the children were called away for supper. His people expected it of their leader, and it was a right that he had fought for, and that was in his blood. But he did have a softer side that he didn't show the world, and that side of him longed for a family, and for closeness and love. He hadn't known that as a child. He hadn't even realised that he'd missed it until he spent more time here in the desert with his people. What he wouldn't give to know the closeness they shared...

He stopped outside the tent they had prepared for Britt, and felt a rush of gratitude for the heritage his people had so carefully preserved. As he fingered the finely woven tassels holding back the curtains over the opening his thoughts strayed back to Britt. They had never really left her.

It wasn't as if she hadn't changed a tyre before—

Famously, she had changed one on the very first day she had met Sharif. But that had been on a familiar vehicle with tools she had used before, and on a hard surface, while this was sand.

As soon as she raised the Jeep on the jack, it slipped and thumped down hard, narrowly missing her feet. Hands on her hips, she considered her options. It was a beautiful night. The sky was clear, the moon was bright, and she had parked in the shadow of a dune where she was sheltered from the wind. It was lovely—if she could just calm down. And, maybe she shouldn't have set out half cock with only the thought of seeing Emir/Sharif again in her head. But she was where she was, and had to get on with it.

She had never seen so many stars before, Britt realised, staring up. What a beautiful place this was. There was no pollution of any kind. A sea of stars and a crescent moon hung overhead. And there was no need for panic, she reasoned, turning back to the Jeep. She had water, fuel, and plenty of food. The GPS was up and running, and according to that she was only around fifteen miles away from the encampment. The best thing she could do was wait until the morning when she would try again to wedge the wheels and stop them slipping. As a sensible precaution, and because she didn't want Jazz to worry, she texted Sharif's sister: *Flat tyre. No prob. I'll sleep 4WD then change it am and head 2 camp.*

A reply came through almost immediately: *I hve yr coordinates. Do u hve flares? Help o—*

The screen blanked. She tried again. She shook the phone. She screamed obscenities at it. She banged it on her hand and screamed again. She tried switching it off and rebooting it.

It was dead.

So what had Jazz meant by that last message? Help was on its way? Or help off-road in the middle of the desert at night was out of the question?

Heaving a breath, she stared up, and blinked to find the sky completely changed. Half was as beautiful as the last time she looked, which was just a few seconds ago, while the other half was sullen black. A prickle of unease crept down her spine. And then a spear of fright when she heard something…the rushing sound of a ferocious wind. It was like all her childhood nightmares come at once. Something monstrous was on its way—

what, she couldn't tell. The only certainty was that it was getting closer all the time.

Her hands were trembling, Britt realised as she buttoned the phone inside the breast pocket of her shirt. Not much fazed her, but now she wished she had a travelling companion who knew the desert. Sharif would know. This was his home territory. Sharif would know what to do.

The elders had invited him to eat with them around the campfire. The respect they showed him was an honour he treasured. Here in the wildest reaches of the desert he might be their leader, but he could always learn from his people and this was a priceless opportunity for him to speak to them about their concerns. They talked on long into the night, and by the time he left them he was glad he could bring them good news about renewed investment and the realisation of their plans. He didn't go straight back to his tent. He felt restless for no good reason other than the fact that the palm trees seemed unnaturally still to him, as if they were waiting for something to happen. He had a keen weather nose and tonight the signs weren't good. He stared up into the clear sky, knowing things could change in a few moments in the desert.

He paced the perimeter of the camp and found himself back at the harem tent where Britt would be housed when she arrived. His mood lightened as he dipped his head to take a look inside. He could just imagine her outraged reaction when she realised where she was staying. He hoped she would at least linger long enough to enjoy some of the delights. The surroundings were so sumptuous it seemed incredible that they could exist outside a maharaja's palace, let alone in the desert. Like his own pavilion, hers had been cleverly positioned around the underground stream. The water was clear and warm and provided a natural bathing pool in a discreetly closed off section of the tent. Solid gold drinking vessels glinted in the mellow light of brass lanterns, while priceless woven rugs felt rich and soft beneath his sandaled feet. The heady scent of incense pervaded everything, but it was the light that was so special. The candles inside the lanterns washed the space with a golden light that gave the impression of a golden room. It certainly wasn't a place to hold a business meeting. This tent was dedicated entirely to pleasure, a fact he doubted Britt would miss. He tried not to smile, but there was everything here a sheikh of old might have required to woo his mistress. The older women of the tribe had heard a female visitor was expected and had approached him with their plan; he couldn't resist.

*Would their Leader's friend be pleased to experience some of the very special beauty treatments that had been passed down through generations?*

Absolutely, he had replied.

*Would she enjoy being dressed in one of the precious vintage robes they had lovingly cleaned and preserved; a robe they carried with them in their treasure chest on their endless travels across the desert?*

He didn't even have to think about that one. He was sure she would.

*And the food...Would she enjoy their food? Could they make her sweetmeats like the old days; the sort of thing with which the sheikhs of old would tempt their... their...*

Their friends? he had supplied helpfully.

'I'm sure she would,' he had confirmed. He had yet to meet a woman who would refuse a decent piece of cake.

His acceptance of all these treats for Britt had put smiles into many eyes, and that was all he cared about.

Their final assurance was that if their sheikh would honour them by entertaining a female visitor in their camp, they would ensure he did so in the old way.

Perfect, he had said, having some idea of what that might entail. He couldn't think of anything his visitor would enjoy more, he had told them.

Imagining Britt's expression when she was treated as a prized concubine was thanks enough, but there was a serious element to this mischief. The older women guided the young, and it was imperative to have them onside so they embraced all the educational opportunities he was opening up to women under his rule. Kareshi would be different—better for all in the future, and on that he was determined.

The peal of the phone distracted him from these musings. It was his sister Jasmina, calling him to say that Britt had decided not to wait until the morning to travel into the desert, but with all the confidence of someone who believed she knew the wilderness—every wilderness—Britt had insisted on setting out by road, just a couple of hours ago.

Issuing a clipped goodbye to his sister, he went into action. No wonder he'd felt apprehensive. Here with tents erected against the shield of a rock face people were safe, but if the weather worsened out in the desert, and Britt was lost—

All thoughts of Britt in connection with the harem tent shot from his mind. She knew *her* wilderness, not his!

Striding back into the centre of the camp, he was already securing the headdress called a *howlis* around his face and calling for his horse, while his faithful people, seeing that he meant to leave the camp, were gathering round him. They had no time to lose. If a sandstorm was coming, as he suspected, and Britt was alone on treacherously shifting sand, all the technology of a modern age wouldn't save her.

Calling for a camel to carry the equipment he might need, he strode on towards the corral where they were saddling his stallion. Springing onto its back, he took the lead rope from the camel and lashed it to his tack. He wasted no time riding away from the safety of the camp at the head of his small troupe, into what Britt would imagine was the most beautiful and tranquil starlit night.

Where had the romance of the desert gone? She had almost been blasted away in a gust of sand in a last attempt to change the tyre. What was it about her and tyres? And this wasn't fun, Britt concluded, raking her hand across the back of her neck. Sand was getting everywhere. Eddies of sand were exfoliating her face while more sand was slipping through the smallest gap in her clothes.

Did she even stand a chance of being found? Britt wondered, gazing around, really frightened now. Visibility was shrinking to nothing as the wind blew the sand about, and the sky was black. She couldn't even see the stars. She had never felt more alone, or so scared. Battling against the wind, she made it to the back of the Jeep and locked her tools away. Shielding her eyes, she opened the driver's door and launched herself inside. The wind was so strong now it was lifting the Jeep and threatening to turn it over. She had never wished for Sharif more. She couldn't care less about their differences right now. She just wanted him to find her.

She had checked the weather before setting out, but could never have imagined how quickly it could change. There was nothing to see out of the window. She changed her mind about Sharif finding her. It was too dangerous. She didn't want him to risk his life. But she just couldn't sit here, helpless, waiting to buried, or worse... She had to remain visible. If the Jeep were buried she would never be found.

There was a warning triangle in the boot—and a spade handle. And the very last thing she needed right now was a bra. She could make a warning symbol. And there were flares in the boot.

Downside? She would just have to brave the storm again.

The wind was screaming louder than ever and the sand was like an industrial rasp. But she was determined—determined to live, determined to be seen, and determined to do everything in her power to ensure that happened.

Once she had managed to get everything out of the back of the Jeep, securing the warning triangle to the handle of the spade with her bra was the easy part. Finding a way to fix it onto the Jeep wasn't quite so simple. She settled for wedging it into the bull bars, and now she had to get back into the shelter of the vehicle as quickly as she could or she would be buried where she stood.

Closing the door, she relished the relative silence, and, turning everything off, she resigned herself to the darkness. She had to conserve power. There was nothing more she could do for now but wait out the storm and hope that when it passed over she would still be alive and could dig her way out.

# CHAPTER TEN

DISMOUNTING, SHARIF COVERED his horse's face with a cloth so he could lead it forward. Attached to his horse by a rope was the camel loaded down with equipment. The camel's eyelashes provided the ultimate in protection against the sand, while he had to be content with narrowing his eyes and staring through the smallest slit in his *howlis*. His men had gathered round him, and so long as he could see the compass he was happy he could lead them to Britt's Jeep. When all else failed magnetic north saved the day.

As they struggled on against the wind he sent up silent thanks that Jasmina had been able to text him Britt's last coordinates, but a shaft of dread pierced him when he wondered if he would reach her in time.

He *had* to reach her in time. He had intended to test Britt as she had tested him in Skavanga when she arrived in the desert, but not like this.

What would she think when he appeared out of the storm? That a bandit was coming for her? It only occurred to him now that she had never seen him in robes before. That seemed so unimportant. He just prayed he would find her alive. He had left the encampment battening down for what was essentially a siege. Custom dictated the tribe pitch their tents at the foot of a rock face to allow for situations like a sandstorm. The best he could hope for where Britt was concerned was that she'd had enough sense to stay inside her vehicle. She wouldn't stand a cat in hell's chance outside.

The scream of the wind was unbearable. It seemed never ending. It was as if a living creature were trying every way it knew how to reach her inside the Jeep. Curled up defensively with her hands over her ears, she knew that the electrics were shot and the phone was useless. The sand was already halfway up the window. How much longer could she survive this?

What a rotten end, she thought, grimacing at the preposterous situation in which she found herself. She could only feel sorry for the person who had to drag her lifeless body out of the Jeep—

She Would Not Die Like This.

Throwing her weight against the driver's door, she tried to force it open, but it wouldn't budge—and even if it had, where was she going?

Flares were her last hope, Britt reasoned. She had no idea now if it was day or night, and before she could set off a flare she needed something to break the window.

Climbing over the seats, she found everything she needed. The vehicle was well equipped for a trek in the desert. There were flares and work gloves, safety goggles, a hard hat, and heavy-duty cutters, as well as a torch and a first-aid kit. Perfect. She was in business.

He had almost given up hope when he saw the flare flickering dimly in the distance. Adrenalin shot through his veins, giving him the strength of ten men and the resolve of ten more. He urged his weary animals on and his brave men followed close behind him. He couldn't be sure it was Britt who had let off the flare until he saw the warning triangle she had fixed onto the top of a spade handle with a bra, and then he smiled. Britt was ever resourceful, and any thought he might have had about her setting off into the desert at night without a proper guide seemed irrelevant as he forged on, his lungs almost exploding as he strained against the wind. Nothing could keep him back. Sharp grains of sand whirled around him, but the robes protected him and the *howlis* did its job. Just thinking about Britt and how frightened she must be made his discomfort irrelevant. His only goal was to reach her—to save her—to protect her—to somehow get her back to the camp—

If she were still alive.

He prayed that she was, as he had never prayed before. He prayed that he could save her as he sprang down from his horse, and started to work his way around the buried Jeep. The vehicle was buried far deeper than he had imagined, and, worse, he couldn't hear anything against the wind. Was she alive in there? With not a moment to lose he yanked at the windscreen with his men helping him. Britt had already loosened it to let off the flare—

And then he saw her. Alive! Though clearly unconscious. She had managed to free the rubber seal on the glass and had forced it out far enough to let off the flare, but in doing so had allowed sand to pour in and fill the vacuum, almost burying her. He waved his men back. It wasn't safe. Too many of them and the Jeep might sink further into the sand or even turn over on top of them, killing his men and burying Britt. He would not let anyone else take the risk of pulling her out.

He dug with his hands, and with the spade he had freed from the bull bars of the Jeep. He was desperate to reach her—frantic to save her. It was the longest hour of his life, and also his greatest triumph when he finally sliced through Britt's seat belt with the *khanjar* at his side, and lifted her to safety in his arms.

To say she was bewildered would be putting it mildly. She had woken up to find herself transported from a nightmare into a Hollywood blockbuster, complete with sumptuous Arabian tent and billowing curtains, with not a grain of sand to be seen. Added to which, there were women clustering around what passed for her bed. Dressed in rainbow hues, they looked amazing with their flowing gowns and veils. At the moment they were trying to explain to her in a series of mimes that she had been barely conscious when their leader carried her into the camp. At which point it seemed they had to pause and sigh.

She must have been asleep for ages, Britt realised, staring around. The bed on which she was reclining was covered in the most deliciously scented cushions, and was enclosed by billowing white curtains, which the women had drawn back. She felt panicked for a moment as she tried to take it all in. Was this the encampment Jazz had told her about—or was she somewhere else?

And then it all came flooding back. The terrifying storm— The sickening fear of being buried alive. Her desperate attempt to set off a flare, not knowing if anyone would see it—

Someone had. She squeezed out a croak on a throat that felt as if it had been sandpapered, and the women couldn't understand a word she said, anyway, so the identity of her rescuer was destined to remain a mystery.

The women were instantly sympathetic and rushed to bring her drinks laced with honey, and one of them indicated an outdoor spa, which Britt could now see was situated at the far end of the tent.

And what a tent! It was more of a pavilion, large and lavishly furnished with colourful hangings and jewel-coloured rugs covering the floor. Burnished brass lanterns decorated with intricate piercing cast a soft golden glow, while the roof was gathered up in the centre and had been used to display a number of antique artefacts. She was still staring up in wonder when the women distracted her. They had brought basins of cool water and soft towels, and, however much she indicated that she could sort herself out, they insisted on looking after her and bathing all her scratches and battle wounds.

It was a nice feeling to be made so welcome. Thanking the women with smiles, she drank their potions and accepted some of their tiny cakes, but she couldn't lie here all day like some out-of-work concubine. She was badly in need of a sugar rush to kick her into gear. And those little cakes were delicious. She was contentedly munching when she suddenly remembered Jazz. Sharif's sister must be out of her mind with worry—

Thank goodness she had a signal. She quickly stabbed in: *safe @camp. sorry if i frightnd u! lost a day sleeping! talk soon* J

A message came back before she had chance to put the phone away: *relieved ur safe. Look fwd 2 mtg u b4 long!* ☺

Britt smiled as she put the phone down again. She looked forward to that meeting too. And now the women were miming that she should come with them. She hesitated until they pointed towards the spa again, but the thought of bathing in clean, warm water was irresistible.

She was a little concerned when the women started giggling as they drew her out of the bed and across the rugs towards the bathing pool, especially when they started giggling and then sighing in turn. Were they preparing her for the sheikh? Was she to be served up on a magic carpet with a honey bun in her mouth?

Not if she could help it.

She asked with gestures: 'Did your sheikh bring me here?' She tried to draw a picture with her hands of a man who was very tall and robed, which was about all she could remember of her rescuer—that and his black horse. She must have kept slipping into unconsciousness when he brought her back here. 'The Black Sheikh?' she suggested, gazing around the golden tent, hoping to find something black to pounce on. 'His Majesty, Sheikh Sharif al Kareshi…?'

The women looked at her blankly, and then she had an idea. She sighed theatrically as they had done.

Exclaiming with delight, they smiled back, nudging each other as they exchanged giggles and glances.

She left a pause to allow for more sighs while her heart thundered a blistering tattoo. So it was very likely that Emir or Sharif, or whatever he was calling himself these days, had rescued her. Her brain still wasn't functioning properly, but it seemed preferable to be in the tent of someone she knew, even if that someone was the Black Sheikh.

She allowed the women to lead her into the bathing pool. She didn't want to offend them and what was the harm of refreshing herself so she could start the new day and explore the camp? The women were keen to pamper her outer self with unguents, and her inner self with fresh juice. One of them played a stringed instrument softly in the background, while the scent rising from the warm spring water was divine. Relaxing back in the clear, warm water, she indulged in a little dream in which she was a young woman lost in the desert who had been rescued by a handsome sheikh—

She *was* a young woman lost in the desert who had been rescued by a handsome sheikh!

And however she felt about him, the first thing she had to do was thank Sharif for saving her life. She had to forget all about who had done what to whom, or how angry she had been about his people's interference in the business, and start with that. She could always tell him what she thought about his high-handed ways afterwards. Sharif had risked his life to save her. Compared to that, her pride counted for nothing.

The women interrupted her thoughts, bringing her towels, which they held out like a screen so she could climb from the pool with her modesty intact. They quickly wrapped her, head to foot, and she noticed now that the sleeping area had already been straightened, and enough food to feed an army had been laid out.

Was she expecting visitors?

One visitor?

Her heart thundered at the thought.

As they led her towards the bed of cushions she caught sight of the lavender sky, tinged with the lambent gold of a dying sun. The women insisted she must lie down on a sheet while they massaged her skin with soothing emollients to ease the discomfort of all the cuts and bruises she had sustained during her ordeal. The scent of the cream was amazing and she couldn't ever remember being indulged to this extent. Being prepared for the sheikh indeed...

She was a little concerned when, instead of her own clothes, the women showed her an exquisite gown in flowing silk. 'Where are my clothes?' she mimed.

One of the women mimed back that Britt's clothes were still wet after having been washed.

Ah… 'Thank you.'

She bit her lip, wondering how the rest of this night would play out, but then decided she would just have to throw herself into the spirit of generosity being lavished on her by these wonderful people. And the gown was beautiful, though it had clearly been designed for someone far more glamorous than she was. In ice blue silk, it was as fine as gossamer, and was intricately decorated with silver thread. It was the sort of robe she could easily imagine a sheikh's mistress wearing. But as there were no alternatives on offer…

One of the women brought in a full-length mirror so Britt could see the finished effect. The transformation was complete when they draped a matching veil over her hair and drew the wisp of chiffon across her face, securing it with a jewelled clip. She stood for a moment staring at her reflection in amazement. At least she fitted in with the surroundings now, and for perhaps the first time ever she felt different about herself and didn't long for jeans or suits. She had never worn anything so exotic, or believed she had the potential to project an air of mystery. I could be the Sheikh's diamond, she thought with amusement.

She tensed as something changed in the tent…a rustle of cloth…a hint of spice…

She turned to find the women backing away from her.

And then she saw the man. Silhouetted with his back against the light, he was tall and powerful and dressed in black robes. A black headdress covered half his face, but she would have known him anywhere, and her body yearned for her lover before her mind had chance to make a reasoned choice.

'So it was you…' Even as she spoke she realised how foolish that must sound.

His Majesty, Sheikh Sharif al Kareshi, the man known to the world as the Black Sheikh, and known to her before today as Emir, loosened his headdress. Every thought of thanking him for saving her life, or condemning him for walking out on her without explaining why, faded into insignificance as their stares met and held.

'Thank you for saving my life,' she managed on a throat that felt as tight as a drum.

She was mad with herself. The very last thing she had intended when she first set out on this adventure was to be in awe of Sharif. She had come to rail at him, to demand answers, but now she was lost for words and all that seemed to matter was that they were together again. 'You risked your life for me—'

'I'm glad to see you up and well,' he said, ignoring this. Removing his headdress fully, he cast the yards of heavy black silk aside.

'I am very well, thanks to you.'

Dark eyes surveyed her keenly. 'Do you have everything you need?'

As Sharif continued to hold her stare her throat seemed to close again. She felt horribly exposed in the flowing, flimsy gown and smoothed her hands self-consciously down the front of it.

'Relax, Britt. We're the same people we were in Skavanga.'

Were they? Just hearing his voice in these surroundings seemed so surreal.

'You've had a terrible ordeal,' he pointed out. 'Why don't you make the most of this break?'

'Your Majesty, I—'

'Please—' he stopped her with the hint of a smile '—call me Sharif.' He paused, and then added, 'Of course, if you prefer, you can call me Emir.'

The laughter in his eyes was quickly shuttered when she drew herself up. 'There are many things I'd like to call you, but Emir isn't one of them,' she assured him. 'This might not be the time to air grievances—after all, you did save my life—'

'But you're getting heated,' he guessed.

'I am curious to know why you found it necessary to deceive me.'

'I conduct my business discreetly.'

'Discretion's one thing—deception's another.'

'I never deceived you, Britt.'

'You didn't explain fully, did you? I still don't know why you left in such a hurry.'

'Things moved faster than I expected, and I wasn't in a position to explain them to you.'

'The Black Sheikh is held back? By whom?'

'I'm afraid I can't tell you that.'

'Isn't that taking loyalty too far?'

'Loyalty can never be taken too far,' Sharif assured her. 'Just be satisfied that your sisters were not involved and that everything I've done has been for the sake of the company—'

'And your deal.'

'Obviously, the consortium is a consideration.'

'I bet,' she muttered. 'I'm glad you find this amusing,' she added, seeing his eyes glinting.

'I don't find it in the least amusing. When a company defaults on a payment risking the livelihoods of families who have worked for Skavanga Mining for generations, I did what I could to put things right as fast as I could, and while you were still in the air flying to Kareshi to see me.'

She knew this was true and blushed furiously beneath her veil. She was used to being on top of things—at work and with her sisters. She was also used to being told all the facts, and yet Sharif was holding something back for the sake of loyalty, he had implied—but loyalty to whom?

It hardly mattered. He wasn't going to tell her, Britt realised with frustration. 'Okay, I'm sorry. Maybe I did overreact, but it still doesn't explain why you couldn't have said something before you left the cabin.'

'I'm not in the habit of explaining myself to anyone.'

'You don't say,' she murmured.

'It's just how I am, Britt.'

'Accountable to no one,' she guessed.

The Black Sheikh dipped his head.

'Well, whatever you've done, or haven't done, thank you—' She was on the point of thanking him again for saving her life, when Sharif held up his hands.

'Enough, Britt. You don't have to say it again.' Glancing towards the curtained sleeping area, he added, 'And you should take a rest.'

Her mind had been safely distracted from the sumptuous sleeping area up to now, and she stepped back, unconsciously putting some distance between herself and Sharif. She needed time to get her thoughts in order. Better do something mundane, she decided, drawing back the curtains. Task completed, she turned to face Sharif, who made her the traditional Kareshi greeting, touching his chest, his mouth and finally his brow.

'It means peace,' he said dryly. 'And you really don't have to stand in my presence, Britt.'

'Maybe I prefer to—'

'And maybe, as I suggested, you should take a rest.'

Now was not the time to argue, so she compromised, sitting primly on the very edge of one of the deep, silk-satin cushion. 'I apologise for putting you to so much trouble,' she said, gesturing around. 'I had no idea a storm was coming, or that it would close in so quickly. I did do my research—'

'But you couldn't wait to come and see me a moment longer?' he suggested dryly.

'It wasn't like that.' It was like that, Britt admitted silently.

She watched warily as Sharif prowled around the sleeping area, his prayer beads clicking at his waist in a constant reminder that she was well out of her comfort zone here. She stiffened when he came to sit with her—on the opposite side of the cushions, true, but close enough to set her heart racing. And while she was dressed in this flimsy gown, a style that was so alien to her in every way, she couldn't help feeling vulnerable.

'The women gave me this gown to wear while they were washing my clothes,' she felt bound to explain.

'Very nice,' he said.

Very nice was an understatement. The gown was gloriously feminine and designed to seduce—which she could have done without right now. Her sisters would laugh if they could see her. Britt Skavanga backed into a corner, and now lost for words.

# CHAPTER ELEVEN

'I AM GLAD you have been given everything you need,' Sharif said, glancing round the sumptuous pavilion.

'Everything except my clothes.' Britt was becoming increasingly aware that the gown the women had dressed her in was almost sheer. 'I believe my own clothes will soon be here.' She had no idea when they were arriving, or even if they would ever arrive. She only knew that her body burned beneath Sharif's stare as his lazy gaze roved over the diaphanous gown—she had never longed for a business suit more.

Sharif's lips tugged a little at one corner as if he knew this.

Turning away, she ground her teeth with frustration at the position she found herself in. Of course she was grateful to Sharif for saving her, but being housed in the harem at the sheikh's pleasure was hardly her recreation of choice—

She had to calm down and accept that a lot had happened in the past twenty-four hours and she was emotionally overwrought. The temptation to do exactly as Sharif suggested—relax and recline, as he was doing—was overwhelming, but with his familiar, intoxicating scent washing over her—amber, patchouli and sandalwood, combined with riding leather and clean, warm man—she couldn't be answerable for her own actions if she did that. Business was her safest option. 'If I'd seen a photograph of you before you came to Skavanga, I wouldn't have mixed you up with Emir and maybe we could have avoided this mess, and then you wouldn't have been forced to risk your life riding through the storm to find me.'

'I don't make a habit of issuing photographs with business letters. And as it happens, I did see a photograph of you, but it wasn't a true representation.'

'What do you mean?' she asked.

'I mean the photograph showed one woman when you are clearly someone very different.'

'In what way?'

Sharif smiled faintly. 'You're far more complex than your photograph suggests.'

She pulled a face beneath the veil, remembering the posed shot. She had been wearing a stiff suit and an even stiffer expression. She hated having her photograph taken, but had been forced to endure that one for the sake of the company journal.

'Well, I haven't seen a single photograph of you in the press,' she countered.

'Really?' Sharif pretended concern. 'I must remedy that situation immediately.'

'And now you're mocking me,' she protested.

He shrugged. 'I thought we agreed to call a truce. But if there's nothing more you need—'

'Nothing. Thank you,' she said stiffly as he turned to go. Her body, of course, had other ideas. If she could just keep her attention fixed on something apart from Sharif's massive shoulders beneath his flowing black robe, or those strong tanned hands that had given her so much pleasure—

'I'll leave you to rest,' he said, getting up.

'Thank you.'

And now she was disappointed?

He was leaving while her body was on fire for him.

Yes. And she should be glad, Britt told herself firmly. A heavy pulse might be throbbing between her legs, but this man was not Emir—and Emir had been dangerous enough—this man was a regal and unknowable stranger, who could pluck her heart from her chest and trample it underfoot while she was still in an erotic daze. She stood too and, lifting her chin, she directed a firm stare into his eyes. Even that was a mistake. Lust ripped through her, along with the desire to mean something to this man. For a few heady seconds she could think of nothing but being held by him, kissed by him, and then, thankfully, she pulled herself round.

'This is wonderful accommodation and I can't thank you enough for all you've done for me. Your people are so very kind. They let me sleep, they tended to my wounds, they—'

'They bathed you?' Sharif supplied.

The way his mouth kicked up at one corner sent such a vivid flash of sensation ripping through her she almost forgot what she was going to say. 'I…I had a bath,' she admitted in a shaking voice that was not Britt Skavanga at all.

'They spoiled you with soothing emollients, and that's so bad?'

'They did,' she agreed, wishing he would look anywhere but into her eyes with that dark, mocking stare. And every time she nodded her head, tiny jewels tinkled in a most alluring way—she could do without that too!

'The women have dressed you for their sheikh,' Sharif observed.

And now she couldn't tell if he was joking or not. Her chest was heaving with pent-up passion thanks to her desire deep down to be angry—to have a go. *He can't talk to you like that!* She wasn't a canapé to whet his appetite—a canapé carefully prepared and presented to the sheikh for him to sample, then either swallow or discard.

'They have prepared you well,' Sharif said, showing not the slightest flicker of remorse for this outrageous statement. 'Would you rather they had brought you something ugly to wear?' he demanded when her body language gave away her indignation. 'Moral outrage doesn't suit you, Britt,' he went on in the same mocking drawl. 'It's far too late for that. But I must say the gown suits you. That shade of blue is very good with your eyes...'

So why wasn't he looking into her eyes?

Straightening up, she wished her jeans and top were dry so she could bring an end to this nonsense.

And yet...

And yet she was secretly glad that Sharif's gaze was so appreciative. Why else would she stand so straight? Why were her lips parted, and why was she licking them with the tip of her tongue? And why, for all that was logical, was she thrusting her breasts out when her nipples were so painfully erect?

'It's a very pretty dress,' she agreed coolly.

'Our desert fashions suit you,' Sharif agreed.

She shivered involuntarily as he reached out to run the tip of his forefinger down the very edge of her veil. There was still a good distance between them, but no distance could be enough.

And now her thoughts were all erotic. Perhaps Sharif saving her life had added a primitive edge to her feelings towards him. The desire to thank him fully, and in the most obvious way, was growing like a madness inside her. Thank goodness for the veil.

'I'll call back later—when you've had a rest,' he said.

She watched without saying anything as Sharif drew the gauzy curtains around the sleeping area. She reminded herself firmly that she might be dressed like the sugar plum fairy, but she had no intention of dancing to his tune. She was here for business, and business alone. She had to be wary of this man. Sharif had spoken to her sisters without telling her. He had taken mineral samples from the mine, and yet he hadn't had the courtesy to share the results of the tests with her. This might be a seductive setting, she reasoned angrily as the curtains around the sleeping area blew in the warm, early evening breeze, and Sharif was certainly the most seductive of men, but, grateful or not, she still wanted answers, and he had a lot of explaining to do.

He was back? She tried not to care—not to show she cared. She must have failed miserably as breath shot out of her when he dragged her close. This was not even the civilised businessman—this was the master of the desert. There was no conversation between them, no debate. And there was quite definitely no thought of business in Sharif's eyes. There was just the determination to master her and share her pleasure.

'Well, Britt?' Sharif demanded, holding her in front of him. 'You had enough to say for yourself in Skavanga. You must have something to say to me now. Why did you really come to Kareshi when you could have wired your test results and I could have done the same? When you could have laid out your complaints against me in an email message without making this trip?'

Why had she listened to Eva? Eva was hot-headed

and impetuous, and was always getting herself into some sort of trouble, while Britt was cool and meticulous, and never allowed emotion to get in the way.

*How had this happened?*

'Why are you really here?' Sharif pressed mercilessly, smiling grimly down into her eyes. 'What do you need from me?'

He knew very well what she needed from him. She needed his hands on her body, and his eyes staring deep into hers. She needed his scent and heat to invade her senses, and his body to master hers—

His senses raged as Britt pressed her body against his. This was his woman. This was the woman he remembered and desired. This was the fierce, driven woman he had first met in Skavanga, the woman who took what she wanted and rarely thought about it afterwards.

'Sharif?'

Could it be possible that he didn't want that part of her? he marvelled as Britt spoke his name. Did that wildcat bring out the worst in him? Loosening his grip on her arms, he let her go. When he had first entered the pavilion he had seen the tender heart of a woman he had started to know in Skavanga—the vulnerable woman inside the brittle shell—the woman he had walked away from before he could cause her any hurt.

'Sharif, what is it?'

He stared down and saw the disappointment in her eyes. And why shouldn't Britt expect the worst when he had walked out on her before?

Everything had been so cut and dried in the past. He'd fed his urges and moved on, but he had never met a woman like this before. He had never realised a woman could come to mean so much to him. The feelings raging inside him when he had found Britt alive were impossible to describe. All he could think was: she was still in the world, and thank God for it. But he had a country to rule and endless responsibilities. Did he make love to her now, as he so badly wanted to do, or did he save her by turning and walking away?

'It's not like you to hesitate,' she murmured.

'And it's not like you to be so meek and mild,' he countered with an ironic smile. 'What shall we do about this role reversal?'

'You're asking me?' she queried, starting to smile.

He closed his eyes, allowing her scent and warmth and strength to curl around his core, clearing his mind. He prided himself on his self-control, but there was will power and then there was denial, and he wasn't in the mood to deny either of them tonight. He wanted Britt. She wanted him. It was that simple. Above all, he was a sensualist who never ate merely because he was hungry, but only when the food was at its best. Britt thought she knew everything about men and sex and satisfaction, but it would be his pleasure to teach her just how wrong she was.

'What are you doing?' she said as he led her back through the billowing curtains.

Settling himself on the silken cushions, he raised a hand and beckoned to her.

'What the hell do you think this is?' she said.

'This is a harem,' he said with a shrug. 'And if you don't like that idea you might want to step out of the light.'

'I'll stand where I like,' she fired back.

His shrugged again as if to say that was okay with him. It was. There wasn't one inch of Britt that wasn't beautifully displayed or made even more enticing by the fact that she was wearing such an ethereal gown and standing in front of the light. He let the silence hang for a while, and then, almost as if it were an afterthought, he said, 'When the women brought that gown, didn't they bring you any underwear?'

Her gasp of outrage must have been heard clearly in Skavanga.

'You are totally unscrupulous,' she exclaimed, wrapping the flimsy folds around her.

'I meant no offence,' he said, having difficulty hiding his grin as he eased back on the cushions. 'I was merely admiring you—'

'Well, you can stop admiring me right now.'

'Are you sure about that?'

'Yes, I'm sure. I feel ridiculous—'

'You look lovely. Now, come over here.'

'You must be joking.'

'So stand there all night.'

'I won't have to,' she said confidently, 'because at some point you'll leave. At which time I will settle down to sleep on *my* bed.'

Britt looked magnificent when she was angry. Proud and strong, and finely bred, she reminded him of one of his prized Arabian ponies. And this was quite a compliment coming from him. Plus, a little teasing was in order. Hadn't she put him through trials by fire and ice in Skavanga? Britt had done everything she could think of to unsettle him while he was on her territory, but now the tables were turned she didn't like it. 'Come on,' he coaxed. 'You know you want to—'

'I know I don't,' she flashed. 'Just because you saved my life doesn't give you droit de seigneur!'

'Ah, so you're a virgin,' he said as if this were news to him. 'When did that happen?'

Her look would have felled most men. It suggested she would like to bring the curtains and even the roof down on his head. She was so sure he had styled himself on some sheikh of old, she couldn't imagine that beneath his robes he was the same man she had met in Skavanga. He should get on with proving that he was that man, but he was rather enjoying teasing her. Helping himself to some juice and a few grapes, he left Britt to draw back a curtain to scan the tent, no doubt searching for another seating area. She wouldn't find one, and he had no intention of going anywhere.

'There's nowhere else to sit,' she complained. 'Until you go,' she added pointedly.

He shrugged and carried on eating his grapes. 'Formal chairs are not required in the harem—so there is just this all-purpose sleeping, lounging, pleasuring area, where I'm currently reclining.'

'Don't remind me! I don't know what game you're playing, Sharif, but I'd like you to leave right now.'

'I'm not going anywhere. This is my camp, my pavilion, my country—and you,' he added with particular charm, 'are my guest.'

'I treated you better than this when you were my guest.'

He only had to raise a brow to remind Britt that she had treated him like a fool, and was surprised when he had turned the tables on her at the lake.

'I came to do business with you,' she protested, shifting her weight from foot to foot—doing anything rather than sit with him. 'If you had stuck around long enough for us to have a proper discussion in Skavanga, I wouldn't even be here at all.'

'So that's what this is about,' he said. 'It still hurts.'

'You bet it does.'

He had left at the right time and, though he wouldn't betray Tyr's part in the business, he wanted to reassure her. 'Well, I'm sorry,' he said. 'It seems I must learn to explain myself in future.'

'Damn right you should,' she said, crossing her arms.

'I'm just so glad you're here—and in one piece.'

'Thank you for reminding me,' she said wryly. 'You know I can't be angry with you now.'

They were both in the same difficult place. They wanted each other. They both understood that if you laid the bare facts on the table theirs was not a sensible match. The only mistake that either of them had made was wanting more than sex out of this relationship.

'So maybe we can be friends?' she said as if reading his mind. 'Except in business, of course,' she added quickly.

'Maybe,' he said. 'Maybe business too.'

After a long pause, she said, 'So, tell me about the tent. Do your people always provide you with a harem tent—just in case?'

'In case of what?' he prompted, frowning.

'I think you know what I mean—'

'Come and sit with me so I can tell you about it. Or don't you trust yourself to sit close to me?' he added, curbing his smile.

She chose a spot as far away from him as possible. Again he was reminded of his finely bred Arabian ponies, whose trust must be earned. Britt was as suspicious as any of them. 'Remember the deer,' he said.

'The deer?' she queried.

'Remember the deer in Skavanga and how relaxed we were as we watched them?'

'And then you'll tell me about the tent?'

'And then I'll tell you about the tent,' he promised.

She hardly knew Sharif, and they sat in silence until—yes, she remembered the deer—yes, she began to relax.

'This pavilion is a priceless artefact,' he said. 'Everything you see around you has been carefully preserved—and not just for years, but for centuries by the people in this camp and by their ancestors. It is a treasure beyond price.'

'Go on,' she said, leaning forward.

'You may have guessed from the lack of seating that this pleasure tent is devoted to pursuits that allow a man or a woman to take their ease. Pleasure wasn't a one-sided affair for the sheikhs. Many women asked to be considered for the position of concubine.'

'More fool them.'

'What makes you say that?' he asked as she removed the veil from her hair.

She huffed. 'Because I would never be seduced so easily.'

'Really?'

'Really.'

'It's a shame your nipples are such a dead giveaway.'

She looked down quickly and, after blushing furiously, she had to laugh.

'Shall I go on?'

'Please...'

'After yet another day of struggles beneath the merciless sun,' he declaimed as if standing in an auditorium, 'fighting off invaders—hunting for food—the sheikh would return...'

'Drum roll?'

He laughed. 'If you like.'

'How many women did he return to?'

'At least a football team,' he teased. 'Maybe more.'

'Sheikhs must have been pretty fit back then.'

'Are you suggesting I'm not?'

She met his eyes and smiled and he thought how attractive she was, and how overwhelmingly glad he would always be that he'd found her in time to save her. He went on with his storytelling. 'Or, maybe there could be just one special woman. If she pleased the sheikh one woman would be enough.'

'Lucky her!' Britt exclaimed. 'Until the sheikh decides to increase his collection of doting females, I presume?'

She amused him. And he liked combative Britt every bit as much as her softer self. 'Your imagination is a miraculous thing, Britt Skavanga.'

'Just as well since it allows me to anticipate trouble.'

'So, what's the difference between my story and the way you have treated men in the past? You think of yourself as independent, don't you? You're a woman who does as she pleases?'

'You bet I am.'

'No one forced any of the sheikh's women to enter the harem. They did so entirely of their own accord.'

'And no doubt considered it an honour,' she agreed, flashing him an ironic look.

'But surely you agree that a woman is entitled to the same privileges as a man?'

'Of course I do.'

Where was this leading? Britt wondered. Why did she feel as if Sharif was backing her into a corner? Perhaps it was his manner. He was way too relaxed.

'So if you agree,' he said with all the silky assurance of the desert lion she thought him, 'can you give me a single reason why you shouldn't take your pleasure in the sheikh's pavilion…like a man?'

Her mouth opened and closed again. The only time

she was ever lost for words was with Sharif, Britt realised with frustration. He was as shrewd as he was dis-
tractingly amusing, and was altogether aware of how
skilfully he had backed her into that tight little corner.
He was in fact a pitiless seducer who knew very well
that, where he might have failed to impress her with
the fantasy of the harem tent, with its billowing curtains and silken cushions, or even the rather seductive
clothes they were both wearing, he could very quickly
succeed with fact. She had always been an ardent believer in fact.

# CHAPTER TWELVE

SHE COULD HARDLY believe that Sharif had just given her a licence to enjoy him in a room specifically created for that purpose. Crazy. But not without its attraction, Britt realised, feeling her body's eager responses. But she would be cautious. She had heard things about Kareshi. And she liked to be in control. What if she didn't like some of these pleasures Sharif was hinting at? Her gaze darted round. She started to notice things she hadn't seen before. They might be ancient artefacts, as Sharif described them, but they were clearly used for pleasure.

She drew in a sharp, guilty breath hearing him laugh softly. 'Where are you now, Britt?' he said.

Caught out while exploring Planet Erotica, she thought. 'I'm in a very interesting tent—I can see that now.'

'Very interesting indeed,' Sharif agreed mildly, and he made no move to come any closer. 'So I have laid you bare at last, Britt Skavanga?'

'Meaning?' she demanded, clutching the edges of her robe together.

'Have I challenged your stand only to find it has been erected on dangerously shifting sand?' Sharif queried with a dangerous glint in his eyes. 'I've offered you the freedom of the harem—the opportunity to take your pleasure like a man—and yet you are hesitating?'

'Maybe you're not as irresistible as you think.'

'And maybe you're not being entirely truthful,' he said. 'What do you see around you, Britt? What do your prejudices lead you to suppose? Do you think that women were brought here by force? Do you look around and see a prison? I look around and see a golden room of pleasure.'

'That's because you're a sensualist and I'm a modern woman who's got more sense.'

'So quick sex in a corner is enough for you?'

'I deplore this sort of thing.'

The corner of Sharif's mouth kicked up. 'You're such a liar, Britt. You have an enquiring mind, and even now you're wondering—'

'Wondering what?'

'Exactly,' he said. 'You don't know.'

'That's no answer to that.'

'Other than to say, you're wondering if there can be pleasure even greater than the pleasure we have already shared. Why don't you find out? Why don't you throw your prejudices away? Why don't you open your mind to possibility and to things we *modern-thinking* people may not have discovered if they hadn't been treasured and preserved by tribes like this.'

'There can't be much that hasn't been discovered yet,' she said, gasping as she snatched her hand away when Sharif touched it.

'Did you feel that?' he said.

Feel it? He had barely touched her and her senses had exploded.

'And this,' he murmured, lightly brushing the back of her neck.

Her shoulders lifted as she gave a shaky gasp. 'What is that? The sensation's incredible. What's happening to me?'

'This is happening to you.' Sharif explained, gesturing towards the golden dish of cream the women had used to massage her skin. 'This so-called magic potion has been passed down through the generations. Not magic,' he said, 'just a particular blend of herbs. Still...'

They had a magical effect, Britt silently supplied. The scratches she had acquired during her ordeal in the desert had already vanished, she realised, studying her skin. She shivered involuntarily as Sharif's hand continued its lazy exploration of the back of her neck, moving through her hair, until she could do no more than close her eyes and bask in the most incredible sensation.

'They put lotion on your scalp as well as on your body, and that lotion is designed to increase sensation wherever it touches.'

And they touched practically every part of her, she remembered, though the women had taken great care to preserve her modesty. She looked at Sharif, and saw the amusement in his eyes. So he thought he'd won again.

She stood abruptly, and became hopelessly entangled in her gown.

'I've heard of veils being used as silken restraints and even as blindfolds,' Sharif remarked dryly, 'but why would you need those when you can tie yourself in knots without help from anyone? Here—let me help you...'

She had no alternative but to rest still as Sharif set about freeing her.

She wasn't prepared for him being so gentle with her, or for her own yearning to receive more of this care. She wanted him—she had always wanted him.

She was still a little tense when he unwound the fine

silk chiffon gown—exposing her breasts, her nipples, her belly, her thighs, with just a wisp of fabric covering the rest of her. She concentrated on sensation, glad that Sharif was in no rush. Everything he did was calculated to soothe and please her. He took time preparing her, which she loved. She loved his lack of haste, and his thoroughness, and knew she could happily enjoy this for hours. Sharif's hands were such delicate instruments of pleasure, and so very knowing where she was concerned.

'And now the rest of you,' he said in a tone of voice that was a husky sedative.

Each application of cream brought her to a higher level of arousal and awareness, so that when he slipped a cushion beneath her hips, she understood for the first time what they were for, and applauded their invention. And when he dipped his hands in the bowl of cream a second time, warming it first between his palms...

And when he touched her...

'Good?' he murmured.

'Do you really need me to answer that?'

And at last he touched her where she was aching for him to touch, but his attention was almost clinical in its brevity.

'Not yet,' he soothed when she groaned in complaint.

He sat back, and she heard him washing his hands in the bowl of scented water and then drying his hands on a cloth. 'You need time to appreciate sensation, and I'm going to give you time, Britt.'

She sucked in a shocked breath. Words failed her. Being on the ball in the office was very different from being...on the sheikh's silken cushions.

'Why confine yourself to once or twice a night?' Sharif said, his eyes alive with laughter.

She didn't know whether to be outraged or in for the journey. When would she ever get another chance like this, for goodness' sake? And with Sharif's dark gaze drawing her ever deeper into his erotic world, and the knowing curve of his mouth reassuring her, there was only one reality for her, and that was Sharif.

'And now you have a job to do,' he said, breaking the dangerous spell. Removing the cushions, he carefully eased her legs down.

'What?' she said, wondering if this was the moment to admit to herself that she would walk on hot coals if that was what it took to have Sharif touch her again.

She followed his gaze to the dish of cream.

Desert robes were intended to come off with the least amount of trouble, Britt discovered as she loosened the laces on the front of Sharif's robe. As it dropped away to reveal his magnificent chest she realised that she might have found the sight of such brute force intimidating had she not known that Sharif was subtle rather than harsh and, above all, blessed with remarkable self-control.

She was glad when he turned on his stomach and stretched out. She wasn't sure she was ready for the whole of naked Sharif just yet. This warrior of the desert was a giant of a man with a formidable physique. Using leisurely strokes, she massaged every part of him, though had to stop herself paying too much attention to his buttocks. They might be the most perfect buttocks she had ever seen on a man, buttocks to mould with your hands—to sink your teeth in—but there was only so much cream to spare, she reflected wryly as he turned. 'Did I say you could move?'

'Continue,' he murmured, settling onto his back.

Okay, so she could do this—and with Sharif watching, if she had to. Hadn't they both seen each other naked in the snow? And was she going to turn her back on Sharif's challenge? Because that was what this was. She had acted big-time girl-around-town, and now he'd called her bluff as she'd called his at the ice lake. He'd come through that with flying colours—flying them high and proud.

*How could she ever forget?*

She took her time scooping up more cream in her hands and spent ages warming it until she really couldn't put off what had to be done any longer. She began with his chest, loving the sensation as she spread the cream across his warm, firm flesh. She moved on down his arms, right to his fingertips where she spent quite a lot of time lavishing care and attention on hands that were capable of dealing the most extreme pleasure—and gasped with shock when Sharif captured her hands and guided them down. They exchanged a look: his challenging and hers defiant.

He won.

Thank goodness.

Sharif had creamed her intimately and she would do the same for him...

Maybe they both won.

She took her time to make certain that every thick, pulsing inch of him was liberally coated with the cream. She was breathless with excitement at the thought of having all of that inside her—

'So, Britt,' he said, distracting her momentarily. 'You're beginning to see the benefit in delay.'

'And what if I am?' she said carelessly.

'Don't pretend with me,' Sharif warned, stretching out, totally unconcerned by his nudity.

As well he might be, she thought, admiring him in silence.

'So what do you think of my golden room of pleasure?' he demanded.

'Not bad,' she agreed. She'd come across perks in business before, but none like this.

'So you like it?' he said with amusement.

'It's fascinating,' was as far as she was prepared to commit. 'Okay, so it's fabulous,' she admitted when he gave her a look.

'But?' he queried.

'It's got such a vibe of forbidden pleasure—how can anyone be here without feeling guilty?'

'Do you feel guilty?'

Actually, no. The cream was beginning to do its work. 'It's just that this is the sort of place where anything could happen...'

'What are you getting at, Britt?'

Her throat tightened. 'I'd like to hear about all the possibilities,' she said.

And so Sharif told her about the various uses of the hard and soft cushions, and the feathers she had been wondering about. She blushed at his forthright description.

'What about your sauna in Skavanga?' Sharif countered, seeing her reaction to his explanation. 'What about your birch twig switches?'

'They are used for health reasons—to get the blood flowing faster.'

She wasn't going to ask any more questions, because she wasn't sure she was ready to hear Sharif's answers.

'Ice and fire,' he murmured, staring at her.

They held that stare for the longest time while decisions were being made by both of them. Finally, she knelt in front of him, and, reaching up, cupped his face in her hands. That thanks she had intended to give him for saving her life was well overdue. Leaning forward, she kissed him gently on the lips.

Sharif's lips were warm and firm. They could curve with humour or press down in a firm line. Both she loved, but now *she* wanted to both tempt and seduce. She increased the pressure and teased his lips apart with his tongue, but just as she began kissing him more deeply Sharif swung her beneath him and pinned her down.

'All that trouble I've gone to with you, Britt Skavanga,' he complained, smiling against her mouth, 'and all you really want is this—'

She let out a shocked cry as Sharif lodged one powerful leg between her thighs, allowing her to feel just how much he wanted it too.

'All you want is the romance of the desert and the sheikh taking you. Admit it,' he said.

'You are impossible.'

'And you are incredible,' he murmured, drawing her into his arms.

'I do want you,' she admitted, still reluctant to give any ground.

'Well, isn't that convenient?' Sharif murmured. 'Because I want you too.'

This teasing was all the more intense because she knew where it was leading. She knew Sharif wouldn't pull back, and nor would she. Somehow her legs opened wider for him, and somehow she was pulling her knees back and pressing her thighs apart and he was testing her for readiness, and catching inside her—

And she was moving her hips to capture more of him, only to discover that the cream had most definitely done its work. One final thrust of her hips and she claimed him completely. When Sharif took her firmly to the hilt, she lost control immediately. She might have called his name. She might have called out anything. She only knew that when the sensation started to subside he took her over the edge again and again.

They were insatiable. No thrust was too deep or too firm, no pace too fast, or too deliciously slow. Her cries of pleasure encouraged Sharif and he made her greedy for more. He never seemed to tire. He never seemed to tire of drawing out her pleasure, either, and each time was more powerful than the last, until finally she must have passed out from exhaustion.

'Welcome to my world, Britt Skavanga,' was the last thing she heard him say before drifting contentedly off to sleep.

# CHAPTER THIRTEEN

HE WATCHED BRITT sleeping, knowing he had been searching for a woman like this all his life. *And now he'd found her, he couldn't have her?* Britt would never agree to be his mistress. And when he married—

*When he married?*

Yes, Sharif's thoughts where Britt was concerned were every bit as strong as that. Selfishly, he hoped she felt the same way about him. But he had always believed when he married it should be for political reasons, for the good of his country. He'd never been much interested before. His council had pressed him into giving advantageous matches consideration, but he'd never had an appetite for the task. He wanted a woman who excited him—a woman like Britt.

Warm certainty rushed through him as he brushed a strand of hair away from Britt's still-flushed face. He would find a way. The Black Sheikh could always find a way. He would never ask Britt to give up her independence. No one knew better than he that privilege came with a price, and that price was freedom to do as he pleased, but with a woman like Britt anything was possible.

Or, was it? Britt was exceptional and could do great things in life. She deserved the chance to choose her own path, while his was cast in stone. And then there was Skavanga Mining, and all the subterfuge with her brother…

He exhaled heavily as business and personal feelings collided. The consortium needed Britt's expertise in the mining industry as well as her people skills, but would she stay with the company when the consortium took over? She had been running the company up to now, so it would take some fine diplomacy on his part to keep Britt on board. Could he find something to soften the blow for her?

His dilemma was this: while he cared deeply for Britt, his loyalty could only be fixed in one direction, and his was firmly rooted in the consortium.

The phone flashing distracted him. It was Raffa to say he had been forced to move money into Skavanga Mining on the recommendation of their financial analysts. Britt could only see this as another plot, when in fact what Raffa had done had saved the company.

'Our money men are already swarming on Skavanga Mining, and we need you on the ground to reassure everyone that the changes don't mean catastrophe,' Raffa was saying.

'What about Tyr?' And the grand reunion he had been planning for Britt.

'Tyr can't be there—'

'What do you mean, Tyr can't be there?' He cursed viciously. Having Tyr in Skavanga in person would have softened the blow for Britt when she discovered Tyr's golden shares had swung the ownership of the company into the hands of the consortium. But now—how was he going to explain Tyr's absence without betraying Britt's brother as he had promised faithfully not to do?

He had to get back to Skavanga Mining right away to sort this out—and he could only do that without Britt's newly discovered emotions getting in the way, which meant returning to Skavanga without her. Thankfully, his jet was always fuelled. 'I'll be there in fourteen hours,' he said, ending the call.

Glancing at Britt, he knew there was no time to waste, and by the time he had woken her and explained as gently as he could about Tyr coming into the equation it could all be over in Skavanga. This was one emergency she would definitely want to be part of, but it was better if he prepared the ground first, and then sent the jet back for her.

She woke cautiously and her first thought was of Sharif. She didn't want to wake him as it was barely dawn. The first thin sliver of light was just beginning to show beneath the entrance to the tent. She stretched luxuriously, and, still half asleep, reached out to find him…

The empty space at her side required she open one eye. The initial bolt of surprise and disappointment was swiftly replaced by sound reasoning. He must have gone riding. It was dawn. It was quiet. It was the perfect time of day for riding. Groaning with contentment, she rolled over in the bed of soft silken cushions, and, clutching one, nestled her face into it, telling herself that it still held Sharif's faint, spicy scent. He'd held her safe through the night, and the pleasure they'd shared was indescribable. The closeness between them was real, and she was content, a state she couldn't claim very often. This encouraged her to dream that one day they might work side by side to create something special, something lasting, and not just for Skavanga, but for Kareshi too.

She stilled to listen to the muffled sounds of the encampment coming to life for another day. She could hear voices calling somewhere in the distance and cooking vessels clanking against each other, and then there was the gentle pop and fizz of the water in her bathing pool as it bubbled up from its warm underground source. Everything was designed to soothe the senses. Everything was in tune with her sleepy, mellow mood. She wasn't too warm or too cold, and her body felt deliciously well used by a man who made every day a special day, an exciting day.

Yes, she was a contented woman this morning, Britt reflected as she stretched languorously on her silken bed, and she couldn't ever remember feeling that way before—

She jumped up when the phone rang.

'Leila?'

She sat bolt upright. When her younger sister called it was invariably good news. Leila didn't have a grouchy bone in her body and had to be one of the easiest people in the world to get along with, and Britt was bursting to share the news about her growing closeness with Sharif. 'It's so good to hear your voice—'

An ominous silence followed.

'Leila, what's wrong?' Britt realised belatedly that if it was dawn in the desert it was the middle of the night in Skavanga.

'I don't know where to start.' Leila's voice was soft and hesitant. 'We're in trouble. You have to come home, Britt. We need you.'

'Who's in trouble? What's happened?' Britt pressed anxiously. Her stomach took a dive as she waited for Leila to answer.

'The company.'

As Leila's voice tailed away Britt glanced at the empty side of the bed. 'Don't worry, I'm coming straight home.'

She was already off the bed and launching herself through the curtains with her brain in gear. 'Hang on a minute, Leila.' Grabbing a couple of towels from the stack by the pool, she wrapped them around her and ran to the entrance of the pavilion where she saw a passing girl and beckoned her over. Smiling somehow, she gestured urgently for her clothes, before retreating back into the privacy of the pavilion.

'Okay, I'm here,' she reassured her sister. 'So tell me what's going on.'

The pause at the other end of the line might have been a few seconds, but it felt like for ever. 'Leila, please,' Britt prompted.

'The consortium has taken over the company,' Leila said flatly.

'*What?*' Britt reeled back. 'How could they do that? I had the confidence of all the small shareholders before I left.'

'But we don't have enough shares between us to stave off a takeover, and they've bought some more from somewhere.'

'The consortium's betrayed our trust?' Which meant Sharif had betrayed her. 'I don't believe it. You must have got it wrong—'

'I haven't got it wrong,' Leila insisted. 'Their money men are already here.'

'In the middle of the night?'

'It's that critical, apparently.'

While she was in a harem tent in the desert!

Had nothing changed? Had she learned nothing? Sharif had walked away from her again—distracted her again. And this time it all but destroyed her. For a moment she couldn't move, she couldn't think.

'I'm sorry if I shocked you,' Leila said.

*Shock?*

'I'm sorry that you've had to handle this on your

own,' Britt said, forcing her mind to focus. 'I'll be there just as soon as I can get a flight.'

She had been stupidly taken in, Britt realised. Sharif had betrayed her. By his own admission, nothing was signed off without the Black Sheikh's consent. He must have known about the share deals all along.

'There's one thing I don't get,' she said. 'How can the deal be done when the family holds the majority share-holding? You didn't sell out to him, did you?'

'Not us,' Leila said quietly.

'Who then?'

'Tyr…Tyr has always had more shares than we have. Don't you remember our grandmother leaving him the golden shares?'

Shock hit her again. Their grandmother had done something with the shares, Britt remembered, but she had been too young to take it in. 'Is Tyr with you? Is he there?' Suddenly all that mattered was seeing her brother again. Tyr had always made things right when they were little— Or was that just her blind optimism at work again? She couldn't trust her own judgement these days.

'No. Tyr's not here, Britt. Neither Eva or I has seen him. The only thing I can tell you is that Tyr and the Black Sheikh are the main forces behind this deal,' Leila explained, hammering another nail into the coffin of Britt's misguided dream. 'The sheikh has got his law-yers and accountants swarming all over everything.'

'He didn't waste any time,' Britt said numbly. While she had been in bed with Sharif, he had been seeing the deal through and speaking to her brother. This had to be the ultimate betrayal, and was why Sharif hadn't been at her side when she woke this morning. He was already on his way to Skavanga. What could she say to Leila— to either of her sisters? Sorry would never cover it.

'It's such a shock,' Leila was saying. 'We still can't believe this is happening.'

There was no point regretting things that couldn't be changed, Britt reasoned as she switched quickly to reassuring her sister. 'Don't worry about any of this, Leila. Just stay out of it until I get back. I'll handle it.'

'What about you, Britt?'

'What about me?' She forced a laugh. 'Let me go and pack my case so I can come home.'

She had been betrayed by her feelings, Britt realized as she ended the call. She was to blame for this, no one else. And now it was up to her to make things right.

She spun around as the tent flap opened, but her hammering heart could take a break. It was the smiling women with her clothes. And whatever type of man their master was, these women had been nothing but kind to her. Greeting them warmly, she explained with mime that although she would love to spend more time with them, she really couldn't today.

It was as if she had never been away, Britt reflected as the cab brought her into the city from the airport. But had the streets always been so grey? The pavements were packed with ice and with low grey cloud overhead everything seemed greyer than ever. After the desert, she reasoned. This was her home and she loved it whatever the climate might be. This harsh land was where she had been born and bred to fight and she wasn't about to turn tail and run just because the odds were against her. Nothing much frightened her, she reasoned as the cab slowed down outside the offices of Skavanga Mining. Only her heart had ever let her down.

Her sisters were waiting for her just inside the glass entrance doors. Whatever the circumstances she was always thrilled to see them. Knowing there was no time to lose, she had come straight to the office from the airport with the intention of getting straight back in the saddle. Thank goodness she'd had a non-crease business suit and stockings in her carry-on bag. She needed all the armour she could lay her hands on.

'Together we stand,' Britt confirmed when they finally pulled apart from their hug.

'Thank God you're here,' Eva said grimly. 'We're overrun by strangers. We have never needed to show a united force more.'

'Not strangers—people from the consortium,' Leila reassured her. 'But he's here,' Leila added gently. 'I just thought you should know.'

'Tyr's here?' Britt's face dropped as she realised from Leila's expression who her sister was talking about. 'You mean Sharif is here,' she said softly. Better she face him now than later, Britt determined, leading her sisters past Reception towards the stairs. 'With his troops,' Eva added as a warning.

Britt made no response. Troops or not, it made no difference to her. She would face him just the same. She could only hope her heart stopped pounding when she did so.

*How the hell had he got here ahead of her?*

His private jet, of course—

Get your head together fast, Britt ordered herself fiercely. She was strong. She could do this. She had to do this. She had always protected her sisters and the people who worked for Skavanga Mining. That was her role in life.

*Without it what was she?*

Nothing had changed, she told herself fiercely.

'Don't worry,' she said. 'I can handle this.'

Eva was right. The first-floor lobby was bustling with people Britt didn't know. Sharif's people—the consortium's people—Sharif had moved them in already. Her temper flared at the thought. But she had to keep her cool. She had lost the initiative the moment she allowed her emotions to come into play, and that must never happen again.

So, Tyr definitely wasn't coming. Sharif had tried to persuade him, but now he put his phone away. Their conversation had been typical of the type Sharif had come to expect from the man who was a latter day Robin Hood. If a worthy cause had to be fought Tyr would drop everything and swing into action. He couldn't blame the man, not with everything that was going on in Tyr's life, but his presence here today would have softened the blow for Britt, whose arrival was imminent. Britt's campaign to save the company was on track, but a happy reunion with the brother she hadn't seen for years was not on the cards. So now she would just be bewildered by what she would see as Tyr's betrayal and his.

He pulled away from the window when he saw Britt's cab arrive. However angry she was he had to keep her on board. Skavanga Mining needed her—

*He needed her—*

He would protect her from further distress the only way he knew how, which was to say nothing about Tyr, just as he had promised, and allow the blame to fall on the ruthless Black Sheikh instead. He would live up to his reputation. Better she hated him than she blamed Tyr for throwing in his lot with the consortium. Tyr had seen it as the only way to save the company in a hurry, and Tyr was right, though Sharif didn't expect Britt to be so understanding; and with Tyr and the other two men in the consortium tied up half a world away, it was up to him to handle the takeover. There had been time to leave a brief message for Britt with the women at the encampment, and he hoped she'd got it. If not he was in for a stormy ride.

'Britt.' He turned the instant she entered the room. His response to her was stronger than ever. She lit up the room—she lit up his life. She forced him to re-evaluate every decision he had ever made, and he always came to the same conclusion. He would never meet another woman like her, but from her expression he guessed she hated him now. 'Wait for me outside,' she told her sisters in a cold voice that confirmed his opinion.

'Are you sure?' the youngest asked anxiously.

'I'm sure,' Britt said without taking her eyes off him.

She looked magnificent—even better than he remembered. A little crumpled from the journey, maybe, but her bearing was unchanged, and that said everything about a woman who didn't know the meaning of defeat. He'd made a serious error leaving her behind in Kareshi. He should have brought her with him and to hell with the consequences. He should have known that Britt was more than ready for whatever she had to face. Her steely gaze at this moment was unflinching.

'Please sit down,' she said, and then she blinked as if remembering that he was in charge now.

'Thank you,' he said, making nothing of it.

Crossing to the boardroom table, he held out the chair for her and heard the slide of silk stockings as she sat down and crossed her legs. He was acutely aware of her scent, of her, but, despite all those highly feminine traits that she was unable to hide, she was ice.

He chose a chair across the table from her. They both

left the chairman's chair empty, though if Britt felt any irony in sitting beneath portraits of her great-grandfather, who had hacked out a successful mining company from the icy wastes with his bare hands, or the father who had pretty much lost the business in half the time it had taken his own father to build it up, she certainly didn't show it. As far as Britt was concerned, it was business as usual and she was in control.

Even now she felt a conflict inside her that shouldn't exist. She had entered the room at the head of her sisters, determined to fight for them to the end. But seeing Sharif changed everything. It always did. The man beneath that formal suit called to her soul, and made her body crave his protective embrace.

So she might be stupid, but she wasn't a child, she told herself impatiently. She was a grown woman, who had learned how to run this company to the best of her ability when it was thrust upon her, whether she wanted it or not. And nothing had changed as far as she was concerned. 'I called the lawyers in on my way from the airport.'

'There's no point in rushing to do that,' he said, 'when I can fill you in.'

'I prefer to deal with professionals,' she said.

He couldn't blame Britt for the bite in her tone. The way that things had worked out here meant she could only feel betrayed by him.

She searched his eyes, and found nothing. What would he find in hers? The same? If her eyes contained only half the anger and contempt she felt for him, then that would have to do for now. She could only hope the hurt and bewilderment didn't show at all.

'I'd be interested to hear your account of things,' she said coldly. 'I believe my brother's involved in some way.' For the first time she saw Sharif hesitate. 'Did you think I wouldn't find out?'

'In an ideal world I would have liked things to take their course so you could get used to the idea of Tyr's involvement. As it was he stepped in to prevent a hostile takeover from any other quarter.'

'And this isn't a hostile takeover?'

'How can it be when Tyr is involved?'

'I wouldn't know since I haven't heard from him.'

'He is still on his travels.'

'So I believe. I heard he took the coward's way out—'

'No one calls your brother a coward in my hearing,' Sharif interrupted fiercely. 'Not even you, Britt.'

Sharif's frown was thunderous and though she opened her mouth to reply something stopped her.

'You realise Tyr and I go back a long way?'

'I don't know all his friends,' she said. 'I still don't,' she added acidly.

Ignoring her barb, Sharif explained that Kareshi was one of the countries Tyr had helped to independence.

'With his mercenaries?' she huffed scathingly.

He ignored this too. 'With your brother's backing I was able to protect my people and save them from tyrants who would have destroyed our country.' He fixed her with an unflinching stare. 'I will never hear a wrong word said against your brother.'

'I understand that from your perspective, my brother has done no wrong. Tyr knows how to help everyone except his own family—'

'You're so wrong,' Sharif cut in. 'And I'm going to tell you why. If Tyr had added his golden shares to those you and your sisters own, the company would still go down. Add those shares to the weight of the consortium and the funds we can provide—not some time in the future, but right now—and you have real power. That's what your brother's done. Tyr has stepped in to save, not just you and your family, but the company and the people who work here.'

'So why couldn't he tell me that himself?'

'It's up to Tyr to explain when he's ready.' Sharif paused as if he would have liked to say something more, but then he just said quietly, 'Tyr's braver than you know.'

She felt as if she had been struck across the face. There was no battle to fight here. It had already been won.

'A glass of water?' Sharif enquired softly.

She passed an angry hand over her eyes, fighting for composure. She felt sick and faint from all the shocks her mind had been forced to accept. The structure of the business had changed—Tyr was involved, but he still wasn't coming home. And mixed into all this were her feelings for this man. It was too much to take in all at once.

Thrusting her chair back, she stood.

Sharif stood too. 'We want to keep you, Britt—'

'I need time—'

'The consortium could use your people skills as well as the mining expertise you have. At least promise me that you'll think about what I've said.'

'Ten minutes,' she flashed, turning from the table. She had to get out of here—now.

*One foot in front of the other—how hard could that be?*

That might be easy if she didn't know she had let everyone down. She allowed herself to become distracted and everything had changed. The company might have been thrust upon her, but she had given it all she'd got, and had intended to continue doing so for the rest of her working life. So much for that.

Bracing her arms against the sink in the restroom, she hung her head. She couldn't bear to look at her reflection in the mirror. She couldn't bear to see the longing for Sharif in her eyes. Everything he'd said made sense. He wasn't even taking over and booting her out. They wanted her to stay on, he'd said. And she wanted Sharif in every way a woman could want a man. She wanted them to have a proper relationship that wasn't just founded on sex. She had run the gamut of emotions with him, and had learned from it, but this was the hardest lesson of all: the man they called the Black Sheikh would stop at nothing to achieve his goal—even recruiting Britt's long-lost brother, if that got him where he wanted to be. And Sharif didn't even want the part of her she wanted to give, he wanted her people skills. The only way she could survive knowing that was to revert to being the Britt who didn't feel anything.

Sluicing her face down in cold water, she reached for a towel and straightened up. Now she must face the cold man in the boardroom whom she loved more than life itself, and the only decision left for her to make was whether or not she could stay on here and work for Sharif.

She could stay on. She had to. She couldn't abandon the people who worked here, or her sisters. And if that meant her badly bruised heart took another battering, so what? She would just have to return it to its default setting of stone.

# CHAPTER FOURTEEN

BRITT RETURNED TO the boardroom to find Sharif pacing. Caught unawares, he looked like a man with the weight of the world on his back. For the blink of an eye she felt sorry for him. Who shared the load with Sharif? When did he get time off? And then she remembered their time in the desert and her heart closed again.

'There is a problem,' he said, holding her stony gaze trapped in his.

'Oh?' She felt for the wall behind her as wasted emotions dragged her down. She could fix her mind all she liked on being tough and determined, and utterly sure about where she wanted this to go, but when she saw him—when she saw those concerns she couldn't know about furrowing his brow and drawing cruel lines down each side of his mouth—she wanted to reach out to him.

She wanted to help him, and, even more than that, she wanted to stand back to back with Sharif to solve every problem they came across, and she wanted him to feel the same way she did.

'I've had to make some changes to my plans.'

'Trouble in Kareshi?' she guessed.

'A troublesome relation who was banished from the kingdom has returned in my absence and is trying to rally support amongst the bullies who still remain. It's a basic fight between a brighter modern future for all and a return to the dark days of the past when a privileged few exploited the majority. I must return. I promised my people that they would never be at the mercy of bullies again, and it's a promise I intend to keep.'

Sharif really did have the weight of the world on his shoulders. 'What can I do?' Britt said. Whatever had led them to this place was irrelevant compared to so many lives in jeopardy.

'I need your agreement to stay on here. I need you to do my job for me while I'm away. I need you to ease the transition so that no one worries about change unnecessarily. Will you do that for me, Britt?'

Sharif needed her. The people here needed her. And if he didn't need her in the way she had hoped he would, she still couldn't turn her back on him, let alone turn her back on the other people she cared about.

'I really need you to do this for me, Britt.'

Her heart hammered violently as Sharif came closer to make his point, but he maintained some distance between them, and she respected that. Her heart responded. Her soul responded. She could no more refuse this man than she could turn and walk away from her duties here. But there was one thing she did have to know. 'Am I doing this for you, or for the consortium?'

'You're doing it for yourself, and for your people, Britt, and for what this company means to them. Hold things together for me until I get back and we can get this diamond project properly under way and then you'll see the benefits for both our people.'

'How long will you be away?' The words were out before she could stop them, and she hated herself for asking, but then reassured herself that, as this concerned business, she had to know.

'A month, no more, I promise you that.'

The tension grew and then she said, 'I noticed a lot of new people were here when I arrived. Will you introduce me?'

Sharif visibly relaxed. 'Thank you, Britt,' he said. 'The people you saw are people I trust. People I hope you will learn to trust. They moved in with the approval of your lawyers and with your own financial director alongside them to smooth the path—'

'Of your consortium's takeover of my family's company,' she said ruefully.

'Of our necessary intervention,' Sharif amended. 'I hope I can give you cause to change your mind,' he said when he saw her expression. 'This is going to be good for all of us, Britt—and you of all people must know there's no time to waste. Winter in the Arctic is just around the corner, which will make the preliminary drilling harder, if not impossible, so I need your firm answer now.'

'I'll stay,' she said quietly. 'Of course, I'll stay.'

How ironic it seemed that Sharif was battling to keep her on. He was right, though, she could handle anything the business threw at her, but when it came to her personal life she was useless. She had no self-belief, no courage, no practice in playing up to men, or making them see her as a woman who hurt and cared and loved and worried that she would never be good enough to deserve a family of her own to love, and a partner with whom she shared everything

'And when you come back?' she said.

'You can stay or not, as you please. You can still have an involvement in the company, but you could travel, if that's what you want to do. I have business interests in Kareshi that you are welcome to look over.'

A sop for her agreement, she thought. But a welcome one—if a little daunting for someone whose life

had always revolved around Skavanga. 'I'd be like you
then, always travelling.'

'And always returning home,' Sharif said with a
shrug. 'What can I tell you, Britt? If you want responsibility there is no easy way. You should know that. You
have to take everything that comes along.'

'And when Tyr comes home?'

'I'm not sure that your brother has any interest in the
business—beyond saving it.'

She flushed at misjudging her brother when she
should have known that Tyr would have all their best
interests at heart.

'And now I've got a new contract of employment
for you—'

'You anticipated my response.' But she went cold.
Was she so easy to read? If she was, Sharif must know
how hopelessly entangled her heart was with his.

Sharif gave nothing away as he uncapped his pen.
'Your lawyers have given it the once-over,' he explained. 'You can read their letter. I've got it here for
you. I'll leave you in private for a few moments.'

She picked it up as Sharif shut the door behind him.
Her nerves were all on edge as she scanned the contents of the letter. 'This is the best solution,' jumped out
at her. So be it. She drew a steadying breath, knowing
there wasn't time for personal feelings. There never had
been time. She had consistently fooled herself about that
where Sharif was concerned.

Walking to the door, she asked the first person she
saw to witness her signature and two minutes later it
was done. She issued a silent apology to her ancestors.
This was no longer a family firm. She worked for the
consortium now like everyone else at Skavanga Mining.

Sharif returned and saw her face. 'You haven't lost
anything, Britt. You've only gained from this.'

That remained to be seen, she thought, remembering Sharif leaving her in Kareshi and again at the cabin.

'I left a message for you in Kareshi,' he said as if picking up on these thoughts. 'Didn't you get it? The women? Didn't they come to find you?' he added as she slowly shook her head.

And then she remembered the women trying to speak to her before she left. She'd been in too much of a hurry to spare the time for them. 'They did try to speak to me,' she admitted.

'But you didn't give them chance to explain?' Sharif guessed. 'Like you I never walk away from responsibility, Britt. You should know I would always get a message to you somehow.'

And he was actually paying her a compliment leaving Skavanga Mining in her care. It was a compliment she would gladly park in favour of hearing Sharif tell her that he couldn't envisage life without her—

How far must this self-delusion go before she finally got it into her head that whatever had happened between them in the past was over? Sharif had clearly moved on to the next phase of his life. Why couldn't she?

'Welcome on board, Britt.'

She stared at his outstretched hand, wondering if she dared touch it. She was actually afraid of what she might feel. She sought refuge as always in business. 'Is that it?' she said briskly, turning to go. 'I really should put my sisters out of their misery.'

'They already know what's going on.'

'You told them?'

'Like you, I didn't want them to worry, so I told them what was happening and sent them home.'

'You don't take any chances, do you, Sharif?' She

stared into the dark, unreadable eyes of the man who
had briefly been her lover and who was now her boss.

'Never,' he confirmed.

A wave of emotion jolted her as she walked to the
door. Sharif's voice stopped her. 'Don't leave like this,'
he said.

She turned her face away from him, unwilling to
meet his all-seeing stare. The last thing she wanted now
was to break down in front of him. Sharif must be given
no reason to think she wasn't tough enough to handle
the assignment he had tasked her with.

'Britt,' he ground out, his mouth so close to her ear.
'Please. Listen to me—'

She tried to make a joke of it and almost managed to
huff a laugh as she wrangled herself free. 'I think I've
listened to you enough, don't you?'

'You don't get it, do you?' he said. 'I'm doing this
for you—I rushed here for you—to save the company.
This isn't just for the consortium. Yes, of course we'll
benefit from it, but I wanted to save your company for
you. Can't you see that? Why else would I leave my
country when there's trouble brewing?'

'I don't know,' she said, shaking her head. 'Everything's happened so fast, I just don't know what to
think. I only know I don't understand you.'

'I think you do. I think you understand me very well.'

She would not succumb to Sharif's dark charm. She
would not weaken now. The urge to soften against him
was overpowering, but if she did that she was lost. She
might as well pack up her job and agree to be Sharif's
mistress for as long as it amused the Black Sheikh. 'I
need to go home and see my sisters.'

'You need to stay here with me,' Sharif argued.

She wanted his arms around her too badly to stay. She

still felt isolated and unsure of herself. She, who took pride in standing alone at the head of her troops, felt as if the ground had been pulled away from her feet today.

'Are you frightened of being alone with me, Britt?' Cupping her chin, Sharif made her look at him and she stared back. He was a warrior of the desert, a man who had fought to restore freedom to his country, and who could have brushed her aside and taken over Skavanga Mining without involving her.

*So why hadn't he?*

'I asked you a question, Britt? Why won't you answer me?'

Sharif's touch on her face was so seductive it would have been the easiest thing in the world to soften in his arms. 'I'm not frightened of you,' she said, speaking more to herself.

'Good,' he murmured. 'That's the last thing I want.'

But if he could know how frightened she was of the way she felt about him, he would surely count it as a victory. And the longer Sharif held her like this, close yet not too close, the more she longed for his warmth and his strength, and the clearer it became that, for the first time in her life, being Britt Skavanga, lone businesswoman, wasn't enough.

'I've got an idea,' Sharif said quietly as he released her.

'What?' she said cautiously.

'I'd like you the think about working in Kareshi as well as Skavanga— Don't look so shocked, Britt. We live in a small world—'

'It's not that.' Her heart had leapt at the thought, but she still doubted herself, doubted her capabilities, and wondered if Sharif was just saying this to make her feel better.

'It's not that—' Her heart had leapt at the thought, even as doubt crowded in that for some reason Sharif just wanted to make her feel better.

'I have always encouraged people to break down unnecessary barriers so they can broaden their horizons in every way. I'm keen to develop talent wherever I find it, and I'd like you to think about using your interpersonal skills more widely. I know you've always concentrated on Skavanga Mining in the past, and that's good, but while I'm away— Well, please just agree to think about what I've said—'

'I will,' she promised as Sharif moved towards the door.

'One month, Britt. I'll send the jet.'

Anything connected with Sharif was a whirlwind, Britt concluded, her head still reeling as he left the room. He ruled a country— He was a warrior. He was a lover, but no more than that. But Sharif had placed his trust in her, and had put her back in charge of Skavanga mining where she could protect the interests of the people she cared about.

A month, he'd said? She'd better get started.

He had to give her time, he reasoned. He would see Britt again soon—

*A month—*

He consoled himself with the thought that in between times he could sort out his country and his companies—

To hell with all of it!

Without Britt there was nothing. He'd known that on the flight when every mile he put between them was a mile too far. Without Britt there was no purpose to any of this. What was life for, if not to love and be loved?

# CHAPTER FIFTEEN

A MONTH WAS a long time in business, and Britt was surprised at how many of the changes were good. With new blood came new ideas, along with fresh energy for everyone concerned to fire off. The combination of ice and fire seemed to be working well at Skavanga Mining. The Kareshis brought interesting solutions for deep shaft mining, while nothing fazed workers in Skavanga who were accustomed to dealing with extreme conditions on a daily basis. Drilling was already under way, and even Britt's sisters had been reassured by how well everyone was getting on, and how much care, time and money the consortium was putting into preserving the environment. They had always taken their lead from Britt where business was concerned and so when she explained Sharif's plan to them, they were all for her trip to Kareshi—though their teasing she could have done without.

'Oh, come off it,' Eva insisted in Britt's minimalist bedroom at the penthouse, where the sisters were helping Britt to pack in readiness for the arrival of Sharif's jet the following day. 'We've seen him now. Don't tell me you're not aching to see your desert sheikh again.'

Aching? If a month was a long time in business, it was infinity when it came to being parted from Sharif.

'He isn't *my* desert sheikh,' she said firmly, ignoring the glances her sisters exchanged. 'And, for your information, this is a business trip.'

'Hence the new underwear,' Leila remarked tongue in cheek.

Business trip?

Business trip, Britt told herself firmly as the limousine that had collected her from the steps of the royal flight, no less, slowed in front of the towering, heavily ornamented golden gates that led into the courtyard in front of Sheikh Sharif's residence in his capital city of Kareshi. She had read during the flight that the Black Sheikh's palace was a world heritage site, and was one of the most authentically restored medieval castles. To Britt it was simply overwhelming. The size of the place was incredible. It was, in fact, more like a fortified city contained within massive walls.

It was one month since she had last seen Sharif. One month in which to prepare herself for pennants flying from ancient battlements, alongside the hustle and bustle of a thriving modern city—but she could never be properly prepared, if only because the contrast was just too stark. And those contrasts existed in the Black Sheikh himself. Respectful of traditional values, Sharif was a forward-thinker, always planning the next improvement for his country.

Excitement wasn't enought to describe her feelings. There was also apprehension. Until she saw Sharif's expression when he saw her again, she couldn't relax. She was prepared for anything, and was already steeling her heart—the same heart that was hammering in her ears as she wondered if Sharif would be wearing his full and splendid regalia—the flowing black robes of the desert king? Or would he be wearing a sombre tailored suit to greet a director of what he had referred to in the press as his most exciting project yet?

Exhaling shakily, she hoped the problems he had referred to in Kareshi had been resolved, because she was bringing him good news from the mine. They were ahead of schedule and there was a lot to talk about. Ready for their first business meeting, she had changed into a modest dress and jacket in a conservative shade of beige on the plane.

Her heart bounced as the steps of the citadel came into view. Somewhere inside that gigantic building Sharif was waiting.

Not inside.

And not wearing black robes, either, she realised as the limousine drew to a halt.

Sharif was dressed for riding in breeches, polo shirt and boots…breeches that moulded his lower body with obscene attention to detail…

'Welcome to my home,' he said, opening the car door for her.

His face was hard to read. He was smiling, but it could easily have been a smile of welcome for a business associate, newly arrived in his country. Forget business—forget everything—her heart was going crazy. 'Thank you,' she said demurely, stepping out.

He was just so damn sexy she couldn't think of anything else to say. Her mind was closed to business, and her wayward body had tunnel vision and could only see one man—and that was the sexy man who knew just how to please her. There was only one swarthy, stubble-shaded face in her field of vision, and one head of unruly, thick black hair, one pair of keenly assessing eyes, one aquiline nose, one proud, smooth brow, one firm, sexy mouth—

Pull yourself together, Britt ordered herself firmly as Sharif indicated that she should mount the steps ahead of him.

There were guards in traditional robes with scimitars hanging at their sides standing sentry either side of the grand entrance doors and she felt overawed as she walked past them into the ancient citadel. Every breath she took seemed amplified and their footsteps sounded like pistol shots in the huge vaulted space. Everything was on a grand scale. It was an imposing marble-tiled hall with giant-sized stained-glass windows. There were sumptuous rugs in all the colours of the rainbow, and the beautifully ornamented furniture seemed to have been scaled for a race of giants. She felt like a mouse that had strayed into the lion's den. The arched ceiling above her head seemed to stretch away to the heavens, and she couldn't imagine who had built it, or how the monstrous stone pillars that supported it had been set in place.

Attendants bowed low as Sharif led her on. Even when he was dressed in riding gear, authority radiated from him. He was a natural leader without any affectation, and—

And she was going there again, Britt realised, reining her feelings in. Each time she saw Sharif she found something more to admire about him, yet his insular demeanor irritated the hell out of her too, even if she accepted that hiding his feelings must be an essential tool of kingship.

'Do you like it?' he said, catching her smile.

She jolted back to full attention, realising that Sharif had been watching her keenly the whole time. 'I think it's magnificent,' she said as a group of men in flowing robes with curving daggers in their belts and prayer beads clicking in their hands bowed low to Sharif.

A hint of cinnamon and some other exotic spices cut the air, a timely reminder of just how far away from home she was, and how they still had quite a few issues to address. She wondered if Sharif would hand her over to some underling soon, leaving their discussions until later. She almost hoped he would to give her chance to get used to this.

'What's amusing you?' he said.

'Just taking it all in,' she said honestly. 'I'm a historic building fanatic,' she admitted, thinking that a safe topic of conversation. 'And this is one of the best I've seen.'

'The main part of the citadel was built in the twelfth century—'

As he went on she realised that Sharif really did mean to be her tour guide. She had no complaints. He was an excellent teacher, as she knew only too well.

He took her into scented gardens while her heart yearned for him to a soundtrack of musical fountains.

'We have always had some of the greatest engineers in the world in Kareshi,' he explained.

And some of the greatest lovers too, she thought. And what else but love could this exquisite courtyard have been designed for? Everything spoke of romance—the intricate mosaic patterns on the floor, the songbirds carolling in the lemon trees, and the tinkling water features. Surely it was the most romantic place on earth?

And as such was completely wasted on her, Britt concluded, as Sharif indicated that they should move on. 'I'll have someone show you your room,' he said.

So that was it. Tour over. Her heart lurched on cue as he raked his wild, unruly hair into some semblance of order. He probably couldn't wait to pass her over to someone else.

'Freshen up and then meet me in ten,' he said.

Oh…

'Unless you're too tired after your journey?'

'I'm not tired.'

'Good. Put something casual on. Jeans—'

She held back on the salute as a group of women clothed in flowing gowns in a multitude of colours appeared out of nowhere. She turned to look over her shoulder as they ushered her away, but Sharif had already gone.


'These are your rooms,' an older woman, who seemed in charge of the rest, explained as Britt gazed around in wonder.

'All of them?' she murmured.

'All of them,' the smiling woman explained. 'My name is Zenub. If you need anything you only have to ask—or call me.' And when Britt looked surprised, she added, 'This is an ancient building, but we have a very modern sheikh. There is an internal telephone system. This room leads into your dressing room and bathroom,' she explained, opening an arched fretted door that might have been made of solid gold, for all Britt knew. The door was studded with gems that seemed real enough, and probably were, Britt concluded, since Sharif had explained that every original feature inside the citadel had been faithfully restored to its former glory.

She was excited to discover that she had her own inner courtyard, complete with fountain and songbirds. The scent from a cluster of orange trees decorated with fat, ripe fruit was incredible while the fretted walls and covered walkways kept everything cool. It was just the type of place to invite exploration—the type of place to linger and to dream. Perhaps it was just as well she didn't have time.

'There are clothes in the wardrobe, should you need them,' Zenub told her as she ushered the other women out. 'And your suitcase is over here,' she added, indicating a dressing room with yet another glorious display of fresh flowers on one of the low-lying, heavily decorated brass tables. 'Please don't hesitate to call me if you need anything else.'

Britt smiled. 'I will—thank you. And thank you for everything you've done to make me so welcome.'

Amazing didn't quite cover this, Britt reflected as the women left her alone in what amounted to the most fabulous apartment. Every item must have been a priceless treasure, and it was only when she walked into the bathroom and smiled that she saw Sharif's hand in the restoration. The bathroom was state of the art too. There were the high-quality towels on heated rails, as well as fabulous products lined up on the shelves. If the harem pavilion in the desert had been a place of pure pleasure, this was sheer indulgence. It was just a shame she didn't have time to indulge. Another time, she mused ruefully, stepping into the shower.

She showered down quickly and dried off. Tying back her hair, she thought, Sharif stipulated casual, so she tugged on her jeans. A simple white tee and sneakers completed the outfit. A slick of lip gloss and a spritz of scent later and she was ready—for anything, she told herself firmly, leaving the room.

Except for the sight of Sharif wearing a tight black top that sculpted his muscular arms to perfection, and snug-fitting jeans secured by a heavy-duty belt, holding heaven in its rightful place.

And why had she never noticed he had a tattoo before? *She'd been otherwise engaged, possibly?*

'Hello,' she managed lamely, while her thoughts ran crazy stupid wild.

'Britt.' He looked her over and seemed pleased. 'You fulfilled the brief.'

'Yes, I did, boss.' She raised her chin and met the dark, appraising stare with a challenging grin.

'Shall we?'

She glanced at the imposing doors, either side of which stood silent guards whose rich, jewel-coloured robes and headdresses reminded her that this was an exciting land full of rich variety and many surprises. But not half as many surprises as the man standing next to her, Britt suspected as they jogged down the steps together. She stopped at the bottom of the steps and did a double take. 'A motorbike?'

Sharif raised a sexy, inky brow. 'I take it you've seen one before?'

'Of course, but—'

'Helmet?'

'Thank you.' She buckled it on.

And yes, there were outriders. And yes, there was an armoured vehicle that might have contained anything from a rocket launcher to a mobile café, but it wouldn't have mattered, because none of the following posse could keep up with Sharif.

Riding a bike was hot without any additional inducements, like jean-clad sheikhs she had to cling to. Sharif was a great rider. She felt safe and yet in terrible danger—in the most thrilling way. By the time he stopped the big machine outside the university he could have had her on the street.

Fortunately, Sharif had more control than she had

and led her through the beautifully groomed grounds, explaining that he wanted to talk to her before he introduced Britt to the students.

'You've got another idea,' she guessed.

'You know me so well,' he said, his dark eyes glinting.

I wish, she thought as Sharif ruffled his hair. 'So, what's it about?'

'We've talked about this before, in a way,' he said, perching on a wall and drawing her down beside him. 'If you agree, I'd like you to start thinking about plans to bring our two countries together by arranging exchange trips between students.'

'Is that why you've brought me here?'

'That's one reason, yes. I want you to see where your diamonds are going.'

She couldn't pretend she wasn't excited. Her world had always revolved around Skavanga, but now Sharif was offering her more—so much more and her heart soared with hope.

'You're the best person for the job,' he said. 'You'll be reporting to me, of course—'

'Oh, of course.' She tried to keep it light.

'Don't mock,' he warned.

He touched her cheek as he said this, and stared deep into her eyes. It was impossible to feel nothing. Impossible, but she tried not to show it.

'Your first task is to work on a way for our people to learn about each other's culture.'

And now the dam finally burst and she laughed. 'Birch twig switches and harem tents? That should go down well with the students—'

'Britt—'

'I know. I'm sorry. I think it's a wonderful idea.' And

she could tell that it meant a lot to Sharif. This wasn't a whim on his part; this was a declaration of sorts—and maybe the only one she would ever get. But they were close. Deep down she knew this. And she wasn't fooling herself this time, because Sharif was sharing some of the things closest to his heart with her, and when he squeezed her hand and smiled into her eyes, she knew how much this meant to Sharif and was honoured to be a part of it.

'You would have to come back to Kareshi, of course,' he said, frowning.

'Of course,' she said thoughtfully.

'Once the changes have been implemented in Skavanga and everything has settled down here, I want you to tour our universities and colleges with me—art galleries, concert halls and museums. I want to share everything with you, Britt.'

'For the sake of the exchange scheme,' she clarified, still lacking something on the confidence front.

'Absolutely,' Sharif agreed. 'We have some fascinating exhibits in the museums. You might even recognise some of them.'

'But you don't expect me to explain those to students, I hope?'

'I don't think they need any explanation, do you?'

She stared into Sharif's laughing eyes, remembering everything in the fabulous pavilion where she had lost her heart. It had never occurred to her that Sharif might have lost his too.

Or was she just kidding herself again?

# CHAPTER SIXTEEN

HE STOOD BACK to watch Britt, wanting to remember every single detail as she met and mingled with the students for the first time. He wished then that he had been less preoccupied and more open from the start, so he could have showered her with gifts and told her how he felt about her. But he had been like Britt—all duty, with every hour of every day filled. They had both changed. He had maybe changed most of all when he had discovered that a month away from Britt was like a lifetime. He'd realised then how much she meant to him and had concluded that it must never happen again.

He wondered now if he'd ever seen her truly relaxed before. Britt Skavanga unmasked and laughing was a wonderful creation. She genuinely loved people and would be wasted behind a desk in an office.

They ate together with a crowd of students who swarmed around Britt. He was almost jealous. Their table was the noisiest, but she still got up and went around every table in the refectory, introducing herself and explaining the scheme she was already cooking in her head. It was as if there had never been a misunderstanding between them, he thought as she glanced over to him and smiled as if wanting to reassure him that she was enjoying this. One of the students commented that Britt came from a cold country, but she had a warm heart.

Cheesy, but she'd warmed his heart. How long had he been in love with her? From that first crazy day, maybe? He just hadn't seen it for what it was. But one of the nice things about being a sheikh was that he could pretty much follow his instinct, and his instinct said, don't let this woman go. He had everything in a material sense a man could want, but nothing resonated without Britt. He saw things differently through her eyes. She made every experience richer. He wanted her in his life permanently and that meant not half a world away. He wanted them to do more than plan an exchange scheme or run a company. He was thinking on a much wider scale—a scale that would encompass both their countries. A life together was what he wanted. He knew that now, and that could only benefit the people who depended on them, and for the first time he thought he saw a way to do it.

'Are you ready to go?' he whispered to Britt discreetly.

'Not really,' she admitted with her usual honesty, gazing round at all the people she hadn't had chance to meet yet.

'You can come back,' he promised. 'Remember— I've asked you to run this project, so you're going to be seeing a lot of these people.'

'But—'

As he held her stare she saw with sudden clarity exactly what he was thinking. Her own eyes widened as his gaze dropped to her mouth.

They were never going to make it back to the citadel. He lost the outriders a few streets away from the university and the security van went off radar in a maze

of side-turnings in the suburbs. Britt yelled to ask him
what he was he doing when he pulled into a disused
parking lot earmarked for development.

'What do you think?' he yelled back, skidding to
a halt.

The scaffolding was up and a few walls were built,
but that was it. More importantly, no one was working
on the site today. Dismounting, he propped the bike on
its stand and lifted Britt out of the saddle.

'Is this safe?' she demanded when he backed her
against a wall.

'I thought you loved a bit of danger?'

'I do,' she said, already whimpering as he kissed
her neck.

He couldn't wait. Neither could she. Pelvis to pelvis with pressure, waiting was impossible. Fingers flying, they ripped at each other's clothes. Blissful relief
as Britt's legs locked around his waist and her small
strong hands gripped his shoulders. Anything else was
unimportant now. They were together. She was ready
for him—more than. Penetration was fast and complete.
There was a second's pause when they both closed their
eyes to savour the moment, but from then on it was all
sensation. He cupped her buttocks in his hands to prevent them scraping on the gritty wall, as he kissed her.
He groaned and thrust deep, dipping his knees to gain
a better angle. Britt was wild, just as he liked her. He
wanted to shout out—let the world know how he felt
about this woman— How he'd felt without her, which
was empty, lost, useless— And how he felt now—exul-
tant. Nothing could ever express his frustration at how
long it had taken him to realise that if they wanted each
other enough, they would find a way to be together. And
that it had to happen here in a parking lot—

'Sharif?' she said.

She was giving him a worried look he'd seen before; he knew she couldn't hold on. 'Britt…'

He smiled against her mouth, loving the tension that always gripped her before release. And now it was a crazy ride, hands clawing, chests heaving, wild cries, until, finally, blessed release. The best. It wasn't just physical. This was heart and soul. Commitment. He was committed to this woman to the point where even the direction his future took would depend on what she said now.

'Marry me,' he said fiercely. 'Marry me and stay with me in Kareshi.'

'Yes,' she murmured groggily in a state of contentment, resting heavily against him. '*What?*' she yelped, coming down to earth with a bump.

'Stay with me and be my queen.'

'You *are* joking?'

'No,' he said, brushing her hair back from her face. 'I can assure you I'm not joking.'

'You're a king, proposing marriage in a car lot when you've just had me up against the wall?'

'I'm a man asking a woman to marry me.'

'Aren't you being a little hasty?'

'Crazy things happen in car lots and this has been at the back of my mind for quite some time.'

'Only at the back,' she teased him as he helped her to sort out her clothes. And then she frowned. 'Are you really sure about this?'

'I'm not in the habit of making marriage proposals in car lots, or anywhere else, so, yes, I'm sure. But you're right—' Going down on one knee in the dirt, he asked the question again.

'You *are* sure,' she exclaimed. 'But how on earth will we make this work?'

'You and me can't solve this? Are you serious?'

'But—'

'But nothing,' he said. 'You can travel as I do. You can use the Internet. I don't have any trouble staying in touch.'

'And you run a country,' she mused.

'I'm only asking you to run my life.' He shrugged. 'How hard can that be?'

She gave him a crooked smile. 'I'd say that could be quite a challenge.'

'A challenge I hope you want to take on?' he said, holding her in front of him.

'Yes.'

'I'd be surprised if you'd said anything else,' he admitted, returning the grin as he brushed a kiss against her mouth.

'You arrogant—'

'Sheikhs are supposed to be arrogant,' he said, kissing her again. 'I'm only fulfilling my job description.'

'So I'd be staying here in Kareshi with you?'

'Living with me,' he corrected her. 'And running a very important project—with me, not for me. You'll be working for both our countries, alongside me. We'll be raising a family together, and you'll be my wife. But none of this will take place *here*, exactly. I did have somewhere a little better than a parking lot in mind.'

'What about the harem?'

'I'll tell them to go home.'

'I meant the tent.'

'We'll keep it for weekends. So? What's your answer, Britt?'

'I told you already. Yes. I accept your terms.'

'How about my love?'

'I accept that too—and most willingly,' she teased him, her eyes full of everything he wanted to see. 'I love you,' she shouted, making a flock of heavy-winged birds flap heavily up and away from the scaffolding. 'And I don't care who knows it.'

'And I love you too,' he said, and, drawing her into his arms, he kissed her again. 'I love you more than life itself, Britt Skavanga. Stay with me and help me build Kareshi into somewhere we can both be proud of. And I promise you that from now on there will be no secrets between us.'

But then she frowned again and asked the question he knew was coming.

'How can I ever leave Skavanga?'

'I'm not asking you to leave Skavanga. I'm asking you to be my wife, which will give you more freedom than you've ever dreamed of. You can work alongside me and raise a family. You can be a queen and a director of a company. You can head up charities and run my exchange programmes for me. You can recruit the brightest and the best of the students you've just met. I'm asking you to be my wife, the mother of my children, and my lover. The only restrictions will be those you impose on yourself, or that love imposes on you. You'll find a balance. I know it. And if you want more time—you've got it.'

They linked fingers as they walked back to Sharif's bike. They were close in every way. Her hand felt good in his. She felt good with this man. She felt safe. She felt warm inside. She felt complete.

# EPILOGUE

'THERE'S JUST ONE thing missing,' Britt commented wist-fully as her sister helped her to dress on her wedding day in her beautiful apartment at the citadel in Kareshi.

'Tyr,' Leila guessed as she lifted the cloud of cob-web-fine silk chiffon that would be attached to the spar-kling diadem that would crown Britt's flowing golden hair.

'Have you heard anything? Has Sharif said anything to you about Tyr?' Eva demanded, her sharp tone mel-lowed somewhat by the hairpins she was holding in her mouth. 'After all, Tyr is a major player in the con-sortium now.'

'Nothing,' Britt admitted, turning to check her back view in the mirror. 'Sharif shares everything with me, but he won't share that. He says Tyr will return in his own good time, and that Tyr will explain his absence then, and that we must never think the worst of him, because Tyr is doing some wonderful work—'

'Righting wrongs everywhere but here,' Eva re-marked.

'You know he's already done that—fighting with Sharif to free Kareshi. And I trust Sharif,' Britt said firmly. 'If he says Tyr will explain himself when he feels the time is right, then he will. And if Sharif has given his word to Tyr that he won't say anything, then he won't—not even to me.'

'So, I suppose we have to be satisfied with that,' Eva commented, standing back to admire her handiwork. 'And I must say those diamonds are fabulous.'

'I'm glad they distracted you,' Britt teased.

'Well, they would, wouldn't they?' Eva conceded. 'And this veil…'

'Eva, I do believe you're looking wistful,' Britt remarked with amusement as her sister reached for Britt's dress. 'Are you picturing yourself on your own wedding day?'

Eva sniffed. 'Don't be so ridiculous. There isn't a man alive I could be interested in.' Eva chose not to notice the look her sisters exchanged. 'Now, let's get this dress on you,' she said. 'The way Sharif runs you ragged with all those projects he's got you involved in, it will probably drop straight off you again.'

As Leila sighed even Eva was forced to give a pleased and surprised hum. 'Well… Who knew you could look so girlie?' she said with approval, standing back.

'Only a sister,' Britt muttered, throwing Eva a teasing fierce look while Leila tut-tutted at their exchange.

'Eva!' Leila complained where her two sisters settled down for a verbal sparring match. 'You can't get into a fight with Britt on her wedding day.'

'More's the pity,' Eva muttered, advancing with the veil.

'The dress fits like a dream,' Leila reassured Britt.

'Stand still, will you?' Eva ordered Britt. 'How am I supposed to fix this tiara to your head?'

'With a hammer and nails, in your present mood?' Britt suggested, exchanging a grin with Leila.

But Eva was right in one thing—the past six months

had been hectic. She had overseen so many exciting new schemes, as well as flying back to Skavanga to manage the ongoing work there. And as if that wasn't enough, she had insisted on having a hand in the organisation of her wedding at the citadel. Some people never knew when to relax the reins, Sharif had told her, with the type of smile that could distract her for quite a while. She wouldn't have it any other way, Britt reflected. Life had never been so rich, and when the baby came…

Tracing the outline of her stomach beneath the fairytale gown, she knew she would keep on working until Sharif tied her to the bed. Actually—

'Man alert,' Leila warned before Britt had chance to progress this delicious thought.

'Don't worry, I won't let him in,' Leila assured her.

'Stand back, I'll handle this,' Eva instructed her younger sister. Marching to the door, her red hair flying, Eva swung it open. 'Yes?'

There was silence for a moment and Britt turned to see who could possibly silence her combative middle sister.

'Ladies, please excuse me, but the bridegroom has asked me to deliver this gift to his beautiful bride.'

The voice was rich, dark chocolate, and even Britt could see that the man himself was just as tempting. Eva was still staring at him transfixed as Leila stepped forward to take the ruby red velvet box he was holding out.

'Thank you very much,' Britt said politely, taking another look at the man and then at Eva. Which one would blink first? she wondered.

'It is my pleasure,' he said, switching his attention back to Britt. 'Count Roman Quisvada at your service…'

He bowed? He bowed. 'And this is my sister, Leila,'

she said, remembering her manners. 'And Eva…' Who, of course, had to tip her stubborn little chin and glance meaningfully from the count to the door.

'I can see you're very busy,' the handsome Italian said, taking the hint, his dark eyes flashing with amusement. 'I hope to spend more time with you later.'

'Was he looking at me when he said that?' Eva demanded huffily, her cheeks an attractive shade of pink, Britt thought, as Eva closed the door behind the count with a flourish.

'There's no need to sound so peeved,' Leila pointed out. 'He's hot. And he's polite.'

'I do like a man who's polite in the bedroom,' Britt commented tongue in cheek.

'Wow, wow, wow,' Leila whispered as Britt opened the lid of the velvet box. 'And there's a note,' she added as the three Skavanga sisters stared awestruck at the blue-white diamond heart hanging from a finely worked platinum chain; the diamond flashing fire in all the colours of the rainbow.

Britt read the note while her sisters read over her shoulder: *I hope you enjoy wearing the first polished diamond to come from the Skavanga mine. It's as flawless as you are. Sharif.*

'Cheese-ee,' Eva commented. 'And he doesn't know you very well.'

Britt shook her head as the three sisters laughed.

When she walked down the red-carpeted steps towards him, the congregation in the grand ceremonial hall faded away, and there was only Britt— Beautiful Britt. His bride. But she was so much more than that and they were so much more together than they were apart.

'You look beautiful,' he murmured as her flame-haired sister and the young one, Leila, peeled away.

Now there were just the two of them he didn't dare to look at her or he'd carry her away and to hell with everyone. It took all he'd got to repeat the vows patiently and clearly when all the time his arms ached to hold her. Britt's darkening eyes said she felt the same, and as she held his gaze to tease him she knew how that would test him.

His control was definitely being severely tested, but that was one of the things he loved about Britt. She challenged him on every front and always had.

And long may it continue, he thought, teasing her back by staring fixedly ahead.

Sharif in heavy black silk robes perfumed with Sandalwood and edged with gold was a heady sight.

*And he was her husband...*

Her husband, Britt reflected, feeling a volcanic excitement rising inside her. Could she contain her lust? Sharif was refusing to look at her and it was only when they were declared man and wife that he finally turned.

Now she knew why he'd refused to look at her. The fire in his eyes was enough to melt her bones. How was she going to stand this? How was she going to sit through the wedding breakfast?

The food was delicious, but even that wasn't enough of a distraction. The setting was unparalleled, but nothing could take her mind off the main event. Candles flickered in golden sconces, casting a mellow glow over the jewel-coloured hangings, making golden plates and goblets flash as if they were on fire, while crystal glasses twinkled like fireflies dancing through the night. It was a voluptuous feast, prepared by world-renowned chefs, but she wondered if it would ever end, and was surprised when Sharif stood up.

'Ladies and gentlemen,' he began in the deep husky

voice Sharif could use to seduce to command. 'The evening is young, and I urge you to enjoy everything to the full. Thank you all for coming to help us celebrate this happiest of days, but now I must beg you to excuse us—'

She still didn't quite understand until Sharif whistled up his horse and held out his hand to her. His black stallion galloped into the hall. As *coup de théâtre* went, she had to admit this one was unparalleled. As their guests gasped the stallion skidded to a halt within inches of its master, and the next thing she knew Sharif was lifting her onto the saddle and holding her safely in front of him.

She gasped as the stallion reared, his silken mane flowing like liquid black diamonds, as his flashing ebony hooves clawed imperiously at the air.

The instant he touched down again, Sharif gave a command in the harsh tongue of Kareshi, and the horse took them galloping out of the hall into a starlit night, and a future that was sure to fulfil all their desires.

\* \* \* \* \*

# HIDE-AND-SHEIKH

## GAIL DAYTON

To those wonderful women from Waco, the best friends a writer could have. Thanks for all your support. I wouldn't be here without you. To Myles, for worrying about me when I don't write, and for twenty-five wonderful years.

**Gail Dayton** has been playing make-believe all her life but didn't start writing the make-believe down until she was about nine years old, because it took her that long to learn how to write coherent sentences. She married her college sweetheart shortly after graduation and moved to a small Central Texas town where they lived happily for twenty years. Now transplanted to an even smaller town in the Texas Panhandle, Gail lives with her Prince Charming, their youngest son and Spot the Dalmatian, where they are still working on the "ever after" part. The "happily" they have down. After a mixed career with intervals spent as a mother, the entire editorial staff of more than one small-town newspaper, a junior college history instructor and legal assistant in a rural prosecutor's office, she finally got to quit her day job in favor of writing love stories. When she's not writing or reading other people's love stories, she sings alto in her church choir and teaches basic sewing as an incentive to finish her own sewing projects, which would otherwise languish. Gail would love to hear from readers. Write her at P.O. Box 176, Clarendon, Texas 79226, USA.

# One

---

She'd found her target. He lounged near the make-shift bar, his perfect teeth glinting as he smiled at some dark-haired bimbette. In the warehouse-cum-nightclub in New York's garment district, lights flashed, strobe-quick and bright, or slower, in garish colors that painted the party goers in even more ghastly shades than they'd painted themselves. Except for that man, her night's mission. The Sheikh of Araby.

Or rather, the Sheikh of Qarif, to give him his true name. As she maneuvered her way toward him, Ellen watched the lights turn his handsome face pink, then sickly green, then dappled blue, but his perfection continued unblemished. He knew it, too.

He threw back that chiseled profile in a laugh that had to be calculated to show off his best features: dark sultry eyes, straight white teeth, high, carved cheek-bones. His picture hadn't done him justice.

Oh, it had amply illustrated his movie-star features, but it hadn't said a word about the sexuality that oozed like honey from his every pore. Ellen kept the wry twist from her faint smile at the sight of the little girl bees buzzing around him. She couldn't let him see past the mask she wore to her real purpose. He might be the best-looking, sexiest man she'd seen in the past dozen years, but he was still her target.

And, as mama always said, beauty is skin deep, but ugly goes clear to the bone. Somebody's mama had said it, even if Ellen's never had. She'd known spoiled, rich playboys. One of them she'd known very well.

Davis Lowe had been born with a golden spoon in his mouth and upgraded to platinum at his first opportunity. He'd swept her off her middle-class feet with his charm and his money and brought her into his world, where she'd met his spoiled playboy friends. Because of Davis, she'd learned these rich men were all the same.

Whether they were from New York or New Delhi, they all expected the world to bow and scrape and cater to their every whim. At least this one offered a nice view.

Finally he reacted to Ellen's laser-beam stare. He looked up and met her gaze. Ellen held it a long moment, allowed a hint of a smile to brush her lips, then she turned away and began to count seconds.

One… She found a place at the sawhorse-and-planking bar, and ordered a gin and tonic. Seven, eight, nine… Would she have to look at him again? The pretty ones were often tougher to get to. Ellen tossed her hair back over her shoulder. Long, straight, dark blond hair with golden highlights, it was one of her best weapons.

"Hello."

*Bingo.* He was hooked. Fourteen seconds. Not her best time, but not her worst, either. If "the look" didn't get them, the hair usually did.

Ellen turned and gave her sheikh a once-over. That high-beam smile of his could prove near lethal at close range. She raised a cool eyebrow. The effect was somewhat destroyed by the fact that they had to lean close and shout full volume to be heard over the pounding music.

"Hello?" she said. "That's all you can come up with? What kind of line is that?"

He shrugged. "It is no line. I said hello. If you want a line, I am sure many other men here would be happy to provide one."

His English was impeccable, overlaid with a faint hint of the foreign, and a fainter hint of a…Southern drawl? He wore a short-sleeved raw silk navy shirt unbuttoned over a plain white T-shirt. A T-shirt that must have been bought a size too small, given the way it strained over the man's lean but well-muscled torso. Khaki slacks finished the ensemble. Not what one would expect from the scion of a royal family, but it looked good on him. Darn good. Did she have the right man? Ellen studied his face again, comparing it to the memorized photo in her head. This *was* her target. No mistake.

She lifted a shoulder in a casual shrug. Cool and calculated would serve her better with this one. He would be used to women falling over themselves to please him.

"I don't need a line." She accepted the drink from the bartender and took a sip, schooling her expression against the taste. Fruity concoctions with paper umbrellas, the kind she preferred, didn't blend with the sophisticated image she wanted to project tonight.

He grinned and pushed his hand back through his thick sable hair. "That is just as well," he said, "because I do not have any idea what to say next. Whatever I say will sound like a pick-up line."

Ellen found herself charmed by his apparent openness and told herself it was an act. It had to be. Nobody with "prince" in front of his name could be this transparent.

"Have you any suggestions?" He propped an elbow on the bar and leaned. The wattage in his smile seemed to go up.

"My name is Ellen." She put her hand out to shake. She had to keep him on a string until she knew she could reel him in.

"Names. Good." He took her hand and squeezed gently. "Call me Rudy."

*Rudy?* Ellen ran through the list of names they'd given her, half a dozen or more, all belonging to the target. Of the few she could actually remember, Rashid was one, and it didn't sound anything like Rudy. Neither did any of the others.

"Rudi, with an *i*," he said. "I prefer the way it looks written that way."

She shook the hand still holding hers. "How do you do, Rudi-with-an-*i*. It's nice to meet you."

Whatever he wanted to call himself made no difference to her. But it did surprise her a bit. Why not use his real name? Unless he was more security conscious than he appeared. Ellen stopped herself from searching the room for bodyguards. She knew where his bodyguards were. She'd sent them there herself.

"So." He glanced down at their still-clasped hands, and the brilliance of his smile suddenly took on a heat that Ellen felt clear down to her toes, which curled in their strappy sandals. "Now that we have the formalities over, why don't we…"

His words trailed off as he bent over her hand and pressed a kiss to its back, a kiss that sizzled across her skin straight to the libido she'd thought long ago starved to death.

Why don't we *what?* Curiosity resurrected her dormant desire. Nothing else had for years.

"Dance," Rudi said.

"Dance?" That's all he wanted to do?

Feeling numb and yet feeling every nerve ending spark and sizzle, Ellen let him lead her by the hand— the same hand he'd kissed—onto the dance floor. Rudi tugged, spinning her skillfully into his arms. Never mind that the band clashed and wailed and thumped out raging heavy metal rock that made the flashing lights shudder with vibration. Rudi held her close and danced what Ellen could only describe as some kind of cross between a tango, a foxtrot and sex with clothes on.

Or maybe the sex part was just in her head.

This dance, seen objectively, wasn't much different from the hundreds of others Ellen had danced. Rudi's hands rested lightly at her waist, her hands on his shoulders. They moved back and forth to the music in the limited space allowed on the crowded dance floor. But with every brush of Rudi's hips against hers, the heat turned a notch higher.

Ellen's hands curved over Rudi's shoulders, shaping themselves to his lean musculature. He was sleek and strong, beautiful like one of those horses they raised in his part of the world.

He laughed, a very male sound, his eyes flashing pleasure at her, and Ellen realized her hands had slipped. Now they rested on the broad slope of his chest. With another laugh, Rudi whipped off the unbuttoned shirt he wore to let the T-shirt beneath show off his physique. Ellen didn't have to fake her approval. She liked the way he looked. Entirely too much.

He snapped out one end of the shirt, reached out and caught the other end so that it passed behind Ellen. Then he used it to draw her in closer, until they touched hip to hip. Holding her only with the shirt pulled snug around her waist, Rudi swayed, his eyes twinkling.

"Join me," he shouted over the crashing music. "Do you not know how to rumba?"

She pushed at him, her fingers curling into his chest. "This doesn't sound like a rumba to me."

Rudi deepened the swing of his hips, his thighs getting friendly with their sensual nudging against hers. "The beat is in your blood. Feel it inside you."

Was it getting hotter in here? Or was he just making her crazy?

He leaned in, until his lips brushed her ear. "Feel it, and let it out."

Rudi did something with his hands, and the shirt around her jumped several inches higher, drawing her slowly in, bringing her breasts toward that white-clad chest.

Confusion struck her. This was a new dilemma. She needed to tempt him, keep him close until the final moment. But she'd never before been tempted herself. She wanted to touch him, to let her breasts settle against that solid chest, and that would be entirely unethical. She wasn't supposed to like her targets.

The music paused to allow the gasping musicians time to catch their collective breath. In the startling, deafening silence, Ellen broke away, tugging the navy shirt from his hands. She stared at him, panting almost as hard as the band. Why? She hadn't done anything strenuous.

Rudi's smile faltered a second, then returned. "Let me buy you a drink." The white of his T-shirt contrasted with his deep tan. He was gorgeous *and* nice. A deadly combination.

Ellen had to get this done and get out quickly, before she got in over her head. It was for his own good. And for hers. They'd both be better off if she just got it over with now.

"I have a better idea." Still holding his shirt, Ellen caught Rudi's hand and led him from the dance floor.

"Where are we going?"

''You'll see.'' She threw him one of her patented mysterious smiles, her hair swinging around her shoulders.

Rudi followed her out of the warehouse, bemused by his luck. Ellen was the most beautiful woman he'd seen in his entire life, and he'd seen a lot of beautiful women. But they never came on to him like this. Not to Rudi.

Only Rashid ibn Saqr ibn Faruq al Mukhtar Qarif could get women at the snap of his fingers. And then it was the money and the power that attracted them, not the man.

Money and power were as much of an illusion as Rashid. Or maybe Rudi was the illusion. Sometimes he wasn't sure which of his personas was the real one. But he did know that the money and the power belonged to his father, not to him.

Down the street outside the warehouse, Ellen hailed a taxi. The streetlight gleamed along her slender, mile-high legs as she got in. Rudi stared, half-hypnotized, until Ellen leaned out the open car door.

''Are you coming?'' she asked, a smile curving her luscious pink lips. A smile that promised nothing and everything at the same time, that dared him to find out what secrets hid behind it.

He shouldn't. He had doubtless terrified and infuriated his family enough, vanishing as he had. The bombs back in Qarif were real. The terrorists were real. But the terrorists were still in Qarif, trying to transform the country into a miniature Afghanistan. This woman could not possibly be a terrorist. Just look at her.

Rudi followed his own suggestion as she waited without a hint of impatience for him to make up his mind. She was a blond goddess, a Valkyrie escaped from Wagner's opera. Her straight dark gold hair spilled over her shoulders like yesterday's sunlight, streaked with the brighter shine of tomorrow's dawn. Long thick lashes shaded eyes whose color he couldn't decipher in the uncertain light. A high forehead, straight narrow nose, prominent cheekbones and full mouth completed her classically beautiful face.

But it was not the beauty of her face or her sleek athlete's body beneath the simple black dress that drew him. Perhaps it was the hint of mischief in her eyes, or the mystery in her smile, the feeling that she played some secret game and he did not know the rules. She challenged him, dared him to play. Rudi had never been able to pass up a dare.

He stepped off the curb and got in the cab. Satisfaction flickered across Ellen's face a brief second before she hid it behind that smile. Rudi did not object. She had won only one hand. He intended to win the game.

"So, Rudi." Ellen leaned back in the corner of the cab opposite him. "What do you do?"

"I dig holes." At least, he wanted to. His family did their level best to keep him in a nice, clean office where he couldn't play in the dirt.

Ellen's eyebrow arched. "Really."

Would she back off now, thinking him no more than a ditchdigger?

"Holes, as in the Lincoln Tunnel?" she asked. "Or holes as in—" She waved at a construction site vanishing behind them, where bulldozers would have clawed deep into the earth to set the foundation before the steel frame started up.

"Holes as in wells. For water, oil—whatever is hiding down there."

Ellen's expression changed, as if she were impressed in spite of herself. At least, Rudi hoped that was what it meant.

"You dig oil wells?" She stretched a long, elegant arm along the back of the seat.

Rudi started to agree, then changed his mind. Tell her the truth, see how that impressed her. If it did. "Actually, I prefer drilling for water. A person cannot drink oil."

"You can't run a car on water."

"Not now." Rudi grinned. "Give the scientists some time. If they ever finish their fusion reactor research, we could be pulling up to the garden hose to fill our cars with fuel."

She watched him with that enigmatic smile on her face, saying nothing. Rudi did not know if that meant she wanted to know more or was bored to tears. But he did not handle silence well.

"Of course, you can make more money drilling oil wells, but…" Rudi shrugged. "The people who need water generally need it more."

Ellen's smile changed, became warmer and yet sad at the same time. This smile still hid secrets, but it seemed more genuine. "You're a nice man, Rudi," she said. "I like you."

Stunned, Rudi didn't realize the cab had stopped until Ellen got out. Scrambling to follow her beckoning gesture, he found himself on the sidewalk in front of an upscale hotel. Ellen linked her arm through his and strolled past the doorman into the gilt-and-marble lobby.

She led him past the desk, past the plush brocade chairs, past the opening to the dimly lit bar, to the elevators between the potted palms where she pushed the up button. Rudi's second thoughts kicked in.

Not that he objected to the idea of going up to Ellen's room and "getting to know her better." But he did not know her. She probably was no terrorist. Then again, she might be. Or she might be a thief, with a partner upstairs waiting to cosh him over the head and steal everything he had in his pockets, which by now was not much, since he had been away from the family coffers for more than a week.

Or she might be the best thing he had ever happened across in his life.

He was used to women throwing themselves at him, wanting to be seen with him for his name, or his money, or because they liked the way he looked. Their motivations had always been transparent to him, and he'd usually been willing to give them what they wanted—a little pleasure for the moment, a little thrill, a little pampering. They were easy. So easy that lately he hadn't bothered.

But this woman was different. She intrigued him. She challenged him by holding her secrets so close. She was all mystery and potential and wide-open possibility.

In which case, he did not want to ruin it by rushing into sex with her. He wanted to know more, know everything about her, how she thought, what made her laugh and cry. That took time. If he went upstairs with her now, Rudi very much feared he wouldn't get that time.

"Ellen, why do we not go into the bar? Have a drink. Talk." He tipped his head toward the dark, cavelike entrance.

Something that might have been surprise flashed in her eyes before it vanished behind that sexy, enigmatic smile. Rudi began to hate that smile.

"Why?" She slid her hand up his arm to his shoulder and trailed her fingers down his chest.

"I wish to talk to you." He caught the hand resting on his chest and kissed her fingertips. Then he touched the corner of her mouth.

Her smile slipped, just a little.

"I want to find the woman behind that smile," he said. "If we go upstairs, I do not think that we will do very much talking."

"Probably not," Ellen conceded with a tip of her head. "But what if there's nothing to find?"

"I cannot believe that. Not with the devil peeking from deep within your eyes."

An expression that was almost alarm flickered in those hazel-green eyes. Then her smile went hot and sultry, and Rudi's entire body stood at attention.

"Talking isn't the way to meet that devil." Ellen took both his hands in hers and backed onto the elevator, drawing him with her. "We can talk later."

"Promise?"

The elevator door slid shut. Ellen brushed against Rudi as she reached past him to press a floor button, and he shuddered at the light touch. His hand settled at her waist.

"I promise," she said.

Rudi had to think a minute to recall what she was promising.

"If you still want to talk, we can talk all you want. Later."

The floor lurched slightly as the elevator stopped and the door rumbled open. Holding his hand, Ellen led him into the hallway. About halfway down, she paused in front of a room.

She looked up at him, the sweet sadness back in her smile. Her hand settled soft on his chest again, and she stretched the mere inch necessary to touch her lips to his cheek in a warm, tender kiss that melted all Rudi's internal organs together.

She glanced away to slide the keycard in the lock. It flashed green and she turned the handle, then looked back up at him.

"I'm sorry," she murmured, "but it's for your own good."

Alarm flashed through him. Was she a terrorist after all?

Then the door was open and Omar, his valet-cum-bodyguard, was hauling him into the room. Frank, the rent-a-bodyguard from the service his family used in New York, stood behind Omar, with a third burly guard beyond.

"Thanks, Miss Sheffield," Frank was saying. "I knew if anybody could find him, you could."

Ellen's smile was gone, replaced by a businesslike

scowl. "I wouldn't have had to, if you bozos hadn't lost him in the first place."

"You are a bodyguard?" Rudi goggled at her.

"I'm a security consultant. Frank and George are bodyguards." She indicated the two locals. "See if you can keep up with him now."

And she was gone, the door slamming shut behind her.

The woman of his dreams had come on to him just to track him down for his family and return him to the dubious safety of his bodyguards.

Rudi started to laugh. He had to—she had outwitted him so cleverly. She had won this round.

But the game was not over yet.

And she had promised him they could talk later, if he wished. Rudi definitely wished to talk much more with Miss Ellen Sheffield.

# Two

Ellen Sheffield was the best at what she did.

At least, she used to be, before she met that too-handsome-for-her-own-good son of a sheikh. His movie-star face kept popping into her head, complete with that obnoxious grin. The one that made him look even more handsome. No matter how hard she tried to dismiss him as a lightweight, tell herself the grin was goofy and the man uninteresting, his voice would whisper in her mind's ear, *A person cannot drink oil.* And she'd wonder if he still wanted to talk.

Because, however many times she told herself she didn't want to see him, she couldn't forget that he had actually wanted to delay going upstairs at the hotel. He'd invited her into the bar. He'd seen past the mask to the person behind her polished facade, the first man to bother looking in years. Maybe ever.

When she was little, she'd been merely "the Sheffield boys' sister." Then she'd grown breasts, and her brothers' friends had done nothing but stare at them. Until her brothers beat them up.

None of the boys in high school had dared ask her out, and with a policeman for a brother, none of the men in the academy had, either. So she'd had no preparation for Davis's practiced seduction when she'd met him at a book signing just after she'd finished her course.

Ellen sighed. Davis had been such an overwhelming experience that she'd agreed to marry him before she realized what kind of man he was. Before she realized what kind of woman he wanted. He wanted a decorative, expensive toy to show off to his friends, not a person. Ellen's opinions, desires, thoughts and wishes had all been dismissed as unimportant. Her career was immaterial. Davis expected her to drop everything and dance to his tune.

When she'd broken the engagement, his "friends" had moved in, all of them wanting the same thing: a beautiful woman to show off. She'd learned then how to use her appearance as a tool, a weapon against them. That skill had benefited her career, both in the police department and since. Vic Campanello, her partner on the job and her current boss, called her his secret weapon. Which was why she'd been tapped to find Prince Rudi the Gorgeous.

She didn't want to think about him, didn't want him popping into her head. He might have noticed the devil in her eyes, but he couldn't care anymore.

Not now, not after she'd put him back into his gilded cage.

Ellen got out of the cab and slammed the door. Then she overtipped the driver because she felt guilty for taking out her guilt on his cab. She had not betrayed Rudi, or Rashid, or whatever the man wanted to call himself. She had probably saved his life. He had no business wandering around New York on his own, not with terrorists stalking Qarif's ruling family, of which Rudi was most definitely a member.

The terrorists had been a problem in Qarif for most of Rudi's life, but lately things had changed, according to Campanello. The old leader had been captured, and the new, more militant leader had vowed vengeance for the captivity, even though he was probably the one who'd tipped the authorities off.

Rudi might be used to the terrorist threat, but that didn't mean there was no danger. Ellen's job was to protect him from that danger, and she had absolutely no reason to feel guilty for doing her job.

Summer flowers bloomed in beds lining the paths, but they might as well have been weeds for all the attention Ellen paid them as she headed into Central Park. She checked her watch and picked up her pace. If she didn't hurry, she'd be late for her meeting.

Swainson Security had been hired to provide security for a music video to be shot in Central Park sometime in the next month, and she was supposed to meet with the producer, the director, the group's manager and whoever else thought they needed a finger in the pie, to check out locations. She much preferred this kind of work to tracking down spoiled dil-

ettantes. Though she had to admit that finding Rudi
had been a challenge. She did enjoy a good challenge.

Campanello had told her this morning he had a new
assignment for her, one that would begin immediately
after this meeting. Maybe it would offer something
tough enough to keep her mind off Qarif's prince. The
fact that the boss wouldn't tell her what the new job
was, however, made her suspect that it might have
something to do with said prince.

Ellen ground her teeth, then curled her lips up in
what she hoped resembled a smile more than a snarl
as the band's manager turned to greet her. Time to
go to work.


Rudi stared at the piece of paper in front of him
on the polished table without actually seeing it or anything it said. It was Wednesday. Hump Day, as they
had called it when he was in college in Texas, and
probably everywhere else in the United States. If he
could make it past Wednesday, it was a downhill slide
to the weekend. Only, the weekend would be no better, trapped as he was by his bodyguards and big
brother Ibrahim.

Rudi felt Ibrahim's glower and ignored it. He
pulled his hand inside the sleeve of his djellaba and
discreetly scratched his thigh. Ibrahim had insisted on
traditional dress for the negotiations today, to remind
the other parties just who they dealt with. Rudi stuck
his hand back out and took yet another sip of water.
Maybe he could escape to the rest room for a few
minutes, if he drank enough water.

He had no idea why he had to be at this forsaken

meeting anyway. It was not as if he could contribute anything but another body. Ibrahim's wife or one of his children now in New York could contribute as much. Rudi would happily trade places with Kalila and escort the children to museums and even opera, while she sat in on her husband's meetings. They were about finance and numbers, dollars and marks and yen and things he knew nothing about. Did not want to know about.

Give him a piece of ground, a "Christmas tree" rig and a couple of roughnecks to handle the steel, and he could bring in the well. He could even tell you if the piece of ground might produce anything, whether water, oil or gas. But high finance could kill him. If Rudi got any more bored, his heart just might forget to beat, fall asleep just like the rest of him. Although if he actually dozed off, Ibrahim would be the one to kill him.

He had sworn off thinking about her. This resolution had lasted about as long as every other resolution he had ever made. Maybe an entire hour. He needed something to do that would keep him awake, so he began to plot his revenge on Ellen Sheffield. Most of the plots involved isolated tents in the desert, paved with thick, soft carpets and plenty of pillows, and thin, gauzy, semitransparent clothing. Better yet, no clothing at all.

Not that the plots would ever come to fruition. It had been ten days since Ellen had turned him back over to the loving, suffocating arms of his family like a runaway schoolboy, and he still had no hint how to find her. Her company "did not give out personal information," as he had been told several times over by the annoying, perky-voiced receptionist. His dream girl might have been just that—a dream—for all he was able to learn about her. He had held her in his arms, only to have her vanish like a mirage in the sands.

"What is your opinion, Prince Rashid?"

One of the suits around the table asked him a question, and Rudi had no idea what he was supposed to have an opinion about. Even if he had heard the discussion, he would not have understood it. He moved his leg out of reach of Ibrahim's potential kick under the table.

"I am in complete agreement with my brother," he said, which was true. Ibrahim knew about this kind of thing. Rudi wished he would take care of it and stop making him sit through this agony.

Finally, after another eternity of congratulations and chitchat and backslapping, the deal apparently made, the meeting ended. Rudi headed for the elevators, only to be halted by his brother calling him back.

"Rashid, are you not joining us for lunch?" Ibrahim looked surprised, maybe even wounded by Rudi's apparent defection. "To celebrate the success of our negotiations. Come."

*Allah forfend.* Rudi stifled his shudder. He could not take another hour of high finance, not another minute. He had been to lunch with these men before. He knew what they talked about.

"Forgive me, brother. It has been a long morning, and I feel a bit under the weather."

"Are you ill?" Genuine concern colored Ibrahim's voice.

Rudi was grateful once more that he was merely the seventh son of his father, and not the ninth and youngest. If young Hasim stubbed a toe, the flags in Qarif went to half-mast. Ibrahim would have panicked.

"Merely tired." Rudi said. "I will catch a cab back to the hotel."

"You will take the car. And Omar."

"Very well. I will take the car." Rudi did not mention that Omar was back at the hotel with a severe case of traveler's trouble, and had only consented to stay in bed because of Ibrahim's own bodyguards. This could be his chance to make a break for it.

Maybe they would send Ellen after him again.

Rudi was whistling by the time he reached the garage.

He slouched in the back seat of the bulletproof, bombproof, escapeproof car, and plotted his escape. Without Omar, or any of the rent-a-bodies, it ought to be relatively easy. He had received a phone call from Buckingham, saying that everything was ready and just waiting for him. He could get the driver to drop him at the hotel, catch a cab to the heliport and take a helicopter to the airport. He could be gone without anyone knowing it. Perhaps they would send Ellen after him again. Perhaps he would allow her to find him.

But not in Buckingham. No one knew about Buckingham, and that was the way he wanted it.

Then he sat up straight, his attention captured by a woman in the park as the car inched along in the near-noon traffic. It was Ellen. It had to be. No other woman could possibly possess that precise combination of sun-kissed hair and million-dollar legs.

She was talking with an odd collection of mostly men. Or rather Ellen stood near them while they talked. She did not seem to be paying much attention, looking at her surroundings, until one of the men put his arm around her. Ellen moved away from his arm, but listened to what he had to say, nodding now and again.

The car moved a few feet ahead, leaving Ellen and the rest of the group walking slowly the other way. Rudi turned to watch, swearing when his view was blocked by a horse and rider.

In that instant, a plan sprang full-grown into his head. He had always wanted to sweep a woman off her feet and carry her away on horseback, like his great-grandfathers had surely once done. He was even dressed for it, in his desert robes.

"Stop." Rudi didn't wait for the driver to comply. The car was barely moving as he opened the door. "I will be back in five minutes, perhaps ten."

He caught up with the horseback rider in a few quick steps, wondering if he ought to rethink his plan. This horse seemed to have little in common with the fiery animals in his father's stables. He caught the beast's rein, startling a little shriek from its rider, a slightly plump, barely pubescent girl with braces and red frizz under a white helmet.

"Hello, might I borrow your horse?" Rudi borrowed Ibrahim's Oxford accent. It seemed to play better dressed as he was. "I wish to surprise my fiancée." The lie rolled easily from his lips. "By sweeping her away in the manner of my ancestors."

The girl gulped and giggled. Rudi captured her hand. "Surely someone of your sensibility would be willing to assist in my romantic endeavors." His ploy seemed to be working on the horse's rider.

"I've only got an hour to ride," she said.

"I only need the barest minute." Rudi glanced over his shoulder. Ellen and her party were retreating deeper into the park. In a moment they would be out of sight. "Please. My heart will be devastated if you do not allow me the use of your steed for a paltry space of time." Maybe those English literature classes he had suffered through had done better work than he had thought.

"My heart is in your hands." Rudi pressed a kiss to the child's hand, and she giggled again, looking past him at a cluster of other riders who had pulled up to stare gape-mouthed at the scene he was making.

She sighed. "Okay. But just a minute." She slid awkwardly from the horse's back.

"Allah bless you for your generosity." Rudi kissed her cheek, knowing it would impress the girl's audience, then swung into the saddle.

The horse recognized a knowledgeable hand on the reins and took exception. It preferred being in charge. But after a brief, stern scolding, Rudi reminded the animal of its manners, and it did as he demanded.

Payback would be sweet indeed.

\*   \*   \*

Ellen walked back toward the fountain with all the video people, only half listening to their chatter of angles and dollies and dance steps as she mentally placed barricades and personnel across park paths and lawns. So hard did she concentrate on blocking out all the extraneous noise that she didn't hear the hoof-beats until they were almost on top of her.

The sudden thunder brought her whirling around to see a horse bearing down on her, on its back a man in the billowing white robes of a desert nomad.

"Crazy son of a—" The producer had no time to finish his oath before diving aside.

Too surprised to move, Ellen watched the man lean toward her, saw his arm stretch out. Before she could react, he'd snatched her from her feet and hauled her up onto the horse in front of him. Her mind was so muddled, she could only think what an impressive feat he'd just accomplished.

Voices rose about them, shouting. "Call 9-1-1!"

"He's crazy! Somebody stop him."

"He's kidnapping her!"

The horse's stride shortened abruptly, then it whirled and galloped back the way it had come. Ellen clung to the man to keep from flying off during the sharp turn, noticing despite herself the lean, almost familiar strength of his body. Who was this nutcase? She was afraid she already knew.

She batted the windblown robes out of her way and looked up into the face that had been haunting her dreams. Rudi.

If the cops arrested him, it could create an international incident. It could get her fired.

"It's okay," she shouted past his shoulder at the video crew. "I know him. He's a friend."

Her words apparently reached them, because the frantic shouting and rushing slowed. The horse didn't. Its rocking gait bumped her against Rudi in a matching rhythm, a rhythm that came too easily to mind in connection with this man. No wonder the body beneath the robes had felt so familiar. Hard as she tried, she hadn't been able to forget the feel of him under her hands. The muscular thighs that had teased her in that blood-boiling dance now flexed and shifted beneath her, guiding a thousand-plus pounds of horseflesh, pushing their way back into her memory.

"Am I truly?" He grinned at her, his teeth flashing white in the afternoon sun as the horse thundered on across the park.

"Are you truly what?" Ellen pried her brain away from the legs beneath her backside and ordered it to get busy with thinking.

"Your friend. You said I was a friend."

"I—" *Think.* She wanted to bang her head against something to see if she could knock a little sense loose, but the nearest something was Rudi's chest, and she knew beyond any doubt that would only make things worse. "I didn't want you arrested."

"Ah." His Day-Glo smile dimmed a fraction.

The horse came to a skittering halt at a signal from Rudi that Ellen missed. He dismounted and tossed the reins to a waiting child before lifting Ellen from the horse's back. But instead of setting her on her feet, he carried her in his arms to a car at the curb. The driver opened the door, and Rudi put her inside, much the same way Ellen had once inserted prisoners into her patrol car. Before following her inside, Rudi called to the girl with the horse.

"Blessings upon you, child." He tossed her a coin that glinted gold as it spun over and over in a high arc. Ellen saw the girl miss the catch and bend to pick it up before Rudi got into the car and signaled to the driver.

"What was that you threw?" Ellen asked.

"A ten-fiat piece."

"It looked like gold."

"It is." Rudi stretched his arms along the seat and the door, looking completely at ease in his exotic garb. He seemed a different person somehow. Strange, foreign, exciting.

"Gold." She had to get a grip on this situation. She had to get a grip on herself.

He made an affirming hum. "I wanted to reward her for the loan of the horse."

"With a ten-fiat gold piece."

He mmm-ed again in agreement.

"How much is that in real money?"

Rudi laughed. "Some people would say that the fiat is real money, since it is actually gold and not your paper greenbacks."

"How much?" Ellen didn't know why she persisted, only that she wanted to know. Maybe her brain was trying to get warmed up.

"Depending on a number of factors, between thirty and fifty dollars, American."

Resentment swelled inside her. Did he think he

could impress her by throwing his money around like that? Or did he think to buy her, the way he'd bought the use of the horse?

"What do you want?" Ellen didn't care if her attitude sounded in her voice.

"A bit of your time." Rudi's voice seemed calculated to soothe, and so rubbed her resentment raw. "You did promise me we could talk, remember?"

She did, and resented even more being put in the wrong. "If you wanted to talk to me, all you had to do was call the office and say so."

"I did. You have not been taking my calls."

He was right again. Another mark against him.

"So talk." She slouched in the seat, tugging at the hem of her dress. It drew his eyes to her legs where they emerged from the short skirt, and his gaze heated the atmosphere.

"I want more than a few stolen minutes in the back of a car," Rudi said.

*I just bet you do.* Ellen shot him a sideways glance and met his gaze looking back. He knew how guilty she felt, the rat, and was playing it for all he was worth. She wanted to kiss that smirk—no. No, she wanted to wipe that smirk off his face. Wipe. She didn't dare think of Rudi and kissing in the same thought.

"I have received a call concerning some business I must take care of out of the city this afternoon. I want you to come with me." Rudi watched her like a cat near an active mouse hole.

Ellen was already shaking her head. "No, I'm sorry. It's impossible."

"Why?" Rudi slid a finger across the curve of her bare shoulder.

She shoved his hand away as she repressed her shuddering reaction. "I have responsibilities. A job. And you have other bodyguards." Her eyes narrowed. "Speaking of which, where are they?"

"Omar is sick, the others are with Ibrahim. The driver is driving."

"That's no good. You should have at least one other guard with you at all times."

Rudi's smile glistened in the car's dim light. "You are with me."

"I'm not your bodyguard."

"Why not? Come with me. I have cleared it with your company. I have cleared it with my family. All is prepared." He paused and gave her a little-boy-pleading-for-a-treat look. "That is, if you agree."

"What if I don't?" Ellen fought against the temptation. If she wanted something this much, it had to be bad for her. But what if this was the new job Campanello wanted her on?

"I will have the driver drop you wherever you want to go." The teasing grin was back. "Preferably after lunch. Grant me at least that much."

She eyed him, all her suspicion sensors on alert. "What about you? If I don't go, who will you take on your trip?"

"Myself."

Scowling, Ellen decided not to argue with him. He was just contrary enough to do what he threatened. If she didn't go, he'd go alone, and that was absolutely out of the question. "I want to call my office, make sure this is okay with my boss."

Rudi's expression didn't change, didn't even flicker as he gave a nonchalant shrug. Either he really had cleared it with everyone, or he was a consummate actor. "Of course. Whatever you think you need to do." He handed her a cell phone from somewhere inside those voluminous robes.

"Thanks. I have my own." Ellen pulled her phone from the bag she'd somehow hung on to when Rudi snatched her up on the horse. She had to think a minute to remember the office number. How could this man interfere so with her thought process?

"Swainson Security." The phone was answered on the first ring.

"Hey, Marco. Is Campanello in?"

"Oh, hey, Ms. Sheffield. No, he's out meeting with those guys about that string concert in October."

"String?" Ellen racked her brain trying to recall any violinists the company had contracted with. "Do you mean Sting?"

"Maybe that's what he said. I just know it was some old guy. But he did tell me to tell you those sheikhs wanted you to head up the detail for—uh—" The rustle of paper shuffling came through the phone. "For one of them. I can't find the paper with the guy's name on it. It was here just a minute ago." Marco sounded stressed.

Ellen glanced at Rudi. She hated being pushed into things. But he was the client, and clients had the right to do a limited amount of pushing. "Tell Campanello I know about it, and I'm on the job."

It had to be Rudi they wanted her with. Campanello had been bugging her about it ever since she'd found the man. Ellen didn't do guard details anymore if she could help it, but it didn't look as if she could help this one. Rudi had boxed her in.

"Got it, Ms. Sheffield."

"I'm going to try to reach the boss on his cell phone, but if I can't, tell him I'll check in again as soon as I can. Everything's under control. I've got Rudi with me."

"I'll be sure to tell him. Rudi."

"Thanks." Ellen flipped the phone shut and tucked it away.

"Marco—another hulking brute like Frank or George?" Rudi's eyes twinkled at her. "Or someone more interesting?"

"Definitely more interesting." Ellen chuckled. "He's sixteen. A friend of one of Campanello's kids. It's his first summer job. He might be hulking someday, after he gains a hundred pounds. He's a good kid. And he only answers the phones during lunch."

"Ah." Rudi leaned forward and gave the driver an address. Ellen didn't hear it clearly. "Speaking of lunch, do you mind if we eat on the way? It will save some time."

"Sure, why not? What's a few crumbs on the upholstery?"

The driver let them off at an uptown building Ellen wasn't familiar with. She got on the elevator with Rudi, forcing herself to go into bodyguard mode. She hadn't done this kind of work in a while, but it had been even longer since she'd been in date mode. Besides, this wasn't a date.

As they traveled upward, Rudi excused himself and stepped away to make a few calls. He was still talking when the elevator stopped at the top floor, and Ellen stepped out first, like a good bodyguard, into the small, glass-walled enclosure.

Correction. This wasn't the top floor. They were on the roof, in the lobby area of a heliport. Ellen had been in most of New York's heliports, but not this one. Rudi shut off his phone and strode to the desk, Ellen at his elbow.

"Your helicopter is waiting, Mr. Ibn Saqr," the clerk said, gesturing out the window.

There it was, a shiny white helicopter just settling to the pad as if conjured up by a genie's magic.

"Shall we?" Rudi bowed slightly, offering his arm.

Ellen ignored it, striding to the door. "Don't waste your gallantry on me," she said, pushing the door open.

The roar of helicopter blades vibrated through the little lobby until Rudi pulled the door shut again. Ellen let him. Let him have his say without shouting.

"Gallantry is never wasted on a beautiful woman," he said with a little bow.

Ellen rolled her eyes and shoved at the door again. She was sick of being beautiful, sick of people who could see nothing else. Agreeing to come on this trip was a mistake. She should have known Rudi would be just like all the other men she'd ever met. She stalked out the door and climbed into the helicopter. Just do the job. Ignore the charm. It wasn't for her, but for the mask she wore.

# Three

----

**W**ind whipped Rudi's djellaba into a tangle as he hurried behind Ellen to the helicopter. He almost shivered in the sudden chill emanating from her. What had he said, what could he possibly have done to plunge her into this icy mood?

He had called her beautiful. What woman could object to that? She was beautiful. Stunningly so. She was also clever, responsible and determined. But beyond that, Rudi thought he had seen a vulnerability in her. A softness beneath the polished surface waiting for someone—the right man—to find it. He wanted to be that man.

The helicopter landed at the airport outside the city where he kept his private plane. Ellen balked as he led her across the tarmac to where the plane waited, engines thrumming.

"Just exactly how far is this place we're going?" she demanded.

"Not far. Wink of an eye and we will be there." He urged her onward, and reluctantly she came.

"Then why do we need to take a plane?"

"So we can get there in the wink of an eye. Without the plane it would be four winks and a snore, at least." Rudi tried teasing to pull her out of that icebox.

She humphed and climbed on board. The plane's opulent appointments irritated Rudi less than usual, because he hoped they might soothe Ellen's mood. Technically the plane belonged to the family, for ferrying various members here and there, but practically it belonged to Rudi. He was, for the most part, the only one who used it. Everyone else preferred to use the larger, even more luxurious model. Rudi liked this one, the smallest jet the company made, because he could fly it himself if he wanted.

The lunch basket was in place on the table, he noted as he paused to pull off his robes. He draped them over one of the seats and headed forward, wearing only the dark slacks and white dress shirt that were his usual attire beneath the djellaba.

"Samuel." Rudi clapped his hand on the pilot's shoulder. "Is everything ready?"

"All set. You're flying yourself?"

"I am." Rudi took the clipboard from the other man. "Take the day off. Take the week off, if you prefer."

Samuel laughed. "Maybe I'd better. You're skipping out again, aren't you?"

Rudi kept his expression bland. "I have a body-guard with me."

Disbelieving, the pilot bent and looked into the passenger cabin. He straightened with a low whistle. "Some bodyguard. I wouldn't mind guarding that body any day."

"That body is guarding me, and from what I hear, she is very, very good at it."

"You'll have to tell me all about it when you get back."

Rudi gave the other man a look calculated to intimidate. It did not work as intended—nothing much intimidated Samuel—but at least he fell silent. "Did you get the flight plan filed for me?"

"Barely. You didn't give much notice." Samuel paused. "Santa Fe again?"

"That is what the flight plan says." Rudi bent over the instruments, beginning his preflight checklist.

"So how come every time you file a flight plan to Santa Fe, you never get there?"

Though his heart pounded with nerves, just as it had when Ellen called her office, Rudi refused to let it show. He trusted Sam with his life, but not with his privacy. No one knew where he was going, and it would stay that way. He had somehow made it past Ellen's phone call without catastrophe striking. He would survive this, too. "I get there. Sometimes."

"Not often."

"Often enough." Rudi straightened and turned to face Samuel. "It is no business of yours, is it?"

"It is if I get fired for not doing my job. You know

I'm supposed to stay with the plane, even if you're flying. I belong in the right-hand seat."

"We have done this for years. No one has ever caught on, and no one will now. If they do, if they fire you, I will hire you."

"You can't afford me." Samuel met Rudi's gaze for a long challenging moment before he looked away. "But it's your business. Just don't get me caught up in it."

"I am doing nothing illegal, nor is it immoral. I simply need room to breathe every now and again."

"Okay, okay. With these terrorists running around back in Qarif, you can't blame a guy for worrying."

Rudi winked. "That is why I am taking a body-guard with me this time."

Samuel winked back. "Sure it is. Right." He drew the word out long with skepticism. He left the cockpit then, and Rudi followed.

"I will see you in a few days," Rudi said quietly, as Samuel stepped off the plane.

"There's a thunderstorm brewing beyond Harrisburg," Samuel said. "Better keep an eye on it."

"Thank you. I will." Rudi hauled up the door and dogged it shut, then turned to see Ellen watching him.

"Isn't he the pilot?"

"I am." Rudi plucked an apple from the basket and bit into it. "Fully qualified with all the required certificates. I learned to fly during my military training several years ago. I flew this plane here from Qarif."

Ellen eyed him as if she were having second thoughts about agreeing to the trip.

"Do you want me to call you a cab?" he asked. "I am going, whether you come or not. So do I go with a bodyguard or without one?"

She sighed and tugged at that wonderfully short skirt. "Go fly your plane. I'm not getting off."

Rudi nodded briskly, careful not to allow any of his triumph to show. He was getting much too good at dissembling. Sometimes it disturbed him, how good he was at it. But not today.

He finished his flight check, radioed the tower and received takeoff clearance. Moments later he was in the air flying west. When he was out of the airport traffic pattern, he engaged the autopilot and stepped back into the small cabin.

"Who's flying the plane?" Ellen looked startled to see him.

"Autopilot. Just long enough for me to get a sandwich and some coffee." Rudi poured from the insulated carafe into his lidded cup. "There is a storm ahead I want to keep an eye on."

"The one past Harrisburg."

"Correct." Rudi winked at her, wondering how much else she'd heard. "I cannot keep anything from you, can I?"

She didn't answer.

He stirred sugar into his coffee and snapped the lid on the cup. "Come up to the cockpit if you like. The view is much better up there."

He picked up a sandwich wrapped in plastic and headed back up front, hoping Ellen would take him up on his invitation. He wanted to talk to her. He would rather have let Samuel stay and do the flying, but he had never allowed anyone to go with him to Buckingham. Until now.

Ellen sat in the soft velour-covered seat staring out the window at fat, fluffy clouds floating past and wondered what in heaven's holy name she was doing in this airplane. She'd been in private corporate jets before, but none so sybaritically luxurious as this one, with the ornate rugs laid over the utilitarian gray carpet and the intricate inlay on the wood-paneled half walls. Nor had she ever been in one alone.

Not that she was exactly alone now. Rudi, her client, the body she was supposed to be guarding rather than lusting after, was on the plane with her. He was just in a separate part of the plane, in the cockpit, flying it. A rich man's self-indulgence, she told herself.

She picked through the lunch basket, mostly to see what was there. She'd been hungry earlier, but no more. Rudi upset her stomach. It couldn't be the combination of guilt, resentment and desire he stirred up in her. But if it was, it was still his fault.

Ellen unwrapped a sandwich and sniffed it. Chicken salad. Very fresh chicken salad. Maybe she could eat a bite or two. She poured a cup of coffee. The first sip set her back on her heels—it was strong enough to stand up and walk out of the cup on its own. But it was good. She added cream and sugar to tone it down a bit, and made up her mind.

Carrying coffee and sandwich, she walked to the cockpit, staggering only once in slight turbulence. Rudi glanced up and smiled when she entered.

"So you decided to come see the cockpit." He gestured at the chair to his right. "Have a seat. Take a look around."

Ellen slid carefully into the seat. She didn't want to touch anything she shouldn't. Her seat had a steering mechanism in front of it that appeared to be locked down. Good. She looked out the window and was mesmerized.

Trees blanketed the rippling ground below them, interspersed with squares and rectangles of bright green or mellow gold, depending, Ellen supposed, on the crops growing there. Blue river ribbons curled through the patchwork, while black roads slashed arrow straight, dotted with fast-moving traffic. And around her—above, below, left, right, before, behind—the sky opened its vast vistas.

She could see clear to tomorrow and back to yesterday. Clouds kept them company like fat, contented sheep. But ahead, a dark line on the horizon shadowed her pleasure in the scene, told her the clouds weren't always contented.

"Is that the storm?" She tipped her head toward it.

"Yes. We will turn south in a few minutes and fly around it." He looked at her. "I do not fly through thunderstorms just to prove how manly I am."

Ellen laughed. "No. You just ride through Central Park on a borrowed horse and snatch women off their feet."

"For fun." A tiny smile tickled the corners of Rudi's lips. "Admit it. It was fun, was it not?"

She shook her head. She might admit it to herself,

but never, ever to him. "You're absolutely outrageous."

"I know." He winked. "And you love it."

Rather than dignify his nonsense with a response, Ellen ate her sandwich.

Before long, they were flying with the dark line of clouds off their right wing, but the storm grew faster than the little jet could fly. The clouds seemed to boil, racing and churning as the pewter-gray froth climbed higher and higher, blotting out the sun. These were angry clouds, throwing lightning back and forth like insults, reaching out to drag Ellen and Rudi into their quarrel.

"Buckle up." Rudi pointed at the shoulder harness attached to Ellen's seat. He already had his fastened, she noticed as she pulled the straps around her and clicked them into place.

"We will get caught in the edges of this storm," he said. "The front is bigger and badder than it looked in the forecast, but we should miss the worst of it."

"Can't we fly above it, or something?" Her hands shook, and she locked them together in her lap. Ellen couldn't believe her nerves were so shot. She'd never had a problem with flying in her life. But then, she'd never been in a plane this small in the middle of a storm that big with her safety in someone else's hands. Her cousin the shrink said she had control issues.

"It is too high. A commercial jetliner would have trouble getting above this one." Rudi shot her a quick smile. "Relax. I have never crashed one yet."

"That's the word that bothers me," she muttered.

"What word?"

"Yet."

Rudi laughed, a big, full-throated sound of pure enjoyment. Then the plane plunged, caught by a sudden downdraft.

Ellen yelped, and Rudi stopped laughing as he wrestled for altitude. The aircraft bucked and jolted like something alive trying to escape a predator's jaws. Ellen squeezed her eyes shut and hung on to the chair's armrests for dear life. She wasn't afraid. But if the plane was going to crash, she didn't want to see it.

Time passed. The jet would level out and climb for a few minutes, then the wind would lash out again with another stomach-floating drop, or a sideways blow, and the struggle would start over. Rudi fought the storm with a fierce light in his eyes that must have been in his ancestors' when they fought the invading Crusaders. Ellen watched him, fascinated.

Except when the downdrafts struck. She couldn't keep her eyes open when the wind pushed the plane toward the ground.

Rain and sleet sporadically battered the little jet. For minutes at a time they would break into the clear, only to have the storm reach out and snare them again. It exhausted Ellen, and she was merely a passenger. She didn't want to think how tired Rudi must be.

Finally, finally the clouds thinned, then dissipated, and nothing shone ahead of them but blue sky.

Rudi took a deep breath and got on the radio. Ellen's ear had been well tuned to pick up the hissing, staticky tones of speech over the airwaves, but pilot talk was full of jargon she didn't know. She understood the English words, the ones like *heading* and *southwest*. The rest of it was beyond her.

"Clear skies ahead," Rudi said when he hung up the microphone. "All the way to California, if we like, according to the weather wizards."

"I guess they'd know." She gave him a lowering look. "We are *not* going to California." It was not a question. Nor was it an option.

Rudi grinned. "No, we are not going to California."

"So where are we going?"

"Not California."

Ellen ground her teeth, then made herself stop. Her doctor blamed the habit for her headaches. "Stop being coy. It doesn't suit you. Where are we going?"

"You will know when we get there. Let it be a surprise. And I am never coy."

"I hate surprises. I'm responsible for your safety. What if these terrorists are waiting for you on the other end of this flight?"

"They are not."

"How do you know?"

"Because even if they knew where we are going, which they do not, they have had insufficient time to get there. And even if they are there, which they are not, they will stand out like a goat in the parlor. You would spot them in five seconds or less."

Ellen scowled at him. "Why won't you tell me

where we're going? And you're about as coy as it's possible for a man to be.''

"Not coy. Clever." Rudi winked.

"Rudi—" She put a threat in her voice. It didn't work.

"Yes, Ellen?" His smile was inoffensive.

"You're ticking me off. So if you're not telling me because you don't want to make me mad, it's too late. I'm already there. Where are we going?" She punctuated the words with silence. She locked her hands around the armrests to remind herself that, as much as she wanted to, she couldn't strangle him.

"Our destination is a surprise."

That again. "I really hate surprises. They always jump up and bite you in the ass." Ellen glowered out the windshield.

"Some surprises are nice. This one is."

She didn't believe a word of it.

"And if I cannot be coy, you cannot be sullen," he added.

"I'm not sullen." Her glare should have singed his ears, if there was any justice in the world.

"Right." Rudi's smug smile shoved her irritation higher.

Ellen needed to get away, out of the same room with him, lest she lose her marginal grip on her self-control and do something best left unthought of. He was flying the plane, after all.

She fought her way out of the seat belt. "I'm going to the little girls' room," she said. *Before I smack you.*

"All the way aft." Rudi glanced up at her, and for

a minute Ellen thought he would say something smart-ass, something that would drive her right off the deep end.

He didn't. "Why do you not take two of the chairs in the cabin and stretch out? You look as if you fought the storm to a standstill single-handedly. You should get some rest."

She didn't know whether to feel insulted because he implied she looked awful or comforted because he showed concern for her well-being. Either one wasn't what she'd expected from a rich, irresponsible, playboy younger son. But then Rudi had been confounding her expectations from the minute she'd met him.

"Aren't you tired?" she asked.

"I am flying." He grinned. "Besides, it is harder to be a passenger than a pilot coming through a storm. When you are doing the flying, you are taking action. You are in control. Not wincing and ducking and closing your eyes. Not that you did any of those things, of course."

Ellen stood up and stepped out the cockpit door to escape the blasted man, then turned back. "I closed my eyes," she said. She believed in owning up to the truth. "And I really, *really* hate surprises."

When Ellen did not come back to the cockpit, Rudi put the plane on autopilot just long enough to check on her. He found her asleep in the cabin. She sat tipped against the wall in a corner, rather than stretched out as Rudi had suggested. Probably because he had suggested it.

Or maybe she had told herself she would just sit

and look out the window a minute, never intending to fall asleep. That would be like her, from the little Rudi knew of her thus far. She refused to be pushed, didn't like to be led and fought to keep control of everything around her, holding it clutched tight in those long, elegant fingers. But sometimes, apparently, her body overruled her.

Rudi indulged himself with one more look at those slender, forever legs before stepping back into the cockpit. Sleep was good, he thought as he buckled himself back in and flipped the switch to manual. She needed it. Besides that, if she slept long enough, she would not give him trouble over their destination.

At least, not until they landed. Rudi was a great believer in putting off trouble as long as possible.

The storm had delayed them. Enough to make Rudi push the plane a little harder than he liked. If he did not reach the landing strip before dark, they would have to go miles out of the way to a lighted airport. Fortunately it was summer, and the sun stayed above the horizon well into the evening hours. Crossing two time zones helped, also.

The sun was low on the horizon when he spotted the notched bluff just past the rusty smear of river bottom. He aimed for the notch and five minutes later he was over the runway, the wind sock indicating a strong south wind, as usual. Grateful he did not have to land facing the sun's dying glare, Rudi circled the field and put the jet on the asphalt strip with only two or three hard bounces. Not the best runway in the world, especially when the cows strayed across it.

Before he could taxi down the runway to the hangar, Ellen burst into the cockpit.

''Where's the exit?'' She knelt to unbuckle his seat harness. ''Stop messing around trying to fix things and get out of there.''

''What are you doing, woman?''

Distracted by her hands playing in his lap, Rudi drifted slightly off course and ran over something left too near the runway, causing the jet to bump slightly. Ellen clutched at him, one arm locking around his thigh to keep from losing her balance. Rudi would have smacked the plane into the side of the hangar if he had not managed to hit the brakes hard enough to stop it.

''Ellen.'' He pushed her gently to the other chair. ''Wait until the plane stops before you start grabbing the pilot's legs. Let me get the plane in the hangar, and then you may play with my legs all you want, all right?''

She peered out the windscreen, her slender neck swiveling as she checked out her surroundings. Her nostrils flared, subtly surveying the air, perhaps for the scent of smoke. Then her eyes narrowed into anger, and she sank into the copilot's chair.

''The way you landed this thing, throwing me clean out of my seat, how was I supposed to know we didn't crash?'' Ellen looked out the window on her side, toward the pink-and-orange sky where the sun had just vanished beyond the distant horizon, then aimed her glare at Rudi again. ''It's sunset. You said we'd be back in the city tonight.''

He brought the plane to a halt inside the open han-

gar. "I never said that." He had been very careful
not to.

"Okay, you let me assume it."

Before he could inform her that her assumptions
were not his responsibility, she had moved on.

"Just where are we, anyway?"

"My place." Rudi shut everything down, then ran
the checklist to be sure. "I could not carry you away
to the Casbah, but I think this is better."

"You said it was a business meeting." Her eyes
flashed fire at him. He'd always thought it a cliché,
but she truly was beautiful when she was angry.

"It is. In town, in the morning." He stood and
edged between the seats, partially through the door,
then offered Ellen his hand. "Coming?"

Rudi held his breath as she looked from his face to
his hand and back again, waiting for her to decide.
She would come—he had maneuvered her pretty
neatly into that. She had to stick with him, at least
for now. But would she take his hand? Rudi did not
think so. Still, he had to take the chance and offer it.

When her slim, cool fingers slid across his palm
and her hand closed around his, the touch jolted him.
It sent his persistent awareness of her presence sizzling into raging desire. Every molecule in his body
wanted her. Not just for sex, though he could not deny
he wanted that, wanted it so much he had to choke
off a groan. But he wanted more.

He wanted to see admiration in her eyes. He
wanted to hear her laugh. He wanted to argue with
her and make up afterward. He wanted to wake up
with her in the morning after a night of hot, mindless,

slow, sultry sex, and have her smile at him simply because she liked him.

And Rudi knew, somewhere down deep in his gut, that if he rushed the sex, he would never get the smile. It might kill him, but he intended to take his sweet time with this woman.

"Well?" Ellen's voice broke into his musing, and he realized he still stood like a fool in the cockpit doorway holding her hand. "Are we going to get off this airplane any time in this millennium?"

Rudi grinned. He loved her sass. "Come along. Meet the natives."

# Four

———

Ellen let Rudi open the jet's door, but she was the first one through it, her hand on the gun in her purse as she descended the narrow ladderway. The hangar, a primitive construct of corrugated tin, was empty.

She walked to the open entrance and looked out into the blue twilight. Open land stretched out ahead of her, broken only by a flat-topped hill in the far distance. Short, scrubby bushes covered the land, almost silver in the dusky light. The black-topped runway became a dirt road about a mile distant, and looped around to the west, toward high rocky mountains.

Foothills, Ellen corrected herself, seeing the sunset-gilded peaks of higher mountains in the distance beyond. She'd never in all her life seen so much…nothing. Or so few people. Like none, besides herself and Rudi. She would definitely be able to spot a terrorist in this vast wasteland. They'd be the only other people out here.

"Where in the world have you brought me?" she muttered.

"As I said—" Rudi spoke at her elbow "—this is my place."

She looked around at the empty, echoing hangar. "Nice house."

Rudi chuckled. "The house is at the base of that rise." He pointed at one of the hills to the west.

"I'm not exactly dressed for a cross-country hike."

"Do not worry. Our ride is coming."

Just then, Ellen heard the growl of a motor. Headlights pierced the gloom as a pickup truck shouldered up out of a fold in the land she hadn't seen, and rumbled its way onto the runway and up to the hangar. Her grip tightened on the automatic pistol still hidden in her purse, and she stepped in front of Rudi. He might know who the pickup belonged to, but she didn't.

The lanky, grizzled cowboy who unfolded himself from the truck certainly didn't look like a Muslim terrorist, however. Rudi's wide smile as he stepped past her reassured her more.

"Bill." Rudi embraced the man and kissed him on both cheeks.

Bill was still wiping off his cheeks when Rudi drew Ellen forward. "This is Ellen Sheffield. She'll be staying with us for a few days."

"Pleased to meet you, Miss Sheffield." Bill shook

her hand with great ceremony, his hand as dry and callused as old leather. "Welcome to New Mexico."

"I—" She had to pause a moment to digest the knowledge that she was in New Mexico. Rudi would pay for this. He most definitely would pay. "I'm pleased to meet you, Mr...." She paused again, waiting for his response to her prompt.

"Just call me Bill. Everybody else does." Bill reclaimed his hand and turned away.

"I'd be happy to. But I'd still like to know your last name."

Ellen could feel Rudi's silent laughter beside her as Bill turned back, eyebrows climbing his laddered forehead.

"Dadgum, boy," he said in a slow-as-five-o'clock-traffic drawl, "if you were gonna wait so long before bringin' a woman home, don't you think you coulda found one who wasn't so snippy?"

"I'm a bodyguard," Ellen said. "The fact that I'm female is immaterial. And I still don't know your last name."

"It's Chandler." Bill gave her a long, slow, head-to-toe once-over. Ellen endured it, as she had all the others in her life. "And you look pretty durn material to me."

He looked at Rudi. "You bring your usual luggage?"

"Yes." Rudi gently tugged Ellen's hand out of her purse and escorted her to the pickup truck. "Has everything gone well here?"

"Right as rain, except we haven't had any. Rain." Bill got in the driver's side and waited.

Ellen eyed the open passenger door of the pickup in dismay. She'd never been in a truck before, and now she knew why. They were not made to get into while wearing a dress. Particularly not a short, snug dress like the lime-green sheath she presently had on.

"Do you need assistance?" Rudi murmured in her ear.

"No, I—um—" Ellen lifted her foot, but the seams of her skirt popped alarmingly before she could get it high enough to set on the step.

Before she could try something else, Rudi grasped her around the waist and lifted her in, then climbed in after her.

"Thanks, son." Bill started the engine. "I figured we'd be pussyfootin' out here till sunup waiting for Miss Bodyguard to figure out how to get in a truck."

Ellen ignored the old Neanderthal. She'd known a thousand men just like him. He wasn't worth the waste of her time to try to prove him wrong.

"How is the beautiful Annabelle?" Rudi asked.

"Anxious to see you again, but she'll keep till tomorrow. She left you some supper." Bill paused while he drove the truck into a gully and out again. "I reckon there'll be enough for the both of you, even if she was only expecting one."

*Annabelle?* Ellen refused to give Rudi the satisfaction of looking at him. She refused to play his game. If he kept a woman in his New Mexico hideaway, that was his business. She was just the bodyguard.

"I am desolate," Rudi said. "I am forced to wait until tomorrow to see my Annabelle? How can I eat when I am deprived of her company?"

Bill snorted. "You may think I'm no-count enough that you can flirt with my wife like that, but I'm thinkin' your bodyguard here can straighten you out right fast."

*Annabelle was Mrs. Chandler.* Ellen caught herself when she heard Rudi's laughter, stopped her glare from shooting at him. She didn't care who Annabelle was. Rudi's flirtations were none of her business. None.

But the shape of the situation shifted again, back to her original assessment of his purpose in bringing her here. Rudi had seduction on his mind.

Well, he could just wipe it right out of there, because Ellen wasn't playing. She was here for one reason and one reason only. To do her job and guard his body.

"How far is it to the house?" she asked.

"Another couple miles," Bill said.

"What kind of security does it have?"

"State of the art." Rudi stretched his arm across the back of the seat, and incidentally around Ellen. Step one of his plan, she was certain. "I do not use motion-sensor sound alarms because of the wildlife, but everything else is installed. Also, the house cannot be approached unseen."

"Good." Ellen nodded her head once, briskly. Keep everything businesslike, and she could keep it under control.

"Relax." Rudi smiled at her. "There is no danger here. Not from terrorists, at any rate."

Ellen shrugged. It was her job to make sure. He was probably right. She couldn't envision terrorists braving this no-man's-land of New Mexico. But it was still her job to stay alert.

She sat up straight in the center of the seat and watched the bushes jolt by, as the truck alternately lurched, crawled and jounced its way along. Rudi's head settled against the back glass of the pickup's cab. When Ellen glanced his way, she saw his mouth had dropped open, and he slept, despite the rattling of his head on the window.

The truck hit a bigger-than-usual rock, and Rudi's head bounced hard. He blinked awake and pulled his arm in, straightening slightly on the seat, as if determined to stay awake. But in seconds his eyes shut again, and his head fell back on the window as he slumped low in the seat.

Ellen sighed. It was a conspiracy. The whole world conspired against her, forcing her into niceness. She was not a nice person. She didn't want to be a nice person. Nice people got dumped on.

And yet. Ellen found herself tipping Rudi's head forward, off the back glass, and sideways. Against her shoulder. She hoped he didn't drool in his sleep. If he drooled, the niceness was over.

Bill was apparently as taciturn as cowboys were reputed to be. The remainder of the trip passed in silence, except for the roar of the motor and the occasional very soft snore from Rudi.

The sky had darkened to a deep navy blue just a shade lighter than the black horizon and stars were beginning to appear when the truck heaved itself up onto an almost-paved road and turned left. The surface was graded and graveled, and much smoother than the rutted track they'd just left. A few minutes later, lights winked on, triggered by motion sensors, illuminating what Ellen guessed to be some dozen acres. Rudi's house sat in the center of the light pool.

Ellen stared. This was no little cabin in the foothills. This was the Ponderosa. It was Tara. Manderley. A house like this deserved a name. Half log cabin, half glass palace, it nestled into the rocks jutting from the hill behind as if it grew out of them. It belonged in this wild place, and yet, somehow, it promised luxuries beyond Ellen's most fantastic dreams. And she could dream some pretty big fantasies.

Bill pulled the pickup to a halt in front of the wide stairway leading up to the entry deck. Rudi jolted awake, springing upright before he blinked. Ellen brushed off her shoulder, brushing away the touch of his head.

"We're here," Bill said. "You need anything else?"

"No. Thank you." Rudi opened the pickup door and slid out, stumbling once before his knees caught and held. He turned and offered his hand to Ellen.

She ignored it, preferring to rely on herself, to bypass his little courtesies. They were all part of the web he tried to weave, a web she had no intention of getting caught in. In fact, she was no slouch at weaving her own webs, which was how she came to know all about them.

"Your keys are in the usual spot," Bill said through the still-open truck door. "She's gassed up and serviced. Ready to roll."

"Thank you, Bill. I will see you tomorrow, then."

Rudi shut the door, and Bill and his pickup rumbled off.

Rudi gave Ellen a little bow and gestured toward the stairs. "Shall we go in?"

Scowling, Ellen started up. "Who knows you're here?"

"Besides my family and the Chandlers?" Rudi climbed the few steps at her side, and led the way across the broad deck to the front door. He unlocked the door. "Only your office, of course."

Ellen didn't bother answering. She reached inside and flipped on the interior light, the gun out of her handbag and in her hand this time, as she stepped into Rudi's house.

She could see almost all of the lower level from the door. A massive native-stone fireplace rose on the north wall. The kitchen, with cabinets matching the unstained pine log walls, took up part of the western side of the house, and Ellen surmised that a bedroom or two lay beyond the doorway on the south wall. A stairway made of split logs suspended from yet more logs rose from near the middle of the room's expanse, leading to a loft above, and possibly more bedrooms. Comfortable, masculine, rustic furniture divided the vast open space into areas for dining, relaxing and conversing according to its placement.

Quickly Ellen checked the rooms she couldn't see into, locating a luxurious master bedroom and bath complete with whirlpool on the first floor, and four more bedrooms upstairs beyond the loft area. Decks surrounded the house, void of occupants save for an

annoyed squirrel. Ellen lifted the cover off the hot tub
on the deck outside the main bedroom, just to be sure.

"Are we safe?" Rudi asked, a smile curving his
lips as he pulled a casserole dish from the oven.

"For now." Ellen put her weapon away. She had
to smile herself at the picture he made. "You look
real cute wearing that oven mitt. Real natural."

"Why, thank you." Again he made that little flour-
ishing bow, still holding the hot dish.

Ellen wished she had said nothing, hadn't even noticed. The oven mitt somehow emphasized his exotic
masculinity, the breadth of his shoulders and strength
of his arms. Didn't the man own a shirt in the right
size? Surely he could find something that didn't strain
at the seams.

Rudi set the dish on the table. "Are you hungry?"

"I guess." Ellen shrugged. "What is there to eat?"

Steam rose, redolent of tomatoes and spices and
things Mexican, as he peeled away the foil. "I do not
know the name of it, but I assure you, it is delicious.
Annabelle could cook a sow's ear and make it delicious."

"Just who are Bill and Annabelle?" Ellen asked,
opening kitchen drawers at random, hunting silver-
ware.

"Sit down." Rudi took her by both arms, turned
her toward the table and gave her a gentle push. "You
are my guest. I will take care of everything."

This was a new kind of seduction scene, watching
a man wait on her with his own hands, rather than
snapping fingers at a restaurant waiter. She kind of
liked it. Not that it would work.

Rudi set a plate in front of her, creamy blue-painted stoneware. Then he set a napkin, cloth, in the middle of the plate and a fork, real silver, on top of the napkin.

"We do not need knives for this," he muttered as he collected wineglasses from where they hung upside down on a rack. He rinsed them out and dried them quickly before setting one at each place. Instead of wine, he pulled two amber bottles from the refrigerator.

The label was unfamiliar to Ellen, unreadable. "What is this?"

"Beer." Rudi found a serving spoon and stabbed it into the casserole. "Mexican beer for the Mexican food. I learned to appreciate it when I was at university." He surveyed the table. "Do you need anything else?"

Ellen shrugged, hiding her pleasure at being asked. Rudi sat down in the chair beside her, at the place he had prepared. He opened his beer, poured it into the glass, then held it up in a toast. "Drink with me."

She drank straight from the mouth of her bottle, then held it out to answer his toast. "What are we drinking to?"

She knew, of course. The toast would be to her, or to both of them, or to beautiful women. But it would be about sex and seduction.

Rudi's perfect mouth curved in that perfect smile. "To conversation," he said.

*Conversation?* Ellen blinked and belatedly tipped her bottle up to her mouth. Damn the man for being able to confuse her. Again.

Maybe that was how he planned to seduce her. Get her all confused until she didn't know which way was up, then pounce when she was helpless. Well, Ellen Sheffield was never helpless. Ever. But she was definitely confused.

Rudi served Ellen's plate with the food Annabelle had prepared for them, and then served his own.

"Eat." He picked up his fork. "I promise you, it is not poisoned or otherwise tampered with." He took a bite, hissing faintly as the fire of the peppers hidden in the meat hit his palate. "It may be a trifle spicy, however."

He could not resist chuckling at Ellen's suspicious expression as she poked at the cheese and tortillas.

"You never did answer my question." She finally stopped poking and took a bite.

Rudi could tell when the peppers hit, but only because tears started in the corners of her eyes. She disguised the rest of her reaction, reaching casually for the beer as if flames were not about to shoot from her ears.

"Is it hot?" he asked.

"Not at all." She cleared her throat, obviously unwilling to either choke or cough. "Bill and Annabelle—who are they?"

"Bill manages the property. And Annabelle cares for the house, and for me when I am here." Rudi smiled.

He found one of the sliced jalapeños and deliberately, making sure Ellen saw him, stabbed it with his fork and carried it to his mouth, where it quickly reminded him why he usually left the peppers sitting on the rim of his plate. He shoveled in a big mouthful of starchy tortillas and beans immediately after the pepper, to dilute some of the burn.

"Do you like it?" he asked, pointing at the food on Ellen's plate.

"Delicious." She blinked back tears.

"If the peppers are too hot, just leave them on the side of your plate." Rudi uncovered another and ate it, even as his conscience and his tongue chided him for his wickedness. "Sometimes women find them more than they can handle."

"No, they're not too hot. They're good." Ellen took his dare, snaring a pepper from her own plate and popping it into her mouth, where she swallowed it virtually whole.

*Rudi, Rudi, you are an evil man.* And he ate another, hoping his digestion could stand up to the assault.

"So, Ellen, now that we can finally have that talk you promised..." He paused to smile, hoping it looked as guileless as he wished it to. "Tell me about yourself. Have you family?"

"And then some." She looked up from her plate where she had been stirring and gave him a shy smile that jolted him clear to his toes. "Although I guess I can't complain. I only have half as many brothers as you do."

"Only four brothers, then. Allah is indeed merciful to you." He grinned, and she laughed. "Are they older or younger than you?"

"I'm the middle child, unfortunately." She sighed.

"Usually it's the middle child who feels invisible, but being the only girl, I wasn't so lucky."

"Be glad you were not. Invisible is not a pleasant thing to be." As Rudi well knew. Being number seven among nine brothers was about as invisible as a boy could get.

"I can't believe you've ever felt invisible," Ellen said. "Not the way your family comes unglued when you're not where you're supposed to be."

"Ah, but there is invisible, as in unseen, and there is invisible, as in seeing only what the viewer wishes to see. I have always been seen as no more than a copy of my brothers. A body to fill in the gap between Hamid and Ahmed."

Why was he telling her this? He had intended to pry out Ellen's secrets, not lay his own out for view, as if asking for her pity. Angry with himself, he stabbed the pepper he had just uncovered and ate it, enjoying the burn.

"Actually," Ellen said, toying with a shred of meat, "I think I do know about that kind of invisible."

Rudi's eyebrows went up, his gaze fastened on her, as his internal detector of secrets signaled wildly. "Because you were the only girl and everyone expected you to be sweet and feminine?"

Ellen looked at him, surprise in her expression. Then she threw her head back and laughed, a full-hearted, joyous laugh such as he had not heard from anyone in too long, and never from Ellen. It was possible she frequently laughed this way, and Rudi had simply not been near her enough to know it, but he did not think so.

"No," she said, wiping her eyes as she took another bite.

Rudi noticed she left the jalapeño on the plate. Then she noticed that he noticed, and she oh-so-casually scooped it up and ate it, coughing only once.

"No," she repeated. "I did everything my brothers did, from baseball to ice hockey. And if anyone tried to tell me I couldn't, I knocked him down.

"Oh, I had Barbie dolls and Wonder Woman boots, but my Barbie dolls went out on bivouac with Steve's G.I. Joes—Steve is my next younger brother—and got blown to smithereens with Roger's firecrackers. Roger is the oldest. We had to steal his firecrackers because we were too young to have any of our own."

Rudi liked this side of her, wanted to know all of it. "Tell me more. Tell me about the Wonder Woman boots."

Ellen's eyes grew wistful. "I loved those boots. I got them for Christmas when I was six, I think. And I wore those boots everywhere, until I outgrew them. Even to school if Mom didn't catch me. I had Danny's old Superman cape. Danny comes between me and Roger. I wore the cape pretty much everywhere, too. Until Danny convinced me I could fly in it."

"He what?" Rudi sat up straight, alarmed. But she must have come to no harm from it, for she sat here before him eating Annabelle's delicious fiery food.

"Well, he didn't really convince me." Ellen's fond chuckle did not do much to reassure Rudi. "I was

pretty sure the cape didn't have any Superman powers. That's why I didn't jump off the roof.''

"Thank goodness." Rudi almost collapsed in his
chair as the relief rushed through him.

"I just jumped out of my second-story bedroom
window.''

"What?'' His heart could not take this jolting.
"You jumped from a second-story window thinking
you could fly because of a stupid red cape?''

Ellen laughed, a gleeful chortle this time. "Don't
forget the boots. The boots were supposed to be these
superpowered pogo-stick things. Like landing on a
trampoline. If I didn't fly, I'd just jump right back to
the window.''

"What possessed you to do such a foolish thing?''

"He dared me.'' Ellen shrugged. "Don't tell me
you never did anything like that, because I won't believe you.''

"I never jumped off a roof.''

She lifted one skeptical eyebrow.

"Or out of a window.''

Her other eyebrow went up. Rudi resisted that cool
appraisal for approximately ten seconds before he
broke.

"Oh, very well. I once tried to dive to the bottom
of the pond in our garden because Fahdlan told me
Aladdin's lamp was hidden there. But the pond was
only four feet deep.''

"How old were you?''

"Four years old. However, I remember it very
well.''

"And who had to haul you out when you almost drowned?"

Rudi shot her a sharp glance. How had she known that? "My brother Ibrahim. And how many bones did you break in your brave leap into the sky?"

"Only two." She grimaced. "Both arms. Danny had to feed me till the casts came off. His punishment for daring me to jump. And mine."

"Do you always accept dares?"

Ellen held his gaze a moment, then she speared a jalapeño, put it in her mouth and chewed very slowly. Tears again gathered in the corners of her eyes, and she had to clear her throat before she swallowed. Rudi watched her throat work, wishing he could kiss his way along the path the pepper took.

"Always," she said.

Rudi had to clear his own throat and remind himself what her word referred to. "I shall have to remember that, if there is something in particular I wish you to do."

He licked his lips and noticed Ellen watching his tongue travel across his mouth. Then she copied the action, and he could only stare at her tongue darting out and across her lips. What madness had possessed him to bring her here?

*That* madness, obviously, but had he been required to give in to it? Too late to change anything now. Impulse had carried him into deep waters once more.

And he did not know whether, this time, he could get himself out again.

# Five

Ellen stared into Rudi's deep, soulful, melting, coffee-brown eyes, framed by the thickest, curliest lashes that no man had any right to possess. What had he just said? Something about things he wanted her to do?

He licked his lips again, and again Ellen fought the tingle at the back of her neck as his tongue traveled across those eminently kissable lips. They parted.

And Ellen caught herself before she leaned toward them.

What was wrong with her? She had to be in control of this little seduction scene, had to keep him off balance and slavering, ready to do whatever she wanted. So how did she wind up being the one off balance?

She glanced down at her plate, intending to distract herself with food, and discovered that some gremlin had climbed onto the table and eaten everything on her plate when she wasn't looking.

"Would you like more?" Rudi asked, his hand on the serving spoon.

Ellen looked at him and almost lost herself in those dark eyes again. She could not do that. Not ever again.

"Much as I've enjoyed our little pepper-eating contest," she said, "I think I've had enough. Which bedroom is mine?"

"Take this one." Rudi gestured toward the first-floor suite.

Ellen's eyes narrowed. "And where, pray tell, will you be sleeping?"

"There are many rooms in this house." He stood and took her hand as she rose, despite her effort to avoid his grasp. "I will have no trouble in finding a place to sleep."

"I don't want to take your room." She let him draw her toward the bedroom door, but stalled outside it.

"My guest should have the best my home has to offer."

"What about the dishes?" Ellen turned back to the kitchen. Rudi stopped her before she could take a step.

"Annabelle will wash them when she comes in the morning. I will put away the remaining food. You are my guest. Please…" He opened the bedroom door and indicated with a graceful wave that she should enter.

"I really don't think—"

"But I do," Rudi interrupted. "If you are going to begin talking about bodyguarding and employment, perhaps I should point out that you will be closer to the entrances by sleeping here on the first floor."

"There is that."

"Please. Humor me."

The mere fact that he wanted so badly for her to stay in the master bedroom ought to be reason enough for Ellen to insist on another room. But she found herself nodding in agreement. "Oh, all right. If you're going to be that way about it."

"I am." He smiled at her. One of his patented smiles that could put furnace companies out of business, the way it seemed to raise the ambient temperature. "I will be sleeping in the bedroom right at the top of the stairs."

She shot him a suspicious glare.

He chuckled. "I assumed you would want to know which room I would take in order to better perform your guarding tasks. To be sure no one creeps in during the night to slit my throat."

He drew his finger across his throat, drawing her eye to it. Strong, muscular, shadowed with the day's beard, and yet vulnerable, his throat matched the rest of Rudi. Ellen told herself firmly that she did not want to press her lips to the faint pulse she saw there.

Rudi leaned toward her.

*Here it comes, the kiss that's supposed to knock my socks off and convince me to share the room with him.* Trouble was, Ellen was afraid Rudi's kiss really would knock her socks off. But she refused to run away from it.

Then he bypassed her mouth and pressed a warm, dry kiss on her forehead. "Sleep well, my dear Ellen."

He turned away, leaving her staring gape mouthed at him.

*Damn him!* She whirled away and slammed the door shut. She could hear him laughing through the closed door and wanted to open it again and yank out a few handfuls of that black, silky hair. How could he do this to her?

Not "how could he" as in how did he dare, but "how could he" as in how in the world *did* he do it?

Ellen knew men. She knew what they wanted, what turned them on and what made them angry. She knew how to push all the right buttons to make a man do what she wanted him to do. She'd learned it well, after Davis. Never had any man been able to push her buttons in return. Until now.

Rudi didn't behave the way she expected. At virtually every turn he surprised her. He was different.

And that was how he had stolen control away from her. She had no set of instructions for dealing with a man like Rudi, no experience in handling a man who would kiss her forehead at his own bedroom door and walk away, leaving her to sleep alone, without even attempting to join her. That innocent kiss had left her tingling and wanting, more than any tongue fight ever had.

She was going to have to play this one by ear, and when it came to Rudi, Ellen feared she was tone-deaf.

The big black SUV turned headfirst into a parking place on the downtown street—the only downtown

street—of Buckingham, New Mexico. Ellen stepped
out onto the red brick pavement, adjusting her sun-
glasses against the brightness of the summer sun.

It seemed harsher here, more glaring than she remembered it being in New York. Maybe because of
the altitude, considerably above New York's sea
level. Or maybe the sun had no pollution to cut
through here. Whatever the reason, Ellen's stylish
half-tint designer shades did not suffice to cut the brilliance.

She hitched up her borrowed jeans, which had been
left in her bedroom before she woke by the efficient
and estimable Annabelle, and stepped up the knee-
high curb onto the sidewalk. The jeans bothered her.
Not because they threatened to slip off her hips and
tangle around her knees with every step, but because
someone had entered the house, entered the *bedroom*
where she slept, and she hadn't known it.

Just because she'd woken twice in the night, terrified by dreams that she'd gone deaf, and then been
unable to go back to sleep was no excuse for screwing
up. It was her job to be alert at all times. Still, she
would never complain about New York City traffic
noise again.

"When is this meeting?" she asked Rudi as he
joined her on the sidewalk.

He checked his watch. "Eleven o'clock."

"So we have a little time before then." Ellen
hoisted the jeans again.

"Yes. Was there something you wished to do?"

His mouth ought to be declared a controlled substance, Ellen thought. It was definitely addictive. She couldn't stop staring at it, wanting to taste. But she forced herself.

Blinking helped. So did looking past his shoulder when she talked to him. She was a protector. She had to keep an eye out for bad guys, not go comatose staring at her protectee.

"If there's anything in this grand metropolis resembling a department store," she said, "I thought I might find something to wear that would stay on."

"That would be a pity." Rudi's voice sounded so sincerely solemn that Ellen risked looking at him. The mischief shining in his big brown eyes made her want to smack him. Not good bodyguard behavior.

"And why is that?" The words grated out between her teeth.

"I was so looking forward to spending the day waiting—perhaps hoping—that Annabelle's clothes would *not* stay on."

She couldn't smack him, but she could at least glare.

Rudi's smile stayed where it was, and he pointed down the street. "I believe there is a store that will have what you are seeking. There are things in the display window other than clothing, but I remember seeing clothing as well."

Saye's was a mix of antiques, gifts and clothes, which would have charmed Ellen if she'd encountered it in New York. Or anywhere that she could go to another store and buy normal clothes. All this store carried was tight jeans in every shade that denim could be dyed, and shirts to match.

The jeans wouldn't be so bad, Ellen decided, if she could find a shirt without a pointed yoke or pearl snaps. The ones without snaps had cute embroidered flowers or teddy bears on them. Ellen did not do cute.

Finally she bought two pairs of jeans that actually fit. Two, because Rudi had told her they'd be in New Mexico at least one more day. She had the store owner put one pair in the sack with the sleeveless, disgustingly cute teddy-bear-print shirt, and she wore the red-checked-gingham, pearl-snapped shirt out of the store with the other pair of jeans. Rudi owed her big time. Making him pay for the clothes was only the beginning. She intended to collect a piece of his hide.

"You look very nice," he said as he followed her out the door.

"I look like Daisy Mae Clampett," she retorted, slapping him in the chest with the sack. "I look like an idiot."

Taking the sack from her, Rudi looked her over, head to toe. This once-over felt different from the others she'd endured. Everywhere his gaze touched she tingled. She wanted to snarl at him, tell him to take his roving eye off her or she would remove it for him. But she couldn't. He'd frozen the words right in her throat with his looking. Or maybe he'd burned them to ashes.

His gaze caressed her, warmed her inside. Good Lord, her nipples were getting hard. Thank God for Victoria and the secrets her bras could hide. This set-tled it. Ellen was going to see Cousin Alice the shrink the minute she got home. She had gone completely over the edge into lunacy.

"The shoes," Rudi said, startling Ellen out of her appalled reverie.

"What?" Her thoughts were still scattered, and she'd lost the broom to sweep them together again.

"Your shoes do not go with the rest of your clothing." Rudi nodded, as if he'd just solved the secrets of the universe.

"Yeah, I realize that high-heeled sandals don't exactly go with gingham." Her voice carried all the disdain she felt for the word. *Gingham.* Even the sound of it made her shudder. "But I didn't see any saddle oxfords around."

"Boots," Rudi said.

She lifted an eyebrow and tilted her head. He was nuttier than she was. "Are you on some kind of quota system? Did somebody ration your words so you have to save them up because you'll run out if you use too many words at once?"

Rudi laughed, so handsome in the sunlight with the mountains as his backdrop that Ellen's stomach curled around, kicked her heart into pounding and jolted something loose lower down that started to purr.

"You need some boots," he said, offering his arm. "I will buy you a pair of boots, and this afternoon we can go riding."

"I don't ride." Reluctantly she slipped her hand into the crook of his elbow, unable to keep from it, unable to resist his charm or that stupid perfect smile.

"Does that mean you never have, or you never

wish to?'' Rudi started down the street, the breeze off the mountains stirring his sable curls.

"It means I don't know how." Nor was she sure she wanted to know, but she wouldn't say that out loud.

"That can be remedied. Riding is not a difficult thing to learn, if one merely wishes to ride for one's own pleasure." He paused, walking in silence for a moment as if absorbed in thought. "Unless, of course, one is afraid of horses."

There he went, pushing her buttons again. "I'm not afraid of horses or anything else."

"Then it is settled. I will buy you boots, and this afternoon we will ride."

"In the open? I don't think so."

"We are in the open now."

"Yes, and the back of my neck is crawling from all the eyes on us." Ellen surveyed their surroundings, but saw nothing out of the ordinary. The few people on the street wore their jeans and boots like second skins, smiled and nodded. Not exactly terrorist behavior.

"You know how remote my home is. The area I will take you to ride is even more remote. No one will be able to reach it without your notice." He opened the door to a store with a neon boot in the window and Ellen went in, grumbling.

"I still don't like it," she said.

"You will like it once you are on your horse." Rudi turned his perfect smile on the salesclerk, a woman somewhere between thirty-five and sixty, with weathered skin that had Ellen wishing she'd been more generous with the sunscreen that morning.

Rudi's smile had its usual effect, and in fifteen minutes Ellen was equipped with a pair of black cowboy boots with fancy red stitching on the tops and extra socks to wear with them. She felt almost like a little girl again, playing dress-up. The boots fulfilled a secret fantasy she'd never known she had.

Then the salesclerk rattled off the total.

Ellen closed her gaping mouth, grabbed Rudi's arm and spun him around as she simultaneously tried to remove the boots from her feet. "I'm not doing this," she said. "That's too much. I can't let you pay—"

"Yes, you can." Rudi pulled a wad of cash big enough to choke an elephant from his pocket and peeled off several bills. Ellen grabbed at his hand, trying to stop him from giving them to the clerk, but with one foot half out of her boot, she nearly toppled. Rudi caught her arm, supporting her and holding her at bay while he handed the money to the clerk.

"Rudi," Ellen whispered. "I can't accept these. They're too expensive."

"If I bought you jewelry as a gift," he said, "I would spend three times the amount. This is a small thing. You can accept the boots, and you will."

"But—"

He cut off her protest. "You cannot ride a horse wearing sandals, nor can you accompany me this afternoon unless you are on horseback. If you do not go with me, I will go alone."

Rudi knelt before her and tugged the boot back on her foot, then looked up at her from that position as he smoothed her jeans down over the boot top. He spoke, his voice bedroom soft, so that only Ellen could hear him, despite the fascinated clerk holding out his change. "If you must, think of this as a business requirement, a purchase necessary to fulfill your employment obligations."

His fingers tickled the back of her knee, and the knee almost buckled. Rudi was stirring up things she'd rather he left alone, making her want things that weren't possible.

"But," he said as he rose to his feet, "know that this gift has nothing to do with business. It is for you, and you alone."

She knew it. That was why she couldn't take them. But if she didn't have the boots, she couldn't ride. Why did he have to do these things to her?

Rudi collected his change and escorted her out of the store, Ellen walking awkwardly beside him. The soles of the boots were slick and stiff, and the heels lower than she was used to. The fit was different, changing her walk. It would be a while before she felt comfortable in her new cowboy boots.

Five minutes later they reached a vacant lot across from the Buckingham schools. Pipe, heavy machinery and unidentified metal parts lay scattered all over the lot in a semblance of order, though Ellen couldn't say what that order might be. In the center of the lot a small derrick sat silent. It looked just like the ones she'd seen in movies, only smaller.

Rudi shook hands with the men waiting there and put on the hard hat they gave him. There was a brief scramble while another hat was found for Ellen, and the meeting in and around the machinery began.

She stood back and played bodyguard, ignoring the curious and speculative glances sent her way. In a few minutes the men got involved in their discussion and mostly forgot her presence. Ellen listened, as she usually did on this kind of assignment.

"We've gone down a thousand feet and still have nothing but dry hole," the short, thickset man said.

"How is the water situation, Mayor?" Rudi asked.

The mayor, a white-haired, red-faced cowboy, thought a moment before speaking. "Not good. We're having to get people to fill up their bathtubs in the morning so they'll have water in the evening when the pressure's down. We've been buying from some of the other towns around, but they're in trouble, too, it's been so long since we've had any rain to speak of. And we can't afford to keep drilling if there's nothing down there."

"The water is there," Rudi said. "I am sure of it. I have studied all of the information many times. It is there, but it is deep."

"We can't afford—" the mayor began, but Rudi waved him off.

"Do not worry about the cost. Keep drilling. I will pay."

"I don't feel quite right about that." The mayor rubbed the back of his neck. "You already did the geological study for nothing, helped us pick the site and bought the land to drill on."

Rudi gestured him to silence again. "I am a part of this community. If I can help, I must. The cost is unimportant. A thousand feet more. If you do not reach water at two thousand feet, notify me, and we can consider then what steps to take.''

Ellen watched Rudi discuss the drilling with the foreman, and followed him around the well site, revising her opinion of him with every step she took. This meeting wasn't to impress her. Rudi had already been on his way here when he swept her onto that horse in Central Park. Except for glancing at her regularly, as if to make sure she was still present, Rudi devoted his attention to business.

This was the real Rudi. Caring, generous, capable. She'd been attracted to him from the beginning, had even liked him. The flight to Buckingham had given her respect for his flying skills, and now she'd found other things to respect and admire him for. Maybe he was more different from the men she knew than she'd realized.

That thought made her very uneasy, because it made her like him even more, and that could be dangerous. She could not afford to let her guard down. Not the one that protected Rudi, and especially not the one that protected herself.

Rudi allowed his horse to dawdle a few paces so he could watch his companion. No. Admit it, his conscience prodded. You encouraged your horse to fall back. But the sight was well worth it.

Strands of long golden hair had escaped from Ellen's ponytail and floated about her face in the breeze. Her hips swayed with the motion of her horse, making it difficult for Rudi to ride comfortably as he watched her. But he could not tear his gaze away.

He wanted her. He had from the very beginning, but if this time alone together passed with nothing more than a kiss…

He would not be satisfied. Far from it. His frustration would reach unmeasured heights. But already he felt that the trip had accomplished its purpose.

Rudi had begun to see the Ellen behind that polished facade, the little girl who would accept any dare to prove herself. She still refused to back down from any challenge, but he sensed something more. Something that would explain the mask she hid behind. Something she would not easily reveal.

Ellen twisted in the saddle and smiled at him, open and friendly. "What are you doing messing around back there? Get up here and tell me what I'm looking at."

Rudi laughed and urged his mount alongside hers. "Land," he said, sweeping his arm across the horizon. "Trees. Rocks. And there—" He pointed as he spotted them. "Antelope."

"Where?" Ellen stretched, standing slightly in her stirrups as she looked. "I don't see—"

"There." Rudi touched her shoulder and directed her gaze. "You are searching too far. They are closer."

"Practically under my nose." Her voice softened when she saw them. "They're beautiful. They almost look painted, with those striped faces."

Rudi watched the brown-and-white animals grazing on the hillside, their short, straight, single-spike antlers dull in the bright light. "They remind me of the gazelles I sometimes saw at home."

"Gazelles? In the desert?"

"At the oases. Qarif is on the coast. More rocks than sand." Rudi surveyed the stark, beautiful landscape around them for a moment. "This reminds me of Qarif to some degree. There is no ocean nearby, of course, but water is the same precious treasure in both places. And in both places, there is more rock than soil."

"And there are antelopes," Ellen said.

"Yes." Rudi smiled. She understood.

"So where are we going?" She scanned the terrain with that radar-beam gaze of hers.

"This way."

Ellen caught him off guard when she hauled her horse to a stop and glared at him. "That's it," she snapped. "I have had all I can take of your cryptic half-truths. You tell me right now where we are going, or I'm knocking your sorry butt off that horse and hauling you back to town. And I don't mean Buckingham."

Rudi blinked at her, surprised by her outburst. But then, why should he be? He had not been truthful with her from the beginning, still was not, and he well knew Ellen did not possess large amounts of patience.

"My apologies," he said. "I have no definite destination. I merely thought that we might ride into the hills where there are trees. I did not intend to be cryptic."

Ellen continued to glower at him.

"And my butt is not sorry," he added. "I have

been told that it is—'' He broke off, as if trying to remember. ''Ah, yes. That it is mighty fine.''

She snorted. With laughter, he hoped.

''What's over there?''

Rudi accepted the change of topic and looked where she pointed, at a low, steep rock face rising sharply from a dry wash. ''A small canyon begins just past that face. I should have cattle grazing in the meadow there.''

His horse stirred, and Rudi brought it easily under control. ''Sometimes I climb to the top of the cliff and watch them.''

''You do not.'' Her retort was instantaneous.

''I do not climb the face, or I do not watch the cows?''

''Either. Both.''

She no longer scowled, but Rudi liked her skepticism even less. She maligned his manhood. ''I have climbed that rock face a dozen times.''

''Yeah, right.'' Ellen actually scoffed.

Rudi wondered how he could wish so strongly to strangle her and to kiss her at the same moment. Fury swallowed up his words, bound his hands. She was fortunate.

''Anyway,'' she said, ''if you did climb it a dozen times, it's probably no big deal. I bet a baby could climb that. A baby still in diapers.''

''You could not climb it.'' He found his voice.

''If you can climb it, I can climb it,'' she sneered.

''You cannot. Not without asking for help.''

''I don't need anybody's help to climb those rocks.''

"Prove it." Rudi reined his prancing mount in a tight circle.

"You prove it first."

"We will climb together. And you will ask for my help." He brought his horse right next to hers, his knee bumping hers as he faced her.

"I won't." She poked at his chest. "Not from you."

"Do you care to make a wager on that?"

"Fifty bucks says I make it to the top without help," Ellen said.

"A poor wager. Hardly worth making." His heart began to pound in his chest as possibilities opened up before him.

"Well, excuse me, your high-and-mightiness. I don't carry bags full of gold fizz-cats—"

"Fiats." He corrected her.

"Whatever. I'm not a moneybags like you."

"Which is why a wager for money does not interest me." Rudi pretended to a nonchalance he did not feel.

"What does?"

"If," he said, crowding his mount deliberately into hers, making it back up a step, "if you ask for my help at any time while you are climbing the rock face, I win. If I win, you will agree to do whatever I ask for all of this night to come." He intended to require answers to all his questions.

"If you win, I'm your love slave?" Ellen's voice was colored with bitterness.

Her words made him burn, now she had spoken them, though his intentions truly did not go in this direction. "I suppose you could think of it that way. I did not."

"Sure you didn't."

"Believe what you will." He shrugged, as if it was of no matter to him.

"So I win if I get to the top on my own, right? What do I win? You as *my* love slave?"

"It sounds—" his attention was caught by the quick slide of her tongue across her lower lip "—sounds fair to me."

"It would. Either way, you get what you want."

Rudi backed his horse, as if preparing to leave. "If you are afraid…"

"Don't try to pull that on me. I know what you're trying to do. And you know I'm not afraid to climb that cliff." She stabbed a finger first at him, then toward the cliff.

"Yes. I know you are not afraid of rocks." Rudi crowded close again, urging his mount forward until he was eye-to-eye with Ellen. Understanding burst in his mind with all the slow-dawning power of a sunrise. "You are afraid of me. You are afraid of what I make you feel."

"Like hell I am." Ellen kicked her horse several times before it agreed to move. "You've got your bet."

He rode after her the few dozen yards to the base of the gray granite rock face. Though it was scarcely thirty feet high and studded generously with footholds and handholds, the cliff appeared twice as high and three times as dangerous, now that his mind visualized Ellen's slender form clinging to its side.

"Ellen, wait," he said, reining his horse in beside her as she dismounted.

"Second thoughts, Rudi?" She sent him a challenging glare. "Too late. Of course, if *you're* afraid…"

He was, but not for himself. "You could get hurt."

"I can get hurt walking through Central Park. I can get hurt going down the stairs in my building." She found handholds and set her foot on the first rock. "But I don't. I can take care of myself."

Rudi swung off his horse and hurried to her. "You cannot climb in those boots."

Ellen paused atop her rock and looked at her feet. "I hate to get my new boots all scuffed up. But too bad. You can polish them tonight when you're my slave." She shot him a wicked grin.

"No. That is not what I mean. The soles are too slick for climbing. They will slip." He held up his hands to assist her down.

"Those dozen times you climbed these rocks, did you wear cowboy boots?" She stood straight, balanced on the sizable boulder, waiting for his answer.

"Yes, but—"

"If you can do it, I can do it."

She started up again, checking each foothold before trusting her weight to it. At least she took proper caution, Rudi thought, following close behind her and just to her left. Even better, this rock face was not actually vertical. Not quite.

Hand by hand, foot by foot, they climbed the cliff. A dozen times, a score, a hundred, Rudi reached out to help Ellen, to lift her past a difficult spot, to catch her when her foot slipped yet again. And each time, Ellen glared his assistance away. His heart pounded like a runaway camel, his breath rasped in his ears, as if he climbed a sheer hundred-foot cliff, rather than this tiny one.

When they neared the top, Rudi scrambled ahead, ready to pull her up if necessary. Once more, Ellen refused his hand, crawling under her own power over onto the sparse grass growing in the gritty soil. Panting slightly, more from the altitude than the effort, he was sure, she grinned triumphantly at him as she got to her feet.

"I won," she said.

Rudi's control broke. He caught her by the shoulders and shook her. "Don't ever do that to me again!"

Then he wrapped his arms around her and held on tight, until his own shaking stopped, however long that might take. She was in his arms, whole and safe. He had not taunted her into killing herself.

"Hey, take it easy." Ellen pushed against him, but he could not let her go. Not yet.

"What's going on here?" Her voice came gentler this time. "Rudi?"

Still he could not release her, could not find words, though his heart finally began to slow.

"Rudi, were you worried about me?" This time Ellen managed to pry herself free, enough to look up into his face. "You didn't think I could do it, did you?"

He said nothing, but she must have seen the truth in his expression, for she tore herself free, stumbling back a few paces, knocking away his hands as he grabbed to keep her from the edge.

"How many times do I have to tell you?" Her eyes flashed blue lightning at him. "I can take care of myself."

"I know. That is—" He gave her a rueful look. "My head knows. But my heart is not so wise. It sees only the danger."

"Oh, please." Ellen rolled her eyes. "Let's leave any talk about hearts out of this. You don't mean it, and I don't need it."

Now Rudi's temper flared, but he kept a tight grip. "You do not know. Neither what I mean, nor what you need."

"And you *do?*" Her sarcasm inflamed him further.

"Yes." He bit the word out.

She answered with a snort of mocking laughter. Most unbecoming. "Just remember, princey." She put her forefinger against his chest and pushed. "I won. Tonight I own you. *Capiche?* I own *you.* Not the other way around."

"Yes." The words gritted between his teeth as he ground them. "I understand." He did not know *capiche,* but he could discern its meaning from the use she made of it.

He would be her slave tonight. Honor demanded it. And while he was her slave, he would do everything in his considerable power to break down the walls of fear behind which she hid.

Rudi glanced up at the sun beginning to descend toward the distant Sangre de Cristo Mountains. "We should go back now. Annabelle will have dinner waiting by the time we arrive.''

''I won.'' She taunted him in a childish singsong. ''Care to make another wager? Want to race down?''

''No!'' The shout burst from his sudden, stomach-clenching fear.

''Why not? Afraid you'll lose? Again?''

Her ridiculous glee would be amusing at another time, but not at the top of a thirty-foot cliff. Rudi caught her arm, hauling her close, letting her see his anger.

''Because the quickest way to the bottom is to fall,'' he hissed. ''I will go down first, and you will follow. And if I wish to help you, I will. And you will accept my help. Do you...*capiche?*''

She blinked, seemingly taken aback by his vehemence. ''Okay. Fine. You're the boss.'' A wicked little smile crept across her lips. ''Until tonight, that is.''

Rudi gave a single abrupt nod. ''Until tonight.''

# Six

As they climbed back down the cliff face, Ellen was forced to admit that she was grateful for Rudi's help. Down turned out to be a lot harder than up. She lost count of the number of times he guided her foot to a better hold, or steadied her when the slick-soled boots threatened to slip. When they finally reached bottom, she had to hold on to Rudi's hands, the two hands that had steadied her those last steps from shaky rock to solid ground, for a few extra moments. Just long enough to make sure her knees would hold.

Halfway back to Rudi's house, reality hit her. She'd won the bet. She had won Rudi for her very own personal love slave for the night. What in the hell was she going to do with a love slave?

Okay, he'd tried to dress it up when he made the bet, just saying that the loser had to do whatever the winner demanded. But when she'd accused him of the love-slave thing, he hadn't denied it. He just hadn't expected to lose.

But he had. He'd lost, she'd won, and now she owned him for the night.

She could handle it. She was the boss. All she had to do was not ask for…that.

Ellen glanced at him, riding easily beside her. He looked good in a cowboy hat and jeans. Very natural. He'd looked just as good in his Arab clothes. *Face it, Ellen. He'd look good in anything.*

*Or nothing.*

She smashed that thought flat with a mental sledge-hammer. Only, it curled up again, coming back to life like the villain in that silly Roger Rabbit movie. The man was temptation on the hoof, the devil with big brown eyes.

His shirt strained at the seams where it stretched across his shoulders, the snaps threatening to pop all on their own. She wanted to find out what was underneath. *No, she didn't.* His hips moved with the rhythm of the horse, his legs stretched wide around its barrel, and she wondered how those legs would feel… She tried again to deny the thought, and gave it up as useless. She did want, and wonder, and all the rest of it.

Sex with Rudi might be different, might be all those bells and whistles and fireworks going off that she'd heard about but never believed. With Davis, back when she still believed in true love and fairy-tale endings, sex had been okay, but nothing to write home about. She'd tried it a couple of times since then, thinking surely it had to get better, surely there had to be something to all those romance-novel descriptions. But it hadn't and there wasn't.

So she just wouldn't go there. She could think of plenty of things Rudi could do for her that didn't have anything to do with sex.

No, she couldn't.

When she looked at him, she wanted to touch him, and when she touched him, she wanted to— She just plain wanted.

She couldn't do this. She didn't need a love slave, didn't want a love slave. But she couldn't back out of it. That had been part of the dare. Rudi had accused her of being afraid of the prize. Of course, he was really saying that she was afraid to *be* the prize. Which was true, though she'd never tell him that.

Unfortunately, winning the prize seemed to be almost more frightening. If she tried to call it off, Rudi would accuse her of cowardice again, and she couldn't bear that. Maybe she was scared of certain things sometimes, but she couldn't let anyone know it.

Rudi had to be the one to back out. He was a sheikh. A prince. He was used to people bowing and scraping before him, not doing the scraping himself. Surely his pride wouldn't let him go through with this slave thing. Ellen sincerely hoped so.

If he didn't back out on his own, maybe she could help him along. Maybe she could be so demanding, so imperious, that he would get fed up and quit. She would have to try. Otherwise, disaster loomed.

* * *

When they arrived back at the house, Rudi took care of the horses, which Bill had trailered over earlier in the day. They belonged to Rudi, but usually they stayed in the barn near Bill's house, where he could care for them more easily. With a last pat of his mare's sleek gray rump, Rudi headed for the house and Ellen.

After a brief search, he found her on the deck outside the first-floor bedroom. Something jolted deep inside him at the sight of the sunlight on her golden hair, here in this place that he loved. The pines rising from the hillside beyond provided a fitting backdrop for her beauty.

"There you are." The expression on her face as she turned and spoke put Rudi on his guard. "What took you so long? I've been waiting for ages."

He might have been encouraged by her words if her face had not told him she plotted something. "The horses required care," he said. "I am here now."

"Did I say you could talk?" She drew herself up into a regal posture. "I don't care about your excuses. I don't care about the horses. I care about me. You're my slave, and you have to do what I say."

His eyes narrowed as he watched her watching him. If he were not certain she planned something devious, her latest words would make him angry. But somehow, he knew that anger was what she intended to provoke. Therefore he must remain calm until he perceived her purpose.

Rudi bowed in apology, remaining silent, as she demanded of him.

"Go get me something to drink," she ordered, waving her hand.

He waited.

"Well?" She raised her brows expectantly.

"What do you wish to drink?"

"I don't care. Something cold."

Rudi imitated Omar's bow again and turned to go.

"No, wait." Ellen called him back. "First, come take off my boots."

He inclined his head in acquiescence and approached her, holding his temper in firm hands. Bending over from the waist, he lifted her foot.

"No." She pushed him away. "You're not doing it right. I want you down. On your knees."

Rudi's eyes flashed to her, and he saw the look of triumph on her face before she hid it behind her mask. Immediately his anger cooled. She wanted him angry. She purposely tried to demean him in order to spark his temper. Why?

Slowly, holding her gaze, Rudi went down on one knee. She swallowed hard. He picked up her foot and tugged the boot off easily. He sent a caress of his thumbs across the arch of her foot, and Ellen gasped. With a hidden smile he set the foot down and picked up her other one. She was not immune to him.

As he removed this boot, still watching her, Rudi saw a flicker of apprehension cross her face, and he understood. She intended to push him until he backed out of the wager. Her pride would not allow her to back down, and she believed that his pride would not allow him to do her bidding.

She was wrong.

He intended to make her feel every one of the things she was afraid of feeling, and he would do it by catering to each one of her whims. This would be a night Ellen Sheffield would never forget.

Somebody had sucked all the oxygen out of the atmosphere. Or maybe she'd just forgotten to breathe. Ellen tried inhaling, just as an experiment, but the air seemed to get caught in her throat somewhere before it actually made it to her lungs.

It was Rudi's fault, of course. His fault for having such big, deep, dark brown eyes, and looking at her with them. Looking at her like that. Not as if she was a trophy, or an expensive toy, or any of the other things men had told her in the past, but as if she was infinitely more valuable than anything in the world. As if she was cherished.

She jerked her foot out of his grip and shoved him with it. ''Go on. Get me that drink.''

Instead of glaring at her, or stomping away, or doing any of the things she expected, Rudi made that gracious, graceful bow of his head and rose smoothly to his feet. The muscles of his thighs bunched, making her bite her lip hard. The pain didn't distract her from the sight, from wanting to see just exactly how those muscles felt beneath her hands.

''Of course,'' he said. And he went to do as she ordered.

What was wrong with the man? Didn't he have any pride? If she had been the one to lose the bet, she'd be slamming doors and throwing things already.

Ellen sighed. Maybe it just meant he was a better

sport than she was. That didn't take much. She hated
to lose. But somehow, some way, she had to make
him back out of this bet. She couldn't take much more
of those bedroom eyes or movie-star muscles.

He returned, carrying an opened bottle of beer on
a tray, and bowed as he served it to her.

She glared at him as she snatched it up and took a
drink, then she slammed it back on the tray. "I didn't
want beer. I wanted a soda. Bring me something
soft."

Still he didn't flare up. *Still,* he just bowed. "As
you wish."

What did she have to do to make the man quit?
She was beginning to feel bad about being so nasty
to him. He was probably just as thirsty as she was.
"Wait."

Rudi turned back, one eyebrow up as he waited for
her next petty order.

"No use wasting the beer," she said. "You can
have it if you want."

His smile was tiny, scarcely a smile at all, and it
turned her insides into something soft and gooey, like
chocolate pudding. She was in deep, deep trouble
here.

"Thank you, *zahra.*"

Now he was using Arabic words on her. It probably
meant "slave driver." He inclined his head in that
minibow that she was rapidly getting sick of, and vanished back into the house.

Moments later he returned yet again, the beer on
the tray now accompanied by a can of pop. Rudi

served her, then set the tray on the bench beside her before collecting his bottle.

Ellen racked her brain, trying to think of something else she could do to stop this stupid situation. Her annoyance with him, with herself, and the whole situation, grew.

"Stop looming over me like that," she snapped. "I hate it when you loom."

Rudi grinned at her, and her heart took off on a race to nowhere. He sat back on his heels, hovering there with his knees near his armpits, and his backside inches off the decking. "First I am coy," he said. "And now I loom. What will you accuse me of next?"

"Did I say you could talk?" Ellen refused to look at that backside, taunting her as it hovered.

His little bow was almost mocking this time, hunkered down as he was. "Forgive me, *zahra*. I exist only to serve you."

"Oh, for—" Ellen sprang from her seat, almost knocking Rudi over. "Don't you have any pride? Any self-respect? How can you stand to grovel like this?"

He rose to face her in one smooth motion. "I do not grovel. I serve." His forehead crinkled, the way it did when he spoke of something serious. "It is a matter of honor. I lost the bet, therefore I must fulfill the wager. Honor is only satisfied by paying my debts willingly, cheerfully and thoroughly. Halfhearted, grudging service will not do."

Ellen's heart sank. With that kind of attitude, she would never get him to quit. She turned away and walked to the deck railing, staring out at the red sunset sky beyond the mountains. She didn't know what to do. She liked Rudi, she really did. But she didn't trust him.

All of her previous experience with men had taught her that they would do anything, say anything to get what they wanted. And what they all wanted was a notch on the bedpost. To be able to point to her and say, "See that beautiful woman over there? I did her."

Some of them wanted to own her, to turn her into a prize they could show off, the way Davis had. But none of them wanted any more than her surface—the face, the hair, the legs, the body. What was inside the package didn't matter to them. Which was why her appearance made such a terrific weapon in the business she'd chosen. They didn't expect to find anything beneath it, and it gave her the advantage of surprise.

Rudi might be different in a lot of ways, but not in that one. He still wanted to notch his post. Ellen didn't dare let down her guard. Liking him, wanting him, just made it that much harder.

She sighed and started to lower herself to the bench, when her thigh muscles screamed. Ellen confined herself to a gasp. She grabbed for the railing, managing to hold on to her soda while all the muscles in her body told her in no uncertain terms just how unhappy they were. Not only had she ridden a horse several miles, an activity using a complete set of muscles previously unknown to her, but she'd climbed an entire cliff. Up and back down again.

"Ellen? Are you all right?" Rudi's silky, sexy voice sounded in her ear.

"Ow." She couldn't manage more as she tried to straighten again. "No, I'm okay." She fended off his solicitude. She didn't need to like him any more than she already did, and she certainly didn't need him this close to her. "I just found a few muscles I didn't know I had."

"Can I help?"

"Aspirin." She nodded her head. "Aspirin sounds good."

Rudi's hands settled onto her shoulders and began to rub, his strong fingers finding the knotted soreness. "I am no expert, but I have picked up some techniques from various massage therapists in the past. Would you like...?"

"Aspirin," she repeated. She didn't dare let Rudi get anywhere near her with those magic hands. In fact, she would tell him to stop what he was doing, right now. Or maybe in just another minute.

"Are you sure?" His breath whispered warm across her ear, and Ellen shuddered.

She made herself duck away, a harder thing to do than flipping a sumo wrestler onto his back. She should know. She'd done both. "Just aspirin." Maybe if she said it enough times, she'd believe it.

"Didn't I smell some of Annabelle's famous cooking when I was inside?" Ellen said, trying to distract him. Or herself.

He bowed and swept a hand toward the house, playing the perfect servant again. So perfect, she wanted to smack him. Or kiss him.

His mouth drew her, mesmerized her, tormented her. It was his best feature, next to his eyes. And his shoulders. And his... Ellen stopped that line of thought. But she couldn't stop thoughts about his mouth, because somehow she couldn't make herself stop staring at it. It looked like such a kissable mouth. So why hadn't he kissed her with it?

Not that she wanted him to kiss her. She didn't. She didn't think she did, anyway. But she did wonder. Not one kiss. He hadn't even tried. Not even last night at her bedroom door. Kisses on the forehead didn't count. And it made her curious what a real kiss from that eminently kissable mouth would be like. Dangerously curious.

"Ellen?"

She heard Rudi speak from somewhere far distant, but she couldn't drag her demented mind from its focus.

"Ellen, why are you staring at—?" Rudi's mouth came closer. His breathing seemed ragged, but no more than her own.

She tried to focus. She really did. But the day's exertion must have tied her brain in as many knots as it had her muscles. She could neither think nor move.

"I must," he murmured.

And his mouth closed over hers.

The touch was light at first, a tentative caress that came again with more confidence. Ellen sighed, unable to summon even a moan, and let her body settle against Rudi. His hand cupped the back of her head as his mouth moved over hers. His arm around her back supported her, holding her in place.

At the touch of his tongue, Ellen opened to him, teased and tasted him. She took possession of his mouth, even as she surrendered her own to him. This was everything a kiss should be, and more. The kind of kiss she'd known had to be out there, but never believed could be found. Not by her. Not until now. Until Rudi.

She heard a groan, and thought it came from Rudi, though it might have been hers. His hand moved from the back of her head to her bottom, pulling her hips in tight. She could feel his arousal press hard against her stomach, and she pressed back.

At that moment her good sense recovered from its exhaustion and lifted its feeble head. What in the world was she doing?

*Kissing Rudi,* her body retorted. Her body wanted to keep on kissing, wanted to follow the tingle his mouth had started and see where it led. But her good sense already knew where this kiss would take her. Right into big-time trouble.

Besides sleeping with her client being unethical as hell, she knew herself well enough to know that her emotions would inevitably get tangled up in Rudi if she had sex with him. And inevitably, she would get hurt. There were too many obstacles between them.

He was a prince. His family had more money than God, or at least more money than Bill Gates, which was probably close to the same thing. She was just Ellen Sheffield, a nobody special who'd had the misfortune to be born with a pretty face.

She couldn't afford to fall even a little bit in love with Prince Rudi, however great the temptation. And

Ellen was firmly convinced that no one had ever been this tempted since that snake waved that apple under Eve's nose in the Garden of Eden.

Ellen pulled away, breaking the kiss gently. Already he was getting to her, making her reluctant to wound even his pride.

"Dinner?" she said. "Aspirin?"

He blinked, cleared his throat. "Yes," he said, releasing her. "Yes. Dinner."

Rudi stepped back, then turned and almost ran into the house. His swift departure might have hurt her feelings if she hadn't already decided this was best.

She followed at the fastest pace her aching body would allow. She'd expected her legs and her butt to hurt after sitting on that horse for so long, but her shoulders and back were killing her, too. Even the muscles running down her ribs below her arms hurt. Heck, even her ears hurt. She was still feeling them as she entered the kitchen.

Rudi closed the oven door and faced her, that disgustingly cute oven mitt still on his hand. "Is something wrong with your ears?"

"They hurt." She hobbled on into the kitchen area. "I didn't think I had any muscles in my ears."

Rudi chuckled. He shook off the mitt and came to inspect. "They are sunburned. You did not think to put sunscreen on them, did you?"

"I sunburned my ears? I have never in my life heard of sunburned ears." Ellen touched them gingerly. The pain was more of a burn than an ache, she realized.

"Did you never go to the seaside as a child?"

"Yes, but I never—" She paused, remembering. "I guess I did sunburn my ears, but the rest of me was so much worse, I didn't really notice." She poked him in the arm. "What happened to my aspirin, slave?"

"Yes, *zahra*." He made that fancy hand flourish with his bow this time. "I live to serve you."

"I can do without the sarcasm."

"What sarcasm?" His expression was wide-eyed innocence. "Every word from my lips is sincere truth." Then he laughed at her disgusted look.

Rudi pulled out a chair from the kitchen table as he passed it. "Sit. I will get the aspirin and some ice in a glass for your drink. It must be warm by now."

"Thanks." Ellen couldn't hold back the groan as she shuffled to the chair. She was positive she heard her body creak when she lowered herself into it.

"I cannot bear to see you in such pain." Rudi opened the aspirin bottle, poured two into his hand and held them out to her.

Ellen took the bottle instead. "Give me that. Those, too." She picked the tablets carefully from his palm, not wanting to touch him more than necessary. She was avoiding temptation just now.

She shook another aspirin from the bottle and tossed all three into her mouth, washing them down with swig of warm pop. Nasty tasting. "This is a three-aspirin ache," she informed Rudi, setting the bottle down on the table with a thump.

"Please," Rudi said. "Dinner is not yet finished cooking. Please, allow me to give you a massage. It will help. I swear it."

Ellen believed him. His magic fingers had done

wonders for her shoulders. But she didn't dare. A massage would mean Rudi touching more than just her shoulders. He would touch her back and her neck and her legs. Probably even her bottom, considering it was one of the places that hurt the most.

At that thought, the leftover tingle from his kiss started up all over again. Between the tingling and the aching, she couldn't think. She could only want.

"I'm not taking off my clothes," she said. *Where did that come from?* She had intended to turn him down when she'd opened her mouth. At least, she thought she had.

"Your jeans are too heavy, and the blouse will be harsh against your skin." His thumbs dug into the knots on either side of her spine and she moaned with the pleasure-pain of it.

When had he gotten close enough to do that to her again? He was right, though. The gingham collar felt rough as he rubbed her neck. Rudi moved it aside and laid his hand on bare skin, easing her aches. It did feel much better that way.

"It is, of course, your decision," he said, his voice low and seductive. "I am merely your servant, and do only as you bid. You may feel safe with me."

*Safe?* Not hardly. But it wasn't Rudi's action that endangered, it was her own reaction to him. Odd as it might seem, given her past experience, she trusted him utterly to go only as far as she invited. She just didn't know if she could keep from issuing a blanket invitation. Something along the lines of *Here I am. Take me.*

"Ellen?" Rudi lifted her to her feet. It wasn't as

painful a process when her own muscles did so much less of the work. He led her to the bedroom door.

"Lie down on the bed," he said. "Leave whatever clothing you feel appropriate, and call me when you are ready."

She went into the room and stared at the massive four-poster bed with its white textured coverlet. This was too hard. If she did as Rudi suggested, as her body demanded, she had sole responsibility for whatever happened. She couldn't blame Rudi for anything other than being himself. Could she handle a massage, or would it make her want more? And if she did want more, was she too afraid of being disappointed or hurt to risk it? Was that what had her dithering in the middle of the room?

"Coward." She hissed the word out loud.

Just because she accepted a massage didn't mean anything else *would* happen. Only that it *could*. She was the one in control tonight. Rudi had said that it was a matter of honor for him to obey her commands. To fulfill her wishes. He would stop if she asked him to. She knew it bone deep, as more than fact.

Ellen grabbed her shirt collar and yanked, popping the snaps open all the way down. She would take one step at a time. She would see how things went, and if she wanted to take the next step… Well then, she would. But she left her bra and panties on anyway as she crawled painfully onto the bed.

"I'm ready."

Rudi started at the sound of Ellen's voice calling from the bedroom. She was ready. But was he?

He took a deep breath, then shook himself, like a sprinter trying to loosen up before a race. Rudi didn't need to get loose, however. He needed tight, iron-hard control. He took another deep breath, closing his hands into fists.

"Rudi?"

"I am coming." He let the air out of his lungs as he reminded himself one more time that Ellen expected him to rebel against her instructions, and that therefore he must obey them perfectly. And he walked into the room.

The sight of her lying facedown on his bed, wearing only wispy scraps of pale blue silk, had him breathing deeply again, this time in hopes of holding his head in place on his shoulders. It threatened to fly away like a balloon. She was more beautiful than even his fertile imagination had pictured. Perhaps because this vision was real.

He put his knee on the bed and Ellen looked up, alarm in her eyes. "The bed is too wide," he said. "I cannot reach you properly unless I am on it with you."

"Oh." She nodded, accepting his excuse. "Okay."

She turned her face into the pillows again, her forehead resting on her folded hands.

Rudi clenched his hands tight once more before relaxing them and setting them on the smooth, silken skin of her shoulders. Then he dug his thumbs in, searching for the corded knots.

Ellen moaned. The sound twisted its way inside him to settle hot and heavy at his groin. This was going to be sheer torture.

He worked on her shoulders, slipping her bra straps out of the way. Then he moved down her back to the muscles between her shoulder blades. Ellen's moans and gasps sang counterpoint to the motion of his hands, arousing him as much as did touching her, for he imagined much the same music as he made love to her.

He massaged her deltoids, muscles he knew would be sore from the climb, and on down her sides.

"May I unfasten this?" He tugged lightly at the hooks fastening her bra, asking permission when he wanted to do as he wished.

"Go ahead," Ellen mumbled past her hands, giving him the freedom he desired.

Rudi had no oils for this massage and regretted his sparsely equipped toiletries. He had never brought a woman—or anyone, for that matter—to his New Mexico hideaway, and had seen no need for more than the basics. He would simply have to make do.

His hands rubbed their way down her back, using Ellen's "music" as a guide to the places that needed his attention.

"Better?" he asked.

"Mmm." She took a deep breath, her back rising with it. "Much."

He let his palms slide lightly over her soft skin, delighting in the feel, in the knowledge that she allowed him this freedom. "Where else? Your arms? Your legs?"

She straightened one of her arms, lifting it slightly. "It might do me some good."

Rudi massaged both arms, one after the other. Then he worked on the leg she raised into the air, rubbing her calves.

"Keep going," she said, when he would have stopped at her knees. She turned her head so the bedding didn't muffle her words. "The hurt goes all the way up. The cure needs to follow it."

"As you wish, *zahra*." *Zahra*. Flower. A perfect description of Ellen, so delicate, so beautiful and fragrant. He would not survive this sweet torture. Touching her like this without promise of release was worse than any torments devised by his ancestors. Scorpions would be more welcome.

The sounds she made as he massaged her thighs intensified his arousal and thus his pain. He knew he should have changed out of jeans into native dress before beginning this. But if he had, his condition would be so obvious, he would doubtless frighten her back behind her mental walls.

"Anything else?" he asked, sitting back on his heels, sincerely hoping he would be given the chance to escape.

Ellen lifted her hips slightly and tightened her shapely buttocks. Rudi's mouth went dry. The tiny scrap of pale blue cloth covering them did not hide anything from his eyes. Any effect on modesty was purely imaginary.

"My bottom is sore, too. From the horse, I guess," she said in a faint, almost girlish voice. "Would you…?"

"At your command."

# Seven

Ellen was on fire. Her whole, entire body burned, head to toe, front to back, inside and out. Every blood cell in every capillary in every tiny inch of Ellen blazed merrily away, and every bit of it was Rudi's fault.

The man was seduction made flesh, and now Mr. Temptation Personified had his hands on her bottom.

Why had she bothered to leave her panties on? They made no difference whatsoever. She could feel the warm texture of his palms right through the thin fabric. As he massaged the soreness away, which surely had not been so bad, the flames skittered around inside her. They collected in her secret places, where they burned higher, wilder.

"May I—?" Rudi's voice went rough and ragged, breaking off before he finished.

"What?" She sounded as ragged as he. If they had that in common, did they have the fires in common, too?

He answered without words, his fingers sliding beneath the elastic of her panties to set off new conflagrations everywhere he touched. Ellen lifted her hips, her good sense utterly burned away. Consequences be damned. She wanted this.

Rudi whisked the useless garment away and cupped her bottom in both his hands. Over the pounding of her heart, Ellen could hear the rasp of Rudi's breath, and she willed his hands to move, to touch her more, to give her the magic she knew they possessed.

He cleared his throat. "What is it you wish of me, my owner? To drive me mad? I have sworn to please you, but I am only a man, made of flesh and blood. I am not a stone."

His hands trembled where they touched her, and yet they did not move, other than a gentle squeeze, as if he still attempted his massage. Rudi spoke of desire, yet he did not act on it. Ellen knew he waited for her decision.

"What do you want me to do?" He sounded almost desperate.

She lifted her head and looked at him over her shoulder. His eyes blazed with dark fire as they locked on hers. No wonder she burned. But she couldn't accuse him of arson, not when she'd been dry fuel to his flame, ready to go up at the first touch.

"Please me," she said, turning on her side and

reaching out with one hand. "Make me feel good. Make love to me."

Rudi took her hand and let her draw him alongside, a smile curving his beautiful lips. "That is a terrifying command to give a man. What if I fail? What if I can merely make you feel 'not so bad'?"

Ellen popped the snaps on the shirt he still wore, feeling underdressed, and set her hand on his sleek, bare chest. "Then you'll just have to try again, won't you?"

He laughed. He caught her hand and pressed a kiss to her palm, the tingle acting like gasoline on those flames. He put her hand back on his chest, wriggled out of his shirt and sent it flying. He picked up her bra where it lay half on Ellen and half on the bed and sent it after his shirt. Then he stopped.

Rudi looked at her, his gaze flashing from her head to her toes and back. Then he urged her over onto her back, and he looked again, slowly. His fingers brushed where he looked, light as a breeze whispering over her skin.

Ellen had been ogled before. She had been looked at with greedy eyes, hungry eyes, envious eyes. Sometimes—once or twice—she had even been naked. She had never had any man look at her like this, as if she was a gift from God, something infinitely precious, to be admired and cherished. There was that word again. Cherished. It was ridiculous, but that was the way Rudi made her feel.

As his hand still swept featherlight over her shoulders, past the side of her breast, over her stomach, touching her everywhere but where she most wanted it, Rudi bent over her. He kissed her lips, a sweet, gentle touch. But Ellen was way past gentle.

Clasping his head between her hands so he couldn't escape, she opened her mouth and invited him to plunder with a quick, hard sweep of her tongue. Rudi didn't need a second invitation. He rolled half on top of her, his shoulders pressing her into the bed as his tongue plunged deep into her mouth and his hand burrowed to cup her bottom. He thrust a jeans-clad leg between hers and pulled her in tight.

He didn't leave much room for Ellen to go hunting for a zipper, but she found it. She had it halfway down before he caught her hand, stopping her.

"Wait." He panted, his forehead resting on hers, his eyes squeezed tight shut. "Do not do that."

Ellen tipped her face up and kissed the end of his nose. "Aren't you forgetting something, slave boy?" she teased.

Rudi groaned. He took two deep breaths and eased her hand away before attempting to speak. "You asked me to make you feel good. And I will, but—I said before, I am only a man. You make me so mad with desire—" He broke off to breathe again.

His words made Ellen a little crazy, too. He wanted her, worse than anyone she'd ever seen. But he was fighting like a demon against his own desires in order to give her what she wanted.

"Please," he said. "If you touch me there, I cannot do as you bid me do. Help me in this one thing."

"Oh, Rudi." Tears gathered in the corners of her eyes.

She'd never heard anything so wonderful, that this

strong, proud man would ask for her help at this moment. She cupped his face in her hands, the sandpaper roughness sweet against her palms, and she looked at him. She looked so deep into his dark eyes, she thought she could see his soul looking back at her. Ellen kissed him.

The minute their lips touched, the flames leapt up again, higher than before, consuming her as they burned. Rudi's hand lay flat against her stomach, warm and heavy. Slowly, so slowly she wanted to scream, his hand moved lower. Her hips rose, acting almost on their own, wanting him to hurry. But he refused.

He kissed his way down her neck, leaving a moist, chill snail trail of Rudi-kisses where he passed. He circled her breasts with those kisses, teasing her with them, the way he teased her below, combing his fingers through her crisp hair.

When she thought she would either scream or pass out, Rudi's mouth closed over the peak of one breast at the same moment his fingers found her hidden nub, and she did scream. Ellen came up off the bed with the explosion. The shocks went through her for eternal minutes as Rudi held her tight, whispering Arabic nothings she hoped were as sweet as they sounded.

Though more than she'd ever known in her life, it still wasn't enough, wasn't all she knew Rudi could give her. She pushed him back, grabbing the waist of his jeans and peeling them off as he hurriedly lowered the zipper the rest of the way. When he was naked, she paused to look at him where he stood beside the bed, glorying in the way he fit together, like that statue of David she'd seen in pictures. Thank goodness he was flesh and blood, rather than stone. Marble was pretty, but not near as much fun.

Ellen opened her arms. "Come here, you."

Rudi smiled and made his traditional obeisance. "At your command, *zahra*."

He paused to retrieve protection, and fit himself into the space she'd made for him, in the circle of her arms and legs, his belly burning against her heat.

He kissed her, deep and passion filled, but this kiss was tender at the same time, and heart-stoppingly sweet. When he ended the kiss, Rudi lifted his head and looked at her, cradling her face between his long-fingered hands. "Are you sure?" he asked.

Such a stupid question didn't deserve an answer. Ellen reached between their bodies, Rudi rising onto his knees to allow her access, and she guided him to her entrance. She locked her ankles behind his back, but before she could tighten them, he surged into her with one powerful thrust.

She was lost, and only Rudi could find her. She was blind, and deaf, oblivious to everything but the man in her arms and the sensations he created as he drove into her. Ellen met each stroke eagerly, feeling the flames leap higher with each one. His muscles bunched and moved under her hands, taut with the effort of his passion. Her cries echoed his, until with a shout, her world came apart again. She heard Rudi's shout a fraction of a second later, felt his body throb and shudder as he reached the same pinnacle. Ellen drifted back to earth, nothing more than white flakes of ash in the breeze.

\* \* \*

He must have dozed. Or perhaps his spirit had simply left his body. Rudi was not certain which, though when he regained his senses, he discovered that he had at least moved to one side so that his weight did not crush Ellen.

Several minutes more passed before he realized what had roused him. A smell, sharp and acrid.

"Smoke!" He scrambled from the bed and rushed into the kitchen to discover the thing he smelled wisping from the edges of the oven. When he opened the door, smoke boiled out, setting the alarm to shrieking.

Ellen appeared in the bedroom doorway, naked, her gun in her hand. "Get down," she ordered.

"It is our dinner." Rudi fanned the smoke away. "Not terrorists." He put on the protective glove and pulled the burned food from the oven as Ellen came to join him.

"Where's the alarm?" she asked.

Rudi pointed to the thing directly overhead, though she surely could have found it by the sound alone. As he set the pan of food on the counter and closed the oven, Ellen pulled a chair over, climbed up on it and pressed the button, switching off the alarm. Then they looked at each other.

Ellen laughed first. "You know, the first time I saw you wearing that oven mitt, I thought you looked awfully cute. But this look is much, much better."

Only then did Rudi realize that the glove was the only garment he wore. He blessed their dinner for burning, for easing that first awkward afterward. He put his gloved arm around her, lifting her off the chair and sliding her down his body to the floor.

"Your attire is also very becoming." He held up her hand with the pistol. "Is this the latest Paris accessory for such occasions?"

She stuck her tongue out at him. Then her face went solemn. "For bodyguards who are so unethical as to get themselves into these occasions, I guess it is."

Rudi sensed her withdrawal and kissed her, trying to put all he felt into the kiss. When she melted against him, he dared to break away for a moment. "Does my owner have any other commands for me? Did I please her?"

Her sly smile made him want to crow in triumph. "It's possible," she said. "But I think we ought to try again, just to be sure."

He began to protest that even a slave needed rest, when he realized that he did not. Ellen proved to be more powerful than any of the concoctions he had heard whispered about among the men at home. Rudi lifted Ellen in his arms and bore her into the bedroom. He paused to deposit the oven mitt and the pistol on the bedside table, then set about fulfilling the instructions of his temporary owner.

Ellen's first thought when she woke up the next morning was that she had been through a beating and left to die. Then she remembered. The horse, the cliff and Rudi.

He still lay in the bed beside her, facedown, smashed into the pillows, arms and legs sprawled as if laying claim to the entire mattress. Just like a man.

She smiled and resisted the temptation to twine one of his sable curls around her finger. She had things to do first. Things she would get to just as soon as a hot shower steamed some of the ache away. Of course, without Rudi's massage, Ellen didn't think she would have been able to move at all. Carefully she slid out of bed and hobbled into the bathroom.

The shower made her body feel almost human again, and the coffee finished the job. Her outsides began to match her insides, which felt superhuman. She couldn't stop smiling, thinking of last night. Rudi was more than she'd ever dreamed possible. His tender seduction had made her believe again. Surely he could never have showed such care for her pleasure if she meant nothing more than a conquest.

She took a quick gulp of the coffee, scalding her tongue, and picked up the phone on the kitchen wall. It might be a little late, but if she resigned now, maybe the fallout wouldn't be too bad.

"Hey, Jan, it's me," she said when the phone was answered in New York.

"Ellen?" The receptionist's voice dropped to a near whisper. "Where have you been? Mr. Campanello's about to start frothing at the mouth."

She frowned. "He knows where I am. Oh, never mind, Jan, just put me through. I'll see if I can calm him down."

"Sheffield!"

Ellen moved the phone away from her ear, but kept it close to her mouth. "Hey, boss."

"Where the hell are you? You're fired, you hear me?" The bellow suddenly ceased and became a near whimper, allowing her to move the earpiece closer.

"How could you do this to me? Those Arab clients have been giving me all kinds of grief, because that prince vanished again. I need you, Sheffield."

"But…" Ellen was confused. "I told Marco I was with Rudi. Rudi said—"

"Who the hell is Rudi?" Campanello was back to bellowing.

Understanding dawned. Rudi wasn't his name. It was just a nickname. She'd thought of him as Rudi for so long that it hadn't occurred to her that she was probably the only person in the world who did.

"Rudi is Rashid. Prince Rashid." She sank into a kitchen chair, hand over her eyes to hide her pain from the squirrels outside the window.

"You're with the prince? That's great! Where are you? Why didn't you report in?"

"I just did. Rudi—that is, Rashid—told me this trip was cleared." Of course it hadn't been. She realized that now.

He had skipped town without telling anyone and had made her an accessory to his flight. He'd taken a risk letting her call in to check, but it had paid off for him. Big time.

"I thought you knew where we were."

"And where is that?"

"New Mexico. A place Ru—Rashid has near the mountains. It's a great safe house." Ellen wiped away the tears, tasting the bitter salt of her own stupidity.

"Good. Looks like we're going to need it. The cops have spotted one of those Qarif terrorists in New York. Here's what I want you to do."

"Wait. I thought I was fired."

"Get outta here. You're not fired. You're a vice president, for cryin' out loud. You're my partner."

"Well, then, I quit."

"You can't quit, either. Partners don't quit on each other. I need you on this one. How long we been together, Sheffield?"

"I don't know. Six years."

"Six years. Practically since you finished the academy and came on the job. Remember? Who was there when you dumped that rat Lowe?"

"You." Oh Lord, was he going to go through the whole litany again?

"Who was there when those jerks in the precinct went after you 'cause you got promoted so fast?"

"You, boss, okay? You don't have to—"

"Who was there when—"

"I got the message, okay?" She broke in on his recital. "It's just—I can't work this job anymore, boss." She tried hard to keep the tears out of her voice, but she didn't succeed. "It wouldn't be ethical."

Silence stretched as Campanello absorbed the meaning behind her words. "Oh, geez, Sheffield. Why'd you have to go and fall in love with the guy?"

"I'm not in love with him." She couldn't be. She was just another notch on the bedpost to him.

"If you slept with him, you're in love with him. I know you. We been through this before. Geez, Sheffield, what happened to my Ice Princess, huh?"

"I don't know." The tears fell harder, let loose by Campanello's rough sympathy. "I lost my mind, I guess."

"Okay, here's what I need you to do—"

"Vic, didn't you hear me? I have to resign from this job."

"Do this first. Then I'll let you quit. You're the only guy I got on the spot, Ellen. I really do need you."

She sighed, swiping uselessly at her eyes. "Okay, boss. But you owe me."

"I always owe you something, Sheffield. What's new?" He paused. "Are you gonna be okay with this?"

Ellen took a deep breath. If Vic Campanello was acting this nice to her, she must really sound in bad shape. "Yeah. I'll make it." She had to.

"Okay, so now can I tell you what I want you to do?"

Her chuckle was feeble, but it was there. Her boss was one of the good guys. "Go ahead."

"We can use this safe house for big brother Ibrahim's family. They think some of those terrorists got out of Qarif, and they think they're probably coming over here. So what I need you to do is this."

As she listened to her instructions, Ellen built back her weak defenses, ready to topple over at the next perfect smile from that snake. To fortify them, she enumerated Rudi's faults. He was arrogant. He was a smart-ass. He had lied to her.

This whole trip had been one big lie. Except for the thing with the well in town. And he'd used that one bit of truth to build all his lies on.

He'd lied when he told her his family knew about the trip. He'd lied when he said her boss knew about it. But the worst, biggest lie was when he had made her believe he cared about her.

He didn't cherish her any more than a lion cherished the zebra it ate. He fussed about her climbing the cliff only because if she fell and killed herself, he wouldn't get his notch. But she had been the one stupid enough to believe every soulful look. And she was still dumb enough to wish they'd been true.

"Stupid," Ellen hissed aloud as she gathered up what little gear she had. "Stupid, stupid, stupid."

She took the clothes. She would need them. But she left the cowboy boots standing beside the bedroom door.

Rudi woke slowly after his night of slavery. He lay cocooned in the sheets for an age, remembering every delicious moment of the experience, before he stretched out an arm, seeking Ellen. The other side of the bed was cool, its occupant long gone.

Slitting an eye open, he saw the sun spots on the floor near the windows, indicating a time shortly past noon. After the night's exertions, he had needed to recoup his energies. The night was over. Now it was time for the day's delights. A shower would make a good beginning. If Ellen would not scrub his back, surely he could convince her to let him scrub hers.

He wrapped the sheet around him in a sort of djellaba and went to find her. "Ellen?"

As he stepped through the bedroom entrance, the door to his house burst open and a riot spilled through it. A riot made up of Ibrahim's four children, their mother, Kalila and, herding them all before him, his brother Ibrahim.

# Eight

"Rashid, are you ready to go to work?" Ibrahim paused near the hotel-suite door and looked back at Rudi.

With a sigh, Rudi rose from the sofa where he'd been sitting, elbows propped on his knees, and threw the folds of his kaffiyeh back from his face. "I *was* working. You took me away from it."

"*Tchah!* You were playing with the woman."

"I. Was. Working." Rudi made each word a complete sentence, knowing even so that his brother would pay no attention.

"Digging holes in the ground is not the work of a prince of Qarif." Ibrahim opened the door and waited for Rudi to go through. "You are a child playing with mud pies. Rashid, you are twenty-eight years old. It is time you stopped playing in the dirt and did the work of a man."

"Digging holes in the ground brought you all of that money you love so much," Rudi said, his anger ready to explode.

"We hired other people to do it. We pay them to get their hands dirty."

"Because none of us know how to do it. Now we know. I know. And I am very good at it."

"You?" Ibrahim's face showed the same affectionate contempt as always. He laughed, cuffing Rudi on the shoulder as he shoved him into the elevator.

The bodyguards followed. Rudi was certain he felt the elevator groan from the weight of muscle and weapons.

"You are good at causing your father's gray hairs and your mother's tears," Ibrahim said, almost sadly. "And at causing a great deal of trouble for me. We should never have allowed you to go to that ridiculous university in Texas. What was it? Texas Engineering—"

"Texas Tech University," Rudi corrected automatically. On the west Texas plains, it had reminded him a little of Qarif's open spaces. Those had been the happiest years of his adult life, because he had been free to study whatever interested him and to make friends of whomever he chose. Those friends had given him his nickname, calling him Rudolph Valentino when they learned his father was a sheikh. It had quickly been shortened to Rudi. He preferred the nickname, because he knew that those who used it saw the man that he was, rather than the man they wished him to be.

As they got into the car, Ibrahim began talking numbers. Rudi understood numbers, but he understood them when related to things like pressure, or the tensile strength of a certain thickness of steel. He had no interest in high finance or manipulating money that existed only in theory. Money was to spend in building things. Or in buying gifts for beautiful women.

*Why had Ellen left the boots?* In the uproar surrounding the installation of Ibrahim's family in the ranch house, and the flight back to New York, Rudi had had no time to think about what it might mean. But now he had more than enough time.

The instant Rudi had seen his brother's family invading what had been his private sanctuary, the one place where he could have peace from his family's demands, he had known that Ellen had discovered his prevarications. *Call it by its true name. You lied to her.* Ibrahim's presence was her return volley in this game they had played.

He understood Ellen's anger upon discovering that neither his family nor her employer had known where they had gone. Her move had been quite clever. Diabolical. His secret hideaway was secret no longer. When he had learned the reasons behind the children and Kalila coming to the ranch, he had no more objections. They would indeed be far safer in the mountains.

So why had she left the boots? Surely she did not think he had offered them as payment for the gift of her body. Had he not shown her how he treasured her? Did not his care for her pleasure before his own tell her how very precious she was to him?

The surprised delight on her face as he introduced her to the wonders of her senses should have told him of her inexperience, but he had been so overwhelmed himself. He found it difficult to believe of a woman in her culture with her beauty, but now, thinking back, he knew it was so.

What if that inexperience had led her to believe that the whole of his intent in bringing her to his home had been seduction? Could she think he cared nothing more for her than that, think he had no more use for her, now he had made love to her? Did she think everything that had happened was merely part of the game?

It was time for the game to end. Everything had suddenly become all too real.

"Stop the car." Rudi reached forward and rapped on the glass separating them from the driver.

"Don't be ridiculous," Ibrahim said as the glass descended and the car slowed. "Drive on."

"I said, stop the car," Rudi repeated. He reached for the door and opened it while the car was still moving.

"Stop the car!" Ibrahim grabbed for him, but Rudi was already out of the car and striding down the street.

When he looked back, Rudi saw Frank and Omar trotting after him. He sighed, then slowed to wait for them.

"Have you come to take me back?"

"No." Frank was panting. "Just stay with you, is all he said."

"Good." Rudi turned, his robes swirling about him, and walked on.

Ellen stared at the paperwork on her desk, trying to make sense of what she saw, but it was no good. She'd left her mind at home in bed. Or maybe she'd left it in New Mexico. On second thought, that had to be the answer. Because while in New Mexico, she had certainly lost her mind.

She could think of no other reason for doing the things she'd done. She had simply lost her mind. And when it had gone missing, her body had needed very little convincing to believe that Rudi was different, when he was just the same as all the other men in the world.

The intercom buzzed at the same time her office door flew open. Rudi strode through it, looking like something out of *Lawrence of Arabia,* with Jan the receptionist and two bodyguards on his heels. Dear Lord, she was not ready for this.

"I'm sorry—" Jan said.

"Leave us." Rudi cut her off, his peremptory tone and the brusque wave of his hand setting Ellen's teeth on edge.

She'd known all along this was the man he was. Why did it bother her now?

Omar backed out of the room, but Frank and Jan hovered.

"Ellen?" Jan said. "I couldn't stop him. I tried…"

Rudi turned and glared, but they held their ground,

waiting for Ellen's decision. She took a deep breath. She didn't want this confrontation, but one thing she had learned about Rudi: The man was as stubborn as a rock. If she didn't talk to him now, he'd probably kidnap her again.

"It's all right," she said. "I'll talk to him."

The minute the door closed, leaving the entourage on the far side, Rudi's expression changed. Gone was the imperious autocrat, and in its place Ellen saw the tender lover of her nightmares.

"Why did you leave so precipitously?" He crossed the room toward her.

Ellen held her position, telling herself that she was not using her desk as a barricade to hide behind. Good thing, because it made a lousy barricade. Rudi walked around it and dropped to one knee beside her chair.

"We could have traveled together," he said.

Ellen shrugged, trying to shrug off the pain with an air of unconcern. "I thought it was better that way. I figured you'd had all the togetherness you wanted."

The puzzled crease between his eyebrows made her want to touch it, to caress it away. She made her hands into fists and pushed her chair back, hoping it would help her resist the impulse.

"How can you say that, *zahra?*" he said. "You know—"

"Stop calling me that!" She cut off his speech, springing out of the chair in her agitation. "I don't own you, okay? I never did."

Rudi frowned up at her, still down on one knee. "What do you think *zahra* means?"

"I don't know." Ellen glanced at Rudi as he rose

to his feet. Maybe if he turned that headdress around so it covered his face she might be able to think straight.

"No, you do not. But what do you *believe* that it means?"

"Owner. Mistress. Slave driver. Simon Legree." She threw her hands up and retreated to the opposite side of her small office. "I have no idea."

"*Zahra* means flower." He came around to the front of the desk, following her.

"I'm not a stupid flower. I don't wilt in the sun." She moved toward the slice of window she shared with the office next door and stared out at the pigeons. "Stop following me."

"Stop running away." Rudi halted in the middle of the room. "The flowers in Qarif do not wilt in the sun, either. They turn their faces to it, welcoming the light. They bloom from strength, with deep roots and proud branches."

Ellen took a deep breath, trying to steel herself against his seductive lies. He had charm by the bucketful, but that's all it was, charm that evaporated when you looked closely.

"Look, Rudi." She turned back to face him and forgot what she was going to say. Why did he have to look at her like that?

"Yes, Ellen?" he prompted.

She took a deep breath and huffed it out. This was going to be hard. "Look. Either tell me why you came here this morning, or let me get back to work."

"I came to see you. To learn why—" He broke off and looked down at his feet. "Actually, I do understand that you were angry because I allowed you to believe the trip had been cleared by your employer. I came…'' He looked up at her then, his eyes locked onto hers. "I came to ask your forgiveness."

Ellen blinked. *Damn him.* She could not let him do this to her again. "Okay. You're forgiven. Anything else?" She stepped toward her desk and picked up a piece of paper, hoping she was holding it right side up, because she couldn't read a thing on it.

"No, that is not all." He plucked the paper from her fingers and laid it on her desk. "Have dinner with me tonight. Have lunch with me now. Have breakfast with me tomorrow morning."

Pain dug spiky fingers into her heart. Why did it still hurt her? "No," she said.

Rudi's hand froze in midair, stopped as he reached for her hand. "No?"

"You heard me the first time." She eased another step away from him.

"But…why?"

Ellen busied herself, straightening papers into semineat stacks. "We had a great time in New Mexico, Rudi. But it's over. We're back in New York, and it's time to move on."

"I do not wish to move on." He caught her arm and turned her toward him. "It is not over. I want to be with you, Ellen. When I am alone, I am half a man. I did not know it until I met you."

She laughed, forcing the sound past the threatening tears. "Do they teach 'How To Use Words for Seduction' in school where you come from? That's a real pretty speech. How many times have you used it?''

"Never. Not before this moment. It is true. It is how I feel. Marry me, Ellen. I cannot bear to be without you."

Shock raced through her, staggered her. Ellen braced a hand against her desk. When she looked at Rudi, she saw the same stunned expression she knew had to be on her own face. He had not expected the words, either.

"You don't mean that," she said.

"I do. Marry me." He said it again. He caught her hand before she could pull it back and held on tight, carrying it to his lips, where he pressed a kiss to the back. "Marry me."

Gathering all her strength, both physical and emotional, she yanked her hand from his grasp. "Rudi, be reasonable. We both know you don't want to marry me."

"Stop saying that. You do not know what I want."

"Do you?"

"Who better? Of course I know."

Ellen circled to the front of her desk again, seeking room to pace. "I don't think so. You don't have a clue who I am. How long have we known each other, when you add it all up? Three days?"

"It seems I have always known you."

"I'm not sure it's even three days. Rudi, you just want what you see." She waved her hand along her body. "But this isn't me."

"It is you," he said. "But only a tiny part."

"It's not me at all. But it's all you see. I won't be your trophy, Rudi. I am not some rich man's toy."

"Is that what you think I want?" Rudi snatched off his headdress and shook it in her face, the gold cords rattling faintly. "This is all that you see when you look at me, is it not? Do not accuse me of your own faults."

He threw the cloth across the room, then ripped off the robe he wore and sent it sailing after the head-dress, standing before her wearing an open-necked white dress shirt and gray slacks. "I am only a man who has done nothing more than ask a woman to marry him."

Taken aback by all the flying fabric, Ellen had to pause to marshal her thoughts. "Why?" she said.

Rudi frowned. "What?"

"It's a simple question. Just one word. You want a couple more words? Fine. Why do you want to marry me? And don't say because you love me, be-cause I won't believe it. People don't fall in love overnight. They fall in lust. That's all this is."

"It is not." He spaced the words out, his hands clenching again and again, as if he fought violent pas-sions.

"I think it is. We had us one fine case of lust."

"You are wrong, Ellen. What we had was far more than mere lust."

Why did he have to keep insisting? "Well, I think I'm right." She rubbed her temples, a headache be-ginning to throb behind her eyes. She had to end this, get her life back.

"Look, Rudi, I'm not going to marry you." She

retreated behind her desk. "I suggest that you sit down and think real hard about your life. You decide what it is you really want, and why you want it."

She paused, but she couldn't stop there. Maybe she was the world's biggest idiot for wanting to believe that at least some of what Rudi said might possibly be true, but she couldn't help it.

"And when you get it all straight in your head," she said, somehow forcing the tears back, "if you still have a place for me in that life you decide you want, come back and see me, and tell me why you want me there. And maybe I'll have a different answer."

Rudi took a deep breath. He rubbed a hand over his mouth before looking up at her. "You will not marry me." It wasn't a question.

"No." She just couldn't take the risk. Not now.

He walked across the room and stared at his robes. "Who was the man who hurt you so badly? The man who wanted to own you for his plaything?"

Cold chills shivered down her back. Who had told him? "What makes you think there was a man?"

"Tell me his name, Ellen." Fire flashed from his eyes as he glared at her.

"Davis Lowe. Wh-why? Why do you want to know?"

"So I can know it, while I decide whether I will kill him."

He hesitated a moment, then crossed the room in two steps and caught her by both arms. Before she could even gasp, he kissed her, not with fierce passion as she might have expected, but deep, slow, wet, and so tender she could have wept with his sweetness.

When he ended the kiss she had not made up her mind whether to push him away or pull him closer.

"And that," he said, "is so that you will know what it is you have discarded." With that, he threw his robes over his arm and strode from her office. Frank and Omar trotted after him.

When the coast was clear, Jan scurried back and peeped through the still-open door to Ellen's office. "Are you okay? What did he want?"

Would Rudi really kill Davis? Maybe she ought to call and warn him. Or maybe not. If any man deserved killing...

Oh, good grief. Davis hadn't done anything worth killing him over, nothing any other man didn't do every day of his life. Of course Rudi wasn't going to kill Davis.

"Ellen?" Jan rapped her knuckles on the door.

"Hmm?" Ellen shook her head, trying to unscramble her brain.

"So what did he want? The cute sheikh."

"Oh." Ellen sank slowly into her chair. "Nothing really. He asked me to marry him. I said no."

"You turned him down?" Jan's squeal of shock reached dog-whistle pitch.

"That's what I said. You want to go after him? Be my guest."

Ellen picked up a notebook full of notes about concert security and leafed through it. She heard the door shut when Jan finally left, and still she couldn't decipher the meaning of anything she'd written. Even though her life was now officially back to normal, with no sheikhs wreaking havoc in it, she couldn't shake the feeling that something had just gone very wrong.

The rest of the day Rudi walked the streets of New York. Omar and Frank walked a few paces behind him, Omar carrying the clothing Rudi had discarded.

Rudi thought as he walked. He thought about the things Ellen had said to him. He thought about the quarrel with Ibrahim that morning, and about all the other quarrels on all the other mornings. He thought about what he wanted for his life.

He had not gone to Ellen intending to ask for marriage. He had wanted only dinner, time spent together, the pleasure of her company. But when she talked of moving on, of ending things, sudden desperation had overtaken him. He could not imagine life without Ellen in it. Sheer panic had brought on his proposal.

Did he love her? Rudi had no idea. He had never thought much about love. He did not know whether he knew what love was, not love between a man and a woman. But the things he had told Ellen were true, and he had not told her half of what he felt.

Without her, he felt hollow. As if he had lost a part of himself. He needed her beside him, the way flowers needed rain and sun and earth to hold their roots. If that was love, Rudi did not like it much.

But perhaps Ellen was right. This feeling might be mere infatuation. If he did not see her, it might go away. The hollow inside him might fill itself, and he would again be whole without her.

How could it fill itself when he hadn't known he was half-empty until he met Ellen? How could he be whole when he lived a life he hated, when he hated the man he was while living that life? He could not ask any woman to share such a life, with such a man.

Rudi walked, and he thought. Until the streetlights went on. Until Frank made a cell phone call, huffing and hobbling several paces behind Omar. Until the car pulled up at the curb and Rudi got in, his decision made.

Two days passed in Ellen's new Rudi-free life. The problem was that, although Rudi's physical presence was conspicuously missing, his mental presence refused to leave her alone. She missed him with a bone-deep ache that worried her.

On the third day Jan buzzed on the intercom and announced that ''a Mr. Eben Socker is here to see you,'' giving Rudi's family name her own unique pronunciation.

Ellen couldn't repress the thrill that ran through her. Rudi had come back. But the thrill turned to depression when she went to her door and saw Ibrahim ibn Saqr striding down the corridor.

''How can I help you, sir?'' she asked, offering him the good chair.

She stayed behind her desk, feeling the need for all the authority, bogus or not, she could get. No wonder Rudi occasionally felt the need to slip free now and again, with this guy pulling the strings. Big brother intimidated her, and she didn't intimidate easily.

''Please, call me Ibrahim.'' He flashed a smile that was a pale imitation of Rudi's megawatt grin. ''Our family name is often difficult for those who do not speak Arabic.''

''All right.'' She laced her fingers together in the precise center of her desk. ''Ibrahim. How can I help you?''

''I wanted to pay this visit to point out a number of things to you.''

''I see.'' The man made her want to grind her teeth, and he hadn't even reached his point yet.

''My brother Rashid appears to harbor some affection toward you. I thought it best if I made it clear that nothing could come of such an attachment. Our culture makes it difficult for a Western woman to adapt, and—''

''Hold it right there, Ibrahim.'' Ellen knew steam had to be coming from her ears. Ibrahim looked a little steamed himself by her interruption, but he would be grateful when she explained. She had to control her tendency toward smart-mouthing with this one, however.

''I'm sorry,'' she said. ''I don't mean to be rude, but your, um, clarification is coming a little late.''

''Oh?'' He steepled his fingers. Rudi had learned ''arrogant'' from one of the best.

''Your brother proposed to me two days ago.''

''I see.''

Ellen knew she shouldn't enjoy watching the man deflate as much as she did. ''Don't worry, sir. I turned him down.'' She told him the good news quickly, to make up for that guilty enjoyment.

''You did?'' Ibrahim looked astonished and relieved at the same time. Then he studied her with renewed appraisal. "Perhaps you are wiser than I thought."

Ellen rose to escort him out, before she strangled him with his power tie. "Did you ever think that maybe Rudi—Rashid is old enough to know his own mind by now? If you keep trying to push him into being somebody he's not, you might wind up pushing him away altogether."

Ibrahim glared at her, a thing he must have perfected sometime in his past. "Rashid is my brother, and by your own words, no concern of yours. Your opinions are not wanted."

"Sure." She offered her hand. "Good luck."

He scowled another moment, as if unsure whether her words meant something more than they appeared to. Then he shook her hand and departed.

The next Monday, Campanello came into Ellen's office. "Sheffield, we need you."

Ellen immediately went on her guard. Her boss never came to her, never said those words in that tone of voice unless he wanted something from her he didn't think he would get. "For what?"

"Prince Rashid's on the lam again."

"And what business is that of mine?" She took pride in the fact that her voice sounded cool even as her heart did panicky acrobatics.

"Okay, I know you resigned from the Qarif job." Campanello started up with that pitiful tone, the one that would make her agree to almost anything just to get him to stop it. "But I really need you, Sheffield. I got the big guy sitting in my office about to blow a gasket. He's convinced you plotted something with baby brother. Maybe he thinks you've got him tucked up your sleeve or something, but he's giving me all kinds of grief.''

"This is my problem because...?'' Her heart was still bouncing off all her other internal organs, churning things up in there until her entire abdominal cavity felt tied in knots.

"Come on, Ellen. *Please.*'' He shut her office door. "You want me to beg? Is that what you want? I'm already begging. You want I should get down on my knees?'' Vic Campanello started down slowly to his creaky, forty-year-old, ex-cop knees. He truly was desperate.

"Damn it, Vic, don't do this to me. Get up.'' Ellen stomped around her desk and hauled him back upright. "You manipulative weasel. If I didn't like you so much, I'd hate you.''

"I'm sorry, Ellen.'' He held on to her hand, watching her closely with those knowing cop's eyes. He'd learned to read her too well, back when they'd been partners, before he bought the business and hired her away from the police department with a big title and puny salary. "I know this hurts you, and you know I wouldn't ask if I didn't have to. I'll keep your involvement as limited as possible. You pinpoint, we'll reel him in. I won't ask you to be the bait.''

"It wouldn't work anyway.'' She shook her head as she lifted her gray suit jacket off the coatrack and slipped it on. "I have a bad feeling about this one, partner. He's not going to be easy to find.''

"Then I hope your intuition is wrong. Because two

more of those terrorists were spotted in town over the weekend.''

Fear drew its icy finger down her spine, stopping her heart in midflip. Rudi had picked a terrible time to skip.

# Nine

It took a good half hour to calm Ibrahim down and convince him that Ellen had had nothing to do with Rudi's disappearance. Finally they got the story out of him. During a Sunday-afternoon visit to Bloomingdale's in full Arabic dress, Rudi's bodyguards had gotten a few paces away in the crowd of shoppers. When they'd caught up with him, they'd discovered another man behind the kaffiyeh.

After some confused dashing around, Frank had realized that Rudi had borrowed a trick from a movie and paid three or four men to come into the store, dressed in kaffiyeh and djellaba, and act as decoys. By the time the bodyguards had caught on, Rudi had vanished.

Over the next forty-eight hours Ellen and Campanello learned that Rudi had gathered several thousand dollars in cash during the past week, and that he had not left New York by air, train, or bus. Nor had he rented a car.

Time wore on. They visited one hotel after another—fancy expensive ones, middle-class ordinary ones, even fleabags. No one recognized Rudi from his picture.

By the time the second week rolled around, Ellen was firmly convinced Rudi was no longer in New York. She didn't think he'd left the country, but she had no logical reason for either belief. She called Buckingham again and again, talking to Rudi's sister-in-law, to Annabelle, the mayor, the bodyguards, to anyone Rudi might have contacted. But none of them knew anything.

The terrorists had vanished as completely as Rudi, as if they had shown themselves merely in order to inform their prey of their presence. Now Ibrahim and his bodyguards wasted half their time looking over their shoulders, and the other half worrying about the family hidden in Buckingham.

Late in the fourth week of the search, Ellen stared at her computer screen, her eyes burning, unable to read anything displayed there. She blinked, and the words became momentarily clear, then blurred again. It wasn't late, only about eight o'clock. Her eyes shouldn't be so tired.

She swiped the back of her hand across one eye, and it came away wet. Her cheeks were wet, too. Both of them.

*Because you're crying, you idiot. Don't be so sur-*

*prised.* The fear and worry she'd been denying surged up like a tidal wave and dragged her under. Unable to fight it any longer, Ellen folded her arms on her desk, laid her head on them and cried like a terrified child.

What if her search led the terrorists to Rudi? What if they had no clue at all where he might be, but her poking and probing told them where to look? Maybe she should stop the searching, just let him go. He had a right to live the life he chose.

But what if she stopped looking and they found him anyway? What if they found him before she did? Rudi was alone. He would make a perfect target for these terrorists, these cowards who had threatened the family members of Qarif's ruler, hoping to force him to accede to their demands.

An image flashed into her mind of a body falling. She thrust it away. Another image followed, one she couldn't banish as easily, one that had haunted her for more than a month. In it, Rudi laughed, head back and teeth flashing, his whole body caught up in his laughter, full of life and his joy in living it.

This time, when the pain and longing swept over her, Ellen gave up. She couldn't fight it anymore. She was in love with Rudi. Hopelessly, desperately lost in love.

She'd thrown away her chance at happiness. He was lost to her. But the thought of the world without Rudi in it somewhere hurt so badly, it had shown her how deep she'd fallen. She had to find him because he had to live. The terrorists could not find him first.

It was not an option. Rudi needed protection, no matter how much he resented the presence of bodyguards.

He had been gone almost a month. Even living frugally, he would be running out of the money he'd taken with him. Ibrahim had told them that on all his previous disappearances, Rudi had returned to the fold when his money ran out. Ibrahim remained confident Rudi would do so again this time. The huge amount of cash Rudi had taken with him had been Ibrahim's primary concern because it would allow for a longer absence. Ellen, however, believed that this exit was different. She was convinced that Rudi had no intention of coming back, not any time soon.

She dialed into a new database and put in her request. Rudi would have to find employment if he wanted to live on his own. He might even try to find work in one of the fields for which he'd been trained. She left her search running and headed home for another night of sleepless ceiling-staring.

The weekend played havoc with Ellen's search and her peace of mind. No one was in at any of the offices or search companies she called. Rudi remained missing. Finally, Monday morning, she got her hands on the documents she wanted, the names of all the pipeline and drilling companies nationwide.

There were hundreds of them, but not the thousands she'd feared. Ellen picked up the phone and began to call, beginning with those closest to New York, asking if they'd hired any new engineers in the past month, making up lies to explain her questions. If a human resources department proved reluctant, she'd change her voice and make up new lies when she called back.

Another week was half over when a helpful assistant to the assistant personnel director for a pipeline company in Tulsa, Oklahoma, told Ellen that a Mr. Rudolph al Mukhtar had started work there only two weeks before. Al Mukhtar was in the list of Rudi's names. Ellen wasn't positive, but it was the best clue she had to Rudi's whereabouts. The only clue.

She thanked the assistant politely as she noted the name and address of the company on a sticky pad, then hung up the phone. Ellen snatched up her purse and headed out the door, barely remembering to remove her headset before it ripped itself off her head.

"Tell Campanello I have a lead," she said to Jan as she hurried past. "I'll call him when I know something."

At her apartment, Ellen packed a small bag, making sure all her permits were in order to check her weapons onto the plane, both the big SIG-Sauer automatic and the smaller Colt revolver. Her phone rang while she was packing, but she let her boss curse at her answering machine. She was going to Tulsa no matter what he said. Letting him rant directly would only make his blood pressure worse.

She had to wait an hour at Kennedy for a flight to Dallas-Fort Worth, which would connect her with a puddle jumper to Tulsa, arriving at 10:00 p.m.

By the time she arrived, she was exhausted. Ellen checked in to a motel not far from Rudi's possible new employer.

Patience at an end, she called directory assistance,

but Mr. al Mukhtar's new phone number was unlisted. Even if she had the number, she couldn't call. What would she say?

*Rudi, I was a fool.*

To which he would say, "And your point is?" He would say, "Too late. You had your chance." Or maybe he'd say, "No, you were right. I only wanted your body. Don't bother me anymore." Or he might damn her for betraying him again and vanish. Again.

She wanted to find him right now, see with her own eyes that he was all right, know that this Rudolph in Tulsa, Oklahoma, was her own Rudi and not someone else's. But she had nowhere to begin except his work, where he wouldn't be until morning.

Ellen forced herself to shower and pick at a bacon, lettuce and tomato sandwich from room service. Then she lay down in the big empty motel-room bed and stared at the crack of neon-pink light seeping through the curtains.

By six o'clock she thought she might have slept two hours with all her tossing and turning. Further pursuit of sleep seemed futile, so she got out of bed, dressed and was in her rental car in the lot across the street from Rudi's possible place of business by seven o'clock. As the hour got closer to eight, the building parking lot filled up with people coming in to work: tall, lean men with weathered cowboy faces, young pretty women in brightly colored suits, balding men in wire-frame glasses and pen-filled pockets.

Then an electric shock ran through Ellen as she recognized the walk, the short, dark curls of the man striding into the building. It was Rudi. She'd know that back, that backside anywhere, whether draped in charcoal worsted wool as it was now, or in nothing at all.

Heat rushed her at that errant thought. She was here to protect Rudi, not jump his bones, she reminded herself. The reminder made her pick up her phone.

"Campanello," he said when Jan rang her through.

"I found him," Ellen said.

"Where?"

"Tulsa, Oklahoma. Gainfully employed with the Atcheson Pipeline Company."

"Don't tell me you're in Oklahoma."

"Okay, I won't tell you."

"Shut up, Sheffield. Does he know you've made him?"

"No." Ellen slid the seat back in her car, wanting to close her eyes for five minutes. But she didn't dare.

"Okay, I'll have a team there by tonight."

"Vic..."

"Yeah?"

Ellen sighed, not sure what she'd wanted to say. "Never mind."

"Don't give me that. You called me Vic. You always got somethin' to say when you call me Vic instead of boss, so you might as well just spit it out."

"I'm worried what will happen if we just swoop in and scoop him up. This isn't like all those other times his brother told us about. Most of those times he was probably at his place in New Mexico, but he can't go there to get away anymore, can he? He never used a different name before, never got an actual job."

"What are you saying, Sheffield? You think he's going to bolt if he spots you?"

She took a deep breath. "I don't know. Maybe. If he doesn't run the minute he sees us, then sometime after he's pulled back in, he'll vanish again. And the next time he runs, he'll be more careful, he'll plan better. Next time, we might not find him."

"Next time, it might not be our job to find him."

"True."

"Big brother's paying our bill."

"Also true. But can't we just watch him here in Tulsa? You could talk Ibrahim into leaving him alone. Rudi's not hurting anything. He's just working for this pipeline company."

"Sheffield, you met the guy. Do you really think anybody can talk big brother into anything?"

"You're right. Stupid idea." She slumped lower in her seat.

"Okay, okay. I'll try. I owe you. No guarantees. And I'm sending Frank and Tom out on the next flight. You can't watch him twenty-four seven." Campanello paused. "Ellen, I'll wait till tomorrow to tell big brother you found him, if you want, if you got something to straighten out with the guy."

"Thanks, Vic. I appreciate the thought, but don't bother." She wiped away a stray tear. "There's nothing to straighten out."

"You sure?"

"Yeah."

About mid morning Ellen got a coffee from the bakery in the strip mall where she was parked and sat on the hood of the rental to drink it. At lunchtime she saw Rudi appear among a small knot of people, laughing and talking to a pretty red-haired woman in the group as they all walked to a car and got in together. Ellen ground her teeth against the wave of jealous pain besetting her and managed to get her car started in time to follow them to a Mexican restaurant several blocks away. They all went inside, the woman virtually attached to Rudi's side.

*What did you expect? You threw him back.*

Ellen told her conscience to shut up as she parked in the store lot adjoining the restaurant. No suspicious vehicles followed, either to the restaurant or back again, but still Ellen waited until Rudi had returned inside the office building before driving up to the take-out window of the Burger Doodle on the corner. She hoped Frank and Tom would arrive soon. Her sleepless nights were beginning to catch up with her.

Ellen woke with a start to someone rapping on her car window.

A plump woman with a face younger than her steel-gray hair peered in at her. ''Are you okay?'' she shouted through the window. ''Can I get you some help?''

A frantic look at the clock told Ellen it was a few minutes after five. Panic set in. She got out of the car and scanned the building entrance across the way.

''I'm fine.'' She spared a quick smile for the wonderful woman who'd awakened her. ''I just fell asleep. Stayed up too late last night.''

''If you're sure...'' The woman turned away.

"I was just waiting for someone." Ellen walked to the curb, trying to see the whole parking lot. Decorative shrubbery blocked much of her view.

People streamed out of the building, heading to their vehicles, lining up at the drive waiting to exit onto the busy street. Ellen spotted the redhead climbing into a pickup, alone. *Good.*

She started across the street, running through a short gap in traffic to the center turning lane. Waiting for a break in the westbound traffic, Ellen saw Rudi leave the building. He walked down the steps and along the sidewalk to the side of the building as cars and pickups whizzed by between them. Twice she started to cross, only to be thwarted. Rudi got farther and farther away.

Finally the light changed at the corner, and she darted across, swerving between cars pulling onto the street. She saw a blue panel van sitting alongside the low hedge separating the parking lot from the sidewalk and glanced in the front window as she pushed her way between the bushes.

Two men, clean shaven, black hair, dark complexions, wearing blue work shirts. She cataloged them automatically in her mental files, still her practice after three years away from the police force. Her primary focus remained on Rudi.

He walked across the drive, heading toward an isolated car, keys in his hand. Ellen broke into a trot.

"Rudi!" She called to him. *What was she doing?* She'd just talked Campanello into trying to talk Ibrahim into leaving Rudi alone. She'd intended to watch from a distance, not chase him down in a parking lot. She had lost her mind yet again.

He turned. The smile faded from his face when he saw her, and Ellen's jog slowed to a walk, then came to a halt. She'd killed his smile.

"Ellen?" Rudi took a step toward her, uncertainty in his expression. But the longer he looked at her, the more his face closed down. "I will not go back."

"I had to tell them where you were, Rudi. I had to." She forced her feet to move again, to walk toward him. "Your brother was on the verge of a heart attack, he was so worried about you."

"Ibrahim always looks like that." Rudi glanced away briefly, before capturing Ellen's gaze again. "It is no good. I cannot live a life that I hate. I hate the man I was becoming—useless, good-for-nothing. A waste of time, my own and everyone else's."

"No, Rudi. You're not like that." She stopped near the back of the car where he stood, its neighbors already gone home.

"I was becoming like that," he said. "If you put handcuffs on me and chain my legs together, you can carry me onto the plane and take me back. But I will not stay. It has become a prison to me."

"I'm not the one you need to be saying this to. I believe you. But you have to come back and tell your brother. Tell your father."

"What does it matter to you? You care only because you are paid to care. Without my father's money, you would watch me die in the street and not lift a finger."

"That's not true!"

"Isn't it?"

As he turned away, keys out to unlock the car, the image of the men in the blue van sprang to mind, and she felt the internal click as a pattern slid into place. The men matched the pictures she'd seen of the terrorists, though they'd shaved off their mustaches as a disguise. Their attention had been focused in this direction, as if anticipating…

"Don't touch the car!" Ellen leapt as she shouted, shoving Rudi onto the grassy median and rolling with him to the far side. Time seemed to slow. Her heart pounded five times, six. Then the bomb blast hit her, knocking her head into the concrete. Everything went gray and blurry.

The explosion startled Rudi. Then it made him angry.

He lifted his head, hoping to see a car or a license plate, and he saw two men getting out of a van, guns in their hands. Rising to a crouch, he glanced at Ellen. She struggled, her legs moving feebly, and she groped in the small of her back, but could not grasp her weapon. She was injured.

Rudi drew the big pistol in her stead and fired at the onrushing men. Wishing he had spent more time at the practice range during his last training session with the military, he fired again as he helped Ellen up and guided her behind a pickup truck in the next aisle.

"Ellen, where are you hurt?" He raked his gaze over her, looking for blood.

"What?" She frowned at him, then flinched as a short burst of gunfire ricocheted around them.

It cut off abruptly, and Rudi could hear the terrorists arguing. He peered over the truck, hearing sirens screaming in the near distance, and saw one of the men gesturing back toward the getaway vehicle, while the other kept swinging his machine gun in Rudi's direction. They had brought harm to Ellen.

Bracing the heavy gun, very similar to his own, on the hood of the truck, he took careful aim and fired at the more belligerent of the two. The man dropped like a rock.

The other turned to run. Rudi fired a warning shot and called for him to stop. "I did not kill your friend," he said in his own language. "But I will kill you. You know that I can."

The man halted. He dropped his weapon and raised his hands in the air, head hunched down as if expecting the fatal shot at any moment. Just then, what seemed to be twoscore police cars came screaming into the parking lot. Rudi laid Ellen's gun on the truck and lifted his hands as well.

"Rudi." Ellen tugged at his pants leg.

"Yes, Ellen?" He knelt beside her, cupping her cheek for support when she did not seem able to hold her head up on her own.

"Are you hurt?"

"No, *zahra*. I am well. Where are you hurt?"

She touched her head, and now Rudi could see the swelling, huge and red, above her temple. He started up to call for the ambulance, but Ellen caught his shirt collar and tugged him back.

"I was so worried," she whispered. The tears in her voice and pooled in her eyes shocked Rudi. He did not understand.

"Because you are paid to protect me," he said, trying to make things clear in his mind.

"Because I'd rather die than let anything happen to you." She tugged at his collar again. "Are you sure you're not hurt?"

"I am not hurt, my Ellen. But you are." He stood, lifting her in his arms. The authorities waited, allowed him to carry Ellen to the nearby ambulance, apparently informed of his role in the incident by the onlookers now crowding around.

Rudi identified Ellen. He identified himself only as Rudolph al Mukhtar. No one here knew any different, other than Ellen and the two criminals. There would be time enough later for the police to know his true name. He rode in the ambulance with her to the hospital, where he gave his statement to the police. He allowed the medical personnel to tend to his scrapes and cuts.

The two terrorists captured were only a small part of the gang of thugs ranged against his father. They would provide valuable information, particularly since they had set off their bomb in Oklahoma, a state with good reason to hate bombers. But it would take time to capture the entire group. And for all of that time, if he allowed Ellen to remain near him, she would be in terrible danger. She had already risked her life to save his. By her own words, she would do it again, as a matter of honor at the very least.

Ellen thought it was her job to protect him. But she was wrong.

When the doctors released her, mostly because she refused to stay "just in case," Ellen went looking for Rudi. All of the things she'd said to him, all of the things she hadn't let Ibrahim say were still true. Nothing had changed. But still, she had to see him, had to see with her own eyes that he was unharmed. She found him with Frank and Tom, his bodyguards, in the waiting room.

"We waited to see if you needed a lift to the hotel," Frank said, getting to his feet. "Besides, the prince wouldn't leave. We didn't figure it would be a good idea to knock him out and carry him off after these guys just tried to blow him up."

Ellen scarcely heard him, all her attention was so focused on Rudi. He looked worn, almost haggard, with circles under his eyes and an incipient beard shadowing his face. Then he saw her and smiled, and all her good, logical intentions vanished like fog in the sunshine, especially when she saw the worry tucked behind the smile. Could he truly care for her?

"Are you well, *zahra?*" His hand rose toward the bump on her head, paused when he glanced at the bodyguards, then retreated.

"Well enough that they turned me loose." Ellen tried to make her smile big enough to encompass all three men, but she failed. It was for Rudi alone.

"The police found your car and brought your bag." Rudi took it from a ferociously scowling Frank and handed it to her. "The rental company will pick up the car in the morning."

Ellen glanced at Frank. He was still scowling. Why?

Rudi took her arm, drawing her attention back. "Are you sure you feel well enough to return to the hotel?"

"I'm fine." The light-headed feeling had nothing to do with banging her head on concrete. It was all Rudi.

His arm beneath hers for support, he directed her steps to the door, to the large sedan waiting outside. Inside the car, Rudi urged her head over onto his shoulder. "Rest," he said.

She let her eyes close. Frank and Tom would watch, would give her time to think. But all she could think of was Rudi: her terror as he turned to open the car door, her relief at finding him safe, her content-ment at this moment nestled close to him, with his hand resting on her knee.

His hand on her knee. The touch warmed all the cold, frightened places inside her. It loosened the knots of worry and set her free. So what if it hurt when he left her? She was hurting now, in her heart much more than her banged-up head. And maybe he wouldn't leave.

She'd sent him away before. Maybe if she asked for a second chance, showed him she believed in him, maybe he would stay. Even if only for a day, that was more than she had now.

Ellen curved her hand around his muscular arm and

snuggled closer. She could feel Rudi's smile against her forehead.

"Are you comfortable, *zahra?*"

"Mmm." She didn't want to waste energy in talking. Not just yet.

Sitting so close reminded her of that one wonderful night, when she'd been able to believe in fairy tales for a few short hours. A night when Rudi had made all her most secret dreams come true. And she wondered.

According to those who knew, lightning often struck the same place twice. More than twice, sometimes. Her free hand slid down onto Rudi's lap and she tucked her fingers between his legs. Rudi tensed a brief second, then he relaxed, and his hand on her knee slid a bit higher. She could feel the fires start to burn inside her again. Whatever else happened between them, she wanted a chance to see if what the experts said about lightning was true.

# Ten

At the hotel, Rudi got out of the car to escort Ellen to her room, ignoring Frank's gruff instructions to stay put. Rudi would allow no one else to care for his tough, fragile city flower. And despite his resolve to remain strong and protect Ellen from her virtues, the drive from the hospital had proved him the weak man he was. He must have one last kiss from her pink, petal lips.

She clung to his arm through the small lobby, hugging it close as they walked up the stairs, Frank trailing behind. The pressure of her soft breast against his arm would drive him mad if he allowed it to. But he was stronger than his passions. One kiss. Then he would leave.

By the time Ellen stopped outside her room and handed Rudi the key, he was offering thanks for

Frank's glowering presence. The bodyguard would not allow Rudi to forget himself or Ellen's injuries. Perhaps it would be better to forgo the kiss.

Rudi slipped the card key through the lock and opened the door, but instead of walking through it alone, Ellen tugged on his arm.

"Ellen, I do not think—"

"Then don't." She grabbed his collar and backed into the room, dragging him after her.

"—this is a wise decision," Rudi finished as the door swung heavily shut behind him.

"I don't care."

In the dim entry light of the cookie-cutter room, Ellen looked up at him. Her expression softened, and for the first time he saw her without disguise or tension, the woman he had somehow known he would find behind her mask—strong, soft, tenderhearted. He could only gaze back into her summer-blue eyes.

Her hand rose, stroked gently across his cheek. "You scared me half to death," she said in a whisper-soft caress of her voice.

"You can see I am not hurt." Rudi caught her hand, intending to set her away from him. Instead he pressed her palm to his lips and held it there.

"I see. But I can't quite believe it." She ran her other hand down his chest, shaping her touch to his form. "I have a whole month of worry to make up for. I feel like I've been searching for you my whole life. I would think I saw you on the street, but it was never you. It's going to take more than just seeing to believe I've found you."

Shuddering with the effort to maintain control,

Rudi could not stop her hands as Ellen moved them from his mouth to the back of his head, from his chest around his waist to his back. He could only hold himself rigidly still as she stepped closer, pressed her sweet body against his. Then she lifted her face, like a flower to the sun, and kissed him.

The first touch of her lips shook him. The delicate thrust of her tongue shattered his control into a million glittering pieces. His arms whipped around her, crushing her to him as he plundered her mouth, tasting deep, needing more. When Ellen added her passion to his own, Rudi was far too weak to resist.

He lifted her in his arms, unable, unwilling to end the kiss. He carried her to the bed, where he laid her gently down. "How is your head?" he whispered. "I do not wish to hurt you."

"The only way you'll hurt me," Ellen said, twining her arms around his neck, "is if you stop. Don't leave me."

"No."

Rudi touched his mouth gently to hers, deepening the kiss as his fingers traveled from button to button, opening her shirt and laying bare her beauty. He couldn't stop kissing her to look. As she had said, seeing was not enough. He had seen her, could still summon her image to his mind, savor the delight of her beauty. He needed to touch her, to curve his hands over the soft, high roundness of her breasts, along the sweet sweep of her waist, over the delicate hollow between her hipbones. Then perhaps he could believe she was real and in his arms.

He stripped away her clothes, then assisted her in removing his own, never ceasing his kiss or the driving thrust of his tongue into her mouth. He tried to wait, to bring her passion equal to his own, but when he sent his fingers delicately seeking her hidden places, he found her slick and ready, waiting for him. Barely able to take time to protect her, Rudi slid home.

At that moment, he knew. Ellen was his home, the only one he needed. She was his heart, the breath in his body, his beloved.

He whispered the words to her in his own language as he loved her with his body, too much the coward to bare his soul in words she could understand. She had already told him she did not, would not believe his words of love, but perhaps if he showed her...

Rudi whispered the truth in her ear, in words she did not know, while his body sang to her songs with a beat as old as life itself. His heart pounded double time as he laced his fingers with hers, holding her in place. He drove deep inside her, striving to touch her soul with each thrust. Her sighs and moans sang counterpoint to his slow, silent tempo. She danced for him, her hips rising to meet him, urgent and demanding. And finally, with a crescendoing cry, she raked her nails across his back.

Ellen throbbed around him, and Rudi lost all semblance of control, pounding into her like a madman. Her pulsing climax continued, driving him beyond madness into a passionate explosion of such power that his mind went white.

* * *

Outside the room, Frank knocked softly on the door, then looked at his watch again. He sighed and pulled out his cell phone.

"Park the car, Tom," he said when his call was answered. "He's still in there with her. After this long, you know he ain't comin' out. Rent the rooms on either side—pull out that diplomat thing if you have to—and get your butt up here."

He hung up the phone and sighed again. Then he leaned against the door, folded his arms across his chest and settled in.

Rudi lay beside Ellen, studying her face by the pink light filtering through the gap in the curtains. Dawn would break soon, and the neon's power would fade. He wondered if dawn's light would fade the power of the things they had known and felt in this room.

He thought not. His love for Ellen would not fade, but it had to change. He loved her. Therefore he could not put her life in danger. He could not allow her to put her body between his and those who would do him harm. Even if she were no longer employed as his bodyguard, Rudi knew it would make no difference to Ellen. If they were together and came under attack, she would act in the same manner.

Huge cracks opened in his heart as his eyes traced the straight line of her nose, the sweep of her eyelashes across her cheeks. He had awakened her twice more in the night, partly to follow the doctor's instructions and ensure that she would wake, but mostly to make love to her again. Each time proved sweeter than the one before. He stored up memories, knowing that much time would pass before they could be together thus, before they could be together at all. Chances were very good that he would never hold Ellen in his arms again.

His mind told him it was better so. His heart agreed, unwilling to put her at risk even as it mourned. Rudi slipped from the bed, careful not to disturb Ellen's slumber, and he dressed. He debated leaving a note, but decided against it. She had never spoken of love, save to deny it. Better that she continue on that path.

Quickly Rudi slipped from the room. Tom rose immediately from the chair beside the door where he had been keeping watch. "Wake Frank," Rudi said. "Tell him to take Ellen home when she wakes. You and I are flying to New York."

Ellen woke to the sound of someone knocking on the door. Out of rhythm with the pounding in her head, it made her head hurt worse. She sat up, and only then realized that she was alone and she shouldn't be. At least, she'd hoped she wouldn't be. But the room was empty. No friendly noises came from the bathroom. Rudi had left her.

"Hey, Sheffield, are you alive in there?" Frank's gravelly basso came through the door as he knocked again. "Open up, or I'm gonna get the manager to do it and make sure that bump on your head ain't put you in a coma or somethin'."

Groaning, Ellen dragged on a T-shirt and yesterday's jeans and went to let Frank in. "Don't talk so loud," she said, padding into the bathroom to splash water on her face. "A concussion has a lot in common with a hangover."

"You sure you're okay, Sheffield? You wanta go back to the hospital and make sure?" Frank surveyed the room, taking in the crumpled sheets, ripped from their previously neat tucking, and turned a bland face back to her. Bless him.

"I'm fine. Where's—" She corrected herself before she could say Rudi. "Where's the prince?"

"He and Tom took the Learjet back to New York this morning."

"This morning?" Ellen looked up from rummaging in her suitcase. "What time is it now?"

"After one. You slept so long, I thought somethin' was wrong." Frank hesitated before continuing. "Prince Rashid said he was going back to Qarif this afternoon."

"I..." Ellen took a deep breath. "I see." She wrapped a clean pair of slacks around her underwear and stood up. "Did they catch the guys who blew up his car?"

"Yeah, I forgot. You were out of it when all that came down. Rashid used your gun to drop one of the guys. Didn't kill him, just shot him through the leg, neat as you please. Held the other guy till the cops got there right after. We weren't but a couple of minutes behind the cops. Followed the ambulance to the hospital."

"Mmm." Ellen turned toward the bathroom, then stopped, needing to know. "So did they say how they found him?"

Frank looked down, cleared his throat, and she

knew. He said it anyway. "They, uh, they followed you."

She nodded and escaped into the bathroom before Frank could see the tears filling her eyes and spilling over to run down her cheeks. She was the one who had brought bombs and destruction down on Rudi. And when the terrorists attacked, he'd been forced to defend himself and her, as well. She had failed, totally, completely, utterly. No wonder he was going back to Qarif. Who could want such a failure?

Ellen stood in the shower long after the last of the soap and shampoo vanished down the drain, trying to wash away the pain inside. It didn't work. The hurt lay too deep. Hot water couldn't touch it. Nothing could.

She journeyed back to New York, the ache numbing her to everything else. Somehow she would get through this. She'd survived heartache before, but before had been different. This time her own failure had cost her the man she loved. The fault was in herself, not in Rudi. He was everything she'd hoped and believed him to be—kind, generous, delightfully unpredictable. Knowing that she'd finally found her Prince Charming, her Prince Rudi, and had nearly cost him his life caused more pain than she thought she could bear.

Until the package with the cowboy boots was delivered to her office. She clutched them to her chest, as if they were stuffed toys, and cried until her eyes ached.

Rudi stared out at the ocean rolling into the sands beyond the palace walls. The moon rode high to his left, veiled by wisps of cloud, silvering the waves below. He thought of Ellen, and he missed her.

He had tried to join in the family conversation at meals, but his thoughts would wander off on their own paths. He attempted to take an interest in the business matters laid before him by Ibrahim or one of his other brothers, but these things had always bored him, and bored him more now. The only thing Rudi had found to capture his attention was the hunt for the terrorist faction that had sent its emissaries to blow up his car.

He sat in on interviews with the two men he had apprehended. He eagerly read every report and chafed to take part in the action. More than once, Rudi asked to be allowed to return to his military unit that was participating in the search, only to be denied. He felt useless, half a man. And so he sat on the balcony and brooded on his loss.

"Why do you sit alone in the dark, little brother?" Ibrahim's voice came from the doorway.

Rudi shrugged. Ibrahim had no interest in the truth.

"You did not eat at dinner tonight. Without food, you will begin to rattle like dry bones and frighten the women away." Ibrahim crossed the gap between them and leaned against the supporting pillar. Rudi could feel him watching and did not care.

"You worry your mother, Rashid," Ibrahim said. "And you disappoint our father."

"I have ordered my life to please them. What more can I do?" Rudi didn't bother to look at his brother.

"You can be happy."

Now he looked, his eyes a slitted glare. "No, I cannot. To make my mother and father happy, I have given up work that I love in order to do things I hate. I have given up my freedom to live like a caged bird, and I have given up the woman I love to live in solitude. How can you ask me to be happy? I am not a nightingale, brother. I am the falcon of our father's name. I will live in this cage you have built for me. But I refuse to like it."

Rudi turned and stalked away, through the house, past the gardens to the guarded beach, feeling Ibrahim watching him still. He needed the vastness of the ocean to ease the bars around him.

Autumn had fallen in New York, crisp and cool. The leaves in Central Park turned red, gold, orange, brown, just right for the video to be shot there today. Ellen gathered up her plans for security around the shoot, stuffed them in her soft-sided bag and pulled on her gray wool jacket with the fake lamb collar, ready to go supervise.

At that moment her intercom squawked "Incoming!" as the door to her office flew open. She jumped, whirling first toward her desk, then to the door.

Ibrahim ibn Saqr filled the doorway, his eyes blazing with anger. The beard was new, but the rest she remembered too well. Ellen glared right back at him. They were through. Everyone was back in Qarif, or was supposed to be. He had no right to be here.

"Sorry," she said, trying to keep the snap out of her voice. "I'm due on-site. You'll have to take your business to Mr. Campanello. If you'll excuse me?"

She walked toward the door expecting, or maybe just hoping, that Ibrahim would back out of the way. He didn't.

His expression softened, the scowl leaving his face, and when Ellen came within reach he caught her chin, tipping it up. She jerked away from his touch. He merely did it again, without comment. This time Ellen endured his scrutiny, too tired to keep fighting. She was too tired for much of anything lately.

"You look terrible," Ibrahim said, without releasing her.

"Thanks. Just what I wanted to hear." She tried to summon up her anger and found a spark. "Now, are you going to let go of me, or am I going to have to break your arm?"

The scowl came back as Ibrahim snatched his hand away. "You are beautiful, but you have the temperament of a viper. I do not understand why Rashid is so obsessed with you."

Loss pierced her, almost made her stagger. With an effort, she hid the pain by replacing it with anger. "Obviously you're wrong. He's not obsessed. He's in Qarif."

"And you are here. He does not eat. He does not sleep. He wanders the palace like a ghost, staring at the sea. He takes no interest in his work, or else—"

"More of that finance junk? Can't you people get it through your heads? Rudi hates that stuff. He wants to build things, to create something concrete and tangible."

Ibrahim glowered, probably because she had dared

to interrupt his high-and-mightiness. "His name is Rashid. Why do you call him this ridiculous Rudi?"

"Because he asked me to." Ellen accepted the stare-down challenge Ibrahim sent her. Moments later, Ibrahim was the one to look away.

"This month," he said, "our father asked him to supervise the drilling of a water well in one of the border villages. Rashid worked so hard, ten and twelve hours every day, that he nearly collapsed when the well was done."

She could feel Ibrahim watching her closely, and she hoped her worry didn't show. Why couldn't these people take care of Rudi?

"The family is concerned for Rashid's health," Ibrahim went on after a moment. "He is haggard, thin, with dark circles beneath his eyes." He paused a moment. "Rashid looks much the same as you."

Ellen shrugged, wishing she'd put on her dark glasses before leaving the building, before leaving the office. She knew how she looked, but couldn't bring herself to do much about it.

"This gives me hope that you hold the same feelings in your heart that Rashid holds for you," Ibrahim said.

She couldn't hold back the bitter laugh. "What feelings? Disgust? Contempt? I don't feel that for him at all."

"Nor does he feel so toward you."

"Oh, please. You don't have to lie. I led the terrorists to him. He had to defend himself when they attacked."

"Because you were injured while saving him from the bomb."

"Another piece of prime stupidity. I know how to fall. I failed, plain and simple. Why else would Rudi have left like he did, if he didn't trust me? If he didn't see clearly what I am?"

Ibrahim stared at her. "Perhaps he thought to protect you. The remainder of the terrorist faction is still at large."

"See? He thinks I can't even take care of myself." Ellen clutched her bag tighter and tried to push past Rudi's brother. "I'm going to be late. They'll be waiting for me."

"Someone else can see to your duties." Ibrahim plucked the soft-sided case from her hands and handed it to Vic Campanello, hovering anxiously in the hallway behind him. "I will pay for your time. I require your assistance now."

He stepped forward, forcing Ellen to back away or get a faceful of power tie, and shut her office door. "Do you care for my brother?"

Ellen shrugged, unwilling to share the secrets of her heart with anyone, much less this overbearing, pompous son of the desert.

Ibrahim sighed, running a hand over his neatly trimmed beard. "You and Rashid deserve each other, for you are both equally stubborn. I was almost eighteen years old when Rashid was born, and have been as much father to him as brother, taking over many of our father's duties because of the business of governing that burdens him. But I neglected to listen to our father's wisdom when he told me to let Rashid fly with his own wings. He is so very different from his mother's other sons...."

He shook his head, then looked up at Ellen. "I also failed to listen to your wisdom, and now I must repair the damage I have done."

"So what does all this have to do with me?"

"Rashid is unhappy. Because he is unhappy, his mother is unhappy, and when his mother is unhappy, our father is, also."

"I fail to see what could possibly have brought you all this way to see me. I'm sorry Rudi is unhappy, but there's nothing I can do about it."

"I believe you are wrong. I believe you are the only one who can help."

"I'm not," Ellen snapped. "I am the last person you should be talking to."

"I offer you the chance to prove what you say." Ibrahim reached into his inner jacket pocket, pulled out an airline ticket and offered it to her. "Come to Qarif. Talk to Rashid, to your Rudi. Ask him whether he sees you as a disgusting failure, or whether—as I heard with my own ears from his lips—whether you are the woman he loves."

Ellen stared at the ticket, but couldn't make herself take it. She couldn't make herself believe Rudi could have said what Ibrahim claimed he had. She didn't dare. Twice already she had lost him. Her heart would never survive a third time.

Ibrahim took the two steps necessary to reach her desk and slapped the ticket down on its surface. The emotional weight behind the slim paper folder made the noise seem to echo through her, and Ellen shuddered.

"Come to Qarif," Ibrahim said. "If you have the courage of your convictions. Come to Qarif, if you dare to take the chance that you might be wrong about Rashid."

She could feel Ibrahim watching her, but she could not take her eyes off that airline ticket. It wasn't the chance that she might be wrong about Rudi that frightened her, but the possibility that she might be right. She didn't dare....

"The date on the ticket is open," Ibrahim said, his voice matter-of-fact. "You may use it at any time. Or you may cash it in, if you do not care enough to come."

Ellen heard the door open and close and knew he was gone, but still she stared at the ticket. It wasn't that she didn't care. She cared too much. And she was afraid. Twice now she'd thought the words *I don't dare.* Ellen Sheffield, the woman who would try anything, who jumped out a window in her Wonder Woman boots, who climbed a cliff thirty feet high with only her hands and feet—this same woman was afraid of a little airplane trip.

Okay, so it wasn't just the flight. It was the man at the end of the flight. Cliffs and window jumping could only break her bones, hurt her physically. Rashid ibn Saqr ibn Faruq al Mukhtar Qarif had the power to rip open her very soul, because she loved him. She loved him enough to remember every single one of his names, for crying out loud. And he didn't love her back.

But what if he did? What if he was just as miserable there in his palace as she was in her tiny highrise apartment? She found it hard to believe, but Ibrahim had given her the means to know for certain. If she had the courage to take him up on his challenge.

Ellen gritted her teeth. Did she dare? She could hear her brothers in her mind, clucking like chickens as they taunted her for her cowardice. She could see Rudi's mocking smile, the challenge in his eyes as he dared her to accept his ridiculous wager, as he told her, "You are afraid of what I make you feel."

He'd been right. And yet, when she had taken his challenge and dared to feel those things, they had been so much more than she could have believed possible. They had made the pain of his leaving so much worse. But to know so much joy, so much delight, wouldn't people pay any price? Didn't they, trying to find it in drugs or drink?

And if Ibrahim was right, if Rudi did care for her—she couldn't think the word *love* for fear she would jinx it somehow. She knocked on her wooden desk just in case. But if he did care, that meant she didn't have to endure the pain, that she could have the joy.

Hope hurt. Ellen had almost become accustomed to the ache of its absence, and now Ibrahim had made her hope again, stirring up the pain. He had dared her. She'd never backed down from a dare before, and she wouldn't start now.

Coward or not, she had to know the truth. With her knees knocking and teeth chattering all the way, she would go to Qarif and find it.

# Eleven

Rudi sat with his face turned up to the sun, eyes closed, basking in the warmth, sheltered by the balcony wall from the chill north wind that had swept through only this morning. He should not have pushed himself so hard while drilling that well. He'd known it while he did it, but the work was the first thing he had found to take his mind off his loss. When he stopped working, Ellen intruded into his thoughts again, so he simply kept going.

The exhaustion that had overtaken him when the water flowed bubbling into the cistern had been a blessing as well, for when he dreamed of her, he dreamed they were happy together. Waking was the nightmare.

Now that he had some of his strength back, he could begin on the next part of the water project, piping it into the homes of the villagers. This time he would pace himself, at least as much as he was able.

He heard footsteps behind him, but didn't bother to open his eyes. He was convalescing. If he pretended to sleep, perhaps whoever it was would go away. The sun's warmth would soon send him to sleep for real.

"Rudi?"

His fantasies were improving. Ellen's voice sounded as if it were on the balcony with him. He brought her smiling face up before his mind's eye.

"Ibrahim told me you'd worked yourself to exhaustion, but I never imagined…"

The chaise where he reclined dipped as weight settled onto it, and his eyes flew open in shock.

This was no fantasy.

Rudi sat up, reached for her, needing to be sure. She caught his hand, gripped it tight. He touched her cheek, devouring her with his gaze.

"Are you real?" he whispered.

She must be. The rosy cheeks of his memory had vanished, replaced by pale hollows, with dark-circled eyes above.

"Ibrahim said I looked as bad as you do." She smiled, and his heart began beating again.

Strange that he had never noticed how it had failed to beat during all the time they were apart.

"But I think he's wrong," she went on. "You look much worse than I do."

"Because I missed you more."

"Did you?"

The uncertainty in her eyes tore at him, and he

reminded himself why he had left. He could not risk her life. He could not bind her with the truth, and yet how could he lie? Rudi answered her with a smile, unable to find words.

Yet his fingers spoke what his lips could not, tracing tenderly over the curves and planes of her face, sharper now with her thinness. He could not stop touching her.

"Why have you come, Ellen? To assist in the capture of the terrorists? We are very close, or so I am told."

"No," she said.

Still he caressed her, smoothing a finger across the sweep of her brow, down the line of her nose, along the ends of her eyelashes, making her smile at the faint tickle.

"Have you come to protect us while we lie asleep in our beds?" he asked.

Ellen shook her head. Then she leaned forward, taking his face between her hands as if to prevent his escape, and she kissed him, a sweet, passionless kiss. "I came on a dare," she murmured against his lips.

*A dare.* He should have known. Rudi thrust her away and stood, striding to the end of the balcony.

Ellen came after him. "Rudi—"

He spun around and put his hand over her mouth, harsh at first, but he could never be harsh with her. His touch gentled, became another caress sealing her lips. He didn't want to hear her reasons for coming. Whatever they were, they could not possibly be what he wished them to be.

''I missed you.'' The words came out, despite his intention otherwise.

Ellen opened her mouth to speak past his fingertips. Desperate to stop her, Rudi did the only thing he could think of. He kissed her.

One hand gripped her shoulder, fingers still alive with the feel of her mouth. He lifted the other to cup her head as the kiss softened, deepened. Ellen's mouth had been open, and he took advantage, his tongue joining in the kiss. Her tongue slid across his in welcome, and somehow, suddenly, his arms were wrapped tightly around her, crushing her softness against his body.

Rudi pressed his arousal hard into the soft cradle between her hips. He wanted her to know how much he had missed her, what her presence did to him. His long native tunic and the light trousers he wore beneath allowed more sensation, more of the feel of her body along his to reach him. He should send her away for her own safety, but he simply could not let her go.

It had been too many long days and even longer nights since he had held her in his arms. He loved her so, wanted her, needed her so. He could not think. He was caught up in the chains of his passion, and he realized, as her hands slipped beneath the bunched-up fabric of his tunic, so was Ellen.

The touch of her hands on his bare skin drove him to madness. Rudi turned her, leaning her back against the side wall of the balcony, and reached for her skirt. Today it was long and flowing, the soft folds lifting easily until he brushed her silken thigh.

He touched lace, then skin above the stocking, and he shuddered. He got both hands beneath her skirt as he kissed her, his tongue stroking in imitation of the act he was so desperate for. This was indeed madness. He retained only a semblance of control as he stroked up and around and down her thighs where they were bared above the stockings. Then Ellen untied the drawstring of his trousers, closed her hand around his aching flesh, and he lost even that semblance.

With both hands he tore the fragile-seeming garment that attempted to cover her sex. Stronger than it appeared, the elastic around one leg defied him, but it didn't matter as Ellen guided him inside her. With one thrust, he seated himself deep, the side of his face pressed against the rough plaster of the wall. His hands cupped her buttocks to hold her tighter. The glorious feel of her wet heat enfolding him told him of his careless neglect of protection, but he did not care. If he got her with child, he would have at least that link to bind her to him, no matter the miles between.

"Rudi," Ellen whispered, and touched her lips to the tender spot beneath his ear.

He captured her mouth in another kiss to prevent her from saying more. She twined her leg high around his back, hooking her toes between his thighs. Rudi groaned. His hips began to move, quickly finding the rhythm his body required. Ellen met him, thrust for thrust, until she sent her cry into his kiss and her climax demanded his equal response.

Long minutes later, when he finally began to catch his breath, Ellen's leg slipped slowly down the back of his until her foot reached the balcony floor. Only then did the realization of what he had done truly hit him, like a boulder to the head.

He had made love to Ellen on a balcony, open to the gardens in view of anyone who happened to look in this direction. He had made love to her standing up, fully clothed—or almost—and in such a hurry that he had not thought about protection until too late.

Rudi groaned, hiding his face in her neck. He could not bring himself to pull his clothing together, for that would require space between them, space that would allow him to see the anger in her face.

But the fingers trailing through his hair did not feel angry. They felt nice. Comforting. Contented. He took a deep breath, inhaling essence of Ellen.

"Rudi?" She spoke again.

He took another deep breath and let it sigh out. They would have to speak sometime. Now was as good as any.

"Yes, Ellen?" His words were muffled by her neck.

"You never did ask what the dare was that brought me here."

She twined one of his curls around her finger. He did not want to move, did not want her to stop, but it was time. He summoned up his resolve.

"No, I did not." Rudi stepped away from her, her skirt falling into place again as he did. He took a moment to retie his drawstring and smooth the tunic down over his pants, aware of her eyes watching him.

Ellen reached beneath her skirt and pulled off her torn undergarment, leaving it lying on the floor where she stepped out of it. His passion stirred as he watched her, desire lifting its head, but he could deny it now.

Her gaze caught his and held it. "I dare you," she said, "to ask me what dare brought me to Qarif."

Rudi shrugged. "What matters is that you are here. Is why of any importance?"

"Are you afraid to ask?"

She stepped toward him, and he backed away. Knowing what she did not wear beneath her skirt made it imperative that he keep his distance.

"Ask me," she said, taking another step.

"Ellen, if we are to talk…" He sent a significant glance downward. "Please, do not come closer."

"*Ask.*" She held her ground, her eyes insisting along with her voice. "I dare you."

"What brought you to Qarif?" He snapped the words out like the crack of a whip.

"Ibrahim dared me."

Rudi waited, refusing to ask for more.

Ellen sank onto the foot of the lounge and looked up at him. The vulnerability in her eyes made him want to kiss it away, but if he kissed her, it would not be enough.

"Ibrahim said I was wrong about why you left Oklahoma in such a hurry. He dared me to come here and prove that he was wrong and I was right."

"And are you? Right?" His heart began to beat harder with hope, though his head knew there was none.

"I don't know." She bit her lower lip to still its

quivering. "I can't— That was some hello you gave me, but I still can't quite believe…"

She stopped and took a deep breath. "Rudi, do you hate me?"

"What?" The word burst from him as her ridiculous question brought him to kneel beside her. Rudi took her hand and held it tight as he searched her face. "How can you believe such a thing?"

"I brought those terrorists down on you. They only found you because they followed *me*." Tears flowed down her cheeks faster than his fingers could wipe them away. "And then I was useless—worse than useless—when they came after you with their machine guns. I'm a failure, Rudi. How can you not hate me?"

"How can I hate you, when I love you, *zahra?*" He sat on the lounge and gathered her in, rocking her gently back and forth. "You saved my life when you pushed me away from the car explosion. You took my injury, my hurt upon yourself."

Rudi touched the spot on her forehead where she had hit it, knocking herself semiconscious, then he kissed it. "Will you not allow me the privilege of protecting my beloved, as a man should?"

Ellen sniffled, wiping her eyes on his shoulder. "You love me?"

"I do."

She punched him gently on the arm. "Then why did you leave? Why did you go away and leave me to wake up all by myself with Frank pounding on the door? I thought you were giving me another chance, and then you were gone before I could even take it."

"I am sorry, my flower." He kissed her forehead again. "I wanted to protect you. Only two of the terrorists were captured in Oklahoma. I feared if they came after me again, the next time they would not simply bump your head. I never meant to cause you any pain. I never dreamed that my leaving would do such a thing."

"You never—" Ellen sat up and stared at him in disbelief.

Rudi smiled, brushing back the hair that had fallen into her face. "You have never said that you care for me, my Ellen. I believe—now—that you do. But you have never said it."

"Oh, Rudi." Fresh tears welled up in her eyes. "I'm such an idiot. I—"

"Just say it. Please?" He needed to hear it. A man should be strong enough to say the truth without needing to hear the same words in return, but Rudi was not so strong.

"I love you, Rudi." She cupped his face between her hands. "I love you, Rashid ibn Saqr ibn Faruq al Mukhtar Qarif. I love you by whatever name you want to use. I love you wherever you are. I love—"

Rudi couldn't wait for more confessions of love. He kissed her, sharing with her all the feelings he'd kept imprisoned inside himself for so long.

"I want you to know, Rudi-Rashid," Ellen said when he finally let her go, "that no matter where you go or what you do, I can find you. I *will* find you. I've already done it more than once, so you know I can. You're never going to get away from me again. So you can just forget that 'I left to protect you' junk.

We'll just have to look out for each other. You got it?''

"In that case…'' Rudi placed careful kisses across her forehead, her eyelids, her cheeks, lining them up in rows. "You should marry me. Since you have already promised that I have no escape. We should be equally bound, do you not agree?''

"Do you mean it?'' She looked up at him, eyes wide with uncertainty.

He sighed, exasperated. "Ellen, I have already asked you once to marry me. This is twice. Do not make me ask you a third time. If I did not mean it, I would not ask it.''

"What about—?'' She waved her hand vaguely at the palace surrounding them.

"We have time to work out the details. Ibrahim dared you to come. My family will not object.'' He took hold of her shoulders and looked her in the eyes, letting his determination show. "I insist that you make an honest man of me. Say yes, Ellen.''

She smiled, and his sudden worry left him.

"Yes, Ellen,'' she said.

Rudi lifted his eyes heavenward to offer a quick thanks before he wrapped her in a close embrace. Holding her tight, he pressed a kiss to the top of her head.

"I love you, *zahra*. And I swear that you will never have to go in search of this prince again. Where you are, there I will be, and wherever we are together, that will be home.''

\* \* \* \* \*

# HER SHEIKH BOSS
## CAROL GRACE

# CHAPTER ONE

"GOOD news."

Claudia looked up from her desk to see her boss, Sheikh Samir Al-Hamri standing in the doorway to her office, his arms folded over his chest, a smile on his devastatingly handsome face.

"The merger's going through?" They'd been working out a deal for months with a rival shipping company in his country of Tazzatine.

"Finally. It's been a long road and I couldn't have done it without you."

Claudia blushed at the compliment. She knew he appreciated her input, her willingness to work long hours and her devotion to the job. What he wouldn't appreciate, if he knew about it, was her devotion to him personally. She tried, heaven knows she tried to treat him like any other boss, but how could she when he wasn't like any other boss?

He was a sheikh, a member of the ruling family in his country, with more money than anyone could spend in a lifetime, dazzling good looks, the best education in the world and even a sense of humor. And generous. How could she forget generous, when he gave her large raises without her asking? The one thing he wasn't generous about was vacations. He didn't take them and he didn't see why she should, either.

Claudia didn't care. If she was on vacation, she wouldn't get to see him every day. Wouldn't get to discuss new shipping routes, the GNP of developing countries, or fluctuating petroleum prices. Who else would want to talk about alternate sources of energy or the future of container ships? Nobody in her knitting group or her book club. But who would have thought these subjects would interest a twenty-eight-year-old former English major like Claudia?

When she first took the job it was just a job. High-paying, demanding and high-energy. But working for Samir had been an eye-opener. His enthusiasm for the field of international shipping, the field he'd been born into and raised to inherit, was contagious. Now she took a real interest in the workings and the future of his family's business.

"Your family must be pleased," she said.

He hesitated a moment then walked to the window of her office and looked out across San Francisco Bay sparkling in the morning sunlight to Alcatraz, Angel Island and the Golden Gate Bridge.

"They are," he said. "Very pleased. It's the end of an era, the end to hostility and competition between the Al-Hamris and the Bayadhis, but…"

She waited for him to finish his sentence. He didn't. Something was wrong. She knew him so well, knew he should be on the phone, calling friends, making plans, sharing the news with everyone including the press. Instead he was just standing there lost in thought.

"What about the papers?" She held up the file with the

contract in it. "Nothing's been signed yet." Maybe that was it. He was afraid to count on the deal until it was official.

"That will happen in Tazzatine in our home office on the twenty-first of this month." He looked over at the photograph of the high-rise, waterfront headquarters of the Al-Hamri Shipping Company surrounded by residence towers, a sports complex and a shopping plaza. "For now, they have our word, we have theirs."

"You should be celebrating. Should I book a table at La Grenouille for tonight?"

He turned to face her. He rubbed his hand over his brow and didn't speak for a long moment. "Sure," he said finally. "Why not? And get two first class tickets to Tazzatine on…" He crossed the room to look at the calendar on the wall. "Say, the fifteenth. Leave the return open."

Claudia scribbled the date on her notepad. "Two?"

"Two. You and I."

Her mouth fell open. "I'm going with you?" She'd never gone anywhere further than an hour or two away to meetings in Silicon Valley or Sacramento with him in the two years she'd worked there. Now she was going halfway around the world? "You're not serious."

"Of course I am. You're the one who wrote up the proposal in the first place. You have the details of the contract in your head. You don't think I'd sign anything without your being there, do you?"

"I…uh…"

"Especially something this important. Who knows what could go wrong at the last minute? Changes to be made? Objections? I need you there. You know I'm no good at details."

He was right. He was the one with the big plans, the overview. He was the rainmaker. She took care of the details. They were a team.

"I think I should stay here in the office. If you need me, you can always call me," she said.

"No good. You have to be there. Don't worry, it's a very modern country. You don't have to wear a veil. Women drive, go shopping, swim, play golf. At least in the capital."

She wasn't worried about wearing a veil or being able to play golf, which she didn't do, she was worried about being in his country, seeing him with his family and knowing beyond a doubt, once and for all, that she was a fool for falling in love with her boss. Any boss, but especially a boss who was in line to rule a small country one day. Whose family had certain expectations for him.

She'd feel like an outsider. Oh, no doubt they'd be nice to her. She'd heard tales of their legendary hospitality. But she *was* an outsider and it would finally sink in as it never had before.

Maybe that's what she needed. A reality check. Time to stop fantasizing that one day he'd look up from his desk, see her and gasp. *"Claudia, you're beautiful,"* he'd say. *"What's wrong with me? I never knew it before but I'm in love with you."*

She shook her head to clear it from this daydream. It wasn't going to happen. He wasn't in love with her and never would be. As far as she knew he'd never been in love with anyone though not from a lack of opportunity. There were plenty of women who would be only too happy to fall in love with him. Women who were stunningly beautiful and socially prominent. She saw their pictures in the newspaper in the society column. She fielded their phone calls.

If he hadn't fallen for any of them, how did someone like her have a chance with him? She was far from beautiful. She was downright plain. His dates wore glamorous designer clothes, hers were practical and straight off the rack. They had their hair and nails done at salons downtown, she did her own. Their families were the crème de la crème of San Francisco society. Hers was far from that.

She had no intention of changing. Even if she wanted to, how could she? What was the point? Imagine what he'd say if she suddenly turned up like some fashionista in a clingy, form-fitting dress, her hair colored and cut by some high-priced stylist, her face covered with makeup and her feet in stiletto heels.

It should be enough that he respected her, counted on her, depended on her. It had to be enough because that's all it ever would be.

"What's wrong?" he said, leaning over her desk to look into her eyes. "You were a million miles away. Have you heard a word I've said?"

"Yes, of course," she said, pushing her chair back and standing. She had to get away from that penetrating gaze of his. Away from six feet plus of masculine charm. Away from that voice tinged with just a hint of a foreign accent despite his schooling here and on the continent. This was not the time to argue with him about going to Tazzatine. Not when she was light-headed and dizzy. "I just don't see the need…" she blurted.

"I don't know what you're worried about. The flight is quite comfortable and it's a fascinating country, a blend of old and new. Full of possibilities."

"I know. You told me about the modern city and the desert, the oases and the horses you raise. I'm sure it's beautiful, but…" She held out her hands, palms forward, as if to push him away. As if she could.

"It's a different world from this," he said. "You have to see it to appreciate it. See everything, not just the offshore rigs or the new skyline, not just the desert, or our family villa in the Palmerie. You'll also have the opportunity to meet the people like my family. And the Bayadhi family. And you'll realize what this deal means to everyone. Yes, you're coming."

All right, maybe she did have to go. Maybe it was the chance of a lifetime to see his world through his eyes. How could she turn him down when he looked at her like that? Those brown eyes so deep and dark a girl could get lost in them. His dark hair falling across his forehead until he brushed it back with an impatient gesture. His jaw clenched tight with determination. Determination. He had enough for ten men. Some called it arrogance, because when Samir Al-Hamri wanted something, he always got it.

"Okay, I'll go," she said.

"I knew I could count on you."

Of course he knew that. When had she ever turned him down for anything whether it was working late, running errands or making excuses for something he didn't want to do? No one said no to Sheikh Samir Al-Hamri. The very idea was preposterous.

"Now I need some coffee," she said, feeling a desperate need to get away and out of his orbit where she was in constant danger of being sucked in and never getting out. "Can I bring you some?"

"Yes, thanks. Cream and two sugars."

She smiled weakly. After two years, he thought she didn't know how he liked his coffee? Thought she didn't know he liked mustard rather than mayonnaise on his sandwich? Thought she didn't know he preferred Merlot to Cabernet, the circus to the opera, Schumann to Stravinsky?

"Oh, and Claudia?"

She turned and paused at the door.

"Another thing. While we're in Tazzatine…I'm getting engaged."

She grabbed the doorknob with one hand while the room spun around so fast she thought she might pass out. She took a deep breath and forced herself to stay standing and remain calm.

"Congratulations," she blurted. What else could she say? "This is a…a surprise."

"Not really. It's been in the works for a long time. Our families are old friends. This is just a formality."

"Just a formality," she murmured. "How nice." Claudia made it to one of the smooth leather chairs against the wall of her office and sat down. Just for a moment. Just to catch her breath. Just until her legs stopped shaking. It was all she could do to keep her features arranged in an expression of polite interest, no more, no less.

"You're getting engaged," she repeated numbly as if that would help it sink in. Maybe she hadn't heard right. He couldn't possibly be getting engaged, formality or not, without her hearing about it. She saw all his correspondence, took all his phone calls and forwarded his e-mail. "Who is she?"

"She is Zahara Odalya." He reached in his vest pocket and

pulled out a picture. Claudia couldn't believe it. He kept a picture of her in his pocket. It made her feel physically sick. Who keeps a photo of his fiancée in his pocket unless he's really in love with her? Her boss in love? It seemed like it. It seemed she had him pegged all wrong.

"Here," he said, handing her a photo of a gorgeous woman with a cloud of dark hair, and a cool expression on her flawless face.

"Oh, she's beautiful," Claudia blurted. How she got that sentence out of her mouth with a lump in her throat the size of Plymouth Rock she had no idea.

"Looks that way."

"You don't know?"

"I haven't seen her for a long time. When I knew her years ago she was a little brat who played with my sister. She went off to school in London while I was in Paris and I never saw her again."

"I'm surprised she isn't married already," Claudia murmured. Anyone who looked like that and was part of Middle Eastern high society should be. What was wrong with her?

He took the photo out of Claudia's hand and studied it with a frown on his face. "So am I. I guess she's been saving herself for me. Why not?" He shrugged. "Everyone agrees it's a good match. Family connections mean everything in our part of the world. You'll see."

No, she wouldn't see. She would not go halfway around the world to see her boss get engaged to someone he didn't love. Or who didn't love him. Or even worse to someone he loved. Or to anyone at all. She might be a loyal employee, but she was no masochist.

"You know, Sam…" It wasn't easy to call him Sam, considering who he was, but he insisted. "I really can't go with you."

He stood there, one eyebrow raised, waiting for her to tell him why she couldn't, so he could tell her why she could. Why she must. Her mind was racing. She had to make it good. He was determined, but so was she.

"I…have a prior commitment."

"What kind of commitment? Your commitment is to me and it's a requirement of your job."

"I know. It always has been, but I'm to be a bridesmaid in my friend Susan's wedding which happens to be right at the same time as this trip you're making." She had a friend named Susan, but she wasn't getting married anytime soon. But how would Sam ever know that? He might not believe her. The look on his face told her he didn't, but he couldn't prove otherwise.

"What a coincidence. Your friend getting married just as the merger takes place. Poor planning on our part I guess. I wonder you didn't mention it before," he said dryly.

"I'm sorry. I guess it slipped my mind. I should have remembered. Because it's June," Claudia said. "Everyone gets married in June."

"Even you?"

Claudia bit her lip. He would have to remind her of her brief marriage, which he only knew about because of the box she'd checked on the application when he hired her. It's not like she ever talked about it or even thought about it very much. "I got married in October and divorced in December. It really doesn't count."

"Is that what this is all about?" he asked, walking to her desk and back again. He always paced when he hit an obstacle in his path as if he could smash it with his feet as he walked. "You had a bad marriage so you're worried about me making the same mistake."

He was so far off the mark she almost laughed.

"I'm sure it won't be the same," she said. Her husband cheated on her even before they got married, then he walked out. There was no way she was going to tell Sam that whole humiliating story. "I'm sure you'll be very happy."

"How can you be so sure?" he asked.

She glanced at the door. Why hadn't she walked out to get coffee before she got embroiled in this no-win argument?

"Because you have no illusions. You're going into this, uh, engagement with your eyes wide-open. You know why you're doing it and so does she."

"And you didn't?"

"I thought I was in love."

"What made you think that?"

She stood and went to the door, determined to get out of the office. "Why does anyone think they're in love?" she asked impatiently. "Their heart beats faster, they daydream, they can't sleep, they can't eat, they can't concentrate. They think they can't survive without the other person."

"Sounds delightful," he said with a sardonic smile. "Glad it's never happened to me."

"You're lucky. You'll never have to suffer."

"The way you did."

She opened her mouth to deny it then stopped. "This is not about me, it's about you. You're the one getting engaged. I'm happy for you. You'll have a lovely party surrounded by your families."

"And you. You'll be there."

"No, I won't. I told you."

"I can't believe you'd even consider this prior commitment. I thought I meant more to you than that. I've always been fair with you, haven't I?" he asked. He leaned back against her desk across the room and leveled the full force of his gaze on her.

She sighed. "Yes."

"I've never asked anything out of bounds. Well, maybe the time you got me out of the bachelor auction by feigning a sudden illness. Everyone felt terrible about it."

"They felt terrible because you missed the auction, not because I was sick."

"That's not true. You got a dozen get-well cards. Now tell me the truth. You owe me that much. There's no wedding. You don't want to come to my country. You don't want to be there when we sign the papers. You aren't interested in my personal life. I understand that and that's okay. But this is primarily a business trip and I want you there. I need you there. Why can't you understand that?"

She did understand. She understood only too well that watching him celebrate his engagement to that beautiful creature in the picture would be like being stabbed in the chest. Might as well throw her in the Gulf with a slab of cement tied to her feet.

"Okay, here's the real reason. I'm afraid to fly. I didn't want to tell you. I thought you would lose respect for me. I know you. You'd make me take fear of flying lessons, or get drugged or see a therapist. But there you have it. I've got acrophobia."

"What is it? Fear of hijacking or turbulence?"

"Yes, all of those."

"Have you seen a doctor?"

"There's no cure for what I've got." The only cure for the common condition of unrequited love was quitting her job, and walking away from the world's sexiest, richest and most gorgeous sheikh. All she had to do was quit. Quit now. Or wait until he was gone, then leave a note on his desk saying…

*Sorry, Sam, but I can't work for you anymore. You don't need me anymore. You have Zahara now. All along you knew someday you'd marry her, but you never said a word. When you get engaged, everything will be different. You won't want to work late or phone me at home when you want to talk about business. Nothing will be the same. And I have to get out while I can.*

No, she would never do that. Never reveal her true feelings. The best thing to do was lie.

"Maybe it's an ear condition. I'll make you an appointment with a specialist."

"That's not necessary. I'm not going. Someone has to man the office here. That's me." The more determined he was, the more she fought back. For once in her life she would not let him override her. What could he do, tie her up and carry her onto the plane over his shoulder while she pounded on his back and screamed for help? Even he wasn't that determined to get his way. Of course he could fire her for insubordination. Which, if he brought a bride to live here with him, might be doing her a favor by saving her the trouble of resigning.

Images of his fiancée dropping in to say hello and disappearing into his office with him for hours on end made her cringe. Zahara or anyone he married for that matter would call every hour, she'd shove Claudia aside to take over his social schedule, then his business. She'd hire someone else because she'd guess that Claudia was in love with her husband. Women have a second sense that way. Oh, how life can change so drastically in a minute. For the worse.

"We'll hire a temp to answer the phone in here. The rest of the staff will be here," Sam assured her. "They'll cope. We're a small family business."

"A small family business? With offices all over the world and millions in revenues?"

"All right, we're a small office of a large business."

"Now I'm going for coffee," she said.

He flicked his hand in her direction as if she was one of his Arabian horses who wouldn't behave. "Go ahead, but consider our discussion over. You're coming with me and that's settled."

When Claudia came back fifteen minutes later she was armed with a sense of calm resolve and his coffee—cream and two sugars—but he was gone. The note on her desk said he had an appointment. She checked his schedule but couldn't find anything written there for this morning.

She sat at her desk, her chin propped in her hand and stared at the portrait on the wall of his grandfather in his regal headdress next to his favorite horse. Not his wife, his horse. If that didn't give her an idea of family life in Tazzatine, it should. Of course things had changed. But if Sam was getting engaged to someone he didn't love, didn't even know, because it was part of a grand plan for his life, then the old ways were still very much alive.

She'd like to see the country. She'd like to gallop on an

Arabian stallion over the dunes. She'd always wanted to sleep in a tent, sip mint tea in the market place, shop for copper pots and take part in the ceremonies that were so much a part of Sam's culture. As long as the ceremonies didn't include his engagement. Sure, he was westernized by his education and his lifestyle, but it was his unique background that made him so much more irresistible than any ordinary man she'd ever met.

If it were just a business trip, she'd be packing her bags by now. She'd be on the phone to the airline. But, it wasn't and surely no woman should have to watch the man she loves get betrothed to someone else.

It was her fault for falling in love with someone so unattainable. What was she thinking? She'd already been ditched and dumped by a rotten jerk. Her ego couldn't take much more, which was why Sam must never ever know how she felt about him.

So far it hadn't been hard to keep her little secret. Even when working late in the office. Even when he drove her home afterward. Even when dropping off important papers at his penthouse condo late at night. But being thrown into contact with him at work and after work in a strange country while he was involved in making plans for his wedding? That was something she didn't need. Not if she valued her sanity. She would not go. No matter what he said she had to get out of it somehow. She hadn't even asked when the wedding was. She didn't want to know.

When the phone rang it was a long distance call from his sister, Amina.

"I'm sorry Samir is not in the office," Claudia said in her personal assistant voice.

"Good, because you're the one I want to talk to, Miss Bradford," Amina said. She lowered her voice. "We have a problem. What I tell you must be a secret. Promise me you won't breathe a word of this to Sam."

Claudia clutched the phone tightly. How could she say no? What was one more secret along with the one she was already keeping?

# CHAPTER TWO

"It's about Zahara. You know who I mean?" Amina asked. She sounded worried. Claudia had never had a real conversation with her before. Maybe she always sounded that way.

"His…uh…fiancée?"

"Yes, her. I don't know what to do. The last thing I want is to alarm my brother. He mustn't hear about this. So if someone else calls from here, tell them he's not there. You see she was supposed to try on the engagement party dress I had made for her last week. She postponed, then postponed again. Finally we settled on today, but she didn't show up. She doesn't answer her phone. My other clients who were all asking about her. 'What's happening with Zahara?' they said. 'Haven't seen her for days. Has she got a secret life or something?' I laughed and said something about her being busy."

"That's probably what it is. She's just busy."

"What woman in her right mind is too busy to try on a fabulous new dress for her own engagement party after I designed it and ordered it from Paris and she spent a fortune on alterations?"

"There's so much to do before a big event like this,"

Claudia suggested. As if she was accustomed to having dresses made for major social events. As if Amina didn't know. Claudia remembered her one and only fitting for her wedding dress and the shower her friend Susan gave her and the rehearsal dinner at the restaurant where Malcolm got drunk. That's when she should have known. That's when she should have pulled the plug on the wedding. She wanted to think she'd changed. That she had more wisdom today than then. Enough wisdom to say no to her boss.

"You don't know her," Amina said. "She has nothing to do. Her servants do it all for her. All she had to do was show up and try on the dress. What's wrong with her? You would think getting engaged to the most eligible man in the country would make her happy, wouldn't you?"

"She's not happy?"

There was a long silence on the other end of the phone. Either Amina was shaking her head or she just didn't know what to say.

Claudia didn't know what to say, either. Should she admit that tying the knot with Sam ought to make anyone delirious with happiness or spout some cliché about how some girls got nervous before a big event?

"What can I do?" Claudia asked at last. Why had Amina called her in the first place? She was thousands of miles away. She was not a friend, not a relative, just an employee.

"Screen his calls. Don't let anyone call and upset the apple cart, if you know what I mean. That includes Zahara. I don't know what she might say. This engagement has been in the works forever. It's fate. Destiny. They're meant to be together. Do you know what it means to our family? Of course you do. You are his most trusted employee. We will be so happy when you arrive. Because Samir has told us how you can fix any problem."

"Well, I'm not sure…" Besides, she thought, what is the problem? If they're really meant for each other, there's no need to worry just because the woman missed her dress fitting.

"He couldn't run his office without you. I don't know what we would do if you weren't coming. If something went wrong and you weren't here…."

Was she talking about the merger or the engagement? Now Claudia was getting confused. It was time for Amina to take a deep breath and calm down.

"Look, Amina, don't worry. Nothing's going to go wrong. All the details have been worked out in advance. The contract is ready to be signed and…"

"Our family has been trying to make this happen for years. We've come close before. Then something always goes wrong. It's as if we're cursed."

"Don't say that. This time it will work." Surely she was talking about the merger.

"Because of you. We never had you on our side before. The fortune teller told me we had to bring in someone new to the negotiations. Someone outside the family. Someone who has never been to our country. Or the deal is doomed. I think she must mean you."

"That's not possible, Amina. She couldn't mean me. She doesn't know me. And I might not…I mean I don't think I can be there."

"You must come."

Determination was obviously a family trait. She'd hate to see a dispute between Sam and his sister.

"Father is very Old-World but he's coming around to see that women have an important place in the business world. At first he was against me starting my own business. But now I think he's proud of my success. I haven't told him yet what the old crone said to me. But she's never been wrong before."

"She can't have meant me. I'm just an employee with no power or clout," Claudia insisted.

"I don't know but she says she has a message for you when you come here. She's really very good about predictions. You'll see."

Claudia wanted to tell her to spare her the fortune teller's predictions. That she wouldn't be there. That everything would be fine—the merger, the engagement. Everything. And her presence or lack of presence wouldn't make a bit of difference. Except to her. Except to her sanity. But she didn't. She couldn't. Not when Amina was so upset.

There was a knock on her office door and Sam walked in. She said goodbye and hung up quickly.

"Who was that?" Sam asked when she hung up.

"My friend Sharon." What was one more lie at this point?

"I hope she wasn't too disappointed you won't be at her wedding."

Claudia sighed.

He smiled because he knew he'd won. He always won. "You won't be sorry about this, Claudia. Now, I have a favor to ask."

Claudia looked up. A favor? Wasn't traveling to his country to be on hand for a merger signing and an engagement favor enough? The confident smile on his face told her whatever it was, he was sure she wouldn't say no. Not after she'd just as good as said yes to his plan.

"I went out looking for a ring for my fiancée. Obviously I can't show up without one, but I have no idea what to buy. You have good taste. Take the afternoon off. Go to Tiffany's. I have an account there. Get me a ring. Something with diamonds. Something large but not ostentatious. You know what women like."

Claudia froze. Just when she thought things couldn't get worse, they did.

Two weeks later, despite every fiber in her body crying out to her that it was a mistake, she was on the plane, sitting in first-class next to Sam who had a stunning five-carat ring from Tiffany's in his pocket and a sheaf of papers spread out on the tray table in front of him.

She had papers to look at, too, but he'd insisted she take the window seat and she couldn't resist looking down at the world below, islands in a blue sea, mountains and forests, imagining the lives of the people down there. Picturing them getting married, having children, growing up, leaving home.

Most of all she wondered how she was going to get through the coming days without losing her composure, without bursting into uncontrollable crying or shouting out how wrong this whole engagement was. But what did she know? She was a divorced woman, an outsider without the background to judge such things. Obviously arranged marriages often worked out better than so-called love matches.

On what grounds could she object?

*This man doesn't love this woman.*

*This man doesn't know this woman.*

*This man doesn't believe in love.*

*This is a business arrangement, not a marriage.*

She could just hear the derisive laughter. The pitying looks the family would give her. How naïve she was, thinking marriage should be about love. Maybe they were right.

One thing she didn't have to worry about was the fiancée and her dress. Amina called again with the message that the problem was solved. No details. But obviously Zahara had appeared, tried on her dress and everyone was relieved, including Claudia.

Yes, what a relief to know Sam would be happily engaged within the week. If not happily then dutifully. As far as she knew happiness had nothing to do with this union. It was a duty. Knowing that didn't help Claudia's state of mind. She had no idea how she was going to handle seeing him actually slip the diamond ring on her finger in the traditional ceremony he'd mentioned. Just the thought of it gave her a pain between her ribs.

If he was concerned about pledging to marry someone he scarcely knew, he didn't let on. The only thing he seemed to be worried about was the agreement between the families. Which was why he was engrossed in the documents in front of him. Making sure nothing could go wrong.

At lunchtime the flight attendant brought them each a Salade Nicoise which Sam had specially ordered. Claudia watched the attendant toss tuna, potatoes and green beans in a light vinaigrette sauce then serve it individually in a bed of butter lettuce. It was absolutely delicious and she enjoyed every bite along with a crusty roll and a glass of chilled white wine.

"You seem to be over your acrophobia," Sam said with a sideways glance at her.

She'd completely forgotten about it. How like him to remember.

"Yes, thank you. It must be first-class." She looked around at the well-dressed passengers, sipping wine or coffee, their laptop computers in front of them. "No one would dare be sick up here."

"First time?"

"First time in a plane in any class."

His mouth curved in a half smile.

"The first time I flew was a trip I made with my mother and my sister when we were very young to our mother's home in France," he said pensively.

"You've never mentioned your mother," she said.

"Perhaps because she moved back to Provence when my sister and I went off to boarding school."

"Then your parents are divorced?"

"Yes. I know what you're thinking. That arranged marriages don't always work out. But theirs was a love match. They met at university in France. But my mother didn't know what she was getting in to. She was swept off her feet by my father. He was very dashing and very persuasive."

"She was always homesick and lonely in Tazzatine. My father didn't know how to deal with her problem. He turned our house in the palmerie into a tropical villa and hired a French chef, but it just made her more homesick than ever. He never understood why she couldn't adjust. I think the only reason she stuck it out as long as she did was because of us children. When we left home for school, she did, too."

"I'm sorry," Claudia said, thinking of him growing up without a mother. Impulsively she put her hand on his arm.

"Don't be. She's much happier now than she's ever been."

"Are you?" she asked. Even though they never discussed

personal matters and it was none of her business, she asked anyway.

"Of course," he said. "You should know that. And so is Amina. She spent last summer with my mother on holiday in the south of France. And I see her when I can."

He shifted in his seat and she took her hand away. Maybe he didn't want her sympathy. Maybe he was sorry he'd confided in her at all. "We have strong extended families in our country. When one person leaves, another fills in. In this case it was my aunt who moved in with us," he continued.

"I see."

"On that trip we took to France I realized then how much my mother had given up to marry my father. And how difficult her life was away from friends and family, a stranger in a strange land. And you wonder why I don't put much store in the idea of love?" he asked. "Look at all the problems it causes."

Claudia didn't want to get into an argument about love. What did she know about it? All love had done for her was to cause her pain, and the worst was likely still to come.

Fortunately he changed the subject. "How does it happen you've never flown before?"

"There didn't seem to be any reason to fly and I was always afraid," she said a little defensively. But now sitting next to Sam who oozed confidence and assurance, she wasn't afraid of flying or anything. Whatever happened, he'd take care of it. The die was cast. She was on her way. There was nothing more she could do about it. No more protests. No more telling him it was really ridiculous for her to make this trip. She had to grin and bear whatever came.

Sure, she was the details girl, but with communications between countries being lightning fast, she could have dealt with any problem from San Francisco. No matter what she said, he had an answer for it. The time for arguing was over. They were on their way.

When the attendant removed the plates, she leaned back in her chair and told herself to enjoy the flight. Enjoy having Sam to herself while she could, discussing his childhood or his country or his family, just the two of them. It wouldn't last.

Not only did she enjoy talking to him for the hours in the air about geography, weather, the shipping business and his plans for the future of the company, but she also enjoyed the hot fudge sundae they served for dessert.

"I've never seen you eat so much," Sam said, a smile on his face. "I don't think I've ever known a woman who wasn't on a diet."

"Now you do," she said. But of course he didn't know her at all. Not really.

"Aren't you afraid you won't fit into your dress?"

"What dress?"

"The one you're wearing to the engagement party."

"I...I don't think I brought anything suitable. I never thought of it but, that's okay, I'd be out of place with all your friends and family anyway."

"My sister will find you something. She has a dress shop and she loves anything to do with fashion."

"Really?"

"You'll like her."

"I'm sure I will."

\* \* \*

Sam was puzzled. From the moment they'd stepped aboard the plane Claudia seemed different. Even though she thought she had acrophobia, she obviously didn't. She seemed to relax once they took their seats. Not the way someone would if they were afraid of flying. Maybe she was relieved to have the bulk of the work done. He'd kept her busy these past weeks, that he knew.

She always worked hard, so did he, but this time they really threw themselves into it, staying late at the office, ordering sandwiches and coffee so they wouldn't have to leave until every "t" was crossed and every "i" dotted. Then just when he thought everything was in order, there was a last minute change from his father's lawyers. He didn't know what he'd do without Claudia.

He watched her adjust her seat and look out the window. He'd made this trip so many times he no longer got a thrill out of the service, the food or the views from thirty thousand feet in the air. He'd forgotten what it was like to experience it for the first time. Until she mentioned it, he'd forgotten about that first flight he'd made with his mother and it made him nostalgic for a few moments.

He leaned toward Claudia to look out the window. He brushed her arm and inhaled the faint scent of roses. Roses at thirty thousand feet? Perfume on Claudia, his no-nonsense assistant? It wasn't possible.

When he got his bearings, he explained to her where they were, pointed out Hudson Bay below, at the ice and snow-covered land formed tens of thousands of years ago. Told her what an incredible contrast it would be when they landed in a country one hundred and fifty Fahrenheit degrees hotter than the one they were above, and almost completely covered with sand.

"What about the oases?" she asked.

"Those are mere depressions in the sand. A spring, a village with a few houses and some palm trees. I hope you won't be disappointed."

"Not at all. I've seen the pictures. They look amazing."

He nodded. It would be interesting to see what she really thought of the palm-fringed, spring-fed Moroccan-style villa where the family went on vacation. Maybe it would strike Claudia as isolated as it had his mother, considering his assistant had spent her whole life in an American city. Maybe its charms would be lost on her, too. He wondered if there'd be time to take her to the villa or if she'd really want to go. Maybe they'd be too busy.

She took out her new camera and snapped some pictures of the view, then she asked more questions. Who owned the land beneath them? Did anyone live there? He didn't know all the answers. He opened his laptop and looked for maps and information to share with her. Then he answered some important e-mail. She opened her newspaper and started a crossword puzzle. Unable to concentrate, he looked over her shoulder.

"Four letter word for mid-east ruler," he read aloud. "Emir."

She wrote the letters in pencil. "Is that you?" she asked.

He shook his head. "An emir is a prince. I'm just a sheikh. In line to be head of our tribe, which is about half the country. But not until my father dies. In the meantime I'm just another hardworking executive who depends on his assistant to do all the hard work."

Her cheeks flushed and turned a becoming pink. She was

always so composed, he liked catching her off guard, surprising her when he could with a compliment she didn't expect. She was the most modest woman he'd ever met. He wondered if she possessed even a twinge of vanity. Except for the scent of roses. He was tempted to ask about that, but he didn't want to embarrass her any further.

"I'm not the only one who compliments you, am I?" he asked. He really had no idea of what her life outside the office was like. Maybe it was just like his. Work, eat, sleep and more work.

"My knitting club thinks I do good work," she said primly.

"Really. What do you knit?"

"Socks. Scarves. Sweaters."

"So that's what you do in your spare time, knit?"

"I don't have much spare time."

"That's my fault. I work you too hard."

"You work just as hard or harder. Maybe after…"

"Maybe after I get married, all that will change. Is that what you were going to say?"

"When are you getting married?" she asked.

"I don't know. Whenever it's convenient, I suppose."

"It's possible your wife will have plans for you. Like where you'll live. What you'll do in the evenings besides work."

He frowned. He simply hadn't thought beyond the merger and the engagement announcement. He had no wish to change his residence, or anything about his life. He didn't want someone bringing in new furniture, making plans for him, or taking up his spare time such as it was. What would Zahara expect? A long engagement, he hoped, postponing any difficult decisions for some time to come. Would she even want to live in San Francisco? Maybe she'd stay where she was, wherever that was. Why not?

He assumed everything in his life would stay the same except his family and Zahara's family would be satisfied. As for the business merger, the company would now be twice as large. Twice as many opportunities. Twice as much clout in the worldwide shipping business.

"As far as work goes, the only changes will be for the better, I'm sure," he said. "You may need an assistant."

She didn't say anything. She probably hadn't considered their workload might be heavier. But she knew him well enough to know that when he wanted something he made it happen. If he didn't want his life to change, it wouldn't. If they needed help, he'd hire more people. Still she looked dubious, or maybe it was just that she couldn't figure out number ten down.

"Four letters, a super model," she murmured.

He said a name that she vaguely recognized.

She slanted a glance in his direction. "You know about models?"

"Tall, skinny girls with bony hips and cheekbones? I know I prefer women with curves. Women who smile once in a while."

Claudia herself smiled at his description.

He had no idea if she had curves or not. Not under the shapeless suits she wore to the office and here on the plane. Too bad she hadn't thought to bring a dress for the party. Maybe he should have told her to. But that wasn't his job to tell his assistant what to wear. Still, he wondered what she'd look like in a party dress. He couldn't imagine.

He thought about Zahara. What had happened to her since the last time he saw her? Did she smile? Did she have curves?

How did she really feel about this engagement? Did she accept it as he did as a done deal? Would she be at the airport to meet him?

She was not at the airport. His father sent a driver, a man who'd been with him for years. Sam looked around and wondered what Claudia thought of seeing a sea of men in white robes all talking at full volume. It must be overwhelming. He thought of his mother and what she must have felt. Ali, the driver bowed slightly and said, "Welcome home," before he picked up their bags from the luggage carousel.

Home? Was this hot, muggy city home? Or was it San Francisco often covered in a blanket of cool, damp fog? Or didn't he have a home anymore? With his suit jacket over his shoulder and his shirtsleeves rolled up, he and Claudia followed Ali through customs and out to the waiting limousine.

Claudia fanned her face with her customs form. She had a sheen of perspiration on her face.

"The limo's air-conditioned," he said. She must be feeling the heavy humidity, so different from the city they'd left behind.

In minutes they were parked in front of the office. He got out of the car, looked up and shaded his eyes from the relentless sun. There were more high-rise buildings since his last visit. And more going up every day. The whirring of cranes, the clanging of steel beams and the chattering of air hammers filled the air. It all meant progress.

He slanted a glance in Claudia's direction. How did it look to a stranger? Was she in culture shock already from the heat and the noise? If so, she didn't show it. She stepped briskly into the cool lobby of the Al-Hamri Building and followed him to the elevator as if she'd been doing it every day of her life.

He left Claudia in the lobby with his father's assistant and went straight to the old man's office where he embraced him.

"Father, how are you?" Just a glance at the old man had Sam worried. He looked older, tired and when Sam wrapped his arms around him he seemed thin and frail. How had this happened in the six months since he'd seen him in Hamburg at the launching of their new container ship? Shouldn't someone have told him if his father wasn't well?

"Fine, now that you're here." Abdul Al-Hamri smiled at Sam and sat down in his large leather chair, the same chair where his grandfather had once sat. Not here. Not in this modern highrise. What would his grandfather have thought if he could see what Sam saw when he looked out the window at the huge oil rigs just offshore and the miles of new buildings?

"How was the plane trip?"

"We were able to get some work done."

"We?"

"I brought my assistant with me. Claudia. She's indispensable in negotiations."

The old man's face was creased in a frown. "Who?

Sam surveyed his father with a worried look. He'd mentioned Claudia before. He knew he had. He'd told him she was coming with him. Was his father's memory going?

"I've told you about her. She's been working with me for two years. She's my right-hand man, so to speak. She understands our situation better than anyone who's not family. I rely on her and trust her implicitly."

His father shook his head.

"Surely you don't still believe a woman's place is in the

home," Sam said. "Not in today's world. Look at Amina, running her own shop."

"I know. I know. Things are changing. Truthfully I would prefer that Amina get married and stay home to raise a family. But she has a mind of her own, like you. Like her mother."

"And like you, Father. She's inherited much of your drive and ambition." Surely it would please his father to hear that.

"God help her," his father muttered. "The country's changing so fast it makes me wonder. Is it all for the best? There's something to be said for the old ways, for tradition. For marriage and family," he added pointedly. "That's why you're here, isn't it? Besides the business agreement."

"Of course." But Sam felt his muscles tense. Back in California marriage was far off. This was just an engagement, but now they were talking about marriage and family and not in the abstract. His father meant *his* marriage and *his* family.

Sam wasn't ready to think about that. Not yet. Now that he was there in Tazzatine the idea of marrying a stranger was far from appealing.

"How is Zahara?" Sam asked politely.

"I don't know. I haven't seen her. Either has her father."

Sam frowned. They hadn't seen her? What did that mean? "Is there a problem?" he asked.

His father shot him a querulous glance. "Of course not. I have been assured that everything is in order."

After just a short conversation Sam realized he and his father were not entirely in agreement on the direction the country was taking, the role of women and the responsibility of their family to their country. But these were issues they could continue to discuss and hopefully come to some accommodation. In their phone conversations they never got into any controversial subjects at all. But face-to-face, it was hard to avoid such topics. It was best to talk business.

"In any case, the contract is almost ready to sign," his father said. "As soon as business is finished your assistant will get a chance to enjoy herself by shopping or playing golf. Amina will take care of her when you and I are busy. There are just a few, last-minute changes they've asked for. I said I would have to run them by you. Then it's just a matter of the signing ceremony. And the engagement party of course. You don't know how happy this makes me. And the Odalyas of course. Ben Abdul Odalya is my oldest friend in the world. We always hoped… Although…"

Sam waited, but his father only stared straight ahead lost in thought.

"Are you sure everyone is happy about the engagement?" Sam said. He was beginning to wonder why his father was so vague about it.

"Sit down," his father said. "There is something I need to ask you."

Claudia felt like Alice who'd just dropped down the rabbit hole and landed in Wonderland. Outside the temperature must be close to ninety degrees with matching humidity and inside this building the air-conditioning was turned up so high she was shivering.

She expected a boom town, she didn't expect the loud noise of jackhammers and so much dust swirling outside on the street, so many white buildings reflecting the dazzling bright sunshine, so many men and women dressed in the latest

European fashions alongside the women in veils and men in the traditional keffiyeh.

After a tour of the offices, a tall, slim young woman in a smart black suit appeared and introduced herself as Amina. She shook Claudia's hand and smiled warmly.

"You must be exhausted after your flight. Where's my brother? Ah, I know, in with Father. Come with me. You're staying in my apartment. You'll want to unpack and rest up before the party."

Party? Surely she wasn't expected to go to a party so soon. "I shouldn't leave without telling Sam." And telling him she was there to work and only to work. Why else had she come all this way?

"We aren't going far. The family apartments are on the top floor. It's more convenient that way, especially for the workaholics in my family." She smiled to soften the implied criticism. "I'll leave word where he can find us. Those men, once they start talking about ships and freight, they lose track of time. I must remind them of the dinner party tonight. The Bayadhis will be there of course as well as Zahara's family. Because we're celebrating the engagement as well as the merger. A lot of strange faces all at once, I know, but I hope you'll have a good time."

A good time at a family affair where the man she loved got engaged to someone else? Not likely. Claudia had no wish to intrude on this happy occasion. Besides she needed some time to pull herself together. She had to get out of it. "Please don't worry about including me. I'll be fine on my own."

"But of course you will dine with us." Amina signaled to a young man upon which he picked up Claudia's bag and walked out the door.

Claudia opened her mouth to make an excuse, but she knew better than to cross a strong-willed member of the Al-Hamri family, whether it was Amina or her brother.

"Very convenient indeed," Claudia remarked when Amina whisked them up in the private elevator to her apartment. It was more than convenient. It was beautiful.

The furniture was antique, comfortable but elegant, very much what a well-heeled single woman might have in New York or even Paris. Amina left her shoes at the door and Claudia did the same. Her hostess told Claudia the carpets and the colorful wall hangings were hand-woven by local artisans. When Claudia admired them, Amina said she'd take her shopping in the souks where she knew the merchants by first name.

Amina threw open the French doors to the balcony to let the sea breeze in. Claudia stepped outside and took a deep breath. What a relief to get away from the chill of the omni-present air-conditioning. The waters of the Gulf glittered in the late afternoon sunlight.

"You must have work to do," Claudia said to Amina. "Please don't let me distract you. I don't need to be entertained. I can do very well on my own."

"I have an assistant in the shop this afternoon," Amina said. "I have been looking forward to this meeting with you. Now that you are here I can breathe easier. So can we all."

"I don't understand. I'm only here in case there are any last-minute problems with the agreement." She hoped the rantings of a superstitious fortune teller had been forgotten.

Amina nodded slowly. A woman in a simple long dress came out to the balcony with two glasses of tamarind juice and small bowls of nuts and olives she placed on a wrought-iron table.

"Thank you, Fatima," Amina said, then waited until the maid had left the balcony and gone back inside before she spoke.

"Problems?" she said with a rueful smile. "Ah, yes, if you only knew."

# CHAPTER THREE

THE GUEST ROOM was done in pale green and soft peach and had its own balcony overlooking the sea below. It was feminine but not a fussy room. A king-size canopy bed was outfitted with one hundred percent Egyptian cotton sheets and butter-soft pale peach blankets. But Amina's real pride and joy was the guest bathroom.

"My aunts scoff and say it's too old-fashioned for their taste. But that is why I like it. I ordered everything from England, the porcelain-glazed sink, the cast-iron claw-foot tub and the white tiles on the wall. I hope you like it."

"Like it? I love it. It's charming," Claudia said. It was more than charming. It was fully outfitted with luxury towels, a fluffy bathrobe, an antique wall phone and a TV hidden behind a mirror. Now she knew she was in Wonderland. The only thing lacking was the mad Queen of Hearts. Would she meet her tonight?

Amina smiled. "I'm glad you like it. I hope you like it so much you will stay a long time."

"Oh, no, I don't think I can. Back in California the work is piling up in our absence. We must get back soon."

Amina nodded, but Claudia wondered if she'd really heard her. Sam's sister seemed preoccupied. She hadn't explained what she meant by that "problems" remark. Instead she opened the walk-in closet in the guest room where a silky negligee hung on a hanger next to a matching dressing gown.

"What will you wear to the party tonight?" Amina asked.

"I…I'm afraid I have nothing appropriate," Claudia said, opening her suitcase, which the servant had deposited on the wicker luggage rack and surveying the contents with apprehension. What had she been thinking, packing only work clothes? She had been under the impression this was a work trip, not a vacation, that's what she had been thinking.

"So you see, all the more reason I shouldn't attend. I wouldn't know anyone and the truth is, I'm not much of a party person." That was an understatement. Even if she'd been told she would have to attend the party, what would she have brought? The fanciest outfit she owned was a dark suit and a silk blouse, not much different from the dark suit, cotton blouse and low-heeled shoes she'd worn for traveling. Or that she wore every day to work.

"Never mind. You'll wear something of mine." Amina looked her up and down. "I dare say we're about the same size, don't you think? In a minute I'll bring in some things for you to try on. You do know I run a dress shop, don't you? It's my job to dress women. I'm not bragging but I like to think I do a good job of it. For me it's not just my job, it's my passion."

Once again Claudia saw the similarity between Amina and her brother. They each had a passion for what they did and she envied that. Amina sat in an armchair covered with luxuriously embossed fabric and tucked her legs under her. "What is yours?"

"My…my passion?" Claudia sat on the edge of the bed. "I knit and I belong to a book club, but mostly I have no time for a passion. I spend long hours working."

Amina frowned. "That is my brother's fault. I must speak to him about that."

"No, please don't. I love my job." As if speaking to Sam would change her brother's work habits.

"Very well," she said. "If you say so. Now I will bring you the dresses for the party."

"I appreciate the offer, but I probably wouldn't fit into your dresses and I wouldn't fit in at your party, either. I don't know anyone and…"

"You're shy, yes?" Amina smiled sympathetically. "That's what Samir told us."

Claudia's eyes widened. "He told you about me?"

"Of course. How hard you work, how devoted you are to him and the company. How he cannot get along without you. And there's the fortune teller who seems to know you as well." Amina tilted her head to one side. "Yes, you are exactly the way I pictured you."

For some reason this wasn't exactly what Claudia wanted to hear. The person she described sounded incredibly boring. Which was exactly what Sam must think of her. She was just a part of the business, one he couldn't do without to be sure, like the fax machine, or the copier. Suddenly she felt very very tired. She looked longingly at the four-poster bed and then at her watch. No wonder. It was midnight in California.

"Lie down," Amina commanded. "Take a nap. Get some rest while you can. Before the fun starts," she added with a smile.

Fun? Hardly, but she was here, and she would have to do

whatever it took to keep her emotions under control. When fatigue finally overtook her she stretched out on the smooth, silky bedspread. Just for a moment.

When she awoke the sun was setting and turning the sea to gold. She felt disoriented, sure it must be morning, but where? Not here.

She looked around to find the room full of filmy dresses in an array of colors, lying on the chair, hanging in the closet and folded at the end of the bed and a stack of shoe boxes on the floor.

Ah, yes, now she recalled. A sinking feeling hit her. Clothes. A party. An agreement. And an engagement.

"There you are." It was Amina, smiling at her from the doorway, wearing a long, loose dress they called the djellaba, her hair pulled back from her face. "Feeling better? You look it. Sam called. He asked how you were doing. I told him you were napping."

Claudia sat up straight and ran her hand through her hair. Sam needed her and she was sleeping. "You should have woken me. Maybe he needed to talk to me."

"Whatever it was can wait," Amina said. "You look rested. Rested enough to receive Durrah, the fortune teller?"

"You mean she's here?" Claudia was definitely not feeling like herself, but what harm could it do to listen to a fortune teller? She knew what she'd say. What they all said. You will meet a tall, dark stranger. You will travel across the sea. And so on. Even though Amina swore this one was special, that she'd already predicted things about her, Claudia was skeptical to say the least.

"First I'd better speak to Sam," she said.

Amina nodded and handed her her cell phone.

"Is everything okay?" she asked when he answered her call.

"More or less," he said. "I'm glad you were able to get some rest. It's going to be a big night."

"So it seems." A big night for him and his family, no doubt, but a horrible long night for her. She must not spoil this occasion by complaining or telling him she didn't want to attend.

"Is Amina taking good care of you?" he asked.

"She couldn't be nicer. She's even provided a fortune teller for entertainment."

Amina grinned and nodded toward the door as if the woman was waiting there.

"Don't tell me you believe in that nonsense," he said sternly.

"It will be interesting to hear what she has to say," Claudia said tactfully with an eye on Amina. She didn't want to discount his sister's fortune teller before she'd even met her.

"I can tell you what she'll say," Sam said. "Because Amina forced me to endure a session with the so-called fortune teller the last time I was here. She'll look at your palm and tell you you have a deep, long line stretching horizontally across your palm, which means you have clear and focused thinking. Which you already know because I've told you a thousand times. What a waste of time."

"Yes, well, thanks for your input. I'll see you soon then."

"I suppose Sam told you his feelings about fortune tellers," Amina said when Claudia had hung up. "My brother is the most cynical of men, as you no doubt know. He doesn't believe in seers, magicians, or anything he can't see and touch. Like love for example. Mark my words, someday he'll fall and when he does I will have the last laugh."

Claudia smiled politely. She had to agree that Sam was

cynical, but as for him falling in love, if it hadn't happened yet, it didn't seem likely.

Durrah the fortune teller was small and dark and draped in a long, colorful garment. Her fingers were covered with jeweled rings. Claudia smiled to herself. This woman couldn't have looked more the part of fortune teller than if she'd been cast and costumed for a Hollywood movie.

Durrah waved to Claudia to join her at the small table where she made herself comfortable in one of the wing chairs and set a deck of cards in front of her. Amina leaned back against the dressing table. "To translate," she explained.

The first thing Durrah did was to study Claudia's palms. Sure enough, she did tell Claudia she had a deep, long "head" line, which meant clear and focused thinking. But she moved on to examine her broken "heart" line and told her it meant disappointment in love.

Claudia, feeling a little uncomfortable, shifted in her chair. Disappointment was not quite the word for what Claudia had gone through. Durrah couldn't possibly know about her divorce. It was just a good guess. After all, most people had been disappointed in love at one time or another. But Claudia was a guest and she must not let her cynicism show no matter what she thought. It would be rude.

When the woman turned to her cards, Claudia was relieved. She had been hitting too close to home when she had zeroed in on Claudia's love line.

"She says there is trouble ahead," Amina said. "Someone is sick."

"Oh, dear. Not someone in your family, I hope," Claudia said.

"No, but it will affect the family."

"What about the merger?" Claudia asked. After all, what could be more important?

"She can't see it. It doesn't mean it won't happen, it just means she's having trouble picturing it." Amina frowned. "Well, no one can be right all the time," she murmured. "But there's more. She wants to tell you there's a man in your future."

"Really?" Claudia asked politely. "Is he tall and dark?"

"Why yes," Amina said. "That's exactly right. She says you will find happiness and wealth beyond your wildest dreams. It will be soon. And it will be nearby."

"Nearby?" Claudia asked, glancing around the room. The woman must be getting desperate.

Amina nodded. "The disappointment you once felt will fade like the broken heart line on your palm. And you will live happily ever after. A long, long life. Now, aren't you happy you came here?"

"As long as we can accomplish what we came to do, then of course I'll be happy," Claudia said. Surely Amina didn't believe that a fortune teller, no matter how gifted she was, was capable of spouting anything but tried and true clichés.

"And now it's time to try on some party dresses," she said, handing Durrah a small purse and showing her to the door.

"Wait." The old woman stopped in the doorway, her jeweled hand held high in the air. Amina translated what she had to say. "A woman can hide her love for forty years but her disgust and anger not for one day." She wagged her finger at Claudia. "Remember this."

Claudia smiled politely but inside she was trembling. Surely the woman didn't know anything. How could she possibly guess Claudia had a love to hide at all? She breathed a sigh of relief when Amina closed the door.

"I'm not sure what that was all about," Amina said, then she threw herself into the process of selecting a dress for Claudia. "Maybe it will be revealed to us in time."

Claudia had never been much of a shopper, but she'd rather try on dresses for hours than hear any more of the fortune teller's ramblings. Who knew what more she'd say about her love life if she had any encouragement?

She'd only known Sam's sister for a matter of hours, but Claudia was once again struck by the Al-Hamri family resemblance and it wasn't just Amina's dark expressive eyes that were like her brother's, or her smooth, ebony hair or her passion for her work. It was her manner, her way of setting an agenda and making decisions for others, like what Claudia should wear to the party.

When she disagreed with Sam, sometimes Claudia took a stand, sometimes it just wasn't worth it. She'd learned working with him to pick her battles. The battle of the party dress was not one she was willing to fight over. She might as well give in this time, wear a dress and go to the party.

Good thing she'd decided to give in, because Amina was busily unzipping dresses, holding them out and insisting Claudia strip down to her underwear. Which she could tell by the look on her face, Amina did not find acceptable. Who wore all cotton briefs besides Claudia? Who didn't wear pretty lacy bikinis or demi bras? Claudia didn't. And she had no intention of changing. But she hadn't counted on the Al-Hamri resolve.

It seemed Amina had a collection of lingerie for sale at her shop on hand right there in her apartment, which she insisted Claudia try on. Next it was the dresses.

Sam rang the bell on his sister's door, but when she didn't answer, he let himself in with his key. His own apartment was just across the hall.

"Hello," he called, "anyone home?"

He followed the sound of girlish laughter down the hall from the bedrooms.

"Amina? Claudia?" he said.

"Back here, Sam," his sister answered.

In her guest bedroom he found his sister sitting on the floor, her arms around her knees looking at a woman he scarcely recognized as his assistant who was standing in the middle of the room wearing a bright red dress. It couldn't be Claudia.

Claudia in a bright red cocktail dress that came just below her knees showing long and shapely legs he'd never noticed before. Because if he'd seen those legs, he would have noticed. Maybe it was the high-heeled shoes she was wearing. Totally unlike her. Where had those come from?

He leaned against the wall and stuffed his hands into his pockets. He was tired, hungry and jet-lagged, and now this. Too many changes in too short a time left him feeling like he'd been thrown off his favorite stallion and landed on his head.

"Like it?" his sister asked.

"Very nice," he said. What else could he say? *I don't want my assistant looking sexy. I can't handle that right now. So take the dress off of her and get her back into her work uniform—dark suit, white blouse and sensible shoes.*

Nice? He would never admit it out loud, but she was

stunning in this red dress that was so unlike anything Claudia would normally wear that he rubbed his eyes in disbelief.

"Where's the fortune teller?" he asked. "I thought that's what you were up to."

"She was here," Amina said. "Just long enough to tell us there's a tall, dark man in Claudia's future as well as wealth and happiness. Isn't that right, Claudia?"

Sam frowned. Claudia in a bright red dress with a tall, dark stranger? This was complete foolishness. Fortunately his assistant was as sensible as she was or her head might be turned. "No one in her right mind would believe that old crone," Sam said. "And Claudia is definitely in her right mind. She's the brightest woman I know." He knew how lucky he was to have her for an assistant. As soon as she got out of that dress, things would be back to normal and she'd be back in the role she always occupied.

"Think what you will, Sam," Amina said. "We'll see who's right. You may have to swallow your cynical comments when the future is revealed."

He held out his hands. "You know me. I'm as open-minded as the next man. If it comes true, I'll admit I was wrong. No one deserves wealth and happiness more than Claudia."

"What about the tall, dark stranger?" Amina asked. "Does she deserve him?"

"If that's what she wants." He looked at Claudia who looked uncomfortable in the extreme. He could not imagine Claudia waiting around for a stranger to lure her away with wealth and happiness. If he did, she might quit and where would Sam be without her? Stuck trying to get by without his right-hand man, that's where.

"I hope you didn't pay much for this ridiculous prediction," Sam said, looking at his sister then at Claudia.

"It's not ridiculous at all," Amina said, her hands on her hips. "Claudia is a lovely woman. She could meet someone special and rich at any time and succumb to his charms. In fact, considering the wealth per capita in our country, I believe she's come to the right place to see her fortune fulfilled. She doesn't belong to you, Sam. She just works for you."

Sam turned to take another look at Claudia. Just worked for him? All right, maybe she did look lovely in the dress. That didn't mean she was any more susceptible to the flattery of a stranger. In fact, she was beginning to look tired around the eyes and her mouth was drooping. This was all his sister's fault.

"Enough of this," he said. "You've had your fun, Amina. Let my assistant get out of this dress."

Amina stood and picked up a hanger. "If you'll excuse us, Sam, we are still looking at dresses. What about this leopard print, for example."

Sam shook his head. A leopard print on Claudia? Things were getting out of hand. Amina held up a strapless dress, then tossed it on the bed and grabbed another. "Champagne peau de soie with scoop neck and bubble skirt, one of my personal favorites."

Amina turned to Claudia. "Which one do you like best?"

Sam stared at her. All she had to do was say—*None of the above. I don't want to wear a sexy party dress. It's not my style.* But she didn't. She said she liked the red one. Had she lost her mind? Clearly he'd been mistaken in leaving her in the care of his strong-willed sister.

Claudia seemed to be unaware of how outrageous she

looked. She was staring at herself in the full-length mirror on the closet door with a strange, puzzled expression on her face. Her cheeks were flushed and her hair was in a tangle, so unlike her usual tailored self he was almost speechless.

"Claudia, don't let Amina tell you what to wear," he said. "She gets carried away with her power over her customers."

"Don't talk to me about using my power," Amina said with a saucy grin at her brother. "I think I know a bit more than you about what looks good on women."

"You love doing this, don't you?" he asked his sister. "You used to dress your dolls, now you dress women the same way."

Amina chuckled. His sister never took anything he said seriously. "Nothing wrong with that, is there?" she said. "Making beautiful women more beautiful. It's a gift I have, if I may say so myself."

Maybe it was her gift, but Claudia was not a beautiful woman. She was practical, smart and intuitive. Not unattractive, but no one would call her beautiful. He should never have left Claudia alone with Amina. Look what happened.

He took a step back. As if he got too close to his assistant in this red dress she was wearing, he might get burned.

"Oh, there's my phone. Be right back." Amina dashed down past Sam and hurried down the hall.

"How did your meeting go?" Claudia asked Sam. "You said you wanted to talk to me."

"Well…" He simply couldn't concentrate with her standing there in that dress. Was he the only one who noticed it didn't suit her at all?

"Have their been any changes?"

"A few." He walked to the French doors that opened to the

balcony and looked out to sea. "The biggest change is in my father. He's not himself. I don't know what to do. He's feeling his age, I'm afraid. Which is why the merger is somewhat worrying. The company will be huge and he'll have that much more responsibility."

"That's too bad. Maybe someone from the other family can step in to pick up the slack."

Sam didn't look convinced. "Perhaps. It's true that control for the new company has to be shared if this merger is to work. But it's going to be hard to give up total control and put trust in others."

"Isn't that true of marriage as well?" she asked softly.

He turned to look at her, struck once again by her intuitive powers. "Of course. I hadn't made the connection, but you're right, as usual," he said. "Maybe that's why I never wanted to get married." *And still don't.*

"It will take some time to reorganize, I imagine," she said.

"The company or the marriage?" he asked.

She didn't say anything. He knew the answer was "both" as well as she did.

"Let's get back to business," he said brusquely. This conversation was getting entirely too personal. "You'll make one of your brilliant organizational charts so we can get an idea where we all fit in…to the company of course." She had a genius for sorting things out and making complicated matters understandable. As long as they had nothing to do with his personal life. He would handle that in his own way. Or put it off as long as possible.

"I'd be glad to. I'm looking forward to meeting your father," she said.

"Good," Sam said. Once his father met her, he'd realize what an asset she was. After he saw her in action, he'd be as impressed as Sam himself was with Claudia's knowledge and perception. "You'll meet him tonight."

He took another look at her from her tousled hair to her high-heeled shoes, hoping he'd made a mistake and the dress hadn't changed her after all. She sounded the same. She thought the same. But she didn't look the same. He'd never seen such a transformation within the space of a few hours. It was Amina's doing. Her fault. On her own Claudia would never have chosen to wear a dress like this.

"So is this really what you're wearing tonight?"

"Amina says the party is a formal occasion, so…"

"She knows fashion and I don't. I just think…"

"It's too much, isn't it? It's too bright, too…too…everything. It isn't really me." Her eyes, which had been so bright, now avoided his. "I feel foolish. I'll change."

"Good idea." All she had to do was get out of that dress and those shoes and everything would be back to normal. He had just breathed a sigh of relief when he heard loud voices, his sister and someone else shouting at each other in Arabic.

Claudia's eyes widened. "Who could it be?" she asked.

"From what I hear, it could only be one person. It's Zahara, and she's very angry."

A moment later a red-faced Zahara stood in the doorway, her hands on her hips, glaring at him. She pointed at Claudia.

"Who is this woman?" she demanded. "Get rid of her immediately or the engagement is off."

Claudia teetered on the strappy high-heeled sandals Amina had given her to try on. She wasn't too steady in these shoes anyway, and with this woman standing there, pointing and glaring at her she was afraid she might just topple over. It was just as she feared, in a matter of seconds, this woman had guessed Claudia was in love with Sam.

But if she was really smart, she'd realize she had nothing to fear from Claudia. Sam would instantly make that clear to her and everyone in the room.

"Zahara, this is Claudia, my American office assistant," Sam said firmly "She works for me. She manages the office. That's all." There, that ought to reassure her. Claudia meant nothing more to him than that. It shouldn't hurt so much to hear him say it, because it was the simple truth. But it did. His words were like a knife through her heart.

Just a glance at the stunningly beautiful woman told her as anything more than words could that Claudia was living in a fantasy world if she thought Sam would ever think of her other than a competent assistant.

"Hah," Zahara said. "I know what I see. I'm not blind. What kind of an assistant appears in a red dress like this? I've never been to America but I know that office personnel do not wear designer gowns. You'll have to come up with a better story than that, Sam."

"It's true," Claudia said. What on earth was wrong with the woman? Wasn't it obvious Claudia didn't fit into the scene here any more than a dandelion fit into a formal garden? No matter what she was wearing she was still way out of their league. She'd never worn a designer gown in her life and if she had a choice she wouldn't be wearing one now. And if she really had a choice, she'd still be back in the office halfway across the world instead of standing here wishing she was invisible.

"I have nothing to do with…anything. I'm here to work, that's all. Really. It's not my dress." She looked at Amina, waiting for her to confirm what she said but Amina seemed more amused than anything and didn't say a word.

Claudia's knees were shaking and she reached down to remove her shoes before she fell over. Was this the kind of family drama they were all accustomed to? If so, she wouldn't last another day in this country.

Sam took Zahara by the arm. "I think it's time for you and I to have a talk, don't you? It's been a long time. We have so much to say to each other." And he smoothly guided his future bride out of the room.

Claudia turned away so she wouldn't have to see them walk out together, the perfect couple, both tall, good-looking, rich and meant for each other. She picked up the shoes and tried to catch her breath. To hear Sam talk so soothingly to his intended fiancée was painful. Just as painful as she'd imagined back in San Francisco.

Why oh why had she come here? She knew it would hurt. She just hadn't known how excruciating the pain would be. She'd known it was a mistake to get on that plane. Why had she let Sam talk her into it?

"Well," Amina said, her hands on her hips. "That was interesting."

Interesting? That was her idea of interesting? "I hope he'll be able to explain to her," Claudia said. "I wouldn't want to cause any trouble between them." Claudia wished she'd never taken off her old clothes now piled on the chair in the corner.

"I'm afraid you already have," Amina said. "But *tant pis*, as they say in France."

"You heard what she said," Claudia said. "It's the dress." Claudia cast a rueful glance at the yards of red fabric. "If she'd seen me when I arrived, she'd never have given me a second glance. I can't believe she thinks I'm some sort of a threat to her. It's ridiculous."

"Is it?" Amina murmured. "I wonder."

"Amina," Claudia said as she unzipped the dress and let it fall around her hips to the floor. "Your brother and I work together. I admire him and I think he appreciates the work I do for him. It's the best job I've ever had and he's the best boss in the world." As soon as the words left her mouth Claudia wished she hadn't sounded so adamant. She wouldn't want her words repeated to Sam or anyone however true they were.

"You mean he doesn't make you work overtime, come in early and stay late at the office?"

"Well, yes, sometimes."

"He doesn't call you at home to ask you about work?"

"Of course, but only when it's necessary."

"He's never stubborn or insists he's always right?"

"He usually is right about most things. If he isn't, we talk about it." Claudia could not let his sister make him out to be some sort of ogre. Not that Sam needed her to defend him, it was just that she couldn't help it.

Amina shook her head in mock despair. "I know Sam and I know I couldn't work for him. All I can say is that he's very lucky to have you." She paused and turned her attention back to the clothes, the subject she loved most. Even more than she liked discussing her brother and his overbearing ways. "What is your decision? The champagne peau de soie or the red?"

"You mean the party is on?" Claudia asked.

"Of course. Sam will say all the right things and Zahara will come around. Mark my words. When my brother wants something, he gets it. Surely you've noticed that in the two years you've worked for him?"

"Yes," Claudia admitted, her heart sinking. What she didn't want to admit was that this engagement meant so much to him that he was off sweet-talking his fiancée right now. For one moment her hopes rose thinking that maybe, just maybe the engagement was off. Not that it mattered. He still would never be hers. Now if only she could get out of going to this party. Though there was little hope of that with Amina around.

"What about the black with the bow across the bodice. That was spectacular on you," Amina said, gathering an armload of dresses to take back with her.

Claudia nodded. She'd tried on so many dresses she couldn't remember which was which. "Fine," she said, feeling as deflated as a hot-air balloon after the party.

"Good choice," Amina congratulated, though actually it was *her* choice. "I'll have my maid run you a hot bath and you can relax until dinner. How does that sound?"

"It sounds wonderful," Claudia said gratefully. Maybe there would be a miracle while she soaked in a perfumed bath. Or maybe by some chance Sam wouldn't be able to convince his fiancée that Claudia was no more important than a fax machine or a scanner. In which case there would be no celebration party. Knowing Sam's powers of persuasion, there wasn't much chance of that.

She was glad for Sam, she really was. Because if you love someone, really love them, you want them to be happy. Why did she think he wouldn't be happy with Zahara? He would.

She was perfect for him. Right background, right family, right financial situation. She was everything Claudia wasn't. And Zahara was beautiful, too. He couldn't find anyone who would suit him better.

For his sake, she hoped Amina was right and he'd calm down his fiancée so the engagement would go off as planned. Because she definitely wanted the best for Sam. Why was it so hard to believe that Zahara was really the best for him? He was the only one who could decide that.

# CHAPTER FOUR

IF CLAUDIA thought she would be overdressed in the strapless black dress with the bow across the bodice, she was wrong. Every other woman in the richly appointed ballroom with the crystal chandeliers was in a formal gown and every man including Sam was in a tuxedo and black tie or dress robes. The hum of conversations around her were in Arabic, English and a smattering of European languages. There was the scent of expensive fragrances in the air. It was all so sophisticated, she wondered how she'd possibly fit in.

Every man was in formal wear, but no other man looked as dashing and sexy as her boss. Surely she wasn't the only one who noticed. And she did notice. Even though she was taken around the room by Amina and introduced to everyone there, her gaze kept straying across the room and landing on Sam. Once he caught her eye and smiled at her.

She had no idea if it was meant to reassure her or to hide his concern. Maybe it just indicated he thought things were going well. If so she was glad for him. If anyone could reassure a nervous fiancée, it was Sam. She wanted so much to talk to him, to find out exactly what had happened, but

Amina was introducing her to friends and relatives and she had no chance to break away.

If Claudia's presence was all Zahara was worried about, then it probably wasn't a big job. But where was Zahara tonight? Why wasn't she hanging on Sam's arm? Why wasn't she accepting best wishes and beaming as a future bride should be? Why was she late for her own party?

There was no reason for Claudia to feel like butterflies were nesting in her stomach. She was just an innocent by-stander, no matter what Zahara thought. If Zahara had only caught a glimpse of Claudia's usual self at the office, she'd know she had nothing to fear. Which is probably what Sam had told her. *Claudia works for me. She's a valued and trusted employee. Nothing more.* And she'd believed him. Who wouldn't?

Amina excused herself to greet a man who'd just arrived and was instantly engaged in an animated conversation with him. From the way her eyes were sparkling, Claudia wondered if it was her boyfriend. She wondered what kind of man Amina would be attracted to. Sam's sister looked spectacular in a teal-blue designer dress that showed off her tanned skin to perfection, but when did Amina ever look anything but stunning?

She wasn't beautiful, but with her personality and her sense of style, she would stand out in any crowd. If the man wasn't someone special or even if he was, then Amina was extremely good at flirting, a skill Claudia was lacking. Maybe if she watched and took notes she'd be ready when that tall, handsome stranger appeared in her life.

Standing alone watching the guests, Claudia didn't know

anyone she could ask for Zahara's whereabouts. Certainly not Sam. He was far away across the room. But she kept her eyes on the door. It was almost time for dinner and still no Zahara.

"So this is the brilliant assistant Samir has told us about." A man about Sam's age introduced himself as his cousin Ahmad and told her he'd gone to school in the States. "What he didn't tell us was that his assistant was so beautiful."

Claudia smiled at this outrageous compliment. If she looked even close to beautiful, it was thanks to Amina, the makeup she'd applied, the hairstyle she'd had her maid do for Claudia and of course the black dress.

"Tell me, Sam's assistant," Ahmad said, "what do you think of our little country?"

"I haven't seen much, but I'm sure I'm going to like it," she said politely.

With his hand on her elbow he walked her to the balcony to see views of the spectacular illuminated sculpture gardens below. "It's hard to believe that only forty years ago all that stood here was a stone fort, sand and palm huts," he said, waving his arm toward the city in the distance. "No hotels, no high-rise buildings at all, no fine art, no gardens. I hope your boss is giving you time for some sightseeing while you're here?"

"It depends on how much work we have to do," she said. "But I certainly hope so. I've heard so much about the colorful markets and the camel caravans."

"Have you?" he asked with an amused smile. "Well, if I know Sam he'll be at his desk all day and half the night. And you won't see a thing but what's on the computer screen. The man is a workaholic. Don't look surprised," he said, tilting her chin with his thumb. "You can't work for my cousin and not know that about him."

"Well, yes," she admitted, feeling a little uncomfortable to be touched by a total stranger whose face was only inches from hers. Maybe Ahmad thought all American girls were easy after spending a few years at an American university. "But I'm still hoping to see something of the desert. I've only seen pictures of the dunes and the oases, but…"

"You should see the city from the water. It's the only way to appreciate the spectacular skyline. I have a sailboat and I invite you for a sail. Are you free tomorrow or are you as much of a workaholic as your boss is?"

"No, I mean, I…I really don't know what the schedule is," Claudia said. "I'll have to ask Samir. I assume there will be work to do. That's what I'm here for."

She was here for work, so how could she even consider sailing with a strange man? Surely that's not what she was supposed to do while in Tazzatine.

"Work, work, always work," Ahmad said. "You're only here once. Or maybe not. Maybe you'll like us and our country so much you'll come often." He winked at her.

"There you are," Sam said to Claudia as he came out onto the balcony to join them. "I was looking for you."

"We were just talking about you, Sam," Ahmad said. "You can't keep this fetching creature holed up in your office all day and night." He gave Claudia's bare shoulder a squeeze. She refrained from stepping backward to escape his touch. No, it wasn't disgust or anger she felt, it was just a slight revulsion. But she was a stranger here and she didn't know what was acceptable behavior and what wasn't.

"It's not right," Ahmad said. "She should at least come sailing with me tomorrow. Say ten o'clock? The winds should be perfect."

Sam looked at Claudia for a long moment, his forehead creased in a frown as if he was asking himself if Claudia had been complaining about him or the work he gave her. The amber lights arched along the ceiling were reflected in his dark eyes. She didn't know what bothered him the most. The idea of her going sailing when she should be working with him or the way she looked tonight. Or maybe something had gone wrong with the engagement. If only Ahmad weren't there, she could ask.

One thing was for sure: Sam must be shocked at the amount of makeup on her face and her new hairstyle, not to mention the black dress. Hopefully he understood this was all his sister's doing and not her idea at all. She'd never even meant to come to this party. But there had been no polite way to get out of it.

"This is a business trip, Ahmad," Sam said shortly. "Claudia knows that. Of course I mean to show her around, but business first."

"He hasn't changed," Ahmad said to Claudia shaking his head in mock despair. Obviously Sam's comments didn't dampen his spirits one bit. "I'll get back to you about this later." With that he bowed slightly and walked away to join a group of young people back in the ballroom.

"In case you're wondering, he hasn't changed, either," Sam said. "The man doesn't know the meaning of hard work. He lives off his inheritance and generally spends his days in leisure. If you want to go sailing with him, by all means go."

"But what about the contract? When do we meet with the Bayadhis?"

"Not until tomorrow afternoon. I was going to…never mind, you should take the opportunity to go sailing. You looked like you were enjoying Ahmad's company. Women generally find him amusing."

From the look on Sam's face, it was clear he found him far from amusing. In fact, downright annoying.

He looked at his watch. There was a long silence while Claudia formed the questions she wanted to ask but was afraid to. Where's Zahara? How did your talk with her go? Is everything okay?

After they'd stood there without speaking for what seemed an eternity, while she waited for him to explain what had happened, Sam stepped back and looked at her. His gaze traveled slowly from her new hairstyle to the tips of the high-heeled sandals she was wearing. His eyes narrowed. She held her breath.

"You look…different," he said at last. No smile. No frown. Just a very intense look directly into her eyes.

She exhaled slowly. What did it mean "different?" Good different or bad different?

"I'm not," she said. "I'm still the same, underneath the clothes and…everything."

"Good," he said brusquely.

Then he suggested they go back inside. "It's almost time for dinner," he said. They both knew no one would sit down to dinner until the guest of honor arrived—the lovely and lucky woman who was getting engaged tonight. Claudia just hoped she could keep her composure when it happened.

"But what about Zahara? Surely we can't start until she arrives."

He didn't say anything. He braced his hands on the ledge of the balcony and stared out into the dark night as if he'd forgotten he'd suggested returning to the ball room. "Of course not," he said at last as if Claudia was crazy to even consider such a thing even though she hadn't.

"Then everything went well? Your meeting with her?" Maybe she was overstepping the bounds between employer and employee, but she couldn't wait another minute to find out.

"Very well. We're in complete agreement, Zahara and I."

Claudia thought she might choke. Complete agreement, he said. How much clearer could it be? How much more did Claudia have to hear before she gave up her crazy dreams? She gave herself a stern lecture. He belonged to Zahara. They were getting engaged. By the end of the night she'd be wearing that beautiful, dazzling five-carat ring Claudia had picked out.

"I'm glad to hear it," she said. "She seemed so upset earlier."

"I know. For some reason she thought you and I were a couple."

"How ridiculous," Claudia murmured.

"That's what I said. Completely. She said she has a sense about these things. She thought I was in love with you."

"*You* were in love with *me?*" Claudia blurted. She wouldn't have been surprised to hear just the opposite, that she was in love with Sam.

He shook his head as if he'd never heard anything so preposterous. "That's what set her off. She's really quite reasonable when you get to know her."

"And beautiful," Claudia couldn't help adding. She didn't say she had no desire to get to know his future bride and to find out just how reasonable she was.

"That, too," Sam agreed.

"Did you get a chance to tell her you didn't believe in love?"

"I didn't think it was the time or place. But I assured her I was not in love with you nor were you in love with me. After all, we work together, that's all."

"So everything is…in order?" Claudia asked.

"Absolutely," he said, turning to go into the ballroom.

Claudia didn't see Zahara come in but the sudden lift of Sam's eyebrows and the half smile on his face told her all she needed to know. He was obviously delighted to see her. And why not? Turning, she saw Zahara looked absolutely gorgeous in a long ivory satin gown that clung to her like it was made for her. Which it was, according to Amina.

No longer angry, she looked serene and calm. Reasonable, Sam had said. An excellent trait for a wife. Heads turned. Of course. Not only was she lovely to look at, but she was the star of the party. She and Sam.

A hush fell over the room as Zahara sailed across the polished marble floor. Claudia would never be able to walk like that in high heels. But Zahara certainly knew how to make an entrance as she came straight over to where Claudia stood with Sam. She kissed him lightly on the cheek and Claudia's heart lurched. How much more could she take? There was not a doubt in anybody's mind these two were meant for each other.

"Did you tell her?" Zahara said to Sam.

"Not yet."

Claudia's gaze moved from Sam's face to Zahara's. Tell her what? She already knew they were about to get engaged. She already figured she'd be let go. She already knew she never should have come here.

"I'm so sorry for this afternoon," Zahara said in a melodic low voice tinged with an intriguing accent. So different from her angry tone a short time ago. "I was not myself. I was worried. I thought…oh never mind what I thought. It was ridiculous. But then we had a little talk and everything is going to be fine now, right, Samir?"

The intimate smile she gave Sam said it all. If they had any problems, they'd solved them. Claudia knew she should be happy for Sam, but she was filled with unbearable feelings of unbecoming envy. How could she help it seeing that Sam and his fiancée had made up and were headed for a happy life together while her life was practically over?

Her job would be finished. She'd go back to California and find another job. But no job would ever compare with this one. No boss could hold a candle to Sam. Why had she ever come here with him? He didn't need her. It was pure torture seeing him with Zahara.

"I'm so happy for you," Claudia said stiffly. As if anyone cared what she thought.

"Thank you," Zahara said. She favored Claudia with a radiant smile.

"I'm sure you'll have a wonderful life together," Claudia added, trying her best to sound sincere. It was the least she could do for Sam.

"I'm sure we will," Zahara said with a glance at Sam who smiled back at her. She was positively beaming now. What had happened during their meeting together? Whatever it was, it had made her very happy. What about Sam? He wasn't the type to smile incessantly. But inside he must be delighted he'd gotten what he wanted. And what he wanted was Zahara. Who wouldn't?

All Sam had to do was assure her that Claudia was no threat to their engagement or their future together. He must have told her she was nothing but a drone, an assistant who worked hard and long but nothing more. He must have painted a rosy picture of their future.

Claudia could see it now. A life divided between two countries. Travel, home, children, financial security and maybe even love. If Sam didn't love Zahara now, he would later. That's how these arranged marriages worked. Divorce was frowned on, so the couples worked out their problems and more often than not, got along just fine. Probably many learned to love each other, which was just a bonus. At least that's how it was supposed to be. If it wasn't, why did it work out so well? With the exception of Sam's parents. But their mistake had been in marrying outside their countries and their cultures. His mother was not from Tazzatine, but Zahara was. They had everything going for them.

When dinner was announced, Sam and Zahara led the parade of guests into the private dining room. Candles gleamed from the tables and the sconces on the wall. White tablecloths, bronze utensils and vases of white roses graced the tables. Sam's cousin Ahmad showed up to escort Claudia. It was better than no one, but it was an effort to smile and make polite conversation with the man. It wasn't his fault. He was outgoing and gregarious; it was her fault for not being able to control her jealousy.

During dinner, over tiny lamb chops, potatoes gratin and petit pois, Ahmad told amusing stories of his and Sam's childhood. Learning to sail on the Gulf, riding horses over the dunes and playing hid-and-seek in the souks. Claudia leaned forward and took it all in. She found their shared past fascinating. Ahmad might be as lazy as Sam said, but he was a great storyteller. While listening, she had no trouble picturing Sam as an adventurous little boy.

But she wondered if Ahmad was right. The Sam she knew really was all work and no play. But maybe if he had someone to take his mind off his work, he wouldn't be that way. Surely Zahara wouldn't permit him to bury himself in his work and neglect her. She'd be the type to drag him off to socialize, which he should do. She hated to concede that Zahara had any good points, but it would be good for Sam to get away from the office. And when she was no longer his assistant, she wouldn't care what he was doing or where he was.

It was hard to imagine life without Sam, but it was about time she forced herself to contemplate it. In between courses Sam's uncle stood and gave a short speech about family and love and marriage and with every word Claudia sank further and further into depression.

She didn't belong here. She never should have come. If only she could be swallowed up by the cold, hard marble on the floor. Instead she had to sit there, smile, nod and appear interested. Her head ached from the effort and she just wanted to go back to the apartment, crawl into bed and escape this nightmare.

His uncle welcomed Sam back and gave up the floor to him. Now it was Sam's turn.

"Greetings to all my friends and family," Sam said

smoothly. He looked so happy and relaxed, Claudia couldn't tear her eyes from him. Even though she knew what he was going to say. It was a kind of terrible fixation. Her gaze glued to his, her mind attuned to his. If she had any sense, any will-power, she would have pleaded ill and slipped away now. But she was frozen there, waiting for doom to strike. Waiting for the noose to tighten. Waiting for her life to change forever.

"As you all know, Zahara and I are here tonight to make an announcement that will surprise some but in the end make everyone happy."

Claudia scanned the faces around the tables lighted by flickering candlelight. There was Sam's family at one table. She could be mistaken, but she thought Amina looked puzzled and Sam's father looked positively dour. What was wrong? Would some really be surprised? She thought they'd be ecstatic to see their dreams of uniting the families come true.

"As much as we dislike disappointing our families, Zahara and I have decided to call off our engagement," Sam said bluntly.

Claudia's mouth fell open. Why hadn't he told her? Why had he led her to believe everything was fine? The obvious answer was that he considered his personal life to be none of her business.

The guests around her table gasped in disbelief.

More than one said, "Oh, no."

Sam looked around the room as if daring anyone to challenge him, or even to ask questions. The tone of his voice left no doubt that he was sincere and that the decision was made. The room filled with hushed murmurs of surprise mingled with shock.

When Zahara got up to join Sam at the podium the room

fell silent again in anticipation. What could she possibly say? "Thank you all for coming. It is a lovely party. Samir and I are grateful for your understanding and your friendship." Then she walked between the tables, her head held high and left the room.

Now the buzz grew louder, like dozens of disturbed beehives.

"What happened?"

"Who called it off?"

"Zahara."

"What? But whose idea was it really?"

"How terrible for the Al-Hamris."

"I can't believe it."

"What's wrong with her?"

"There's someone else."

"No!"

"Yes."

"What shame on her family."

Claudia sat staring at Sam as he went back to the table where his family was still sitting. The dinner continued. The salad course was next. It consisted of mixed greens, nuts and dried fruit in a lively vinaigrette. But who could taste anything after that stunning announcement? Claudia pushed the lettuce around on her plate.

Ahmad seated at her right appeared unmoved by the whole spectacle and was eating his salad with gusto.

"I knew it wouldn't work," he said smugly. "Never marry a workaholic."

"You mean that's why she's backing out?" Claudia asked, setting her fork down.

"Who says it's her idea?" he asked, sipping his nonalcoholic sparkling beverage. "Maybe Sam realizes he'd make a terrible husband and is doing the poor girl a favor." He made this remark with a knowing smile. "Whatever the reason, you and I are the only ones here who don't appear to be shocked by Sam having the nerve to question his family's wishes. Am I right?"

"I guess so," she said.

"Sam's in big trouble, believe me. His family isn't going to be happy about this."

"Just because he's called off his engagement?" Claudia asked.

"Oh, it's more than that. It's flouting tradition. It's sticking it to your parents. It's like telling them you know more than they do. Not that I don't give Sam credit for standing up for himself. I don't know if I'd have the nerve. You would, wouldn't you?" he asked, leaning toward her.

"I don't know," Claudia murmured. "It's nice if everyone agrees." Maybe if her parents had met Malcolm before the wedding they would have seen something she hadn't and warned her. She kept thinking of Ahmed's remark that Sam would be a *terrible husband*. He was wrong. Sam couldn't be a terrible anything. He was sensitive, kind, supportive...

But what did she know? She'd made a big mistake herself and what had she learned in the mean time? What would she do differently? She'd imagined herself in love. At least Sam and Zahara realized they weren't in love and called it off before it was too late. Or did they? How did it happen? What did it mean? Would Sam eventually tell her?

Waiters circulated bringing the cheese course around to the tables, serving wedges of smooth, a locally made pungent goat cheese, fresh Italian Asiago, a rich Camembert and a tangy blue mottled Roquefort and several other cheeses she'd never seen before with fruit and an assortment of crackers. And after that, coffee and a cake layered with fresh raspberries and whipped cream. If only Claudia could have appreciated it, but her stomach was tied in knots.

Ahmad, her dinner companion, unmoved by the family drama, or just enjoying seeing Sam being the talk of the party, and not in a good way, continued to eat and enjoy the dinner until he'd polished off every last crumb of cake and drunk two cups of coffee.

People were saying goodbye and exchanging hugs and kisses, men as well as women. Clearly the party was winding down. Would it have finished so early if the outcome had been different? Or would they continue to celebrate until late in the evening? Claudia had no idea. Not only was she a stranger in a strange land, but she was also completely unfamiliar with black-tie social events of this kind in her own country. Never mind broken engagement parties.

"What next?" Ahmad said, pulling Claudia's chair out for her. "You haven't had a taste of our nightlife. Let's get out of this gloomy atmosphere. I'll show you a side of the capitol you won't find mentioned in any tourist guide."

"Thank you," she said, eyeing the door with longing. "But I'm very tired."

"Ah, jet lag," he said. "I have a sure cure for it. Partying till dawn."

"I don't think so," Claudia said. All she wanted to do was collapse in Amina's guest room on that divine bed and sleep until the sun shone in on her in the morning. Or until Sam needed her for work. Her feet hurt, her brain was having trouble processing all the events and her face and lips felt too numb to talk anymore.

"Come on, Sam's beautiful assistant," he said, taking her hand and pulling her toward the door.

"No, really…"

"She said no."

Claudia turned to see where the voice had come from and there was Sam on the other side of Ahmad, glaring at him.

"Fine," Ahmad said. "I was just going to see her home."

"I'll do that," Sam said.

Ahmad shrugged. "See you tomorrow then," he said to Claudia. And he went off to party until dawn, leaving her alone with Sam as they made their way to the door. Now was her chance to find out what really happened.

"I don't understand," she said when she couldn't hold the words back another minute. This was not the time to mince words. "If I had something to do with your breaking off your engagement I should know about it."

"You?" Sam said. As if that was the strangest idea he'd ever heard. "Of course not. It's complicated, but that outburst in front of you had nothing to do with you. Zahara was hoping to break off the engagement and was hoping to force the issue by pretending to be outraged by your presence. As if you and I would ever be involved in that way."

Claudia bit her lip to keep from crying. She was tired, drained and ready to fall apart. The disbelief in his voice when he said *you*? had hurt her as much as a slap in the face.

Before she could say another word, his father caught up with them.

"What does this mean?" he demanded, grasping hold of his son. "This is a cruel disappointment to me."

"Father, I'm sorry. I wanted to tell you first. I tried to find you but every time I looked for you you were busy with someone else. In any case I promised Zahara I'd keep it a secret until tonight."

"I don't understand. We've planned this moment for years. Both our families are overjoyed. It is the dream of a lifetime, uniting the families. Everyone is in agreement and then voilà, it's over." His voice shook. "How can this be? You owe me an explanation, son."

Sam nodded and put his hands on his father's shoulders. Claudia looked around for a way to escape this family dispute in which she was an outsider, but she was trapped in the alcove outside the ballroom.

"Zahara is in love with someone else," Sam said. "She called off the engagement. She knows her father will be furious, so I agreed to present a united front to spare her if I could. In any case, after talking with her, I really feel that it's for the best."

"The best?" his father said, his eyes wide with disbelief. "How do you young people know what's best?"

"We can only try," Sam said, "to do what we think is right. This is a big decision. And not an easy one. Zahara will have a battle on her hands."

"Why? What happened? Who is it? Who has taken away my son's fiancée?" he asked. His eyes filled with tears. Claudia felt sorry for the old man. All his hopes dashed by one impulsive almost-fiancée. She was struck by how important tradition was here. How shocking it was for his father to find he'd been disobeyed. And Zahara. What was her father saying to her right now? Knowing it was her decision. Would she be disgraced? Disowned?

Claudia was trying her best to understand a culture where tradition was so important. More important than love or free choice was the respect owed to the older generation.

"The man is someone who works for her family," Sam said quietly.

"A laborer?" his father asked, shocked. "A servant? Oh, this will never do. I feel sorry for the family. What a disgrace. Wicked girl. Disinheritance is too good for her."

"It doesn't matter who he is," Sam said. "All that matters is that she's made her decision which I support."

Claudia wondered how much Sam really supported her decision. Was he hurt? Or was he relieved? Or was he simply caught in the middle, trying to please everyone, trying to make the best of a bad situation? So he wasn't the one who'd called it off. It was Zahara. She'd given up Sam for someone else. Who? Who could possibly compete with Sam for her heart?

"Father, you of all people should understand," Sam said. "You know what it's like to break the rules and marry outside our society."

"Yes, and look what happened. Your mother never fit in. We thought love would be enough. It wasn't. It still isn't. I should have listened to my father. He told me I was making a mistake, but I was young and foolish and refused to be reasonable. I paid the price. And so did you and Amina." Tears formed in his eyes.

Sam patted him on the shoulder. "Don't blame yourself. You provided us with the best of everything. And if you'd married someone else, I wouldn't be here," Sam said with a half smile. "Nor would Amina."

His father shook his head. With a glance at Claudia he said "This must be your assistant."

"Yes, this is Claudia."

"You must think we are a strange family," he said to her. "An engagement that never takes place. A family torn apart." Just then Amina came rushing up and took in the situation immediately. She put her arms around her father.

"Come, Father, it's time to go home. I have the car waiting. Everything will be fine, you'll see. You'll feel better in the morning." She gave Sam a sharp glance but didn't speak to him. Had she guessed it would never work? Or had she known?

# CHAPTER FIVE

As soon as his father left, Sam led Claudia outside the imposing building. While they waited for the valet to bring his car from the parking garage he paced back and forth, saying nothing. He was so lost in his own world he didn't even seem aware she was there.

Claudia didn't speak, either, not with him in this mood. The look on his face told her he was a thousand miles away. He was obviously upset. But what had upset him? The confrontation with his father or the broken engagement?

"It was hard to hear that my father is sorry he married my mother," Sam said at last, his voice strained.

"Surely that's not what he meant," Claudia said.

"You heard him," he said. "It's enough to discourage anyone from getting married. He said love was not enough."

"He was upset," Claudia said. She had to clench her hands together to keep from smoothing the frown on his brow. "I can't believe he really meant it."

"Oh, he meant it all right," Sam said grimly.

"He was shocked and disappointed, and he was making a point, that's all."

"I know what the point was. He should have been talking to Zahara, not me. He doesn't need to warn me. I'm already convinced. Love and marriage are not for me."

"I think he wants you to get married, but not for love. That's why Zahara seemed like a good choice for you."

"You think I'm a hypocrite, don't you?" he asked, his eyes narrowed. "Knowing how I feel about marriage and love, I was still willing to go through with it."

"It doesn't matter what I think. I don't belong here. I don't understand your customs, but I do understand you felt pressured to do what your family wanted."

"Just so you know, I can't say I'm sorry she called it off," Sam said. "You know me as well as anyone, Claudia, can you really see me married? Tied down? A family man with obligations and a wife who demands I spend time with her instead of at work?" He shuddered as if the very thought was an anathema to him. Then he pinned her with his penetrating gaze, daring her to disagree.

Fortunately the car and driver arrived and she didn't have to answer his question.

In the car, he continued. "You don't have to say anything. I know what your position is."

Claudia turned to him in the backseat, her eyes widened in surprise.

"Love is everything," he said. "Love makes the world go round. Isn't that what you think?"

"Something like that, yes."

"Even after what you've been through?"

"I'd rather not talk about what I've been through. It has nothing to do with your situation."

"Marriage is marriage," he said brusquely. "You called yours off, my fiancée called mine off before it happened. Before things got even more complicated than they were. What happened to you? It might shed some light on the situation."

"I'd rather not," she said stiffly, then turned away and looked out the side window.

There was a long silence as the driver took them down the quiet streets back to the Al-Hamri Building. When Sam finally spoke, he opened a new subject.

"So you're really going sailing with Ahmad?" he asked.

Claudia took a deep breath and tried to act like this was a normal conversation. "I suppose it would be rude to say no. Unless you have work for me to do."

"I'll be meeting with my father in the morning about all kinds of matters that don't concern you. If he's calmed down, that is, and can speak about something besides his supreme disappointment in me. Once we get the broken engagement out of the way we can get back to business."

"Your father was really angry."

"As a foreigner, it must be hard for you to understand."

"I felt sorry for him."

"What about Zahara? Did you feel sorry for her having to marry me when she was in love with someone else? Did you feel sorry that I had to marry anyone when you know my feelings about the institution as a whole? How it goes against everything I believe?"

"Yes," she said, her brain confused and tired. "I mean no. I don't know."

"Of course you don't," Sam said. "You're an outsider. You

have no concept of family honor or tradition. Forget I even asked you."

Claudia winced. His words stung.

"As for tomorrow," he continued, "you should take advantage of the opportunity to go sailing and get out on the water." Although the words were encouraging, the look on his face was not. It all boiled down to the fact that he wanted her out of the way while he dealt with his family.

After two years of working for Sam, she could interpret his expressions pretty well. He didn't like the idea of her sailing with his cousin, that was obvious. But he didn't want her hanging around doing nothing. What did he want from her? Ever since they'd arrived in his country, he was not the Sam she used to know. Sure, he was a demanding boss, but she always knew what to expect from him. Not any longer.

The cool air coming from the air-conditioning in the limo was soothing to her flushed skin and her overwrought brain. She didn't want to talk or smile anymore. She simply wanted to close her eyes and forget the problems of the Al-Hamri family.

Why had she come here? She had no role to play, at least not so far. Everything she said was wrong. Everything she suggested was not welcome. She was a fifth wheel, one no one knew exactly what to do with. Send her sailing? Sightseeing? Dress her up and make her socialize? Fit her into the work schedule whatever that was?

Sam was sitting so close to her in the wide backseat the black tuxedo pants brushed against her bare leg. She shivered. It had nothing to do with the air-conditioning.

"Your announcement came as a great shock to your father.

Too bad you couldn't have warned him in advance," she said, even though she knew he didn't want to talk about it.

"We've been through that, Claudia. Zahara asked me to keep it a secret and I had to respect that." He looked out the window and she couldn't see the expression on his face. She knew he was relieved more than anything else. He didn't have to get married. Not now, not ever.

"I hope…I mean, I understand about Zahara following her heart, but is this really what you want?"

"How can you ask?" he asked, annoyance in his voice. "I'm simply not the marrying type. Never was, never will be. So of course I'm relieved. Vastly relieved. Father will get over it. He has to." Sam turned and gave her a tight smile. "Don't let our family problems interfere with your visit to our country. They don't concern you. Go sailing. Try to enjoy the country while you're here. It may be your only chance."

She knew what he meant. This whole trip was such a disaster, he probably wouldn't want to return anytime soon and when he did, he certainly wouldn't bring her.

"Don't you sail?" she asked after a brief silence. If he was brokenhearted, he certainly didn't show it. But knowing him, he wouldn't. If it were her and her engagement had just been terminated, she'd be sobbing hysterically right now.

"I did. My cousin and I took lessons together, along with tennis, golf and skeet shooting. I even had a boat on San Francisco Bay until I found I had no time for it."

Claudia didn't know about the boat. What else didn't she know about him? Plenty, it seemed. "Your cousin thinks you work too hard," Claudia remarked. She'd never uttered a single critical word to Sam in the two years she'd worked for him. She hoped he wouldn't take this as criticism. It didn't come from her.

"And I think he doesn't work hard enough. We're all entitled to our own opinion."

"Maybe the answer is somewhere in between," Claudia suggested. Suddenly she was so tired, she couldn't hold her head up. She lay her head back on the leather seat cushion and closed her eyes.

Back at the Al-Hamri Building, Sam got out first and reached in to help her out. His hand was warm and his grip was firm. His hair had fallen across his forehead giving him that rakish look she loved so much. She was a little unsteady on her spike heels, so she didn't pull her hand from his as she knew she should do.

It was late. She was tired and he must be, too. This was no time to get carried away with the moment. He wasn't getting engaged, but he was still her boss. Nothing more, nothing less. No matter how right it felt to have her hand in his. It wasn't right at all.

No one spoke as they rode up in the elevator, standing so close and yet so far apart. She couldn't think of a single thing to say. If she did say something now, it might be the wrong thing. He'd already as much as told her she didn't understand his family, his country or his situation. He was probably right. On the top floor, he opened the door to Amina's apartment for her.

"I need an aspirin," he said. "I know where she keeps them." He walked down the hall to the bathroom while Claudia collapsed on the big white couch in the living room and took her shoes off.

When he came back he stood across the room on the dark

polished teak floor and looked out the window at the twinkling lights reflected in the water. He'd loosened his tie and his expression was unreadable in the dim light from the wall lamp.

"Aside from the surprise announcement and the argument with my father you had to witness, I hope you enjoyed the party," he said.

"It was very nice. I'm not used to such a formal occasion. I wasn't sure what was expected. I hope I didn't make any mistakes. Use the wrong fork or say the wrong thing."

A wry smile touched on the corner of his mouth. "Hardly," he said. "Everyone wanted to know who you were."

"Only because everyone else knew everyone."

"No, because you looked…well, different." He hesitated before the word *different*. As if that wasn't the word he wanted. Maybe he meant outlandish, or bizarre or foreign or out of place.

"I was wearing Amina's dress and shoes." She smoothed the skirt. "I *was* different. Tomorrow I'll be myself again." But she wondered if she'd ever be herself again. Not as long as she was in this strange country.

"Good," he said. "I wish I could believe everyone else will be back to normal, too, but I'm afraid the whole city will be gossiping about what happened. It's a small country, a small city and a small society. Since our families are prominent in Tazzatine, the whole country will consider it their business, too. There will be gossip, count on it. I'll be blamed."

"Why? You didn't break it off."

"No, but no one knows for sure. You and I know it's because she believes in love and fairy tales and happily ever after."

Claudia smiled. She wanted to shout, *She's right. Love*

*does exist. Whether you want it to or not. Whether it makes sense or not.*

Let him think she was happy for Zahara. When it was her own selfish self she was happy for. "I always enjoy hearing about a happy ending," she said blithely. It was clear Sam's heart was not broken. Even his ego seemed intact.

"A happy ending?" he said with a raised eyebrow. "That unfortunately remains to be seen. She's going to have problems marrying someone so much below her status. But she's a strong-willed woman. I admire that about her."

Claudia felt the air go out of her lungs. How much more did he admire about Zahara? Surely he couldn't be blind to her beauty. Surely the advantages of such a marriage had occurred to him. Maybe he wasn't as relieved as he claimed. How many times had he used the word? Perhaps he was trying to convince himself as well as her.

She studied his face and tried to remember exactly what he'd said. It was possible he was really disappointed but was covering it up as best he could. And when Sam did his best, it was quite good indeed.

If Claudia thought she could ever match up to Zahara either in looks or willpower, she was wrong. What would she do if she was in love with the wrong man, a man her family didn't approve of? Would she be able to break off an engagement, one that had been in the works for years thus disappointing not one but two prominent families? Fortunately that was not her problem and it never would be.

"It's been a long day," Sam said, running a hand through his hair. "I'm going to bed now and I'd advise you to do the same." He raised his hand in a kind of wave then turned and left.

She watched him close the door behind him and felt terribly let down. For no reason. She'd been to a party. She expected to barely survive the evening but it was over and she had. She'd looked more glamorous than she ever had before or ever would be again and she found out Sam was no longer engaged. She should be happy. Instead she felt like crying. It made no sense at all.

The next morning the maid opened the shutters to a brilliant sunny day. No surprise there. According to her research the country got three hundred plus days of sunshine a year. The maid smiled at Claudia and set a tray on her bed with a glass of fresh squeezed orange juice, a flaky croissant and a large cup of steaming café au lait.

"Miss Amina says to wake you and say you should meet her at the rooftop pool for a swim before it gets too hot."

Before Claudia could protest she hadn't brought a swimsuit with her, the maid opened the closet and brought out several for her to choose from.

There was a maillot, two colorful bikinis and a black racing suit for her to choose from as well as a short white terry-cloth cover-up.

Claudia wanted to ask, But what about work? What about the contract? What am I doing here? I can't spend all day swimming and sailing, can I?

The maid would probably smile and say, why not? But what would Sam say if she asked him? He hadn't seemed at all happy about his cousin's plan to take her sailing. But what did he want her to do?

After she finished her delicious breakfast, she stood on the balcony in the peignoir Amina had given her and took a few pictures of the city below her, the tree-lined boulevards, the steel and glass buildings and the azure sea. She couldn't get over the idea that the new city was transformed from a small settlement of palm huts only a few years ago.

What would happen next to this country? What new buildings, parks, museums and gardens would appear in the next decade? What new industries would appear? What new business opportunities? What new families would emerge? Maybe Zahara would set a new standard by marrying out of her social circle. Whatever happened, Sam's family would be a part of the future.

A swim would feel wonderful. And get her ready for a day of work, not play. After trying on all the suits, and staring at herself in the full-length mirror, she went into a case of shock.

She couldn't wear a bikini. She couldn't even wear a one-piece, high-cut suit. Nor did she feel right dressed like a competitive swimmer. She shook her head and sighed. Then she took a deep breath and put on the bright pink and purple bikini. If she was going to be daring, if she was going to be someone she didn't recognize, why not go all the way? Obviously this was what one wore in the privacy of a private pool, so why fight it? Surely she and Amina would be alone up there.

But they weren't. Sam and Amina were sitting on the edge of the pool, their heads together, their feet dangling in the crystal clear water. The deck was lined with comfortable chaises lounges and umbrellas with striped awnings. Graceful palms fringed the pool and citrus trees in pots, laden with fruit just begging to be picked. Claudia hesitated to interrupt, so she took advantage of the lush foliage to stand in the shade for a moment.

"I knew it," Amina was saying to Sam. "I knew something was wrong all along. Poor Father."

"Thanks for taking him home," Sam said. "I hope he'll come around."

"What else can he do?" Amina asked. "He blames old man Oldalya for not being firm with his daughter. He hopes I won't disappoint the family and run off with one of the servants the way Zahara did."

"Any chance of that?" Sam asked.

"Hardly. It's you he's worried about. He doesn't need to be does he? You're not the type to go falling in love with the wrong woman."

"Falling in love? You know me better than that," he said. "On the other hand, I'm just as glad to be off the hook."

"You get off scot-free, don't you? Unless you're holding out on me and concealing a broken heart. Come on, aren't you even a little disappointed? Aren't your feelings hurt some-what? Think of it, she chose a stable hand over you."

Claudia leaned forward to hear his answer. This was just what she wondered. If Sam had any ego, and she knew he had plenty, wouldn't he be just a little bit hurt to be dumped so quickly for someone everyone assumed was his inferior?

His sister softened her remark with a playful slap on his shoulder, then she hopped into the pool and stood waist deep in the turquoise water.

"You think I have no feelings?" he asked.

"You might," she said. "But if you do, they're buried too deep to find them."

Sam, obviously not in the mood for this kind of probing psychology of his innermost thoughts, jumped nimbly to his feet. "Maybe they're at the bottom of the pool," he said lightly. "I'll have a look."

Claudia couldn't tear her gaze from his broad, tanned shoulders, his narrow waist and long legs as he loped toward the diving board. The man had muscles she had only guessed at. She knew he belonged to a gym in San Francisco and that he always made time for a run in the morning in Golden Gate Park, but she'd never seen a physique like his, not even in photographs of famous athletes. Her heart thudded so loudly she was afraid they would hear it.

How anyone in her right mind could turn him down boggled her mind. But then Zahara didn't know him like she did. Didn't know how smart he really was, how insightful and how deep was his appreciation of his country and his family. What a superb companion he could be for the right woman. Whoever she was, it was not Zahara and it was not her.

Others might think they knew him, knew his qualities, but it was only after two years of daily contact with Sam that she really felt she knew him inside and out. And yet…and yet, here he was surprising her by his banter with his sister. It just made her love him more.

For a brief moment the sight of his gorgeous body in his trim swimsuit as he strode across the Moorish tile surface of the pool deck made her feel so light-headed she thought she might pass out before she'd even said hello. She reached for the edge of a sturdy deck chair to steady herself.

She felt a twinge of envy at the siblings' easy repartee. What if she'd had a sister or brother instead of a lonely childhood as an only child? Amina and Sam didn't see each other very often, but she could see that they'd picked up their close relationship without skipping a beat.

How nice it would be to have someone so close. Someone you knew so well. Someone who shared your background, the memory of a mother who'd left you and a father who could be strict but caring at the same time. Someone to tease and joke with.

She knew Sam had the ability to compartmentalize. So she shouldn't be surprised he could joke with his sister even in the midst of everything that was happening like the merger and the broken engagement.

Sam stepped on the diving board where he tested its springs by jumping up and down.

"See anything?" his sister asked.

"I was right," he said, shading his eyes with one hand. "There they are. My feelings. No wonder I haven't been in touch with them." Then he looked up and cocked his head in her direction. "Claudia?" he said, sounding surprised.

She tried to pretend she'd just arrived and hadn't been eavesdropping on them. She tightened the sash on her cover-up and walked casually toward the pool.

"Come on in," Amina said, waving to her from the shallow end. "You're just in time to race my brother to the end of the pool. He's entirely too arrogant and needs to be beaten."

"I'm afraid I'm not the one to do it," she said.

"Let me see which suit you chose," Amina said.

Claudia took a deep breath and unbelted her robe. She'd come this far, there was no turning back now, no matter how vulnerable she felt. After all, Amina was clad in an even tinier bikini.

"Good choice," Amina said with a smile. "I thought you'd like that one."

Sam lost his balance, tripped and hit the water with a huge splash. Instead of a dive, he'd stumbled and dropped like a stone.

When he came up for air at the end of the pool, he shook the hair out of his face and blinked. Was that Claudia in a bikini? He choked on a mouthful of water. What was happening? First she dazzles his friends and relatives last night and today she shows up in a bikini. This was all Amina's doing and she had to stop. Claudia was his assistant. She was going sailing with his cousin today. It was getting hard for him to know where she fit in anymore.

"Where did that come from?" he demanded of his sister in a low voice. First the dress, now this. How many more shocks could he take?

"I assume you're referring to the swimsuit," Amina said. "It's part of a new line I'm carrying. You can't imagine how popular they are. I can hardly keep them in stock. Women come to Tazzatine because it's a shopper's paradise. They get to buy the most fabulous clothes and naturally wear them. Not that bikinis are worn on the public beaches, of course not. But in hotels and private pools, why not?"

Why not? Sam asked himself. On anybody but Claudia he couldn't object. But seeing her in nothing but a few scraps of cloth made him extremely uncomfortable. He tried to look away but he couldn't.

"I think she looks great, don't you?" Amina asked just

as Claudia walked to the deep end and slipped into the water.

"You don't understand, Amina, Claudia is here to work with me."

"I understand that you work way too hard and so does she. She probably never complains but she should. You're not in California now. You may have forgotten, but we have a different lifestyle here. We take time to enjoy life. Don't tell me you don't need a break. You already look better than when you arrived."

He shook his head at his sister. As if it would do any good. She'd always had a mind of her own and she still did. While they were talking, Claudia seemed intent on getting exercise by swimming energetically back and forth and he was spared from staring at the shapely body he had never known existed under her work clothes. How did she feel about exposing so much skin in broad daylight? He couldn't ask. It was none of his business.

"If you don't have anything to do, you should take Claudia sightseeing."

"I'm afraid she's busy and I'm meeting with Father," he said, admiring her neat strokes out of the corner of his eye. "Ahmad is taking her sailing."

"I didn't know that," Amina said with a frown. "Why didn't someone warn her? He'll flirt with her and talk her arm off. I'm sure you could get her out of it if you wanted to. Tell Father you're busy, say you need her because you have work to do, but then change your mind."

"I can't do that. You know you're just as devious as ever. Did it occur to you that maybe she wants to go?" It had certainly occurred to him. Ahmad could be charming and fun so he'd been told. "You're the one who says we should all relax and have fun," he told his sister.

"That means you, too. Take Claudia to walk the corniche, to see the old fishing village and the craft shops. She'll have much more fun with you than Ahmad."

"I'm not sure about that. I can't spend half the day just wandering around the city like a tourist."

"Why not? You might have a good time. You never know."

When Claudia came up for air, he asked her what she wanted to do today.

"I'm here to work," she said. He was glad to hear her say it. But maybe she wanted to go sailing instead of working and she was afraid to admit it thinking it wasn't appropriate. Maybe she found Ahmad amusing. The water dripped off her hair onto her bare shoulders and the top of her bikini just covered her breasts.

Again he tried to look away but it was impossible. The whole scene was so strange he wondered if he was dreaming. This was not the way he pictured this trip at all. His engagement was off. He'd barely recovered from that shock when his assistant had shown up at his pool half naked, which had him reeling.

"You heard her," he said to his sister. "She feels the same as I do. We're not here to play." If only Claudia would get back into her old clothes, then everything would return to normal and he could concentrate on business. But the world seemed determined to thwart him at every turn. He had more control over events back at the office in San Francisco.

His trusted valet was at the edge of the pool gesturing to

him. What now? He braced his arms on the tiles, and pulled himself out of the water.

"Sorry to bother you, sir," Karim said, "but your father called on urgent business." He handed Sam the phone. A minute later his father was on the line.

"There's been a delay with the merger. Old man Bayadhi is in the hospital. Not sure what it is. Maybe a heart attack. Did you notice last night? He hasn't looked well."

"What does this mean?" Sam asked.

"I don't know." His father sounded tired. "I've had enough of these ups and downs. I'm going to concentrate on something else for a change and I need your help."

"Of course," Sam said. As long as it didn't have to do with the canceled engagement, Sam would agree to anything.

"I have my eye on a prize camel I hear is for sale this week. If I felt better I'd head off to Sidi Bou Said and from there on to the camel market."

"Shall I go for you?" The idea was appealing. Sam was tired of the ups and downs as well. "It may not be bad strategy to pull back for a while. Let Bayadhi recover if that's what he needs and let them think we're not all that eager for the merger."

"I knew you'd agree," his father said. "The old coot may have a dozen more objections to the agreement. I hear he's sent me a list of changes he wants made. I haven't seen it. I wouldn't be surprised if he's out for a week or more. He may be faking it just to put off the merger. To try to get more out of us. As for me, I don't feel like traveling just now. Take your secretary with you, maybe get some work done. But don't fai to come back with my camel. I've called ahead, the house will be in order."

"A week or more?" Sam said. He'd thought longingly about Sidi Bou Said, his horses, the family house, the dunes and the desert, but how could they justify taking off for a week's vacation unless he really could get something done there. With Claudia along it made sense. They could go over the contract there just as well as here.

"Your secretary should see something of the country before she leaves. Otherwise she'll believe Tazzatine is all five-course meals, glass houses and high-rise office buildings being constructed."

"Fine," Sam said. "We'll be ready to go in an hour."

Claudia got out of the water and wrapped herself in her terry robe, which made it much easier for Sam to explain the change of plans. Of course he couldn't tell her what to wear, especially with his sister around filling her head with fortune tellers and emptying her closet to dress her as if she were a doll.

"The old man is sick?" Amina said. "That's just what Durrah predicted. Maybe now you'll believe in her." Amina looked at Sam then at Claudia. "And that's not all. That tall, dark stranger in her future? It could be Ahmad."

Sam shook his head. "Since she's already met him, how could he be a stranger? Amina, forget the fortune teller. Claudia is far too sensible to believe in that nonsense."

"Yes, Sam, we know your feelings on the subject. In any case, I'm staying in town," Amina said, "but Claudia must go with you to see the desert."

"That's what Father said," Sam said. He turned to Claudia. "I'm afraid you'll miss your sailing date."

"I don't mind," she said.

"Then it's settled, Amina will let Ahmad know your change of plans. The Bayadhis are sending over a list of changes to the contract. We can just as easily work on them at the villa. Better perhaps, without any interruptions."

Amina sent a knowing look in her brother's direction. See, her look said. It's all working out for the best.

# CHAPTER SIX

CLAUDIA would have been ready immediately, but Amina insisted on packing a suitcase for her and filling it with clothes she didn't know she'd need. But Amina was probably right. She knew what life at the family compound was like and Claudia didn't. She was happily raiding her closet for riding clothes, loose cool robes, shorts, tank tops and sandals and light cotton sleepwear. And of course two swimsuits to choose from.

Once the car was filled with the luggage, Claudia, Sam and the chauffeur, they headed out of town on a six-lane super-highway.

They passed a large billboard with a picture of a fatherly figure in a white djellaba and some Arabic script written above it.

"My uncle," Sam explained. "His Highness Sheikh Mohammed Ben Ali Maktoum. You were asking what an emir is? He was one, and a fine one. He died a few years ago but he's still much admired."

"What does it say?"

"It's a proverb. 'If you have much, give of your wealth. If you have little, give of yourself.'"

"Which did he give?"

"Both. He ruled with honor and established a foundation with his money."

"Will that be you someday?"

"With my face on a billboard? I don't think so. I wouldn't want to scare the wildlife or small children," he teased.

Claudia smiled. She could just see Sam's gorgeous face smiling down on the admiring populace. "What I mean is will you rule the country someday like he did?"

Sam shrugged. "It's possible. But I'm afraid I don't have his political savvy. Besides he married into a prominent family and united the country." He slanted a glance at Claudia. "I know what you're thinking. If I'd married Zahara…"

"Well?"

"No," he said, hitting the seat cushion with his fist for emphasis.

Claudia's eyes widened. She gripped the edge of the seat.

"How many times do I have to tell you how happy I am, how relieved I am that I'm not getting married. To anyone. I realize now what a huge mistake it would have been. I plan to celebrate my freedom every day from now on. What more can I say besides marriage, commitment and fidelity are all out of the question. No merger, no family pressure, no inheritance, no power is worth it."

"I see," Claudia said. Only a fool would fail to see. That's how clear he'd made himself. "Anyway, your uncle sounds like a wise man."

"He was. We miss him. The whole country misses him. He had many other wise sayings, which have been collected and published." He looked at his watch. "This is turning out to be an entirely different trip than I imagined. I hope you're not bored."

"Hardly. I'm supposed to be working, instead I'm having a paid vacation, seeing things I never expected to see in my life. It may be old to you, but to me everything here is new and fascinating."

"I'm glad you came," he said soberly. "Seeing the country through your eyes has given me a fresh point of view and clarified a few things for me."

He didn't say what things, but she wondered. Did he think of returning to live here for good? Did he wonder what would happen when his father died? Would he then take over for him? Maybe he wouldn't make an advantageous marriage and unite his country, but he could still do some very useful things.

Soon the road dropped down to two lanes and began winding into bare lunar mountains.

"Sandstone," Sam said, with a gesture toward the cliffs in the distance. "Once we cross the mountains, we're in pure desert."

He was right. They left the mountains behind and as far as she could see, the road stretched straight as a ruler across the sand. How far was it to their oasis at Sidi Bou Said?

"Those are Bedouins," Sam said, pointing to men in hooded shirts herding goats along the side of the road. "The nomadic ones who control the desert. They know where the water sources are."

"Isn't it hot for them to live out there?"

"They're used to it and if they need to, they can take refuge in the rocky ravines. They carry their tents of goat or camel hair with them. It's been their way of life for centuries. They prefer the nomadic life."

"I can understand their wanting to live on their own, away from the crowded city."

"How so?" he asked, slanting a curious glance at her as a huge truck carrying drilling equipment passed them. "You're a city girl, aren't you?"

"Yes, and I love my place in San Francisco…it's close to everything. Museums, parks, coffee shops. But if I were a Bedouin I'd want space to breathe. No cement, no tall buildings blocking the light."

"How would you like living in a tent?"

"I don't know. I've never been camping."

"Look over there," Sam said. "The oil derricks always remind me how much the country has changed." He pointed to a series of pumps on the horizon.

"Life at Sidi Bou Said is far from camping," he said. "Wait till you see the compound. You'll understand why my father likes to get away to it as often as possible."

"What about you?"

"I'm glad he suggested it. It's been a long time since I've been there. It's a good place to unwind. Maybe that's why Father suggested we go. But of course the whole reason he wants me here is to attend the camel market and buy one for him."

Claudia didn't think Sam looked like he needed to unwind. He looked relaxed and Westernized in his casual khaki slacks and knit shirt. He looked like he would be at home anywhere. Paris, London, New York, Tazzatine and of course, San Francisco.

"But is it home to you?" she asked.

"I don't know if I have a home." One corner of his mouth quirked in a half smile, but he sounded a little sad.

Though he didn't know if he had a home, Claudia tried to picture him at home in traditional robes here in his country. Maybe he never wore them. She kept thinking of how he looked in his swimsuit and she wondered if they'd be swimming at the compound. She hoped not.

If she had another view of Sam's half bare body, his smooth tanned skin, broad shoulders and his damp hair slicked back from his face, she didn't know how she was going to keep her lust for him under control. It was one thing to work side by side with him and quite another to take a quasivacation with him.

She acknowledged once again she shouldn't have come on this trip. No matter how fascinating or mind-altering. It was turning out worse for her self-control than she imagined. First dealing with the fact he had a fiancée. Then the cancellation of the engagement. Then the fortune teller and the swimming pool. And now this trip out of the city. Who knew what further temptations and disappointments she'd have to endure?

"Who will be at the compound?" she asked. Hopefully many other guests and distractions so she wouldn't be on her own with Sam.

"Just us and the servants. It won't be very exciting. First I spoiled your sailing date and now I've abducted you to an oasis so I can buy a camel for my father. Hardly what you expected, is it?" He gave her a half smile that made her wish he'd smile at her more often. But if he did, how would she get through the next few days without falling even more hopelessly in love with him?

Her goal was to avoid situations that led to any kind of intimacy, and if she did, she might come out of this alive. She told herself things would be better when they were actually doing work. But when was that going to happen? When would they sit down and go over these changes he'd mentioned? What if the situation changed while they were off in the desert? Just the two of them. She pressed her thumbs against her temples in an effort to rid herself of the impossible dreams that threatened to crowd out reality.

"Anything wrong?" Sam asked.

She dropped her hands. "Oh, no, just a little headache." And a little heartache, which is worse. Much worse.

He reached into his briefcase and took out a small bottle of pills. He shook two out and handed them to her, brushing her palm with his fingers. Then he gave her a bottle of chilled water from an ice chest behind them.

She swallowed the pills and wondered how it was possible for him to be so thoughtful. A man who'd been waited on all his life still knew how to make someone like her feel better.

She wondered how he really felt. Was he tired of the city, tired of dealing with a broken engagement, his sister and high society, tired of playing tour guide for her? If he was frustrated by the delay in negotiations, he didn't let any of it show. She knew he was good at riding the ups and downs of business; she didn't know how he'd handle disappointments of a personal kind.

A short time later, Sam told the driver to pull off the road to stop for tea next to an encampment of nomads. Before the servants could build a fire to heat the water, the chief of the Bedouins had spread out hand-woven carpets for them to sit on, brewed a pot of mint tea and passed a basket of fresh dates for the guests.

"So this is the desert hospitality you've told me about," Claudia murmured to Sam who was sitting next to her.

Sam nodded. "They're poor and they don't know us but we are welcome to share what they have."

"Would they mind if I took their pictures?" she asked.

After negotiating and slipping coins into their host's palm, Claudia photographed Sam and their hosts.

Then she sipped her tea thoughtfully while Sam and the desert men engaged in an animated discussion. It could have been about the price of goats or oil production, she had no idea.

"I can't imagine this happening anywhere else in the world," she said to Sam. "Stopping by the side of the road and having people make tea for strangers. It's a wonderful custom."

Sam put his hand on her bare arm. And suddenly her temperature rose. Her face flamed and she couldn't catch her breath. "I'm glad you appreciate it," he said. "It takes a stranger to see our country the way you do. I take these things for granted. I shouldn't."

She was a good swimmer. She'd proved that to herself and anyone else who noticed this morning. But when she looked into his deep, dark eyes she knew what it was like to be in danger of drowning. She tried to take a deep breath, but her heart was racing.

"Are you sure you're okay?" he asked. "You're not having a heat stroke?"

"Oh, uh, maybe I did get too warm."

He frowned. "This is my fault for dragging you out here and making you drink hot tea. I wanted you to have the Bedouin experience. But it's too warm. We'd better get you back to the air-conditioned car." He helped her to her feet, took her hand and led her back to the car.

Claudia should have protested. She should have said she

was fine, just a touch of heartache, but of course she didn't. She just let herself give in to being taken care of for a moment. She let him worry about her and hold her hand all the way back to the car. She should be ashamed, but she wasn't. Back in the car, she closed her eyes and let the cool air wash over her while she gave herself a stern lecture.

*He's not for you. If you don't know it now, you're hopeless and there's something seriously wrong with you. It's not heat stroke and it's not a broken heart. It's pure runaway imagination. And some kind of dumb hope in the impossible. Just because he doesn't have a fiancée and doesn't want one, doesn't mean he wants or needs someone to love or to love him. He's the most independent, self-sufficient man in the world. Remember you've already suffered a broken heart. You don't need to put yourself through that again.*

What she needed was a good, strong dose of reality. No doubt it would be delivered when she needed it most.

But reality was not to be found at the house in the Palmerie. Everything about it was magical, something which was apparent from the moment they entered the stone gates of the villa. After the heat of the unrelenting desert, they were suddenly in a cool, green grove of palm trees where a group of servants stood waving and waiting for them. Flanking the entrance were two ancient cypress trees soaring to the sky, and just inside a huge bright magenta colored bougainvillea covered a pergola.

"It's beautiful," Claudia murmured. It was more than beautiful. It was enchanting. Like something out of a fairy tale.

"I'm glad you like it," Sam said. "Come. I'll show you around. If you're not too tired."

"Oh, no. Not at all."

As they walked, she breathed in the sweet scent of orange blossoms. To one side of the house was the Moorish tiled swimming pool where a Carerra marble fountain sent a stream of water splashing into it.

"I hope you brought your suit," he said.

She sighed. "Yes, Amina packed for me." She could only hope Sam would be too busy for any swimming.

"Then she's thought of everything," he said.

Everything but the fact that Claudia was in love with her brother. She couldn't have thought of that.

"On the other side of the garden is the guest cottage. It's where my parents spent their honeymoon. If you like you can stay there, though I thought you'd prefer a room on the second floor of the main house."

"Of course. The main house is fine."

"You look like you've recovered completely from the heat," he said, studying her face.

"Who wouldn't recover in this lovely place," she said, tucking a strand of hair behind her ear. Though she'd never worn her hair down to the office, Amina had braided it for her before they left today, and she felt young and cool and free in a way she had never felt before. Sam probably wouldn't have noticed if she'd had it cut in a Mohawk. "I wouldn't have missed the tea for anything."

"You have to watch out for the sun. It's quite intense. Here in the Palmerie at least we have shade."

"It's like something out of the *Arabian Nights*," she said, gazing around in rapture at the sight of orange, lemon and apricot trees loaded with fruit. The sky above them was the most intense blue she'd ever seen.

"The nights are beautiful here, too. You can see more stars

than any place else I know. No city lights to interfere." He looked around as if seeing it for the first time.

"How long has it been since you were here?" she asked.

"Too long. I'm glad it worked out this way. Father was right. Coming here now was the right thing to do. Thanks for being so flexible. That's what I've always appreciated about you."

She managed a small smile. He appreciated her flexibility. It was better than nothing. She was a fool if she thought he'd appreciate anything else like her new clothes or her hairstyle. Oh, yes, he did appreciate her brain and her talent for analyzing contracts. That should be some comfort to her.

"Now for the house," he said, leading the way to the arched front entrance. "Long ago Father remodeled it in traditional Arabian style thinking my mother would appreciate it. It has three main areas—the large living room, a dining area and a master bedroom."

Hearing that made Claudia wonder how his mother could ever have left this beautiful place. Homesickness must have been a terrible affliction for her. The main living area had a hand-made marble floor surface called Tadelakt and portraits on the wall that had belonged to Sam's grandfather.

"It's like an art gallery," she said, gazing up at the pictures on the rough-surfaced wall. "Is it all right if I take photographs of them?"

"Of course. Of anything you like."

Her fingers itched to get her camera out and visit the grounds quietly on her own, taking pictures so she'd never forget this house and grounds.

Before they could tour the compound, the servants appeared with trays and motioned for them to come onto the terrace for refreshments. They sat under a tented canopy surrounded by lush greenery and drank fresh, cold lemonade squeezed from fruit from their own trees and ate small, hot flaky spinach turnovers. On the table were bowls of pine nuts, almonds and pistachios.

"Where's the office?" Claudia asked, after quenching her thirst with the tart lemonade.

"In the other wing of the house. I'll take you there next. I'm glad Amina or cousin Ahmad aren't here—they'd say you're as bad as I am, looking for work before you've even unpacked."

"But that's what I'm here for. That's why I came. I'm here to help you."

"You are helping me. You're helping me see things the way they are. If you weren't here I wouldn't appreciate this place the way I should. I wouldn't see my cousin for who he is or realize that I'm better off without Zahara, no matter how right it seemed at the time."

"I made you realize that?" she asked, her voice so high it was almost a squeak. "I never said a word."

"You didn't have to. All I have to do is look at your face and I know what you're thinking."

Claudia pressed her lips together and looked away. It couldn't be true. If it was, he'd know how she felt about him, and he didn't. He couldn't.

He reached across the table and took her hand in his. Her heart thumped loudly. Claudia wondered if she was dreaming.

"Don't ever play poker," he said, tilting his head to give her a long look. "You'd never be able to hide your hand from your opponent."

Was she dreaming or was this Sam sitting across the table,

holding her hand and teasing her. She'd known him for two years, and yet she'd never seen this side of him. Maybe no one had except his sister.

If he only knew how good she was at concealing her feelings for him, he wouldn't say that.

He turned her hand over in his and traced a line in her palm with his finger. Goose bumps ran up and down her arm. "So what did the old girl have to say when she read your palm?" he asked. "Besides the part about the tall, dark stranger."

"Oh, just the usual," Claudia said. But she was so unnerved by the touch of his hand on hers she couldn't remember what Dhurra had said at all. "Um, long, happy life. That kind of thing."

"I'll tell you what I see," he said. His thumb was making circular motions on her palm making her unable to say another word or even think straight.

Claudia leaned forward. She should take her hand back. She should stand up. She should get to work. Go to her room. Unpack. She should do anything but sit here as if he'd cast a spell over her. Or maybe it was the oasis that had done it. But she didn't move. She couldn't.

"This, of course is your fate line," he said. He looked up and met her gaze.

"How do you know?"

"When we were small Amina and I had a nanny who was an expert. She had her book of palms, which she studied. It had pictures of all these lines. She told Amina she would wear beautiful clothes and that I would follow Father into business." He smiled as if they were both in on a little joke.

"I know you and I know you're skeptical of these seers. And yet you have to admit she was right."

"Because she predicted the obvious. Amina has always loved dressing up and my destiny was to follow in Father's footsteps. Nothing magic about that. But at the time we were impressed. We were young and we thought she was not only old but very wise. She used to say fate controls your life. I don't believe it anymore, but let's just see if I remember what the fate line reveals." Again his fingers began sensuously tracing the lines of her palm.

Claudia's throat was clogged, her vocal chords had shut down. His hand that held hers was firm and strong.

"Ah, here it is. The angle of the line says that you surrender your interests to those of others like myself. That's why we work so well together. You give your all to me and the job, don't you?" He looked up to meet her gaze and held it for a long moment. She didn't know how to answer so she just shrugged.

"If I remember right this is the marriage line," he said, turning back to look at her palm. His thumb moved to stroke the most sensitive part of her palm. She felt her heart melt as if she'd left it out in the desert sun.

"Very interesting. You have more than one line. More than one marriage. This is the first." He held up her hand to show her. "And this is the second. The lines that meet the marriage line but don't cross it mean children, four children."

"Stop," Claudia said. "I have no plans to ever remarry and I don't plan on any children. This is complete nonsense. You don't believe it any more than I do." She snatched her hand back.

"Maybe I was wrong," he said. "Maybe there's something to it after all. You've been married, that's marriage number one."

"I thought you were going to show me your office," she

said, getting to her feet. She was feeling desperate to get this trip back on kilter. "I thought we had work to do."

"That was before I saw your hand," he said with a roguish smile. "But if you insist. I'll have to tell Amina that you're a bigger workaholic than I am. Is that what you want? Very well. Come with me."

He stood and stretched, giving her a tantalizing glimpse of his flat tanned stomach. "It's a complete office, though maybe it shouldn't be. Father and Amina hate it when I go in and close the office door. They insist this house should be for rest and relaxation. Maybe when I'm older I'll agree. In the meantime we'll have a look at the papers Father gave me and decide if the changes are reasonable. Then we'll check in with our office back home."

"Home?"

"I meant San Francisco. Frankly I don't know where home is. Maybe it's here." He paused and looked around at the trees, the brilliant flowers and the bubbling fountains that sent water cascading from a brass pipe. He took Claudia's arm and looked at her so intently she didn't know what to expect. "I envy you, Claudia, you have a home in a city you can go back to. You know exactly where you belong."

"But you're at home in many places. Here, in the city, in the States or wherever you are."

"Could you be at home here?" he asked suddenly. His gaze didn't waver, as if her answer was important to him.

"I…I don't know. It's a beautiful place, but it doesn't feel real to me. It's like a dream."

He nodded and dropped her arm. "Let's get some work done," he said. He was suddenly all business. As if they'd never left San Francisco. As if he'd never seen her in a cocktail dress or a bikini. As if he'd never read her palm. Then they went to his office, which was cool and air-conditioned. He spread out the contract with the changes pencilled in. "See what you make of it," he said. "While I check in with our office."

Claudia immediately zoned in on the pages in front of her, writing comments in the margins. She was aware that he'd switched on his computer and read his messages. When she finally looked up she noticed he was leaning back in his chair, watching her.

"What do you think?" he asked.

"There are a few problems. I have some ideas. Let me go through the whole thing first, then we can talk about it. See if you agree with me."

He nodded, but he continued to stare at her.

"What's wrong?" she asked.

"I don't know. Maybe it's all that talk about my being a workaholic. Maybe it's this place, but I can't concentrate. I've always appreciated you, Claudia, but I didn't realize how much I depend on you until now."

Claudia shifted in her chair and turned back to the contract. He made her nervous, looking at her like that. He wasn't himself and she thought she knew why. Say what he would, he was upset by his broken engagement.

Finally he picked up the phone and called his father. Claudia didn't know if she was supposed to listen, but she did. It sounded like the merger was still in limbo. After he hung up, she talked about the contract with him and suggested several ways they could get things moving again, such as some incentives for the Bayadhis to participate.

"We should remind the Bayadhis of the advantages of the merger. Perhaps they're not aware Al-Hamri Shipping has just taken delivery of four new bulk carriers. We know they have a contract with Australia to ship ore to China. How will they get it there without our carriers? As far as we know, leasing is not an option for them right now."

"Brilliant," Sam said. "I'll call Father back."

"Wait. Let's come up with some more advantages for them."

They spent an hour tossing ideas back and forth just as they always did, then Sam called his father back. She heard him giving her full credit for most of the suggestions. It gave her a warm glow hearing him speak. Sam was never one to take credit for anything she'd thought up.

"Father was impressed," Sam said. "But we won't really know if it worked until the agreement is signed. In any case, you've earned your salary this month," he said. "In fact, I think you deserve a raise."

"Sam, you just gave me a raise last month," she protested with a blush.

"Which you deserved as well," he said. He stood and walked around the room, looking at the pictures on the wall, the plaques and the awards and the trophies as if he'd never seen them before.

"Time for a break," he announced. "That's enough for today. You haven't seen your room yet. Amina would never forgive me if she knew I'd taken you to the office first."

She followed Sam up the stairs where he left her alone in the guest room that was decorated in warm yellow and cool blue tiles. She found the servants had unpacked for her so she changed into cropped pants and a short-sleeved T-shirt, which were both a little snugger than what she usually wore. They were Amina's and though Amina and she were about the same size, Sam's sister wore her clothes tighter than Claudia did. Of course Amina's wardrobe was totally different from Claudia's, which was part of the reason Claudia was having a hard time figuring out who she really was.

She took her camera and climbed up the steps to the roof garden that overlooked the palm forest. There she snapped picture after picture. When she got home she'd print them out and make a montage for her wall. It would remind her of this amazing place that she'd never see again. Her memories would be bittersweet. The engagement, then the breakup. The party, then the solitude of this desert refuge. The luxury, the servants, the kindness of Sam's family.

The silence of the palmerie was broken only by the palm fronds whistling in the soft breeze and the chirping of the brightly colored birds that flitted from tree to tree.

For the first time today she was able to completely relax. She knew she needed a break from Sam. Every day, every hour and every minute spent in his company brought her closer and closer to the one man she could never have. She had to constantly be on guard, afraid she'd say something that would enable him to guess how she felt about him. Every time he looked into her eyes, held her hand, read her palm, or exchanged ideas made her wonder if one of these times she'd slip and confess.

If this trip to his homeland had showed her anything, it was that she was an outsider. One thing after another. The reaction of his father to the broken engagement. The importance of family. The possibility of Sam's picture appearing on billboards as the benevolent sheikh. She would never ever fit in. That's why she came here, she reminded herself. For a reality check. Well, she was getting it.

In their office in San Francisco it was easy to forget he was a sheikh and she was a commoner from another country. There he was just another executive and she was his trusted assistant. They worked together and that was all. But here the lines were blurred between work and play. It didn't seem to bother him, but it disturbed her. It made her discontented. It made her want more. It made her into a different person.

Sam might not feel the same, but he most likely needed a break from her, too. It must be tiring to always be explaining, translating and showing her around. He'd just said he was tired of working. As for her it was tiring to be on her guard all the time, afraid to let her feelings show. She couldn't imagine anything worse than raising his suspicions and feeling his pity for his poor, deluded assistant who couldn't control herself.

Sam went to his room on the second floor and changed into cargo shorts, leather sandals and a T-shirt. He could go back to the office and do some more work, but he didn't really want to be dragged back into work today. Not without Claudia, and he'd already taken too much of her time. For the first time in months he felt like stepping back from the problems of shipping lanes, contracts, revenues, and this merger. He never took vacations. Never felt the need.

It must be the oasis. He hadn't been here for a long time. It was having a strange effect on him today. Maybe it was the influence of his father who always loved this place above all others. Maybe it was because his mother had felt more at home here, though not enough to stay.

Why hadn't his father known that before he married her? As Claudia said, it was not reality. It was like a dream. Of course she couldn't live here. She was an outsider just like his mother.

Having Claudia here and seeing it through her eyes made him see the place as he'd never seen it before. As his mother must have seen it. It was a beautiful oasis, but it was not home. The look on her face as they drove through the gates said it all. She'd fallen under its spell, too. But for how long? After a few days most visitors got restless.

Some found it isolated. Some too rustic. Some too hot. Those who were vulnerable to its charm loved it for the gardens, the pool, the fountain and the trees and most of all, the solitude. Claudia seemed to appreciate it all. He couldn't get over how she'd changed.

His usually stiff and proper assistant had looked positively dreamy-eyed when he showed her around. He had a picture in his mind of Claudia picking a yellow hibiscus flower from a vine and stopping to listen to a songbird.

But what if she knew this was her home and she couldn't leave. What then? He knew the answer. He'd seen it all happen to his mother. First the romance, the excitement, the thrill of a different country. Then reality hit, family pressures, different customs, the longing for home and she had to leave. His father had never gotten over her departure.

Was it true Sam was a workaholic and now he was paying the price? Was it that he was married to his work the real reason why Zahara wouldn't marry him? Or did she really believe she'd found true love with the family groom? Why else would she risk her family's disapproval by making such a drastic decision that would affect the rest of her life? Not just hers, but her family's as well.

He had to admire someone who'd take a risk like that. Even though he didn't believe in love, Zahara obviously did. Every woman he knew did. Take Claudia. She'd been in love and had married the man. Then she got a divorce. Her marriage line said she'd marry again. She should. She'd make some lucky man very happy.

He didn't go back to the office. He'd wait to hear from his father and he and Claudia would go back to work together. Here in the desert he would let the warm air wash over him like the wind blew across the dunes and shaped them into lush curves of golden sand.

He looked up and there was Claudia on the balcony above him with her camera held out in front of her. It had to be Claudia, and yet he scarcely recognized her. She not only looked like a different person, but she acted like a different person, too.

As long as he'd known her, he had no idea she was interested in photography. He had no idea what she was interested in at all. He'd just found out about her knitting and her book club. From where he stood he could see her face was flushed and her hair had escaped the braid she was wearing and framed her face in soft tendrils.

Was this the same woman who sat at a desk all day in her office in San Francisco? She was so involved in her picture taking, she didn't see him down there, so he continued to stare at her and wonder at the change in her. Or was he the one who'd changed?

"Come down," he called to her when he was no longer content to just look at her.

She looked down from the balcony and nodded.

He found he was impatient for her company. She hadn't seen all of the place yet. Showing her around was more fun than he'd had for months. She appreciated everything he offered, from food to flowers, to birds and fruit, to people and the pictures on the wall. Now he wanted to see what she'd think of his prized possessions.

"Hurry. I have something to show you."

# CHAPTER SEVEN

"WHAT is it?" she asked when she joined him on the terrace.

He was distracted to see her once again in casual clothes. Different clothes from those she wore this morning. Her shirt and pants hugged her body giving him yet another opportunity to see that she did indeed have curves. Well, what did he expect? She was a woman. They weren't in an office. She could wear whatever she wanted.

When he didn't answer she followed up with another question. "Any more news from the office?"

"Nothing," he said. "It's too soon." He didn't tell her he hadn't even checked and didn't want to. "I'm going to go see my horses. I thought you'd like to see them, too."

"I would," she said, her eyes lighting up. She looked that way whatever he showed her. It must be the sheltered life she'd led. She hadn't even flown in a plane until he brought her here. He had a feeling she'd never tire of seeing new things, having new experiences. And he'd never tire of showing them to her.

He didn't know why he'd never taken her on business trips before. He'd always thought he didn't need her. She was always available on the other end of the telephone if anything came up no matter what time of day it was in California. Now he realized what she'd missed. What he'd missed by not having her with him. He'd missed her insight and her enthusiasm.

He'd also missed seeing things through her eyes. She was sensitive and intuitive. He knew that—he just didn't know what a difference it would make to his viewpoint. On the other hand, with her here, he wasn't even thinking about the merger. It wasn't her fault, and yet maybe it was. She was the one who'd come up with the new ideas. Sometimes he wondered if he even cared. It had seemed so important less than a week ago. Now, what did it matter?

He took her to the stables, which were behind the main house in a grove of trees. Sighting their master, a half dozen proud Arabians, some white, some gray, two bays and a magnificent chestnut whinnied loudly and came racing to the fence.

"Oh, Sam," Claudia said, leaning against the fence. "They're beautiful. They know you, don't they? They're glad to see you."

"Of course they know me," he said, reaching out to stroke their purebred wedge-shaped heads one at a time. "Claudia meet Jaden, El Moktar, Thunder, Pasha, Ranger and Araf."

"Can I pet them?" she asked.

"Go ahead. They'll appreciate it. And give them a lump of sugar." He slipped the sugar into her hand. "These Arabians are bred for intelligence, speed and endurance, but I wouldn't have a horse that didn't have a good disposition. They're one of the few breeds so good-natured that the U.S. Equestrian Federation allows children to exhibit. Do you ride?"

"I took lessons when I was a child. There are stables in the park in San Francisco. I'm afraid it was quite tame, always on the trail, always with an instructor. Afterward we had to brush the horses, feed them and give them water. But they were nothing like these stunning creatures."

Sam grinned. He was as pleased with the compliments as if she'd complimented members of his family. In a way, the horses were just that.

"I chose these horses, I bred them. I'm as proud of them as if they were my own children, which is a good thing, since I probably won't have any children," he said ruefully.

"That would disappoint your father, wouldn't it?" she asked, holding out her hand to give one of the horses his sugar.

"Let Amina provide the grandchildren," he said, reaching into his pocket for a carrot for his favorite mount. "He'll have to make do."

"Because of Zahara breaking off with you?" she asked, leaning forward to rub her hand on the horse's head.

"Because I'm not the marrying type," he said. "You know me well enough to know that."

"I don't necessarily agree with you," she said after a moment.

He turned to look at her, wondering if she was serious. Curious to see what her viewpoint was.

"I think you could make some woman very happy. Whether she would make you happy is another matter."

"You *do* know me, maybe better than anyone. You can bet my family continues to think I'm too selfish and self-centered to ever marry. Especially after this latest fiasco."

"Am I right in assuming you are not brokenhearted?"

"How can I be brokenhearted if I have no heart? Or so says my sister."

"I think you keep your heart hidden."

"Hmm. If I do, it's for the best, wouldn't you say? Otherwise with a fiancée breaking up with me this way my ego would surely be damaged. Enough about me. What made your marriage fail?"

"I'd rather not talk about it," she said stiffly.

"In other words, it's none of my business," he said. He didn't know what made him suddenly so curious. He'd known she was divorced. He'd never given it much of a thought before. "Let's go for a ride."

"I…I don't know if I'm up to it. I'm really not much of a rider."

"I think Thunder would be just right for you. He's strong but gentle. Arabians are sometimes called hot-blooded, which means spirited and bred for speed, but they're also sensitive and intelligent. We call Thunder the great communicator, since he seems more attuned to his rider than the others. I'll have him saddled up for you."

"If you're sure I can do it," she said.

"Absolutely." Sam wasn't completely sure she'd like riding, but he knew Thunder and he knew he was the best choice for a beginner. He called to one of the stable boys who saddled both Thunder and Sam's favorite Jaden.

Claudia put one foot in his outstretched hand and he boosted her up so she could reach the stirrups. With his hand on her firm hip she swung gracefully over the horse's broad back. When he looked up and met her gaze, he felt a shaft of desire hit him like a bolt of lightning. Desire for his assistant? Impossible. What was wrong with him today? It must be the oasis.

He took a step backward. The oasis or he was having a

reaction from his thwarted engagement. Although he'd never felt a single flicker of attraction toward Zahara, who was a beauty by any standard.

And yet he was standing there staring up at Claudia on her horse wondering what was happening. Wondering how he had been so unaware of how her eyes sparkled when she was excited. And how had he not noticed her very attractive body all this time. She was small and compact with a shape that was full and ripe combined with a manner that was unassuming and modest in the extreme. She seemed totally unaware of how she looked whether in his sister's cocktail dress or the casual shirt and pants she was wearing now. If she wasn't aware of her attraction to men, then how could he have been? But something had changed. It was her or him. Or maybe both of them.

While he stood there consumed with contradictory thoughts and feelings and questions that had no answers, she finally broke the eye contact and began talking softly to the horse and rubbing him behind the ears. Almost as if Sam wasn't there. As if she knew what to do because she'd been riding all her life.

He mounted Jaden and they did a slow trot out the back gate into the palm grove, riding slowly between the trees. Sam went first and turned in his saddle to keep an eye on Claudia. There was nothing like being on his horse to make him feel as if he'd really come home. He hadn't realized how much he missed the communication he had with this animal. How much less complicated it was than communicating with a person. Thank God for Zahara falling in love with someone else. Otherwise where would he be now? Stuck in an engagement to please everyone but himself.

How did he ever think he would communicate with a woman he hadn't seen for twenty years? It was ridiculous. He didn't want to contemplate the consequences of a marriage to a stranger.

He was glad they'd come here to the Palmerie. What a perfect place to leave the world behind and concentrate on the basics of life. Horses, trees, water and family. And then there was Claudia. Claudia who knew exactly where she belonged and it certainly wasn't here.

They left the palmerie and Sam led the way to the dunes on the other side of the compound. The horses dug their hooves into the sand and climbed to the top.

"Are you okay?" Sam called to Claudia. He was glad to see Thunder slow down to take the sand dunes a step at a time instead of racing up and down like a more hotheaded animal would have done. He must know he had a novice rider on his back. Otherwise he would have raced Jaden and Sam to the top.

"So far, yes," she called.

Sam waited until she caught up with him.

"Go on," she said. "You want to run. I'll wait here."

He hesitated then he nodded and gave his horse the command. They took off. The sand blew in his face, the hot wind tore at his clothes and he forgot everything but the feeling of power and strength. When he returned to where Claudia was waiting, the sweat poured off his face, but he couldn't help grinning.

She grinned back. "You're a natural. But you've been riding all your life haven't you?"

"Yes, but it's been a long while since I've been here. Too long. I forgot what it feels like. Next time we'll get you and Thunder running, too."

They cantered slowly back to the house and left the horses with the groom at the stable.

He felt more alive than he had in months. Every muscle felt used. He reached up to help Claudia down from her horse. She slid effortlessly into his arms as if she belonged there. She looked at him, questions in her eyes that he couldn't answer. She licked her lips and there it was again, desire, white and hot and unexpected. He bent down and kissed her and the world spun around. Her lips were soft and sweet and he wanted to kiss her again and again. He heard her gasp with surprise.

"I'm sorry," he said, stepping backward. "Forgive me. I don't know what got into me. It must be this place. Or something else." He looked around as if he wasn't sure where he was. "That was a mistake."

She nodded, then she left the stable so fast he wasn't sure what had happened.

Sam showered and changed clothes. He only hoped Claudia understood that the kiss meant nothing. Only that she was an attractive woman and he was a frustrated man. That's all. Of course she would. Not only was she attractive, but she was sensible.

He went to the kitchen to confer with the cooks. By dinner everything would be back to normal. They'd talk about business and the kiss would be completely forgotten. If he kept replaying it now, it was just that he had nothing else to focus on.

There in the kitchen he heard the servants say they were having guests to dinner, a Bedouin nomad and his son who were passing through and assumed his father was with them

Which reminded him that his father was intent on buying the prize-winning camel and these men would tell him where, when and how.

Claudia went up to her room to get ready for dinner. Her knees were trembling so much she could barely climb the stairs. She'd never been kissed like that before. She'd dreamed of Sam kissing her, but it was better than any dream. And yet it was about as real as a dream.

She walked around the lovely guest room wondering what she should have done. She'd wanted to throw her arms around him and kiss him back. But he'd pulled back and apologized before she knew what was happening. He was sorry he'd kissed her. He'd made that quite clear. Whereas she wasn't sorry at all. She blinked rapidly to keep from crying.

She stared at the clothes Amina had packed for her wondering what was appropriate to wear for dinner. Fortunately the servant girl who'd unpacked her clothes for her knew. She laid out a long, loose traditional cotton gown with embroidery at the neckline. It was Amina's of course and it was beautiful, cool and comfortable and it fit perfectly.

Amina had thought of everything. Except that her brother would kiss his assistant. No one could have expected that. Claudia was still shaking both inside and out. Even after her shower. She knew it meant nothing, but why did he do it? Probably just a reaction from his broken engagement.

She looked in the mirror. She looked different and she was. She'd been kissed. Her cheeks were pink, her lips were red. Her hair was wild. Without Amina to braid it, she had to let it fall to her shoulders in loose waves.

After she got dressed, she stood on the balcony of the guest room as the sun set over the palm grove. She told herself this was all a beautiful dream and when she woke up she'd be back in her office, wearing a suit and low-heeled shoes.

She'd be answering the phone and writing messages for Sam. He'd treat her like an employee as usual and not a desirable woman. A trusted and valued employee, to be sure, but there was a difference in the way they interacted here. A big difference. If only he hadn't kissed her, she could pretend everything was the same.

She couldn't procrastinate any longer. She walked slowly down the stairs and heard voices.

"Ah, Claudia," Sam said, watching her enter the living room. "Meet our guests."

The guests who both wore turbans and loose robes had come to see his father and while disappointed, agreed to join them at the long table for dinner.

Claudia breathed a sigh of relief. They wouldn't be alone. They wouldn't have to think about the kiss. They'd be distracted. No awkward conversation over dinner where they both tried to pretend nothing had happened. Instead all the attention was on the men with their leathery, weather-beaten faces who described their travels while Sam translated for her.

The first course was tiny kebobs, which were served on small plates with forks, although the guests simply picked them up in their fingers. Next a huge platter of couscous wa brought to the table and each person helped himself to the light yellow, saffron-flavored grain.

In between courses, the old man named Azuri shared information about the camel races and camel market to be held in two days across the desert. Claudia watched and listened. Even though she couldn't understand a word and had to wait for Sam's translation, it was fascinating for her to study the dynamics, the facial expressions and the occasional shout of excitement or disbelief from both guests and host.

When Sam heard a prize camel would definitely be on the market, he told Claudia that was the one.

"Father has wanted this camel, Zaru, for a while. He's known to be the fastest camel in the country. Always wins these races. But the owner would never sell. Now Father won't rest until he has bought this camel for himself."

"What will he do with him?" Claudia asked.

"Stable him here and race him whenever he can. Be the object of envy of everyone in the country. Enjoy the pride of ownership. If he could own Zaru nothing else would compare. My engagement, the merger, anything."

A few minutes later, the salad was served and Sam said to Claudia, "I have to go to the market at Wadi Halfa and buy the camel for him."

They left her an out. She didn't have to go.

"Will it be expensive?" she asked.

"It doesn't matter," Sam assured her. "He wants it and that's all there is to it. He's been talking about Zaru for years."

This conversation about camels went on and on and was followed by small cups of strong mint tea and honey pastries.

While the two men were discussing the route they would

take when they left later that night, Sam turned to Claudia. "I'll leave tomorrow. There are two ways to get to Wadi Halfa. By Land Rover on a road which is the long way, or by horse which is overland and shorter."

"I can guess which one you'll take."

"What about you?"

Startled, she set her tea cup down. "Me?"

"Don't you want to see some authentic camel races, the market, the Bedouins? Don't you want to sleep in a tent?"

She studied his face, knowing without a doubt the excitement she saw in his eyes had nothing to do with her and everything to do with this trip. The kiss that had rocked her world might as well have never taken place. His forgetting it had ever happened hurt like an ache in her side that would never go away. All his attention was on the trip. He'd invited her along as a tourist. That was all. She could say no, but she wouldn't do that. Instead she swallowed her disappointment.

"Well, yes," she said, "but…"

"Then it's settled," Sam said. "The servants will go ahead in the Land Rover with the supplies, and you and I will leave tomorrow on horses. It's a beautiful ride. And much more interesting than going on the road. It's only a few hours over the dunes. Whereas the car has to go around the mountains on a track, we can cut through."

"Cut through? A few hours on a horse? I've never ridden that much."

"We'll stop to rest. We'll take plenty of water and food. You'll see the desert as no other foreigners do. Only the nomads. You'll have a chance for some outstanding photographs of ancient rock paintings."

She felt herself swept along by his persuasive description. How could she say no? How could she stay here when all the action was happening somewhere else? No use worrying about a repetition of that kiss. She would forget it just as he had. There would be so much going on, it would be just the distraction she needed.

How could she choose to go by Land Rover when he was going on horseback? It was just as it always was. Sam was able to convince her and just about anyone else to do just what he wanted whether they had objections or were the least bit hesitant. Except for Zahara. He couldn't convince her to marry him instead of the man she loved. But maybe he hadn't tried very hard.

In this case, of course she wanted to gallop over the dunes with him at her side. Of course she wasn't going to say no to the adventure of a lifetime. To play Lawrence of Arabia without the risk of being attacked by unfriendly natives.

Here the natives were all friendly and hospitable. Her only enemy was herself. All she had to do was keep reminding herself that Sam did not invite her along on this trip because he couldn't stand to be separated from her. He invited her because he had the hospitality gene. He'd also had it imparted to him at an early age. He could no more be rude or inconsiderate to a guest than to mistreat a horse.

She had to think of this trip as a travelers' dream and not a lovers' rendezvous. And she had to keep her emotions under wrap. If she couldn't, she ought to stay here or at least go in the Land Rover with the servants. That would be the safe thing to do. The prudent thing to do.

But Claudia wasn't feeling prudent. His enthusiasm was

contagious. She was in the desert. She was meeting real nomads. She would see camels race and be sold at market. At the same time she was safe and sound with the only man in the world she'd ever love. It was only her heart that was in danger. Very grave danger.

That night Sam put a duffel bag with her clothes in the Land Rover along with the tent, cooking equipment and sleeping bags, which would be driven to the compound at Wadi Halfa by his father's servants. The next morning the two of them took off, their saddlebags filled with bottles of water, dried fruit and bread.

It was early and the air was cool and fresh. The horses seemed as excited and eager as Claudia. Sam, too, looked better than she could remember. He was tanned, relaxed and smiling and eager to talk about their destination. It was a sure way to avoid saying anything personal. No palm reading. No unnecessary touching. No kissing. Those were the unspoken rules.

Seeing him on horseback, at peace with the world, she didn't know how any woman in her right mind could turn him down. She didn't know how, but she was just glad Zahara had done it. Not for her sake, but for Sam's. He never would have been happy with her and all Claudia really wanted was his happiness. At least that's what she told herself.

Their horses walked slowly side by side as Sam explained that Wadi Halfa was under the jurisdiction of a sheikh who would host the event.

"We'll sleep in our own tent, but we'll be his guests."

"And if you buy the camel?"

"I will buy the camel or else die trying," he said. "In which case the sellers will deliver him to my father. But we're no the only one who wants Zaru. He's famous. We may have a fight on our hands." Her concern must have shown on her face, because he reached out to pat her on the shoulder. The kind of friendly gesture you'd give to a colleague or an underling. She was neither. When Sam was around, she didn't know who she was.

"Don't worry, we'll get him. You brought your camera, didn't you? You can show Father the pictures of his new camel winning the race, which he most certainly will do."

Claudia nodded. It was the part about sleeping in the tent that worried her. He said tent and not tents. He couldn't possibly mean they'd be sharing a tent, could he? She didn't have time to worry because a few moments later they were galloping across the dunes.

It was exhilarating with the warm wind tearing at her hair and clothes. Exhilarating but tiring, too. Her hips were sore from bouncing up and down in the saddle and her face was burning. Her hair had come loose and the perspiration was pouring down her temples.

After the dunes Sam turned down some narrow trails through rocky ravines. Fortunately Thunder was remarkably sure-footed and didn't miss a step.

Sam stopped by a spring and dismounted. "Let's take a break," he said, reaching up to help her down. She was so tired she slid off the horse and brushed against Sam's chest as she landed. Oh, no, not again.

Up close she could see herself reflected in his sun goggles and notice the faint creases at the corners of his mouth. He put his hands on her hips to steady her but even when she landed safely he didn't take them away for a long moment.

Which was lucky because she was shaking all over, either from the ride or from the close contact with Sam.

Behind his glasses she thought she saw some emotion flicker in his eyes. He leaned forward. She held her breath. Waiting. Wondering. Would he kiss her again? Would she kiss him back this time? Her lips tingled. Only a few inches remained between them.

He lifted his hand and tucked a strand of hair behind her ear. His touch left a trail of sparks on her skin. Then he dropped his hand as if he'd been burned and the moment passed as quickly as it had arrived. It was just as well. They both remembered what had happened the last time she'd dismounted and neither wanted it to happen again.

They sat on rocks and drank from the cool, fresh spring water, splashing it on their faces as well.

"How do you feel?" he asked.

"Okay. Well, maybe a little sore." She didn't realize how much her bottom hurt until she rested against the warm rock. "I've never ridden this much or this far before."

"We're over halfway there," he said. "You're doing fine."

His encouraging smile and words almost made her forget the pain in her backside. She pulled her hair back and tied it up to get it off her neck. She ate a few crackers and an orange from her saddlebag and then they were off again.

In the distance they saw a camel train headed in the same direction as they were. Sam slowed his horse and pulled up next to her.

"They're probably going to the market as we are," he said. "Many rulers have tried to force the nomads to change thei ways, to move to town and to speak our language instead of their own."

"But in some ways, they have changed. Didn't your guests last night travel in a four-by-four?" she asked. "They weren't riding camels."

"You're right. That's one way some have welcomed change. Others regret the old days when they had complete control of the desert. Only they knew where the water sources were. They protected the caravans and raided caravans that didn't pay up. When the first Europeans saw them they were impressed by the romantic lifestyle. They painted pictures of the Bedouin on his camel with his sword at his side. Then and now what's really important to them is to be who they are and control their own destiny."

"I'd say that's what's important to all of us," she said.

He nodded thoughtfully. "Trust you to come up with a universal truth," he said with a smile. Was it her imagination or was Sam smiling more these days? It must be the change of scene. The vacation from the office. If he was worried about his father, the merger or anything else, he concealed it well.

"Which reminds me, I promised to show you the cave paintings. I'm afraid we've passed them now—we'll have to do it on the way back."

As they got close to Wadi Halfa the sounds of traditional music from stringed instruments came drifting across the sand. Banners swung in the wind. Men dressed in turbans and shimmering veils came riding out to greet them.

They'd arrived and just in time. When Claudia got off her horse, she could barely stand.

When she winced, Sam turned to her with a worried look. "What's wrong?" he asked.

"Nothing, just a little sore."

"I brought some salve, just in case. It works miracles. First we must greet our host."

The host was an imposing figure, well over six feet tall, he was covered in a white robe with the traditional headdress.

"Welcome," he said. "Come and have a cool drink and rest from your trip. I know why you've come," he said, a smile creasing his leathery face.

# CHAPTER EIGHT

CLAUDIA didn't need to worry about the sleeping arrangements. The servants who'd gone ahead in the Land Rover had set up two tents for them and her suitcase was there along with a cot made up with sheets of the best Egyptian cotton, and hand-knotted carpets covering the dirt floor. They'd filled a pitcher with cool fresh water and Claudia washed her face and tried to forget how sore she was.

They'd already spent a half hour sitting in the sheikh's tent on a pillow on the ground while drinking tea and eating olives. All the while she'd shifted her weight back and forth on the pillow but nothing could relieve the pain she felt where her bottom hit the saddle. Claudia managed to smile and hopefully say the right things, but it wasn't easy.

She changed out of her dusty travel clothes and flopped down on the cot on her stomach. Riding across the desert was thrilling but exhausting and she didn't want to move for a long long time. Or get back on a horse for a long time, either. Just then Sam pulled the flap to her tent open and peered inside.

"Ready?" he asked. "You don't look ready."

"Just resting for a minute," she said, staying where she was. "Ready for what? Not another ride just yet."

Sam stepped inside her tent. "No, but it's the first race of the day. You'll get a chance to see Zaru in action."

"Will he win?"

"I almost hope not. It will just cause more attention, have more people bidding on him. Make the price go up. On the other hand…"

"You'll be rooting for him, I'm sure."

Sam walked to the cot and stood over her. "Sure you're okay?"

"How could I not be?" She sat up and gestured at the interior of the tent. "All the comforts of home."

"Except for showers and bathrooms, which are a short walk across the compound as you saw."

"If this is the way Bedouins live, I can see why they don't want to give it up."

"I'm afraid most nomads don't live this way. But it's the sheikh's responsibility to make his guests feel welcome. And it's my responsibility to make sure you don't suffer from that long ride. How do you feel really?"

Claudia debated whether to insist she was fine, but he must have seen something in her expression, because he brought out a small jar from his pocket. "I know you, Claudia, and I can tell by the look on your face you're hurting. It's understandable and this is the magic emulsion guaranteed to make pain disappear."

She held out her hand for the jar, but he told her to turn around and get back down on the cot. She tugged at her pant just an inch or two below her waist and Sam sat on the edge of the cot. *I know you Claudia, and I know you're hurting,* he'd said. As long as he didn't know she was hurting on the inside as well.

"Bruises. They look terrible," he said. "You must be in pain and this is no time for modesty. I'm going to apply this cream and you'll see, you'll feel a lot better." With that he edged her cargo pants further down and she buried her flaming face in the cool sheets.

His strong fingers rubbed the lotion in and produced a kind of warming, cooling, stinging and soothing feeling all at once. She sighed, wishing he'd never stop.

"Amazing," she murmured into the pillow as she felt the potion do its work. "You're a genius."

"It's not me, it's the cream."

He could say it wasn't him, but it was. It might be a miracle cream, but she could tell he had a magic touch.

"What is it?" she mumbled, feeling like she could dissolve into a pool of ecstasy. The touch of his hands on her lower back and the curve of her hips was nothing short of erotic, but that was because of Sam. Any time he touched her, whether deliberately or accidentally she lost her balance, forgot to breathe and felt like she might faint.

"It was made originally for horses."

She swiveled her head to look at him. "Horses? And you're using it on me?"

He grinned at her surprise. "Don't worry. You're not the only filly I've used it on. I wouldn't treat you as a guinea pig. I've used it myself. And on others."

Claudia wondered what others he'd used it on.

\* \* \*

The races took up the rest of the day. The excitement in the air was contagious. Hooves pounded the sand and the air was full of screams and shouts. As expected, Zaru won the race and everyone was talking about him. Still, Sam didn't seem that worried about his price going up. In fact he was as proud of the camel as if he'd already bought him for his father. Claudia took pictures of Sam posing with Zaru after the race.

Someday she would look at these pictures just to assure herself it wasn't all a dream. She'd really been to this exotic place. She'd really camped with Bedouins and ridden a horse across the sand. She'd really seen Sam stand next to a prize-winning camel with his white shirt hanging open showing his gorgeous bronzed chest, his smile a flash of white teeth. He'd read her palm and he'd kissed her.

Yes, these were memories she'd treasure forever. If she looked different from her former self wearing someone else's clothes and her hair loose and untamed, he was just as different from the man who wore a shirt, tie and suit every day to the office.

The camel market was to be the next day. The rest of the day was spent socializing and examining the camels for sale as well as prized horses. Claudia followed Sam around and he introduced her to old and new friends. He translated much of the conversations, but not all, and she wondered what they thought about her. Did they understand why he'd brought her along with him? Sure, she might be his assistant in America but they must wonder what use she could possibly be at a camel market. She wondered herself.

"You really don't need me here," she said to Sam. "But I'm glad I came. It's fascinating."

"I thought you'd like it," he said. "And I do need you here to cheer on Zaru with me. How else would he have won the race?"

"Is it true camels are normally bad tempered?"

"Like people, some are," he said. "Let's go look at Zaru up close." After asking around they learned where the prize camel was staying with his owners.

There he was, chewing contentedly from a bucket of oats, obviously enjoying the honor accorded to a winner.

After Sam spoke to the owner, he reported to Claudia. "He says Zaru is good-tempered, patient and intelligent. You won't find him kicking or spitting. In fact he says camels don't deserve their bad reputation. Zaru is worth every penny the new owner pays for him. He's a purebred with all kinds of papers and he should live forty years or more. The owner says you can have a ride on him. See for yourself."

"He's quite a salesman, isn't he?" Claudia asked. "I'd love to ride, but…"

"Just around the circle."

She hesitated. She didn't want to add to her pain, but when else would she have a chance to ride any camel, let alone this prize-winning beast.

"Maybe, but I take his picture first, if it's okay."

She got permission and this time she got up close to capture the camel's soft, doelike expression and his long double row of curly eyelashes. Sure enough, he merely gazed calmly at Claudia without a thought of spitting or kicking her.

"I think he likes you," Sam said with a grin.

"Or maybe he's just basking in his fame."

The owner, thinking Claudia had accepted the offer, had the camel go down on his knees so she could mount.

She exchanged a long look with Sam. Would he think her a coward if she didn't go? Might she always regret it if she missed this opportunity?

He gave her a thumbs-up sign and she had no choice. He expected her to take chances. He wanted her to experience it all. She couldn't let him down. With Sam in his country she was a different person from the assistant back home. A braver person. A person who took chances. Who wore different clothes and almost kissed her boss back when he kissed her.

She walked up and spoke a few soft words to Zaru, then threw one leg over his back and he rose to his feet slowly making soft moaning sounds.

"Am I too heavy?" she asked Sam, flinging her arms around the camel's neck.

"Don't worry. It doesn't mean anything. The moaning is just like the grunting and growling of a weight-lifter."

When she was up on the camel's back, high in the air, the owner led them slowly around the compound. The rocking motion was soothing and didn't seem to make her bottom any sorer than it already was.

A few minutes later Sam took her picture with her camera, the camel kneeled down, she got off and thanked the owner profusely.

Sam told him he'd see him tomorrow. Both knew there would be delicate negotiations over the price of the camel. Claudia wondered how much Sam was willing to pay.

"Maybe we shouldn't have admired Zaru so much, so openly," she said as they walked away. "In terms of driving a bargain."

Sam agreed. "We may have made the price go up."

"Maybe that was our mistake in the negotiations with the Bayadhis. We were too eager for the merger. Maybe we should have played hard to get."

Sam nodded slowly. "Exactly what I told Father. You and I are on the same wavelength as usual. Let's be sure to use the strategy to our advantage. For now, we're only dealing with a camel. Given his reputation, he'll be a costly addition to Father's stable no matter what. And it was worth it to see you ride him. You looked quite at home up there. Are you sure you didn't take camel-riding lessons in the park, too?" he teased.

"Actually camels might be easier than horses to ride," she said. "It almost felt like riding a rocking horse. No bouncing, no jarring."

"They're called the ships of the desert for that very reason, they sway and pitch like a ship."

Maybe that's why her bottom wasn't any worse for wear. She hadn't been riding a camel, she'd been on a ship of the desert.

An hour later dinner was served under an open-air tent. Servants passed trays of lamb that had been roasted on a spit and filled the air with a mouthwatering smell. Claudia and Sam joined the other guests and sat cross-legged on goat-hair carpets while served by women in multicolored, long dresses, their hands decorated with henna dye.

The next course was *Fatoush* salad, made of pita chips, tomatoes, cucumber, onion and parsley and flavored with lemon, which made a cool and refreshing accompaniment to the succulent lamb. The flat bread they called *nan* was hot and crisp straight out of a stone oven and spiced with sumac. All the food was washed down with icy soft drinks.

Children chased each other through the encampment, laughing and shouting. Between courses guests got up and greeted friends. Sam introduced her to at least a dozen men, some in traditional dress, some in casual European clothes.

"Do you know all these people?" she asked.

"I do now. Some are friends of my father. They're all asking about him. Wondering how he is. Asking why he isn't here, too. But the real reason they're stopping by is to ask who you are." He cocked his head to one side and narrowed his eyes as if he wasn't too sure who she was.

"I suppose it's unusual to travel with your assistant from the States."

"So unusual they don't believe me," he said.

"Really?"

"They naturally assume you're my wife. They congratulate me on making such a good choice." He grinned at her.

Claudia's face reddened. "Of course you told them how you feel about marriage."

"If I did, they'd be shocked. They'd treat me like a mental patient. They'd ask why."

"What would you tell them?"

"Just what I tell you. I don't want to share my life with anyone. I'd make a terrible husband. I'd be just like my father always at work. Always at the office. Only I'd feel guilty which my father never did. Do you know I hardly ever saw him during my childhood? He was always traveling, always socializing with business people or relatives. He assumed my mother would take care of us, which she did. But why bothe getting married and having children if you don't have to and now I don't have to. Zahara has done me a huge favor. I agreed to marry her, showing how accommodating I am and now I don't have to. Can you imagine how relieved and happy I am?"

Claudia nodded. Relieved. He'd said it again. Either he was trying to convince himself or her. Or he really was.

"In order to stop the questions," he continued, "it might be easier if we just pretended to be married. But then I'd have to sleep in your tent. You wouldn't want that, would you?"

Claudia bit her lip. His eyes gleamed with amusement. He was teasing her again and she didn't know how to take it. How would they ever get back to being boss and secretary again?

"And to show your respect you should probably walk five paces behind me. Could you do that?"

"If you like," she said with a demure smile.

"If you were my wife, you wouldn't even be here, you'd probably be at home."

"What would I be doing?"

"Taking care of our eight children. Weaving. Gossiping with the other wives. That's what my mother couldn't take. My father was off at the camel races or christening a new ship. The men had all the fun and she was treated like a concubine and nanny all in one."

"I don't blame her. But surely times have changed?"

"Yes. Quite a bit. Look around. There are plenty of women here. Just as interested in the races and the markets as the men. But it's too late for my parents. They've gone their separate ways."

He sounded like he'd come to terms with his parents' divorce, but Claudia wondered if the hurt still lingered.

The servers came around with small cups of hot, strong coffee and plates of honey pastries. He sipped his coffee, then he asked her a question.

"How would you feel if you had to stay home and miss all this?" He gestured to the rows of tents, the camels tethered outside, the stable of horses at the edge of the field, and in the distance the shifting sand dunes turning gold in the sunset.

She didn't want to speculate on what she would have done had she been his mother, confined to the home while homesick for her own country. Maybe she would have left, too, once her children were off to school. But if she'd truly been in love…It was hard to imagine. "I'm having a wonderful time. I wouldn't have missed it for the world. I can't believe I'm here."

He gazed at her over his coffee cup, his eyes gleaming with approval. "Good. I thought you'd like it," he said.

"Like it? Riding horseback over the dunes. Eating roasted lamb and watching the camel races. I'll never forget it." She sighed contentedly. "Never."

"Could you live here?" he asked. "Not out here, but in an oasis like Sidi Bou Said?"

Surprised, she set her cup down. He'd asked her a similar question the other night. How could she answer? What could she say? The truth was she'd live anywhere he did. "It's a wonderful vacation spot, but…"

"Don't look so alarmed. It's just a rhetorical question. Of course you couldn't. No one could unless they grew up there. Even then, there are difficulties. Forget I asked you."

"Could you?" she asked.

"I don't know. I've been asking myself. Not that I have to. It's too remote for someone involved in business. Despite the internet access. I guess I sometimes wonder if I have a home and where it is."

There was a long silence. Sam seemed lost in thought, maybe wondering about where he would eventually live and how he would hold out against family expectations.

They got up to leave when two women approached Claudia and pointed to her hands while chattering loudly.

"They want to dye your hands in a pattern like theirs," he said. "Don't worry, it's not permanent. Are you game?"

"Sure, if they want to," she said. Why not go for the whole Bedouin experience?

"They'll take you to their tent and I'll meet you later."

Claudia had the feeling Sam needed some time to himself. He seemed eager to pass her off on the women and she didn't mind going in the least. Soon she'd be back in San Francisco where life was predictable and pleasant, where she was unlikely to meet women in long gowns offering to tattoo her hands or camels racing across the sand.

The women mixed the dark red powder with water and with a tiny stick they painted a pattern on her hands. Then while it dried they served tea and a kind of cookie and sang and danced around the tent. Claudia wished she knew what they were saying when they spoke to her.

Maybe they were asking questions about her just as Sam said. She wanted to tell them this was all business. Sam meant nothing to her. But maybe they wouldn't believe her. Maybe the fortune teller knew more than Claudia thought.

Maybe like Durrah she'd seen more than Claudia wanted

her to. Maybe everyone knew how she felt despite all her efforts to act like she didn't care about Sam. As long as everyone didn't include Sam, she didn't care.

Night was falling as she left the women's tent with her hands covered in intricate patterns of dye. She was walking back to her tent when Sam caught up with her.

"Ah," he said, taking her hands in his to examine the work the women had done. "Now you look like you belong."

"They're amazing artists," she said, staring at his large warm hands holding hers, wishing he'd never let go. But he did.

"It's getting dark," he said. "This is the moment I've been waiting for. It's time for some serious stargazing."

He gathered a large carpet and a bottle of water and they walked a good twenty yards away from the tents and the animals. He spread the carpet out and they lay down flat on their backs. The gas lanterns and the rumble of voices from the compound seemed miles away.

"I don't know if you've ever tried stargazing back in San Francisco or in any big city, but the only thing you can see there with the naked eye are the brightest stars and the moon."

"But if we could see the stars, would they be the same ones we're looking at now?"

"More or less, because we're almost the same latitude, the city light pollution is the reason you can't see much in San Francisco. That's why it's good to get out here, away from it all for many reasons, and see the sky in all its glory."

"Then we won't need a telescope?"

"I'd like to have one someday, but look, there's the Big Dipper and the Little Dipper. The handle of the Little Dipper points to the North Star."

The stars were brilliant in the black sky. Claudia didn't think she'd ever seen a sight so dramatic.

Sam took her hand in his and pointed the way to the North Star. This time he didn't let go. He kept her hand in his as if it were the most natural thing in the world to lie there under the starry sky holding hands and talking about the stars.

"Makes you feel small and insignificant, doesn't it?" Claudia said breathlessly.

"You feel it, too?" he asked, squeezing her hand.

She tried to say yes but when she opened her mouth no sound came out. It was more happiness than she'd ever expected or wanted. Alone under a desert sky with the man she loved. It didn't matter that he didn't love her or that this moment wouldn't last. She knew that. She also knew enough to live in the moment. To make memories that would last a lifetime.

Sam warmed to his subject, when he found how little Claudia knew about the heavens. He explained how important the constellations were to farmers and nomads.

"For example most farmers know they're supposed to plant in the spring and harvest in the fall, but where the seasons are not well defined like around here, where the weather is pretty much the same year-round, how is anyone supposed to remember when to take the goats to pasture or harvest the dates? The answer is the constellations. Take Scorpius there. Does it look like a scorpion to you?"

"I think so," she said. But she was having a hard time paying attention. Who could blame her when her every nerve ending tingling with the smell of the campfires burning back at the camp, the warm breeze on her face and the scent of sandalwood soap that clung to Sam's clean shirt. Underneath was the carpet and sand. Above were the heavens, unreachable, untouchable and yet, and yet…

"Scorpius is only visible in the summer, so if you were a farmer without a clock or calendar, you could look for him in the night sky and you'd know what to do."

It was a good thing there wasn't going to be a test on Astronomy 101 later, because she was afraid she might forget some of the fine points of his lecture. Oh, she was listening all right, but it was the sound of his voice alone that had the power to distract her and make her want to feel his arms around her, his lips on hers.

"Then there's the North Star," he continued, warming to his subject. "At the handle of the Little Dipper. Very useful if you're lost out here in the desert."

She murmured something affirmative but all she could think about was what it would be like to honeymoon in a desert tent with only horses, camels and the starry skies above? Of course it would be nice to throw in a few servants, too. The kind who provided cold drinks and hot food and a tent over your head.

"Where were you and Zahara going to honeymoon?" Claudia asked.

"What? I don't think we'd thought that far ahead," Sam said, sounding surprised. "Why do you ask?"

"I was thinking this would be an ideal spot, it's so…beautiful." She almost said "romantic," but stopped herself just in time.

He laughed and let go of her hand. "You don't know Zahara. I don't know her very well, either, and even though she wants to marry the groom, I think her taste would run more to the Ritz in Paris than a tent in the desert. I hope he'll be able to provide for her. As you know, thinking you're in love and actually being in love are two different things."

"I thought you didn't believe in love."

"I don't, but you do."

"Yes," she said softly.

"Even after what you went through?" he asked, turning his head to look at her hoping that his time she might answer and tell him what had happened to her.

She turned to face him. She didn't want to talk about her marriage, but in the dark of the night, under the starry sky, she thought maybe it wouldn't hurt so much.

"I made a mistake," she said. "I married the wrong man. I was young and stupid. He cheated on me with a friend of mine before we were even married, but he confessed and said he'd never do it again. I believed him because I wanted to. I believed it was my friend's fault, so I cut her off, sick at heart she'd do that to me. I had to make a choice, him or her. I chose him."

Her throat clogged with tears and she couldn't speak. The memories came crowding back. The hurt, the anger and the feeling of being betrayed.

"Claudia, I'm sorry. I shouldn't have asked." Sam reached for her hand again and held it against his chest. She could feel his heart pounding.

"No, it's all right," she said, staring up at the sky again to get her bearings just as travelers once did as they crossed the desert.

"Anyway I married him and then it happened again. A different woman this time. This time I wouldn't listen to him. At least I learned that much. And it was over. All over in a few months. I can't tell you how shocked my parents were.

They believe marriage is forever. They blamed me for tossing him out. They thought I ought to forgive him again."

"I don't," Sam said. "You did the right thing."

"I know that, it's just…" Again the tears filled her eyes.

"Don't cry," Sam said, sounding alarmed. He propped himself on his elbow and gently wiped her tears with his handkerchief. "I never should have asked you about it. The man is an idiot. He never deserved you. I can't bear to think of him hurting you like that."

"I'm not hurt anymore," she protested. "I'm fine. In fact I feel better that I told you. You must wonder why I believe in love when you don't. Sometimes I wonder myself," she said, her lips quivering. If it weren't for Sam, maybe she wouldn't. But she knew what she felt for him was completely different from what she had felt for Malcolm.

She sighed a ragged sigh. Time to get back to the stars.

"What's that one up there?" she asked, sitting up straight. She was determined to get back in the mood by paying more attention.

"Orion the great hunter. He's stalking Taurus the bull and behind him is his dog Canis Major who's chasing Lepus the hare." He sat next to her, put one arm around her shoulders and guided her hand to point to the sky.

The nearness of Sam, the sympathy he felt for her, the warmth of his arm and the side of his body pressed against hers made her tremble all over. She felt like she'd joined the galaxy and was glowing like a star. Surely her face must be radiating as much heat and light as a heavenly body.

It's just an astronomy lesson, she told herself. Along with my true confession. No reason to get so excited. She told herself to stop fantasizing about Sam. Stop pretending this was a romance. He'd listened to her story and she felt better than she had. But this was still a business trip no matter how many confidences they exchanged. He was being kind to her. She understood him and he understood her better.

"Too much for one lesson?" he asked.

The answer was yes, it was too much for one lesson. Too much for one woman who had no experience with real love. She thought she'd been in love once, but she knew now she was wrong. This was a whole different feeling. Sam was unlike any man she'd ever known.

"How did you learn all this?" she asked.

He leaned back on his elbows and let his arm drop from her shoulders. "My sister and I had a tutor once when my father didn't want to send us away to school. Maybe he somehow knew that once we were gone my mother would go, too. Anyway, Marcus taught us everything, math, science and languages. He was an amateur astronomer and he took us out stargazing every night. We thought it was wonderful. But when I tried to look at the sky from my roof deck in San Francisco, it was no where near as clear. So I gave it up. But I haven't forgotten the lessons."

"Oh, look, a shooting star." Claudia tilted her head back. "They're not really stars, are they?"

"They're meteorites, just small pieces of rock. Marcus used to say they were the bonus we got from stargazing. If you stay out for a half hour or more most nights you'll see a shooting star or two. Our tutor was a member of the International Meteor Organization, which made him an official meteor watcher. He was quite passionate about them."

"Like your sister is passionate about clothes and you're passionate about your horses or the shipping business."

"And you?"

She wrapped her arms around her knees. "That's what your sister asked me. I wish I knew."

Of course she did know she was passionate about Sam, but that was beside the point and this was hardly the time to confess. Never was the time for her to confess that. In fact, there wasn't a good time to ever tell anyone.

If only this astronomy lesson could go on forever. What could be more romantic than the black sky above lit with stars, the soft sand beneath them and Sam listening to her recount her sad marriage after sharing his passion for the heavens with her? It was as close to heaven as she would ever get. Did he feel it, too? Whatever he felt, she understood him better than ever. And she knew better than ever why he would never commit to love and marriage.

"Come on," he said, getting to his feet. "It's time to turn in. It's been a long day."

A long day? It had been an incredible day. It was a day filled with sights and sounds she'd never forget. Sights and sounds made more memorable because she'd shared them with Sam. If only he felt the same about her.

# CHAPTER NINE

SAM awoke to the smell of steaming, dark roasted coffee carried in to his tent on a tray by a young man in a long robe and a turban wrapped around his head. He smiled, said good morning in Arabic and left a basket filled with flat bread and dates on a small wicker table.

Sam got up and looked outside. No surprise that it was another warm sunny day in the desert. A perfect day for another camel race. This one would be more important. There would be more competition today. If Zaru won again it would make the price go up for the camel. But how could he not cheer for him? It was almost as if he was theirs already.

Claudia would cheer with him. She seemed to care as much as he did. In the past he'd been with family at these events and they all enjoyed the festivities. But seeing Claudia react was something else. Her dazzling smile, her flushed cheeks and the look in her eyes when she rode that camel were sights he'd never forget.

He had no idea she would be so eager for new experiences, so brave about riding a horse across the desert. How could he? She was his secretary, she sat at a desk and was incredibly efficient and smart. That was all and that was enough. That was all he wanted.

But now? What did he want? Part of him wanted this trip to never end. To continue the discoveries, to find out what else made her eyes light up. What made her able to take chances. How far would she go?

What he knew was that she wore her emotions on her sleeve and he never tired of watching her reactions.

How she'd changed since they'd arrived in this country. Would it have happened to anyone? Surely not. Most women would have avoided being dragged into a family crisis, a broken engagement and a postponed merger. Most women would have gotten on the first plane home instead of attending a camel race. But not Claudia. She looked like there was nothing she'd rather be doing. In fact, she'd said as much.

How many women would want to spend an evening lying on the sand looking up at the stars listening to him drone on about the constellations, repeating the lessons he'd learned so long ago? He couldn't think of a single one. How many would confess to being betrayed by their husband? He was touched by her confiding in him. He wanted to kill the man who'd made her cry.

Sitting there with his arm around her shoulders showing her stars felt so natural and right, he hoped she felt the same way. How anyone could treat her the way her husband had was beyond belief. He clenched his jaw so tight it locked in place, just thinking of the man who'd cheated on her.

He had no idea if Zahara liked stargazing. It didn't matter anymore. He certainly couldn't picture her on a camel. Couldn't imagine her hair blowing in the wind or getting sunburned like Claudia. Claudia didn't seem to have a vain bone in her body.

Zahara was no longer part of his life and the relief he felt when she'd called off the engagement had only intensified over the past two days. Since she intended to marry the family groom, she must like horses, but he couldn't picture Zahara riding across the desert like Claudia had. The thought of how easily he'd committed to marrying Zahara made him realize how lucky he was to still be free. Free to marry whoever he wanted.

Of course he had no intention of marrying anyone at all. It wouldn't be fair to them. He thought of his mother, back in France, finally living the life she wanted, at home in her own country, speaking her own language, surrounded by friends and family. Her memories of this country were bittersweet. And his father was still bitterly uncomprehending of why she'd left. How could anyone know if marriage would last? There were no guarantees. Not money or common interests, or family ties. Sam was prepared to take risks in business, but not in his personal life.

As he got dressed in a loose white shirt and long cargo shorts he had a feeling today would be just as full of events and maybe a few surprises. He smiled thinking of showing Claudia the souks set up in tents outside this morning. Would she be tempted to buy an amulet, cushions, dresses or earrings? He wanted to buy her something to remember this day, this trip. But he had no idea what she liked.

Strange that he'd known her for two years and yet he couldn't picture her in jewelry or indulging in anything that wasn't practical. In some ways, he felt like he was just getting to know her. Did she just think of him as her boss, someone she had to humor and go along with what he decided? A week ago that would have been fine. But not now. They were more than boss and secretary now. They were friends. He shouldn't have kissed her. But he couldn't help himself.

When he made a knocking sound outside her tent, she called, "Come in."

"Sleep well?" he asked. She looked fresh and wide-awake sitting on the edge of her cot with a coffee cup in her hand. "Don't answer that, I can tell, you are…definitely well rested." He couldn't tell her she looked amazing this morning, so unlike her San Francisco self he couldn't stop staring at her. She'd been changing constantly ever since she arrived in his country and now with her hair damp and in long waves, her eyes gleaming, her skin with a sheen from the desert sun, the transformation was little short of stunning.

Of course he would be stunned. Back in the office, she'd appeared every morning in a suit and sensible shoes, her hair pulled back from her face, ready for a day's work. How could he possibly have imagined there was a beautiful butterfly ready to emerge from the cocoon? No wonder he couldn't stop staring at her.

"I had time for a shower," she said. "I feel great."

"You look great," he said. Great was not the word for it. She looked like a ripe, sun-kissed tropical fruit. It was all he could do to keep from taking her in his arms and kissing her again. He wondered if she'd taste like summer and sunshine.

What was he thinking? One day in the not too distant future they'd be back in the office in San Francisco and all this would be in the past. He couldn't do anything to risk his relationship with Claudia. He couldn't get along without her back there. He must not upset the careful balance they had. They worked so well together. It would be unthinkable to get carried away and do something he'd be sorry for.

He never let his emotions run out of control, as his family knew so well. There should be no problem now. And yet…and yet…No matter what he thought, there was some sort of change going on inside his head. He could blame it on the weather, the sun, the sand or this rapidly changing country he belonged to. Or he could blame it on Claudia.

He had to take care their relationship didn't change just because they were in a different country. The status quo was his goal, but it seemed to be slipping away by the hour.

"But what about your sore bottom? Need another treatment?"

She flushed. "Much better thanks to your magic potion."

"Think you'll ever be able to ride again?"

"Of course. I'm looking forward to it. Now that Thunder and I get on so well. How much longer will we be here?"

"Hopefully we can wrap up the acquisition of the camel by tomorrow. It must be tiring for you living in a tent like this."

"Not at all. It's very comfortable. And what an experience. For you it's nothing, but for me? I'll have something to remember for the rest of my life."

"I'm sure you'll have more than that. Who can say what the future holds?" Who knew indeed? "You'll have all kinds of adventures, get married again. Who knows?"

The idea of Claudia getting married and leaving him gave him pause. He'd never find anyone to take her place. But what could he do? She was a free agent.

She shook her head. "No matter what you read on my palm, I'll never get married again. Now you know why. I'm over it now, but that doesn't mean I'd ever take a chance on love again."

"You'll change your mind," he insisted more to himself than to her. "You're lovely, smart and clever. Some tall, dark stranger will make you an offer and you won't be able to refuse."

She stood for a moment then sat down again. She looked so surprised, he wondered if he'd never complimented her before?

"And you're still young."

"Almost thirty."

Enough of this disturbing conversation. He wanted to enjoy the day. There wouldn't be many more like this. Eventually they'd have to go back to work. Why was he having so much trouble concentrating on work? He'd been to the desert before He'd seen camel races. But he'd never been so distracted.

He set his cup down and stood. "Ready? I want to show you the souks. The markets they've set up in tents. You can find anything you want provided you want a camel saddle o a sword or a drum."

"I'll bring some money then."

He shook his head. "Your money isn't good here. If you war something I'll buy it for you. I owe you for coming with me.

Outside the tent she turned to face him. "What do yo mean? This is the best vacation I've ever had. I keep pinchin myself. I'm in the desert. I rode a horse and a camel. Do yo know how amazing that is?"

"I know you didn't want to come."

"Oh." She looked away and a faint blush colored h cheeks. "Did I say that? I was a different person back the I wouldn't miss this for the world. Someday when I'm old a gray and living somewhere in an apartment in San Francisco I'll have a photo album to remind me of the time I went to the desert."

He tried to picture her being old and gray, but he couldn't. He definitely couldn't picture her growing old alone. Anyone who saw her on vacation, letting down her hair, wearing a ball gown or shorts that exposed her lovely long legs would immediately desire her for their own. If he weren't a sheikh, if he weren't from another part of the world, if he believed in love…

"You'll have more than the photos," he said. "There has to be something out there in the souks that catches your eye." He grabbed her hand. "We'll find you a souvenir or two or three."

They wandered from tent to tent as Claudia tried on agate beads, brass bracelets, tested cushions stuffed with feathers, silver earrings and amulets to ward off evil spirits. She shook a tambourine and tapped on a goatskin drum. She took pictures of the merchants in their stalls and Sam used her camera to take pictures of her wearing a turban and veil.

Sam wanted to buy it all for her, but he restrained himself. He was waiting for the perfect necklace, the best beads and the purest gold, so they kept going, picking up a few small items, bargaining, laughing and talking with the merchants.

A tall merchant with a long white beard held up a beautiful leather bag dyed deep red and decorated with fringe.

"The fringe is not necessary," he explained to them. "It's about decoration, but it's also about movement. When you are riding with this bag hanging from your horse, the fringe is moving. When the wind is blowing your robes are blowing, too. We love beautiful things. We find beauty in movement. We also love power and respect and we try to include these

in our craft. Do you understand?" he asked, holding the red
bag out so they could see the fringe to advantage.

Claudia nodded and ran her fingers over the soft leather of
the bag. Which was all Sam needed to buy that, too. Then he
proceeded to buy silver earrings and some rings and a bracelet
from the best silversmith.

Claudia tried to protest, but he insisted and when she wore
the silver on her arm and her ears and saw it flash in the sunlight,
he knew he'd done the right thing. He took more photos of her
with the silversmith. These were pictures he had to have.

Of course she must have smiled as his assistant back in the
city, but not like this. Or if she had, he hadn't noticed. Not
noticed how Claudia's face lighted up when she was happy?
What was wrong with him? He was a different person then.
So was she.

"I think the desert agrees with you," he said soberly as they
strolled past piles of cured leather and silversmiths working
in the sun.

"I think so, too," she said, looking around. When she turned
her head her earrings flashed in the sun. "The air is so dry, so
pure, you can see for miles. Like last night. I'll never forget
the view of the stars. Thank you for that. And thank you for
listening to my sad story. I don't usually talk about…about
what happened. But last night…" Her voice faltered.

"You're welcome," he said, taking her hand in his. When
what he really meant was to thank her for trusting him enough
to tell him about her past. Thank her for letting him share his
passion with her. For letting him buy jewelry for her and for
sharing this day with him.

"Let's get something to drink," he said. They ducked into

a tent where they sat down at a rough table in the shade to eat
juicy chunks of watermelon and drink more mint tea. Juice
stained her lips and he couldn't help wondering how she'd
taste. When she noticed him staring at her, she looked away.
He had no idea what was happening to him. What was clear
was that whatever it was had never happened before.

Before they left the souks Claudia confessed she loved the
glazed earthenware they served the couscous in but didn't
know if she could get it home with her. "And the copper
cooking pots. They're beautiful."

"You should have them. We'll buy whatever you want and
send it home in the Land Rover."

"I mean all the way home to California."

"We'll pack them up and take them on the plane with us."

What was she thinking? How would she have room for it
all in her tiny apartment kitchen? But Sam was so generous
she couldn't say no. All she did was mention something she
wanted and suddenly it was hers. How could she recreate this
atmosphere or this style of cooking back in California?

Maybe she should just enjoy this experience now and
realize that soon it would be over. This trip, this place, this
feeling of closeness to Sam would be just a memory. She'd
have her pictures and her souvenirs, but they just might make
her sad knowing that it was all over like a dream.

Still his enthusiasm was contagious and he went overboard
buying pots and dishes for her. He hired a young man to carry
the goods and on their way out of the souks they passed the
spice market. The pungent smell of coriander, cumin and
saffron wafted through the air. Before she knew it, Claudia

was watching the merchants scoop out the powders into bags and weigh them, then wrap them up for her.

As they loaded everything into the Land Rover, she said "I'll have to get the recipes from your cook at the house, so I'll be able to use these things."

"I didn't know you could cook."

"Of course. Although I've never eaten anything like what I've had since we arrived. At our book club we always have a potluck dinner that's themed to the book we read. For instance when we read *Reading Lolita in Tehran* we all made Persian food. Maybe I'll make a complete dinner with my new spices and pots when we get back." She could make the dinner, but who would come besides her book club or the Knitwits, her knitting club? She couldn't very well ask Sam. After all, he was her boss. Something she was having trouble wrapping her mind around right now.

No matter what had happened here in Tazzatine, when they returned, it would all be the way it was. Every touch of his hand, every smile they'd exchanged, every look between them would be forgotten and they'd be back to normal.

Normal. What a dreadful word. What it meant was early mornings at the office to catch up on the messages that had arrived the night before. Sure, she and Sam would talk, but they'd talk about cargo ships and docking and fees and financial statements. Then there'd be lunches brought in and eaten at her desk, dry sandwiches, nothing like the cumin scented rice or racks of succulent marinated lamb she'd been eating since she got here.

Back to her old office appropriate outfits. No gorgeous borrowed gowns, no handsome men inviting her to sailing. No bikini worn at a rooftop pool. No exotic nomads living in tents.

Claudia forced herself to smile and not think about the future. "When is the next camel race?" she asked. "We don't want to be late."

A new and larger circular track had been plowed in the sand. Sam pointed out that this was an official race, more important than the one yesterday. Much lower in prestige than the King's Cup in Dubai but if Zaru continued to improve, he might someday race there, too.

"How fast can they run?" she asked.

"Forty miles an hour, or twenty-five miles an hour for an hour. This won't last that long."

"What if Zaru doesn't win?" she asked.

"I almost hope he doesn't, then he won't be so expensive," Sam murmured, looking over his shoulder as if for prospective competitive buyers.

But when the race started he cheered louder than anyone. "Go, Zaru," he shouted.

"Come on, Zaru." Claudia yelled until she was hoarse but Zaru was nowhere near the finish line.

"What's wrong?" Sam said. "Maybe he doesn't have the speed. Maybe Father won't be so keen on my getting him."

"But you said he'd be cheaper if he doesn't win."

"I didn't expect him to come in last," Sam said with a frown.

"Look, he's catching up," Claudia said. She jumped up and down and shouted encouragement. She'd never been to a race of any kind, certainly not a camel race. If she'd known how much fun they were she might have gone to a horse race. Zaru continued to gain. She noticed Sam was just as enthusiastic as she was. He'd grabbed her hand in the excitement and they cheered together.

When Zaru pulled ahead of the pack they were giddy with excitement. Sam grabbed Claudia and kissed her. This time she kissed him back. It took only seconds for both of them to realize it was a big mistake. They'd crossed the line for the second time. If the first time was an accident, what was this?

"Sorry," Sam said, breathing hard. "He won and I got carried away."

"Me, too." Claudia was trying to catch her breath. It was a hot day, the perspiration was dripping off her face and Sam had kissed her. And she'd kissed him. Something she'd wanted to do since forever. She'd felt the kiss down to her toes. He was sorry. He'd gotten carried away. That was all. She couldn't breathe. Couldn't speak. She'd gotten carried away, too. But she wasn't sorry. Not at all.

"Let's go find Zaru," Sam said, running his hand through his hair. If he was affected at all by the kiss, he'd gotten over it fast. He looked pleased, but only because his future came had won the big race. That was cause for celebration. It was only a brief kiss exchanged between friends. In a few minutes he would have forgotten it. As for Claudia, it would take her a little longer, maybe a lifetime. She couldn't believe she'd actually kissed him back. Had he even noticed? She hoped not.

They met Zaru and his rider and owner in his stall where he was basking in his glory, munching from a bucket of wheat and oats and drinking water.

Claudia didn't understand any of the bargaining, so she just sat on a small leather three-pronged stool and watched and listened as the men talked. She didn't have to understand what Sam was saying. The sound of his voice resonated in her head, caused a vibration deep inside her.

She watched him knowing he wouldn't notice her. He was too intent on making the deal. She'd seen him like this before, but it wasn't about camels, it was about finding a berth for his ship, paying the docking fees or looking for an alternate port or buying a new ship. He was a supreme negotiator. Fair and honest but aggressive, too. As everyone knew, Samir Al-Hamri always got what he wanted.

She knew he was determined to buy the camel at any cost, and she knew the owner was determined to get the best price so she could imagine how the conversation went even though she didn't understand a single word.

Finally all parties stood and shook hands. They put their arms around each other and kissed on the cheek. Sam told her on the way back to the main tent he was pleased with the deal.

"Then he's yours?" she asked.

"Father's. They'll deliver him next week."

"I didn't see any money change hands."

"No, but we have a bargain. They trust me to pay and I trust they'll deliver the camel."

The rest of the day was spent in traditional dancing, singing and playing music on drums and lute.

For Claudia it was a letdown. She'd been so excited to see Maru win, then watch Sam succeed in buying the camel she felt drained of energy. Did her letdown have anything to do with that kiss after the race? She refused to consider it. Obviously Sam had forgotten all about it. To him it was a spur-of-the-moment event, a celebration. Nothing to get excited about. Nothing to treasure or remember.

He was more interested in the weather forecast. The wind had picked up and the sand was blowing. The sun was a hazy orange ball in the afternoon sky. She was sitting on a small carpet, a hat pulled down over her ears to keep the sand out of her hair, watching the women dance when Sam came and told her the old-timers were predicting the *simoom*.

"What's that?" she asked, noting a worry line had formed between his eyebrows.

"It's a severe sand storm. The *simoom* can move dunes, obliterate roads and even obscure the sun. Our best bet is to leave now and outrun it. I don't want to be stuck here with only a tent for protection. Are you game or do you want to go in the Land Rover with the servants? You'd definitely be more comfortable."

"How would you get the horses back?"

"I'd ride mine and lead Thunder."

"I'd rather go with you," she said.

"I was hoping you'd say that," he said with an approving smile.

He wanted her to go with him. It wasn't much in the way of compliments, but it was something and at this point, she'd take whatever she could get.

"Change clothes," he said. "Cover up completely, as best you can. Just in case."

He didn't say in case of what, but she'd heard somewhere about a wall of sand that could travel at sixty miles an hour. If she had to be in the middle of a sand storm, she wanted to be with Sam. If she was honest she'd admit she wanted to be with him in the middle of rain, hail, snow or sleet or a warm summer day. She just wanted to be with him.

# CHAPTER TEN

"Are you sure you're ready for another long ride?" Sam asked as the grooms saddled their horses.

She rubbed her hip. "I'm much better, thanks to your magic ointment." And his magic touch, or course, but she didn't mention that. "And I'm used to the horse now."

"Good, because we need to make time."

After thanking their host, saying goodbye to others who were also preparing to leave, they were off across the dunes. Sam turned to look behind them where the sky was dark on the horizon.

"What do you think?" she asked.

"It doesn't look good. I'm glad we left when we did."

Claudia didn't ask any more questions. She concentrated on following Sam as closely as possible, trying not to imagine what would happen if a wall of sand hit them at sixty miles an hour.

She glanced over her shoulder to see the sand spraying up from the ground. No matter how fast they rode it seemed to be after them like a ferocious beast. The sand filled their eyes and ears with grit despite their hats and sand goggles. She tried to call to Sam but the wind blew her words back into her face.

He turned to look at her and wave then he galloped on ahead finally pulling off in a ravine between two boulders. She breathed a sigh of relief to be out of the relentless wind. He helped her down, gave her a drink of water from his carafe.

"Are you okay?" he asked, putting his hands on her shoulders. She couldn't see his eyes behind his glasses. She didn't want to know how worried he was. If he was, and he must be with this kind of storm.

"Yes," she said. But she was tired of fighting the wind and the sand.

"We can't take time to rest, we have to stay ahead of it."

"Is that what we're doing?"

"So far. It could be worse. Much worse. Sorry about missing the cave paintings."

She nodded and got back on her horse. It seemed like days but it was only hours later, long hours of hard riding when they arrived back at the gates of the villa at Sidi Bou Said. When she dismounted, Claudia felt her knees buckle. She'd been straining so hard, trying to keep up, trying to keep the sand out of her eyes and ears that she almost collapsed. "We made it," she muttered. But Sam didn't hear her and this time he didn't catch her when she slid off her horse. He was too busy talking to the grooms.

"They say Father wants me to call him right away," he said. "Something's up. I'll have a quick shower and call him." He tilted her chin with his thumb and surveyed her face. "You were superb out there. No one could have done better." He traced his index finger along her jawline. She felt the fine grains of sand on her skin. "Get your clothes off. Wash up."

Claudia nodded and went upstairs to have a long shower

his words echoing in her head. *Superb. No one better.* She let the cool water run through her hair and over her body. She scrubbed her skin and washed her hair over and over. It took forever to finally get the sand off every part of her body. Then she toweled off briskly until her skin was prickly.

She found one of Amina's outfits, an all-cotton shirt with matching shorts and sandals and went downstairs. The house was quiet except for the servants who had prepared a cool eggplant and tomato salad with olives and lemon.

They set a table for the two of them on the patio in the arbor under the fig trees. She was famished but she didn't want to eat without Sam. Passing by the office, she heard his voice.

When Sam appeared on the patio his dark eyes were gleaming. His hair was still damp from the shower and he smelled like soap and leather.

"You look better," he said, his gaze taking in her hair, her shirt, shorts and legs. "How do you feel?"

She felt sore, tired yet super-charged at the same time. "What's happened?"

"Father says the Bayadhis are ready to come back to the table. We should head back to the city tomorrow."

"What happened?" she asked eagerly.

"They were intrigued by your idea of considering the benefits of our ships on their contracts. So you get the credit. If it works out."

"There's no guarantee," she said.

"Not yet. But Father is tired of the uncertainty. I'm afraid it's taken a toll on him. Which is why we must get back. He's talking of retiring. Especially when I told him I'd bought the camel. He sees himself as devoting himself to camel-racing.

He wants the merger to go through, but he's ready to give up responsibility. He already had too much."

"What does that mean?"

"It means if it goes through I'd have much more to do. Both here and around the globe. I'd be taking over his job as well as my own and who knows what else."

"Would you be based here in Tazzatine?" she asked, trying to conceal the fear that threatened to tear her whole world apart. Sam gone. Sam in Tazzatine. Claudia a world away. She knew he could never be hers. All she asked was to see him every day.

"Probably. At least part of the time."

"You don't seem upset."

"I'm not that surprised. I knew it would happen sooner or later. This is sooner, but I understand why he wants to get away from the stress. And maybe I'm ready for a new challenge. Are you?"

"Me? I…I don't know."

"You'll have a bigger job, more money, more perks."

She didn't want more money and more perks. She wanted Sam. It wasn't that unexpected that he would one day take over for his father. But not so soon. Her mind was spinning.

"But if the merger doesn't go through…"

He shrugged. "Then Father will have to keep the office going here and I'll come back to California. But I trust you to come up with a solution."

"I'll try," she said.

"If anyone can bring the two sides together, you can. Father will have to agree if he wants this deal to work. We'll leave first thing in the morning." Sam gave her an encouraging smile. He had faith in her. He thought she was smart and perceptive. She appreciated that. She only wished he found her desirable as well. She might as well wish the skies would shower her with meteors every night.

They sat down at the table and she tried to eat, but her stomach was tied up in knots. The pressure Sam put on her seemed unbearable. He had way too much confidence in her. He thought she could run the office in California. He thought she could talk the Bayadhis into agreeing to the merger.

While she sipped her iced tea, he piled a mound of salad on their plates, but then he, too, seemed to lose his appetite.

She tried to eat, but the food seemed to stick in her throat. She tried not the think of the decision that was hanging over her like a wrecker's ball and the delicate negotiations ahead.

Sam acted like nothing had happened. Instead of eating, he talked animatedly about Amina and the family news he'd received from his father. Everything but what was most important. Maybe he thought he was keeping her from worrying. Instead she worried even more. How could she make the merger take place if the families were too far apart?

Why should she try? It would be best for her if it all fell apart. She could arrange it so it looked like she was trying, but leave a loophole that the Bayadhis were sure to notice. It would end the merger and she would get Sam back. But she knew she couldn't let him and his family down. And she couldn't quit her job. Not yet.

Sam watched Claudia out of the corner of his eye while he ate his salad. He knew he'd given her a big job. He also knew she was up to it. He needed her as he never had before. He had no choice. If the merger didn't go through it would be a failure for the family business. His father would take it personally. If it did go through, he'd have a big job. So would Claudia. He'd have to be here and everywhere else, too. He couldn't do it without Claudia working for him in an office across the world.

She was ideal for the job of running the San Francisco office. She knew more than she thought she did. She was better at some things than he was. He'd miss her. He'd miss his right-hand woman and he'd miss the companion of these last few days, the other Claudia. The one who'd worn a bikini at the pool, the one who'd braved the sandstorm because he told her they could make it. The one he'd kissed and who'd kissed him back. But there was no way he could have them both.

He couldn't forget the kiss. He didn't know why. She didn't mean to kiss him any more than he'd meant to kiss her. The first time was a mistake, the second time was because he couldn't help himself.

Why couldn't he get over it? He'd kissed dozens of women and yet he couldn't remember a single kiss or even the names of the women. Maybe it was just that it was so unexpected. He couldn't be in love. According to Claudia love made you lose your appetite and your concentration. All right, so he hadn't been eating or sleeping well or thinking well, either. But that didn't mean anything.

If he'd fallen in love with Claudia it would be inconvenient to say the least. And where would they live? He'd asked her twice if she could imagine herself living here. She'd said no. He was not going to repeat his father's mistake and bring a bride to be homesick and lonely here or anywhere.

Claudia had kissed him. That much he knew for sure. He

couldn't believe it really happened. But it had and he had to deal with it. He was an expert at dealing with things that didn't fit into the norm. Everyone who knew him knew he was pragmatic and adaptable. But that kiss was not like anything else that had happened to him and he hadn't adapted to it yet.

He also couldn't reconcile the two sides of her. He didn't know who she really was. Maybe she didn't, either. He just knew she had to say yes to his plan. It made perfect sense. There was no one else he'd trust to run the office. This way he'd get to see her sometimes. He'd fly in for a meeting in San Francisco, they'd talk, have lunch and he'd be off. Just like old times. Only not at all like old times.

Maybe if he kissed her again he could get it out of his mind. He'd realize a kiss is just a kiss. On the other hand, if he wasn't in love, he must have some strange disease. Not only could he not eat or sleep, he couldn't concentrate on anything except for Claudia. These were symptoms he wouldn't want to share with any doctor. He'd just laugh and tell him what he didn't want to hear. He was in love.

"I have an idea," she said suddenly, interrupting his thoughts. "I need to look something up on the Internet."

He put his fork down. "Go ahead. I've got some calls to make."

She nodded, her gaze fastened on something in the distance. "I'm not sure I can find it, but if I do…It's just something I read somewhere."

Claudia was up half the night. They didn't talk until the next morning. He stopped by the office to offer his services, but she said she needed to be alone and work something out.

"What did you find?" he asked.

"A new maritime law the European Union has just passed. It might help us. I need to do some more research, and make some calls when we get back to your office. Don't tell your father yet."

"I won't, but I know you. You wouldn't say anything unless you were pretty sure."

He grinned at her and her heart skipped a beat. "Sam, if this works and the merger goes through…"

"I know what you're going to say."

She swallowed hard. "You do?"

"You're going to ask for a raise and a vacation. Ask me—you can have anything you want." He leaned forward and cupped her chin in his hand. Then he very slowly kissed her on the lips. His lips were warm and sure. She put her arms around him and kissed him back. He moaned and held her close.

"Claudia," he said, pulling back to look into her eyes. "What will I do without you?"

Speechless, she shook her head.

He kissed her again. She couldn't have backed away, she could have protested, but she didn't.

She knew she'd regret it. She knew she should keep her distance, but she wasn't made of stone. Soon she'd be gone from this magic place and this would all be a memory. Nothing more. Was it so wrong to take whatever she could get now?

He said she could have anything she wanted. Anything but him. She couldn't tell him now she was leaving. He was too happy. Too hopeful.

On the return drive, they held hands and Claudia watched the scenery go by knowing she'd never see it again. Her head was full of conflicting thoughts. The challenge of making the merger work, and if it did, the reality of losing everything she wanted. Her job and Sam. Not that he'd fire her, he'd promote her, but she'd have to quit. It was clear. She couldn't work for him anymore.

The two families met the next day. The air in the Al-Hamri office was cool, almost frigid and so was the atmosphere at first. The Bayadhi family sat on one side of the table, the Al-Hamris with Claudia on the other. Each side was prepared to get what they wanted or walk away from the table.

Claudia was dressed in new clothes furnished by Amina from her boutique: a slim linen skirt and matching jacket. Her bare legs were tanned and she wore leopard print ballet flats. She felt like a different person than the woman who'd stepped off the plane only two weeks ago. The admiring look Sam gave her told her he thought so, too.

She studied the faces across the table. The old man who'd been Sam's father's rival all these years and three of his children, who would run the company someday, maybe even today. But what company? The new merged company or the old one they were hanging onto?

Sam had greeted everyone warmly. She always admired how cool he was under pressure. He claimed he wasn't worried. That he didn't feel any pressure.

"I know you and I know you have everything under control," he'd said before the meeting. He put his hands on her shoulders and looked into her eyes, a smile tugging the corners of his mouth. She summoned all her willpower and smiled back at him with confidence. This was it. It was in her hands.

If all went well she would save the merger. And she'd say goodbye to Sam. He'd stay here. She'd go back to San Francisco. She'd quit her job. She couldn't take it anymore, loving him and knowing he thought of her as an employee and nothing more.

Or she could withhold her information and let the merger fail and they'd go on as they were. Then at least she'd have Sam from nine-to-five every day and sometimes on the weekends or late at night. Was it better than nothing?

"Ready, Ms. Bradford?" Everyone was looking at her. She opened her briefcase, took out her laptop and motioned for the Bayadhis' lawyer to go first.

He said what she knew he'd say, that merging the two companies would violate a European Union Maritime Law that would prevent them from doing business within the EU.

"I'm sorry, but for obvious reasons, the merger would not do any good for either party," he said and closed his briefcase with a final snap. The Bayadhi family were almost out of their chairs, when Claudia asked for a moment to respond.

Sam's father looked at her expectantly as if to say, now what are you going to do? Sam, however, just kept his dark gaze steady. They'd been through these negotiations before, but she'd never had anything personal at stake before.

It was now or never. Agree with them, and let the merger fail or come up with a solution and let her life change forever. No more job. No more Sam. No more Tazzatine. No more desert or oases, or horses.

She took a deep breath. "There is a way around this new regulation," she said. "In a similar case two years ago concerning a shipping company which changed its registration from Liberia to Bermuda. In this way bypassing Section 243 of the EU Maritime Code regarding shipping registration. We can do the same because Bermuda has just received a special exemption."

The Bayadhis looked at each other. They asked for time to reconsider. Fifteen minutes. They shook hands and walked out of the room.

"Claudia, that's brilliant," Sam said, clasping her hand in his.

His father sat in his chair for a long moment, before he stood and congratulated her. "Sam was right about you," he said. "You've saved the day. They can't say no now."

"They can," Sam said, "but I don't think they will."

When the Bayadhis came back in the room they were all smiles. Sam's father was right. They couldn't say no. They had no more reason to say no. It was time to celebrate. The Al-Hamris hosted a reception in their office, which Sam had planned, and had ordered fruit drinks and an array of delicious finger food, both savory appetizers like flaky stuffed pastries and little sugared tarts; he was so confident that they would be called for. Several others from both companies joined them and the excited talk was all about expansion, new offices, new routes and new personnel.

"You'll be the one to draw up the new organization chart," Sam said, handing Claudia a glass of sparkling juice as they stood apart from the others at the window looking out at the harbor where an Al-Hamri ship was unloading freight.

Tell him, tell him now, she said to herself. Tell him you'll do the chart but after that, you will be gone. Gone from his office, gone from the company and gone from his life.

"What will you do with the bonus I'm giving you for

saving the day? Where will you go on your vacation I'm giving you? Wherever it is, I'll go with you."

She shook her head. "I don't need a bonus, Sam, I was just doing my job. And I've just had the best vacation of my life. I'll never forget this time in your country. I'm just happy it worked out so well. But I ought to get back to San Francisco soon." Her heart fell thinking of facing the city without him there.

"There's no need to rush. We need to celebrate. Really celebrate. I mean to take you sailing and sightseeing here in the city. There's something I want to tell you. Ask your opinion about."

"Ask me now. You've already done enough for me. And I've been gone long enough." Though her lips were trembling, she forced herself to smile politely. It was the only way. He must not guess how she felt.

"I understand," he said. "You're homesick. I should have realized it's not been easy dealing with us foreigners and our strange customs. By all means, you should leave whenever you want to." His voice was suddenly cool and detached. If it was anyone else she would think she'd hurt his feelings. But Sam claimed he didn't have any.

"Tomorrow," she said.

"Tomorrow," he repeated with a frown.

"There's something I have to tell you right now," she said. "I hope you won't take offense."

"Of course not. You couldn't possibly offend me after all we've been through together. Tell me anything."

"Could we go somewhere else?" she asked, glancing over her shoulder at the small groups of smiling employees who represented the new, premier shipping company, all talking excitedly about the plans.

# CHAPTER ELEVEN

BEFORE Sam left the party, his father motioned to him and murmured in his ear. "She's a wonderful woman," he said. "Don't let her go."

Sam nodded. "I won't," he said. But how could he make her stay when she didn't want to. This was the twenty-first century. Women all over the world had rights and power. Claudia had more than most. She was smarter than most. More desirable than most. And he wanted her more than he'd ever wanted anything. But she obviously didn't want him. He couldn't blame her. He could only offer her a different life than she knew or wanted. And that never worked. He knew more than he wanted to about that kind of experiment. And Claudia had already told him twice what he didn't want to know.

He led her to the elevator and up to his penthouse apartment. A few moments ago he was on top of the world, he was going to tell Claudia he was in love with her. He was going to ask her to marry him and then he realized how wrong it would be. She'd never last here any more than his mother had.

He had a hollow feeling in the pit of his stomach that his world was going to fall apart. And it wasn't just that he'd skipped breakfast today. Claudia looked like she was going to announce the end of the world.

What did she have to say? Whatever it was it wasn't good.

He flung the doors to the balcony open and the sun streamed in. The view was as spectacular as ever, but he couldn't appreciate the sight of Al-Hamri ships or the blue waters or the winding corniche along the seaside. He rubbed his hands together. Claudia looked so pale he was afraid she was sick.

Alarmed, he said, "Sit down. Are you all right? Are you sick?" He took her hands in his. They were cold. "What's wrong? My God, Claudia, tell me what's wrong?" He couldn't stand to see her suffer. He couldn't stand to lose her.

She snatched her hands back. "Nothing. I'm fine."

She walked around the room as if she didn't know where she was going. A feeling of despair threatened to overtake him. His desperation was growing by the minute.

"What is it?" he said. "I must know now."

A moment later she stopped pacing and faced him. "I'm leaving, Sam."

"No, don't go yet. Let's talk this over."

"It won't work. I'm leaving the job. I can't work for you anymore."

"You're quitting?" he asked dumbfounded. "What have I done?"

"Nothing. You've been the best boss in the world. But I need to move on. Do something different." She licked her lips. The lips he wanted to kiss.

"You're not happy here, I can understand that." There it was, out in the open. "It's too different. My mother felt the same way."

"I am happy here. I love your country—it's an exciting place to be. It's beautiful and exotic but I can't stay."

"You don't have to stay. You can work wherever you want. We have offices all over the world. But don't leave the company. Don't leave me. I need you. I love you."

She staggered backward and bumped into the leather couch. Now she looked like she was going to faint.

"It's a shock, I know," he said. "I feel shocked myself. It's about time I realized what's been happening to me. I've fallen in love with you." He smiled at her, but she didn't return his smile. He was going to have to do better. She had to believe him. She had to.

"Sam, you can't be in love with me. You don't believe in love."

He grabbed her shoulders and looked into her eyes. What could he say? "I know. I know what I said. But I was wrong. I have all the symptoms, the ones you told me about. I can't eat, I haven't slept for days. And my heart…" He took her hand and placed it on his heart. "Feel that."

"Oh," she said, her eyes wide. "Sam, are you all right?"

"No, I'm not all right. I won't be all right until you tell me you love me and you'll marry me."

"This is all my fault," she said. "Those symptoms I told you about, I didn't realize you'd take them seriously."

He grabbed her hand, and leveled his gaze at her. "Listen to me. You have to hear me out before you turn me down again. I'll tell you how serious I am about you. You've taught me to appreciate my country in a way I never did before. You see the good side of everything and everyone. I've never had such a good time as I've had with you here. I've been working with you for over two years and I thought I knew you. I knew how smart you were, how hardworking and how dedicated, but I never knew how beautiful you were, how you look with your hair wet, or in a sandstorm or in a ball gown. And how you manage to meet every emergency with good humor. You amaze me. You dazzle me. You enchant me." His voice dropped. If she didn't believe him he was lost.

"Sam, stop," she protested, her cheeks bright pink. "You don't need to flatter me."

"It's not flattery if it's the truth. And I need to tell you how I feel about you. Because if I don't…you'll never know. You'll think I'm the same, cold, uncaring boss you always knew."

"I never thought that," she said soberly, blinking back a tear.

"What I'm trying to say," he continued, "is that I don't know when it happened. When I fell in love with you. Maybe it was when you rode across the desert with me, or got up on that camel, or lay on the sand looking at the stars. I resisted. I told myself it wasn't possible. I didn't believe in love, but you know that. I told myself it was a reaction from Zahara's rejection. But I was wrong. It was you. It was always you. It just took me forever to realize it."

"I…I don't know what to say."

"I think I know how you feel. You're afraid of making a commitment. You think because your first marriage didn't work, you don't want to take another chance."

Claudia shook her head. She wanted to believe Sam, but how could she? How could she believe he could have changed so much so fast? She'd been in love with him for two years, and he'd fallen in love with her in a few days. Was that possible? She'd felt his heart pound. "I'm just worried…" she said.

"Of course you're worried. You're worried you'll b

homesick like my mother was. I told you we don't have to stay here. We can live anywhere."

"That's not it. I could live here happily. Everyone here has been wonderful to me. Your home in the oasis is a magical place. The capitol city is booming and I'd love to be a part of the boom. I think I've fallen in love with your country."

"But not with me. I understand. I've sprung this on you too soon. Too suddenly."

Claudia choked on a laugh. Suddenly. He thought he'd come on to her too fast. A sense of wonder and happiness filled her heart. He loved her. He really loved her.

"Sam," she said, putting her hand on his rapidly beating heart again. "I've been in love with you for two years. I don't know when it happened. Maybe it was the night we worked late on the strike at the docks and you drove me home at midnight. Or maybe when you gave me such a glowing recommendation or when I got you out of the charity auction. Or when you brought me flowers on my birthday."

His smile sent sparks shooting in the air. "Then you're over your heartbreak. You're willing to take a chance on love again?"

She nodded and put her hands on his shoulders, returning his smile with her own. Her eyes filled with happy tears and she said, "I love you, Sam. I always have and I always will. I'll marry you and live wherever you want to live." He kissed her then, a deep, thrilling kiss that sealed the promise that their love would last forever.

# EPILOGUE

CLAUDIA'S wedding day at Sidi Bou Said in the oasis was as perfect as it could be. Teams of chefs had arrived from the capitol the day before and the smell of spices and roasting meats came wafting from the kitchen.

Amina was there in a flowing caftan as her attendant. She was also there to fit Claudia's white wedding dress on her and to style her hair in a way that made her look natural and glamorous at the same time.

"There," Amina said with a satisfied smile as she placed a single white rose in Claudia's hair. "You look beautiful." She stepped back to admire the dress, the hair and her future sister-in-law.

"So the fortune teller was right," Amina said. "There was a man in your future and you found wealth and happiness."

"Yes, I did," Claudia said, her cheeks flushed and her eyes glowing. "I must thank you for your part."

"Don't thank me. I did nothing. It was you. I knew you were right for Sam the minute I saw you."

Claudia went out on the balcony and looked down at the guests assembled in the walled garden. Water cascaded from the fountains. Hydrangeas bloomed against the gate. Servants stood just inside the tall, arched windows, ready for the wedding feast. The musicians were playing traditional songs on the lute and guitar.

Sam was standing at the flower-covered bower looking more handsome than ever in his black tuxedo. As if he felt her eyes on him, he looked up and met her gaze. For a long moment she stood there, feeling the connection between them stronger than a rope of steel. There were people everywhere but for one moment it was only Sam and Claudia alone. They had each other and that was all they needed. The electricity between them fairly sizzled.

Finally Claudia turned and followed Amina down the stairs as the musicians played the wedding march. She walked down a path of cream limestone through a Moorish courtyard on her way to marry the tall, dark, handsome sheikh of her dreams. And after a honeymoon in a tent in the desert, they would live happily ever after. It was guaranteed. The fortune teller said so and she was always right.

# MILLS & BOON®
## The Sheikhs Collection!

This fabulous 4 book collection features stories from some of our talented writers. The Sheikhs Collection features some of our most tantalising, exotic stories.

Order yours at
**www.millsandboon.co.uk/sheikhscollection**

# MILLS & BOON®

## Let us take you back in time with our Medieval Brides...

**The Novice Bride** – Carol Townend

**The Dumont Bride** – Terri Brisbin

**The Lord's Forced Bride** – Anne Herries

**The Warrior's Princess Bride** – Meriel Fuller

**The Overlord's Bride** – Margaret Moore

**Templar Knight, Forbidden Bride** – Lynna Banning

Order yours at
**www.millsandboon.co.uk/medievalbrides**

0116_MB519

# MILLS & BOON®

## Why shop at millsandboon.co.uk?

Each year, thousands of romance readers find their perfect read at millsandboon.co.uk. That's because we're passionate about bringing you the very best romantic fiction. Here are some of the advantages of shopping at www.millsandboon.co.uk:

* **Get new books first**—you'll be able to buy your favourite books one month before they hit the shops

* **Get exclusive discounts**—you'll also be able to buy our specially created monthly collections, with up to 50% off the RRP

* **Find your favourite authors**—latest news, interviews and new releases for all your favourite authors and series on our website, plus ideas for what to try next

* **Join in**—once you've bought your favourite books, don't forget to register with us to rate, review and join in the discussions

Visit **www.millsandboon.co.uk**
for all this and more today!